DYING TO TELL

KERI BEEVIS

Print ISBN 978-1-912986-90-3

For the real Natalie Mcardle
And in memory of her son, Joe

Lust. Control. Fear. Silence.

The Bishop stared at the body on the floor, emotions bubbling inside him. He hadn't meant to kill her. It had been an accident.

They had been kissing, things were getting heated, and he had been caught up in the moment. One second she was in his arms, her hands eagerly slipping into his jeans; the next she was motionless on the ground, wide eyes staring up at him, but no longer seeing.

He nudged her shoulder with the toe of his trainer, hoping she would move, knowing she wouldn't, and dread coiled in his belly.

It had been an accident, but he knew they wouldn't believe him.

He shouldn't have brought her there. The move had been reckless and rationality replaced with need. She had offered herself to him and he had known better, but still he had taken. He hadn't meant for things to end this way.

Silence. Frustration. Panic. Anger.

She had brought this upon herself. He wasn't to blame.

They would say it was his fault though. He could already feel the accusation in the weight of their stares; knew they would judge him and find him guilty without taking time to understand what had really happened. Like before.

He had too much to lose.

It had been an unfortunate accident, a mistake, and he had to take care of it.

No-one could know what had happened. She would have to disappear.

A door opened behind him.

He had been so caught up in the moment he had forgotten that they weren't alone.

Footsteps sounded on the stairs and he heard a sharp intake of breath.

'Oh my God. What have you done?'

He stepped back numbly as the girl rushed into the room, watching her futile efforts to resuscitate the one already dead.

They couldn't find out. No-one could ever know.

They would never believe him. He had to make this problem go away.

Moving quietly up the stairs, he locked the door and pocketed the key.

The girl glanced up having heard the key twist in the lock, her anger turning to fear. Her eyes were wide, her pretty mouth trembling, stirring something deep inside him.

. . .

Anger. Regret. Acceptance. Lust.

It all came full circle.

'I'm sorry,' he whispered. 'But I can't let you go.'

1

TWELVE DAYS LATER

For Lila Amberson, the past week had been defined by two moments. In the first she had been a passenger in Mark Sutherland's car, out on her first date in over four years, the next she had awoken in hospital with tubes poking out of her body, her left leg elevated in a sling, and her brother Elliot sitting beside her, his nose buried in a comic book.

Lila had tried to speak, but her throat was so dry she barely managed a feeble croak. Elliot's head had shot up, eyes widening, and the comic book had fallen to the floor. She wanted water, tried to tell him again, but he had already rushed from the room.

HE RETURNED moments later with a doctor and two nurses, who had poked and prodded at her, flashed lights in her eyes. Lila had tried to tell them to stop, frustration and fear knotting as she attempted to comprehend where she was and what was happening to her. Eventually the doctor addressed her directly.

'Can you hear me, Lila? If you can, please nod or blink twice for me.'

Ignoring the second part, Lila tried to answer him. Damn it, why wasn't her voice working?

'Don't try to talk yet. Just a simple nod or a double blink.'

She focussed on his eyes; grey irises that were strikingly pale against his skin, managed to move her head slightly in a nod. What was happening? She looked for Elliot, saw him standing towards the back of the room.

'Lila, you're in hospital.'

But why, she wanted to scream.

The doctor was addressing her again, his voice reminded her of Hugh Grant. He waited until he had her attention before continuing. 'You were in a car accident and you've been unconscious.'

Car accident?

She remembered being on the road in Mark's car. Their date was over and it hadn't gone well. He was taking her home, but she didn't remember getting there.

Was Mark in hospital too? When had the accident happened? How come she couldn't remember?

There were too many questions she needed answers to, but her voice wouldn't work and so she had no choice but to lie in the bed, hooked up to tubes, listening to the plummy voice of the doctor as he told her to be patient, that she was in good hands and he was optimistic for her recovery.

THE REST of that first day was a blur. Elliot stayed with her, but told her nothing. She wondered briefly if her mother was there, but then chided herself for being stupid. Tina Davenport wouldn't interrupt her honeymoon with her fourth husband for something as trivial as a car accident.

Lila slept, her dreams filled with floating in water, and in the darkest moments suffocating, hands around her neck, the world about to go black. When she wasn't sleeping, she was replaying the date with Mark in her head.

She hadn't wanted to go, but Beth had talked her into it. Mark was a friend of Beth's boyfriend, not long out of a relationship and looking to date again. Eventually Lila had agreed to go out with him just to shut her best friend up, but as the night drew nearer, Lila was nervous. She had been shown a photo of Mark and he looked pleasant enough, but she was woefully out of practice.

Ready early, she had paced the length of her tiny flat anxiously, wishing she had an excuse to call things off. It was just drinks she had told herself when she agreed to meet up, nothing serious and she could leave at any time, but then Beth's boyfriend had arranged for Mark to pick her up from home and things became that little bit more scary.

Lila couldn't recall much about the evening of the date. She could picture Mark's face, remembered that he had been wearing a slick grey suit with tight trousers and shoes with pointy tips, that she had felt a little self-conscious and underdressed when he'd picked her up. He had a strong Norwich accent and he kept pronouncing her name wrong, calling her Lee-la, not Ly-la, despite her correcting him, which had pissed her off. They had driven out to the coast and she had been edgy about that, thinking it too far for a first date, and they had argued, she remembered that too, though couldn't recall what the fight had been about. And then there was the journey home, Mark driving too fast, Lila asking him to slow down. She knew she had wanted to get home, that she never wanted to see him again.

IT WAS NOT until the following day that she learned she wouldn't ever see him again. Mark had been killed in the accident.

Her voice had come back during the middle of the night. Elliot had been asleep on the chair in the room that was far too small for his gangly frame, his glasses had slipped down his nose, and he had awoken with a jump when she had called his name.

She had questions, too many questions, and had barraged him with them, her voice still croaky and sounding foreign to her.

Elliot had seemed reluctant to say too much, making excuses to find Doctor Lucas, and Lila had been left waiting impatiently until they returned.

'What happened?' she demanded as they approached her bedside.

'You were in a car accident,' the doctor told her patiently.

'I know. You already said that, but what happened?'

'You don't remember?' Elliot glanced warily at the doctor.

'I remember I was out...' She paused, coughing, her throat dry. 'Can I have some water please?'

Elliot glanced at the doctor again, filling a plastic cup from the jug when he was given the okay.

'Sip it slowly,' Doctor Lucas urged when she gulped at it, choking.

Lila did as instructed. She took a moment, tried again. 'I was on a date... Beth had fixed me up with him. Mark.' Lila paused. 'Is he in the hospital too?'

Another exchanged look between Elliot and the doctor.

'I'm afraid your friend didn't make it, Lila.'

'Didn't make it.' She repeated the doctor's words slowly, letting their relevance sink in. 'He's dead?'

'He died at the scene. There was nothing we could do for him.'

Lila was silent for a moment, not sure how she felt about that.

'What happened?' she asked again, this time calmer. 'I mean, how did it happen?'

'You hit another car.'

'Where?'

'Filby Broad,' Elliot told her. 'Both cars went into the water.'

'What about the other car, the people inside?'

'You were the only survivor.'

When Lila stared at the doctor, he elaborated. 'Both drivers died at the scene. You were very lucky, Lila. You were pulled from the water.'

She had more questions, but exhaustion hit suddenly, plus she needed time to fully process what she had been told. People had died. Mark was dead. Although she had barely known him, hadn't even particularly liked him, part of her grieved for him. And the other car… Doctor Lucas had only mentioned a driver, so she assumed there had been no passengers. Lila was relieved, grateful that she had survived, but with that came guilt. Why had she been the lucky one?

ELLIOT REMAINED HER CONSTANT COMPANION, only leaving her room for a few hours a day, while Tina sent a text. Elliot had tried to brush over it, telling Lila she had called several times for updates while she had been in a coma, and Lila knew her mother well enough that she shouldn't be surprised, so was annoyed at the stab of hurt. Lila should have known to expect nothing more.

SHE WAS CLIMBING the walls by the time she was finally released, departing the hospital in a wheelchair, the crutches she had been practising on during her daily rehabilitation exercises on her lap as Elliot pushed her across the car park to his battered Volvo.

Lila heaved herself out of the wheelchair, balancing on the crutches as he shifted armfuls of papers and files from the front passenger seat, dumping them into the back. His car was a tip and looked ready to fall apart. As she waited, she glanced around the car park, couldn't shake the feeling that she was being watched. It was stupid. There were other people about, but no-one was paying any attention to her and Elliot. It was probably just a reaction to finally being out of the hospital. She remembered the dreams she'd been having the last few nights; hands around her throat, squeezing.

Were they an after-effect of the accident too?

She let her brother help her into the car, winced when he threw her crutches on the back seat. She wasn't used to being reliant on other people, knew it was going to take some getting used to. Elliot was trying his best and she needed to be patient. Her geeky younger brother was more used to having his head buried in a science book than playing nursemaid. She expected him to leave after he had dropped her off home, so was surprised to find his stuff all over her living room, suggesting otherwise.

'I'll take the sofa,' he insisted, when she told him there was no need to stay. 'I don't think you should be alone. At least for the first few days.'

Lila understood. Tina Davenport had failed on all fronts as a mother, more interested in ploughing her way through husbands than taking any interest in her children's lives, and as siblings, they had always looked out for one another. Lila's flat was only small, but maybe it would be nice to have the company.

'Okay,' she agreed. 'But I'll warn you now, that sofa isn't very comfortable to sleep on.'

'I'll manage.' Elliot gave a tight smile. 'I'd rather stay close where I can keep an eye out for you.'

Something about his words chilled her. 'What do you mean?'

'Nothing. It was just a joke.'

Lila thought back to the dreams she'd had in the hospital, the hands around her throat, and shivered. 'Did something happen? While I was in hospital?'

Elliot glanced at the floor. A sure giveaway sign that there was something he was keeping from her.

'I've been having this dream.' Lila subconsciously put her hand to the throat and rubbed. 'Someone trying to hurt me.'

When Elliot eventually glanced up and met her eyes, she screwed up her nose, feeling stupid.

'Forget it. It's probably all the pills.'

'I thought there was someone. I went to the loo and they were in your room when I got back. I thought... no, it was stupid. They probably just had the wrong room.'

'What? Did you report it?'

'Of course.' Elliot's tone was indignant. 'Nothing had been tampered with. I think the doctor thought I had imagined it. You know me. I probably overreacted.'

Lila stared at him. He didn't really believe that, she was certain.

Had someone tried to hurt her while she had been in a coma? The hands around her throat. It may have been a dream, but still she shuddered.

THE GIRL WAS awake and out of hospital. That wasn't good, as it presented a huge problem. She was never supposed to have woken up.

While she remained alive, she posed a threat; her memory could return at any time and that made her extremely dangerous.

She was a loose end and one that needed taking care of as soon as possible.

2

The broken leg made things difficult, but Lila could still manage, and it was irritating having her brother hovering over her trying to help, but awkwardly getting in the way. She tried not to grumble though, knew he was doing his best, and that much of her frustration was down to being stuck in her flat.

And it wasn't just the boredom. Work was worrying her and she was conscious she needed to get back on her feet as soon as possible. She hadn't dared look at her bank balance since the accident. It was fine being told she had to rest, but bills still had to be paid.

For now, she tried her best to be a good patient, reading what information she could find online about the accident.

Mark had hit another car head on and both vehicles had left the road, ending up in the broad. Lila was the only survivor, thanks to a local man who had been travelling home when he witnessed the crash and pulled her from the water.

Richard Gruger: the man who had saved her life. Lila was keen to thank him and Elliot promised that he would drive Lila over to meet him, but not until she had fully recovered. He didn't understand that to Lila answers were more important. Richard

Gruger had been there and may be able to fill in some of the blanks.

The victim in the other car, Stephanie Whitman, had been just seventeen, and guilt gnawed at Lila's stomach. It wasn't her fault, rationally she knew that, but still she had survived while a girl fifteen years her junior had lost her life. It didn't seem fair. Stephanie's distraught father, Henry Whitman, was quoted several times, insisting his daughter was a cautious driver who adhered to speed limits. It seemed he held Mark responsible for killing Stephanie. Henry Whitman: Lila thought the name sounded familiar, but it didn't click until one of the articles mentioned his business, Whitman Homes. Henry Whitman was pretty big news and one of the richest men in the county.

Her messenger pinged. It was from Elliot and she glanced at his suggestion to pick up a takeaway curry on his way home from work. Lila replied with a thumbs-up emoji then grabbed her crutches and hobbled through to the kitchen for a bottle of lager.

As she took a swig, she spotted the bag next to the toaster, knowing it contained the things the hospital had returned to her. After getting back home, she had retrieved her keys, purse and ruined mobile phone, before setting it to one side, figuring she would sort the rest later. Grabbing the bag, she hopped over to the sofa, dumping the crutches and setting down her lager, before emptying the bag on the coffee table and sifting through the bangles she had worn for her date, her tiny handbag and compact mirror, lipstick and a packet of chewing gum.

A delicate chain caught her eye and she snatched it up, the silver locket that hung from it looking unfamiliar. It wasn't hers, so how had it ended up with her stuff? She opened the locket, studied the black and white photo inside. It was of an older woman with greying hair. Engraved on the locket was the letter S.

Stephanie Whitman? It had to be. Their personal effects must have gotten mixed up.

She would have to find out an address for the Whitmans, knew they would want their daughter's locket back. Maybe she could send a sympathy card with it.

She stared at the locket; thought of Stephanie's smiling face from the news articles, and, deep in thought, Lila slipped it in her pocket. She would figure out the right thing to do.

THE RIGHT THING TO do probably wasn't to turn up at Stephanie Whitman's funeral, but it had seemed a good idea when Lila had thought of it.

Elliot told her she was crazy to go, but Lila felt it was something she had to do. Of course he thought he had talked her out of it and didn't realise she had headed to the bus station after he had gone to work.

Stephanie Whitman had lived with her parents in the village of Cley next the Sea, on the North Norfolk coast and Lila had read in the papers and online about her funeral, knew it was taking place at the local church. The journey from Norwich took over an hour, involving a change of bus. Although she was familiar with the coastal road, recognising the windmill with its white sails that she had photographed many times, usually at sunset in skies of gold or pink, she had never seen the church on her visits, knew that it was on a road that led further inland.

The bus dropped her in a narrow street of pretty terraced houses that sat a stone's throw away from open fields of green. The village was set back from the sea, but as she made her way along the country lane that led to the church, the salty scent clung to the air. For an able-bodied person, the walk was only ten minutes, but with the crutches it took far longer and Lila hadn't anticipated how difficult she would find the journey. She paused midway, a little out of breath, in pain, and sweat beading under her dress, and she glanced at her watch, aware the funeral would already be underway. The cool grey May sky was the only relief and even that turned on her when the clouds darkened then spat with rain.

AFTER WHAT SEEMED LIKE AN AGE, she spotted the Three Swallows pub in the distance and several cars parked alongside the verge. A little further behind the pub was the towering church.

She cursed as she passed another bus stop; annoyed that she hadn't taken the time to find out there was one much closer. As she started the incline towards the church, mourners spilled out of the door and anxiety twisted in her stomach.

She paused for a moment, wondering what the hell she had been thinking. This was private and she wouldn't be welcomed. Reaching in the pocket of her denim jacket, she felt the locket, remembering she had come all this way to pay her respects, to return the locket to Stephanie's family. Lila couldn't turn back.

Apprehensively she edged closer, the immaculate black suits, dresses, hats and heels making her feel woefully out of place. She glanced down at her own black dress, which hung above her knees, and her one scuffed boot, conscious that she didn't fit in with these people.

Nerves eventually won out and the closest she dared get was the wall inside the front gate. There she remained, an outsider watching as the coffin that held the body of a girl she hadn't known, but would forever be tied to, was carried through the graveyard, and Lila tried to decide if she would be able to pluck up courage to approach Henry Whitman when he returned to his waiting car. She recognised him from press pictures as he stood graveside beside a sobbing woman, back ramrod straight, his expression grim. He wasn't going to welcome Lila at his daughter's funeral.

This was a bad idea. Elliot was right. She shouldn't have come.

She should slope away quietly and post the locket with a note of condolence.

As she made up her mind it was best to leave, a man standing to the side of the mourners glanced in her direction, eyes narrowing in recognition as they locked onto hers. And before she could react, he was heading purposefully towards her, long strides eating up the ground between them, looking royally pissed off.

'WHAT THE HELL are you doing here?' he hissed.

Lila took a defensive step back, almost losing her footing as her crutch hit an uneven patch of grass. 'This *is* Stephanie Whitman's funeral?' Her voice sounded far more confident than she felt and her heart was thudding. 'My name is–'

'I know who you are, *Lila Amberson*.'

He spoke her name with scathing sarcasm. Who the hell was this man and how did he know who she was?

'I just wanted to pay my respects.'

He gave a bitter laugh. 'You wanted to pay your respects? Why? You didn't even know her.'

'No, you're right, I didn't,' Lila agreed quietly over the lump in her throat. 'But it felt the right thing to do.'

Blue eyes that had until now been cool heated up unexpectedly, the man's frown deepening as anger coloured his cheeks, and Lila shrunk back as he took a step towards her, conscious that he dwarfed her by at least five inches. When he spoke, his words were clipped.

'The *right* thing to do... The *respectful* thing to do would have been to stay away. Your boyfriend killed my sister. Did you really think we would welcome you here?'

'He wasn't my boyfriend.'

Lila kicked herself for the irrelevance of her comment. This man... Stephanie Whitman's brother, had flustered her. She hadn't expected such a hostile reaction.

And how exactly did you think they were going to react? Invite you back to the house for tea to show you Stephanie's baby pictures?

She hadn't thought this through and she certainly shouldn't have come to the funeral.

Before she could say as much, he caught hold of her arm, his grip firm, fingers digging into flesh, as he pushed her towards the gate.

'Ouch, you're hurting me.'

'You need to go. Now. I don't want my mother seeing you here. Not today.'

'Let go of me then! I'm gone.'

'Go!' he hissed, giving her a gentle shove as he released her.

Lila steadied herself on her crutches, sucked in a shaky breath. She wanted to defend herself, point out that it had been an accident and that Stephanie's death hadn't been her fault, but she couldn't find the right words and it wasn't appropriate.

'I'm sorry,' she said instead, her heart thumping and her legs unsteady as she turned inelegantly on the crutches, keen to get away, aware Stephanie's brother was watching her go. Tears pricked at the back of her eyes and she blinked furiously, annoyed that his words had gotten under her skin.

She ordered herself to focus on the view as she descended the stone path leading down from the church. Even on a dull day, it was so pretty with stone cottages spaced around the neatly mown green on the other side of the road. It crossed her mind briefly that it would be a nice location to shoot, but just as quickly she realised she would associate this place with Stephanie Whitman and that day's unpleasant encounter. Better to forget Cley and the Whitmans and focus on getting her own life back on track.

HE STUDIED the local news sites as he drank his tea, looking for any updates.

The main story was still the car accident and the death of Stephanie Whitman. Her father was determined to keep her in the headlines, blaming the driver of the other car.

That was good. If he kept distracting the reporters then other stories would be flying under the radar.

It needed to stay that way.

3

L ila had plenty of time to brood over what had happened.
Not fancying the half-mile walk back to the coast road, she decided to chance the bus stop outside the Three Swallows pub, but was struggling to find information as to when the next bus actually ran.

She weighed up her options: make her way back to the coastal road (something she wasn't sure she could face as the long walk to the church had exacerbated the pain in her neck and shoulder); a taxi, but she could ill afford that option; or persuade someone to come pick her up. Elliot was working in London for the day and wouldn't be home until late. That left Beth or Natalie, but they would be at work.

As Lila made the decision that she would have to wait it out for the bus, thunder rumbled overhead and the spits of rain turned heavy. There was a bus shelter that offered some cover, but it wasn't enough to protect her from the downpour. Lila glanced at the pub across the road. It was her only option.

Negotiating crutches on a road that was slippery with water wasn't easy and, although only a short distance, by the time she reached the door, she was soaked.

. . .

THE PLACE WAS EMPTY, albeit for one barmaid and an old chap who sat at the bar with his back to her. Lila made her way to the toilets and attempted to dry herself using paper towels and the hand dryer. She was a mess and just wanted to go home. Knowing that wasn't an option, she made her way back out to the bar and ordered a Coke.

'Can you tell me when the next bus is back to Holt?'

The barmaid set down Lila's drink, rang up the order on the till. 'There's one going in about twenty minutes outside The Fruit Fayre. It's about half a mile down the road.'

'What about the stop outside?' Lila asked, handing over a fiver.

'The next bus won't pass through here until later on this afternoon.'

Lila's heart sank, still she forced a smile and thanked the barmaid, ignoring the curious stare from the old man sat at the bar, who looked like he was probably a regular so was no doubt familiar with everyone who came through the door and was wondering who the hell she was. She managed to put her purse away, attempted to pick up the full glass of Coke while balancing on her crutches.

'Here, let me help you with that.' The barmaid came out from behind the counter, took the glass from her.

Lila chose a table in the corner, away from the old man's prying eyes. Despite her mop-up job, her clothes were still damp and uncomfortable, and she sat in the cool quiet pub, her neck and shoulder throbbing, sipping at her Coke, trying to figure out what the hell to do, knowing that she would never make it back to the coast road in twenty minutes, so was stuck in Cley village for at least another hour. She listened to the rain pelting against the windows, wishing she had never been stupid enough to come to Stephanie Whitman's funeral.

Lila's phone had been wrecked in the accident, but fortunately Elliot had come through for her, loaning her his old one until she could sort out a replacement. He had also given her sim card to a friend, who was trying to recover her photos for her. Although Lila used her cameras when working, she still had numerous shots on her phone she didn't want to lose. As Elliot's phone was, for now, her only source of entertainment, she checked her e-mail and Facebook accounts, looked at the weather forecast, dismayed to see the rain was set to stay for the rest of the day.

Bored, she typed "Richard Gruger" into Google.

She had already looked up her rescuer after learning his name, so knew which one of the three Richard Grugers he was, that he was fifty-two and a headmaster at a private school in Suffolk. There were a handful of search results for him, mostly relating to the accident, and just one image. Fair, cropped hair and dark eyes. Non-descript in many ways, but a face she would never forget.

Her thoughts turned from Gruger to Stephanie's brother, and anger gnawed at the guilt in Lila's belly. She hadn't caused the accident, had been a victim, the same as his sister. The police hadn't ever said Mark was responsible. How dare Stephanie's brother speak to her as if she was a criminal?

Lila hesitated, googled "Stephanie Whitman" and reread the articles about the accident. Henry Whitman was the only family member to comment in the press. One article mentioned her mother, sister, and a twenty-year-old brother. The man who had attacked her at the church had been older, maybe in his thirties.

She logged into Facebook again, typed Stephanie's name into the search engine, The girl's face appeared, pretty, smiling, looking like she was having fun, and the guilt returned.

Stephanie's page had been turned into a memorial and was filled with comments from her friends. Lila read half a dozen of them, feeling like an intruder. She briefly scrolled through her seven hundred and thirty-six friends, wondering how on earth someone could know that many people, then clicked on her photos, wading her way through dozens of selfies and shots taken at a black tie affair, where Stephanie looked pretty in sunny yellow as she posed with her parents, sister and one brother. The man from the funeral wasn't there.

So who was he?

Lila found him eventually in an album created two summers earlier, titled "Beach Barbecue", Stephanie in the middle of a group hug between him and another guy, all with wide grins on their faces. The caption below read "Awesome catch up with my brothers from another."

The comments below identified the brothers as Jack and Tom Foley, while another picture in the same album told her Jack had been the brother Lila had encountered at the funeral. In the photo he was on the beach with Stephanie, giving her a piggy-back, and they wore identical grins.

Hearing voices, Lila glanced up as the bar began to fill with people wearing black. Stephanie's family was holding her wake at the pub. Jack Foley had been angry to see Lila at the church. He wasn't going to welcome her presence here.

As the thought crossed her mind, he entered the pub, deep in conversation with the other man from the beach photo, whom she now knew was his brother, Tom.

As he spoke, he glanced in Lila's direction, making eye contact.

The light-brown dishevelled hair and blue eyes were the same as the photo, but the wide crooked grin had been replaced by a scowl. Could this day get any worse?

She slipped her phone in her bag, left her almost-full glass of Coke on the table and pushed herself up on her crutches. She wasn't going to get into another fight with him. She would rather endure the rain and her pains, and walk back to the coast road.

He was still standing close to the door and she avoided eye contact as she crossed the bar, aware he was watching her.

'You don't have to say anything,' she hissed quietly. 'I'm going.'

'Why are you even still here?' Despite the scowl, the anger had gone from his tone and he sounded weary.

'I'm waiting for the bus, but it's fine, you don't have to worry. I'll wait somewhere else.'

'In the rain?'

'It's fine.'

Of course it wasn't fine and she was soaked again within seconds of stepping outside the pub. She glanced briefly at the bus shelter, which didn't even have a seat, knew her only real option was to walk back to the other bus stop. Trying her best to huddle into her jacket, her teeth chattered with the cold as she walked. As far as stupid ideas went, this had to be one of the worst she'd ever had. The bus would already have gone, her clothes were soaked, the cast on her leg too, and her calf muscle throbbed underneath, while the pain in her shoulder was getting worse.

When the Land Rover pulled up alongside her, she barely registered it at first, the rainwater plastering her fringe to her forehead, and dripping into her eyes.

The window wound down and Jack Foley stared at her.

'Get in.'

'I'm fine where I am, thank you.'

'Really?'

Lila had tried for indignant and dismissive, but was aware she probably looked pretty foolish from the inside of a dry car. 'Go back to your sister's wake. I need to get to the bus stop.'

Jack hooked a brow. 'You've missed the bus. Next one won't be for another hour. Get in and I'll give you a ride to wherever you're going.'

'I don't want to put you out.'

'You already have,' he told her bluntly.

When Lila shook her head, started to move away, he eased the car forward, keeping pace with her. 'I don't want you going back in the pub but, mad as I am at you, I'm not going to leave you outside in the pouring rain. So get in the car, let me take you to wherever it is you're going then stay the hell out of my life. Deal?'

There was no dignified way out. Lila didn't want to accept the ride from him, but she would look petty and ungrateful if she didn't. Besides, the thought of waiting another fifty minutes in the rain wasn't pleasant. She negotiated her way round to the passenger seat and climbed in the car, balancing the crutches between her knees.

'You can put them on the back seat.'

'They're fine.' They weren't. They were a hindrance and she nearly bashed herself on the chin when she fastened her seat belt. She wouldn't admit to that though. She just wanted this ride over with.

'Suit yourself.' He gave her a pointed glance. 'Where to?'

She didn't want him taking her all the way back to Norwich. This situation was uncomfortable enough without prolonging it. She could get him to drop her in Holt, but she would still have to endure another hour in wet clothes. The café where she worked was only about six miles further along the coastal road. He could drop her there. Natalie would be able to give her a change of clothes and she could catch a ride home with Beth.

'Can you drop me off in Cromer?'

His eyes narrowed. 'Cromer?'

'I work there.'

He studied her for a moment, the frown softening slightly. 'Sure thing, Cromer it is.'

NEITHER OF THEM spoke during the journey, Lila focussing on the rain-splattered passenger window, while Jack scowled at the road ahead. She was grateful that he turned the heating up, though it didn't stop her shivering. The radio was playing in the background, *Happy* by Pharrell Williams. Lila couldn't help smiling at the irony.

'Where am I dropping you?' he asked as they passed the town sign for Cromer.

'There's a café called Nat's Hideaway, down near the pier.'

'I know it.'

He indicated left, took the turn and pulled up outside the café, waiting silently for her to get out.

Lila paused, her hand on the door handle. 'I doubt it means anything, but I really am sorry about your sister.' She waited for a reaction, saw the muscle in his jaw tighten. He didn't look in her direction.

'Go.'

Lila gave a resigned sigh. She had tried and could do no more. She awkwardly climbed out into the rain, balanced on her crutches. 'Thank you for the lift,' she told him as she pushed the door shut.

Jack didn't react, the car pulling away before she'd barely released the handle.

Lila shook her head in frustration; watching him go, before heading into the blessedly warm empty café.

'GOOD GOD, Lila, you look like a drowned rat.' Lila's boss, Natalie Mcardle, stepped out from behind the counter, surprise and concern knitted on her face. 'What the hell are you doing here?'

'It's nice to see you too and thank you for the compliment. It's a long story and before I tell you, can you loan me some dry clothes please?'

'Beth?' Natalie yelled back into the kitchen. 'I need you to cover the counter.' She glanced at Lila's crutches. 'Go wait in the kitchen. You're not going upstairs with those. I'll go get you a towel and something to change into.'

She was gone before Lila could thank her.

As Lila hobbled towards the kitchen, Beth appeared, her mouth dropping open in a similar expression to the one Natalie had worn. 'Jesus, did you swim here?'

'Long story,' Lila repeated, her teeth still chattering from the cold and the damp. 'Nat's gone to get me some dry clothes.'

'I'd hug you, but I think I'll wait.'

Beth Fielding was Lila's oldest friend and had been on the phone to her every day.

Lila grinned. 'That's probably a wise idea. Listen, Beth. If I hang around here until your shift finishes, do you think you could give me a lift home?'

'Sure thing, this bad weather's keeping everyone away and Natalie's going to close up at three.'

'Great. If we're going early, is there any chance we can make a detour?'

Beth looked dubious. 'To where?'

'I want to go back to Filby Broad. I need to see where it happened.'

4

'Where have you been?'

Alyssa Whitman stepped into Jack's path as soon as he walked back into the pub.

'I had something to take care of.'

'It was that woman at the funeral, wasn't it, the one with the crutches. I saw you speaking to her. Who was she, Jack?'

'She was a snoop, just like you.' He kept his tone light. 'I asked her to leave and I made sure she did.'

As Alyssa mulled over his words, he gave her arm an affectionate squeeze and brushed past her to the bar.

'I recognised her. It was her, wasn't it, the woman in the other car.'

Jack paused, swore under his breath at his nosy half-sister who didn't miss a trick.

'Just drop it, Alyssa. She's gone.'

'Does Mum know?'

'No, and she's not going to. I took care of the situation. She's gone and you're not going to say anything.'

'Why was she there?'

To pay her respects, that was what Lila Amberson had told

him. Jack hadn't let her elaborate, wanting her gone before his mother clocked her. Perhaps he had been a little too hot-headed, should have given Lila a chance to explain why she had come.

'I don't know. It's not important. I told her to leave.' He didn't bother to add that in order for Lila to leave he'd had to give her a lift to Cromer.

'Who's leaving?'

The question came from Giles Buchanan, who sidled into the conversation, his free arm snaking around Alyssa's shoulders.

Jack and Alyssa answered at the same time.

'No-one.'

'That Lila woman in the accident.'

'Really?' Giles glanced from one to the other, his piggy eyes narrowed, though his tone was amused. 'And what did Henry and Kate think of that, I wonder.'

'Mum and Dad don't know she was here. Jack sent her away so she didn't upset Mum.'

'And as she's gone, they don't need to know she was ever here,' Jack added.

'Gotcha.' Giles winked, gave a smarmy smile. 'Your secret is safe with me.'

Jack scowled at him, barely hiding his disdain. He could think of a hundred more suitable boyfriends for Alyssa, but it didn't seem like Giles was going anywhere. He worked with Jack's step-father and already had the Henry Whitman seal of approval.

'She had a nerve, didn't she, daring to show up here?' Giles continued, smoothing his already-slicked-down hair with his chubby fingers. 'What do you think she wanted? Money, I imagine. I looked into her... you know, after the accident. I wanted to know who had played a part in taking our Stephanie from us. She calls herself a photographer, but she works in a diner too, because let's face it, we all know photography isn't a proper job.'

'Isn't it?' Jack bristled, remembering how he'd endured similar comments about his own career before his first bestseller. Nobody had thought writing was a real job.

'Photography is more of a hobby,' Giles continued, too thick-skinned to pick up on Jack's annoyance. 'So she's a waitress with aspirations to be a photographer and she doesn't have two pennies to rub together; no wonder she's making a beeline for our family. I can tell you she is thinking *ka-ching*!'

Our family. Oh yes, Giles was making himself right at home.

'Is this true, Jack?' Alyssa was looking at him, seeking confirmation.

'No, it's not. She's not after money.'

'She told you that?' It was a question, but Giles didn't wait for Jack to answer, instead turning to Alyssa. 'I should go talk to her, warn her off. I'll bet Lila Amberson was here because she is viewing your parents as her cash cow. Let me go set her straight.'

'Jesus, drop it, Giles.' Jack snapped. 'Lila Amberson isn't after anyone's money. She came here to pay her respects. It was a stupid thing to do, I think she realises that now. She's gone, so drop it.'

'What?' Jack added, annoyed when both Giles and Alyssa stared at him, mouths open.

'You're defending her,' Alyssa pointed out.

'I'm not defending her. I'm saying she's not a gold digger.'

'You don't know that.'

'Yes, I do, so drop it, both of you. She's gone. Let's move on.'

'We should sue her.'

'For Christ's sake, Giles, stop.'

'Okay, okay.' Giles held his hands up in a truce.

'I need a drink,' Jack muttered.

'A drink? That sounds like a wonderful idea.'

Recognising Tiffany's voice, Jack turned as she snuck an arm around his waist, pulling him in for a kiss. She was damp from the rain, her lips cool.

'You finally made it then.' His tone was only half joking. She had promised she would be there in time for the service and it pissed him off that she hadn't made it, even though deep down he had known that would happen. Tiff was always late, regardless of how important the occasion.

She rolled her eyes dramatically. 'Jack, you know I would have been there if I could. The train was delayed and I had trouble getting a cab. And you know...' She trailed off, trading hugs and air kisses with Alyssa. 'Sweetie, how are you holding up? I still can't believe this happened.'

Leaving the two of them to it, Jack made his way to the bar, ordered a gin and tonic for Tiff and a double whisky for himself. He would leave the car there and catch a taxi back for it in the morning.

The conversation with Giles had soured his mood, had him questioning why he *had* defended Lila Amberson. It had to be Stephanie. He was at the funeral of his seventeen-year-old half-sister, a place he had never dreamt he would be, had watched her body being lowered into the ground. Emotions were running high and losing her was making him soft. He wasn't thinking clearly. Perhaps Giles was right. Maybe it was about money.

No, he didn't think so. Lila had stood out from the rest of the mourners with her hippy dress, denim jacket, one scuffed boot and crutches, and Jack suspected it was true she didn't have a whole lot of money, but his gut told him that she was genuine, and that her reasons for showing up at Stephanie's funeral, although misguided, had been because she wanted to pay her respects. Her reaction when he had confronted her had been shock, hurt, even embarrassed, but she hadn't counter-attacked; something he would have expected her to do if she had a motive.

Plus she had bussed to the village and made her way to the church on crutches. Although he had dropped her in Cromer, he knew from the news articles he had read she lived in Norwich. That was a long journey for someone still recovering from a serious accident. If her intentions were financially driven there were easier ways.

And he had been an arsehole to her.

Of course it was too late to take it back. Lila Amberson was out of his life and he'd made it clear he wanted it to stay that way. There was no point regretting his words. Better to move on.

'ARE you sure this is a good idea?'

It was the fifth time Beth had asked the question since Lila had told her where she wanted to go, despite the fact they were almost at Filby.

'I need to do this.'

The rain had stopped, but the roads were still slick with water, the sky filled with dark clouds threatening another downpour, as Beth eased the car round the bends. Lila's mind had been set on returning to the scene of her accident, but uneasiness cloaked her, tensing her muscles, as they passed through the pretty village filled with hanging baskets and floral displays in vivid colours. As they came through the other side and the houses gave way to trees, she spotted the bridge up ahead.

For a moment she was in the car with Mark. He was driving too fast, and she was begging him to slow down. She had thought it was because he was still mad at her, but then he glanced briefly in her direction and she saw the raw fear on his face.

The flashback was frustratingly fleeting and only served to unnerve her further.

'Stop the car.'

'I can't. We've got traffic behind us.'

'Stop the car.'

'Give me a second.'

'Just stop the bloody car, Beth.'

Doing as instructed, Beth hit the indicator then the brakes, pulling abruptly to the side of the narrow road a few metres before the bridge. The van that had been hugging her tail honked angrily before swerving to pass.

'What the hell's going on, Lila?'

'I need a moment.'

'I can't sit here. There's a car park the other side of the bridge. I'll pull in there.'

Beth earned herself another honk from an angry trucker behind her as she pulled away. As they crossed the bridge, Lila saw the flash of water then the skid marks and the fallen trees and bushes where the accident had happened, now littered with half a dozen bouquets of flowers, and her insides turned to ice. Beth slowed, indicating for the car park, received another honk from the trucker, who wound down his window and yelled a curse about women drivers as he passed.

'Wanker.' She stuck her fingers up at him as he zoomed off up the road.

As Beth pulled into a wooded clearing that served as a car park, Lila had another even briefer flashback. She had been there before, the night of the accident, and was sitting in Mark's car, alone, watching the dark trees.

'Lila? Lila, you're scaring me.'

She snapped to, realised they were parked, the ignition off, and it was still daylight, even if the dull afternoon was making the clearing appear dark.

'Are you okay? You've gone pale.'

'I had a couple of flashbacks.' Lila folded her arms, rubbing at the goosebumps under the baggy sweater Natalie had lent her.

Beth's eyes widened. 'Of the accident?'

'Not the actual accident, but before.' When Beth stayed silent, waiting for her to continue, Lila elaborated. 'I was in the car with Mark and we were fighting. He was driving too fast and I was trying to get him to slow down, but he wouldn't listen. Then I saw his face and he looked really scared. I don't know what scared him, Beth.'

'Are you sure that's what actually happened? Maybe the flashback is muddled with fragments of other things, you know what I mean, like in a dream.'

'I don't know. It was his face. Something had spooked him.'

'You said a couple of flashbacks. What about the other one?'

Lila hugged herself tighter. 'It was here in this car park, but it was only me in the car. I don't know where Mark was.'

'Was this before or after the first flashback?'

'I don't know. It's like I get this brief snapshot of a memory and then it's gone and I can't remember what else happened.'

'What did the doctors say? Will your memory come back?'

'Maybe.' Lila shrugged in frustration. 'It's early days. They say to give it time.'

'Then you have to learn to be patient.'

'You know I'm not good at that.' Lila opened the car door, reached for her crutches.

'What are you doing?'

'Getting out.'

'Are you crazy? The ground's too muddy. Your crutches are gonna sink, you're gonna be a mess, and I had my car cleaned last week.'

'Please, Beth. I want to see exactly where it happened. I need to.'

'We drove over the bridge. You saw it.'

'But not properly.'

Beth shook her head. 'No way, Lila, that road's too busy to cross on crutches.'

'It's a country lane.'

'It's a busy country lane, with cars and trucks going fast, and no proper pavement. I'll drive to the entrance of the car park. You can see everything you need to from there.'

'But...'

'You get out of the car, I'm leaving you here and you can find your own way home.'

'You wouldn't dare.'

Beth raised her chin defiantly. 'Try me.'

Lila considered for a second, knew her friend well enough to not call her bluff. Lila pulled the door shut, slumped back in her seat. 'Can we agree on a compromise?'

'Which is?'

'Richard Gruger, the man who pulled me from the crash, lives a couple of minutes from here. I'd like to see if he's home so I can thank him.'

Beth was quiet for a moment. 'Do you have his address?'

'Yup.'

'Okay, but then we're going home. Deal?'

BORED WITH STUDYING, Aaron Gruger switched off his computer, got up from the desk chair, stretched lazily and yawned. Time to have a break and maybe sneak in a bit of Xbox. His father was away at a teaching conference – thankfully – and his mother out shopping, so they would have no idea he was skiving.

He headed downstairs to the kitchen, poked his head in the fridge and took out a can of Coke, pulled the cap and downed the drink in one, burping loudly before crunching up the empty can and dropping it in the bin. He burped again, yawned again, stretched again, and glanced out of the kitchen window at the wide lawn surrounded by trees. It had been raining heavily for most of the afternoon.

Aaron had grumbled like hell when his parents had first moved to Norfolk. The house they had picked was in the middle of nowhere with a shitty bus service and hardly any shops. He missed being able to go out whenever and wherever he pleased and the first couple of years had been hell. Then he had turned seventeen, got his driving licence and realised it wasn't so bad. The space and quiet had its advantages and the woods and countryside were great for riding his quad bike. He liked the old house too, that it was big enough to escape his father when he was in one of his moods.

Luckily his father wasn't home much, claiming to spend most of his time over at the school where he was headmaster and Aaron went to sixth form. Aaron wondered if his father might be having an affair, though kept his suspicions quiet, knowing it would break his mother's heart if it were true. Judith Gruger lived to please her husband and son, and she put them first in every respect.

Which was why when the time came, Aaron was dreading telling her of his plans.

He was eighteen and his life had already been mapped out for him. A levels in a couple of weeks, university, and a job with one of the city's accountancy firms: it was what Richard Gruger had planned for him, but it wasn't what Aaron wanted.

He was academically smart, always had been, and the A levels would be a breeze. He didn't need the study time, but his father insisted. His mother tried to enforce it in his absence, though Aaron knew he could twist her arm if need be. The only reason he didn't was because he didn't want to get her in trouble with his father. So he dutifully studied, knowing that after the A levels there would be no university, that he wanted to go travelling, learn more about who he was and what he wanted from life.

Maybe he would return, knowing university and a job in accounting was the answer, maybe he wouldn't, but it was his choice to make. While he was looking forward to breaking the news to his father, he was dreading telling his mother.

He was about to head back upstairs to his room, turn on the Xbox, when the front doorbell chimed. Aaron scratched his belly through his T-shirt, cocked his head in curiosity. Given the remote location of the house, they didn't get many cold callers, and his parents were private people so rarely had friends stop by. Possibly another reporter, but they had dwindled in the last week or so and it was unlikely.

Intrigued, Aaron made his way into the hallway, viewed the security camera, immediately recognising the face peering into it.

Lila Amberson: the girl responsible for his father's current bad mood.

Most people would enjoy being touted as a hero in the press, but not Richard Gruger. He hated publicity, good and bad, and was not at all happy at being paraded on the front page of the local papers as the man who had saved Lila's life.

It was a good job he wasn't here, as he would likely blow a gasket. He wasn't though and Aaron was intrigued to meet Lila, the sole survivor of the crash. The story had been all over the papers since it had happened, mostly thanks to Henry Whitman. Something Aaron would like to shake his hand for. It had been fun watching his father growing more and more outraged at the coverage.

He threw open the door, greeted Lila with a wide smile. 'Hello there.'

'Hi, umm, is Richard Gruger home?'

'I'm afraid he's away on business.'

She looked disappointed, but that was probably for the best. Disappointed was definitely a step up from the reaction she would have been sporting had his father been home.

'Okay, umm, I guess you're his son?'

'That's right. Aaron. Nice to meet you.' He held out a hand, waited as she balanced awkwardly on her crutches to take it.

'Hi, Aaron. Nice to meet you too. I'm–'

'Lila Amberson... yes, I know. Word travels fast in this neck of the woods. You're something of a local celebrity, you know.'

'Okay.' She actually blushed. 'Everyone seems to know who I am today.'

There was a hint of dry humour to her tone, which Aaron

appreciated. She was prettier than her picture in the paper, though still a little battered from the accident, and her dark hair fell like a silk curtain to a couple of inches below her shoulders, dark eyes too, slightly exotic in shape, and a wide mouth with a generous top lip that definitely hit the sexy radar. Too old for him – what was she, thirty-one, thirty-two – but then what was wrong with older?

He glanced past her to the car where her friend waited in the driver's seat and he gave a wave. The friend gave an impatient little wave back, but didn't get out of the car.

'Would it be possible to leave a message for your father? I'd like to pop back and thank him in person if I could, but I appreciate he's a busy man.'

'Of course I'm happy to pass on a message. Would you like to come in for moment or are you in a rush?'

'I…' As Lila glanced hesitantly back at her friend, there was the sound of a second engine. Aaron watched as his mother's car pulled to a halt on the driveway.

As Judith Gruger climbed from the driver's seat, Aaron shouted out. 'You'll never guess who stopped by to see Dad!'

Lila turned to face her. 'Mrs Gruger?'

His mother studied her for a second and he saw the moment recognition hit. Instead of smiling at Lila though, she scowled. 'What are you doing here?'

'I… I stopped by to see your husband. I–'

'He's not here!' Judith snapped.

'Mum!'

'I just wanted to say thank you.' Lila's tone though still a little shaken, had a harder edge to it. 'He saved my life.'

'We're private people, Miss Amberson, and this is private property. I would appreciate it if you and your friend would leave.'

'Mum,' Aaron repeated. 'Stop it!' What was wrong with her? Why was she being so mean to Lila? Was this his father's doing?

'I'm sorry,' he mouthed to Lila, stepping past her and going to Judith. He touched her arm, was shocked to see she was shaking.

'Mum, what's wrong?'

'She needs to go please, Aaron. Make her go. Your father won't like it.'

'Dad's not here.'

'Please, Aaron.'

Reluctantly he turned back to Lila, saw she had already hobbled her way to the car and was getting in the passenger seat. He hurried over.

'Lila, I'm so sorry. I don't know what's got into her.'

Lila gave him a smile, though it didn't touch her eyes, looked forced. 'It's okay. It's not your fault.' Then she squeezed his arm and for a moment the smile seemed genuine. 'Will you please tell your father I stopped by? Tell him I said thank you?'

Aaron returned the smile, wondered if he would ever see her again. 'Of course I will. You have my word.'

———————————

5

Lila spotted her landlady's fat ginger tabby, Clyde, as soon as Beth pulled up outside Lila's flat. He was sitting outside the courtyard gate patiently waiting for her and ran up to the car meowing a greeting as Beth cut the engine.

'Hey there, gorgeous boy.' Lila already had the car door open and was scooping him up, burying her nose in his furry neck as he purred like a freight train. She turned to Beth. 'Coffee?'

'I'll pass if you don't mind. It's getting late.'

Thanking her friend for the lift, Lila put Clyde down on the path and got out of the car. As she made her way up the pathway through the pretty front garden, Clyde running around her feet as she negotiated her crutches, she longed to get out of the clothes Natalie had lent her. Elliot wouldn't be home for another hour, leaving her plenty of time to sink into a hot bath.

Her flat was the ground floor of a converted Victorian house. Her landlady, Primrose Vincent, an avid Norwich City football fan, Guinness drinker, and collector of the creepiest Victorian dolls Lila had ever laid eyes on, occupied the upstairs.

It wasn't The Ritz, but Lila loved her little home, appreciating the quirky layout, the pretty courtyard garden and the city centre location. She also liked her eccentric landlady and was happy to help her out when needed, aware that her rent had barely increased in the years she had lived there. Plus of course, Primrose didn't seem to mind that Clyde spent almost as much time in Lila's flat as he did at home, which was good, as Lila appreciated the feline company.

Yes. It wasn't The Ritz, but it was close enough.

She left the taps running, pouring in a generous amount of her favourite peachy scented bath creme, and hopped through to her bedroom to undress. She had a few more weeks with the cast on her leg and couldn't wait to be shot of it. At least the bruising was starting to fade on her face. The ugly blue-black marks from where she had been flung against the seat belt were the worst. Those would take longer to heal and she was glad that they were mostly hidden under her clothes.

Back in the bathroom, she took a sip from the half glass of wine she had managed to carry through then turning off the taps, she eased herself into the bathtub, cursing when she slipped, sloshing water over the side of the bath and wetting her cast. Her left leg hooked over the side, she eased back, tried to relax, and instead spent a few moments indulging in a pity fest. Damn this awkward bloody cast, damn the ugly bruising, damn the pain the accident had caused. All she wanted was for her life to get back to normal. Was that too much to ask?

A slamming reminder followed the pity fest that Mark and Stephanie would never get to go back to normal. They were gone forever. No second chances for them.

There had been so many people at Stephanie's funeral, family, friends and colleagues, whose lives were all affected by her loss. She had been so young, her life still ahead of her.

Lila's thoughts turned to the visit to the Grugers. Richard Gruger's wife had been so hostile. All Lila had wanted to do was say thank you, but instead she had been ordered off the property.

Jack Foley's anger towards her was understandable, but Mrs

Gruger's was unexpected. Her husband had been away. Would he have greeted Lila with the same hostile reaction or would he have been more welcoming?

And then there was the incident at the hospital that Elliot thought he had witnessed. Her brother had an overactive imagination. Had he overreacted?

Unable to relax, Lila climbed from the bathtub and reached for a towel.

She sat on the edge of the bath for a few moments, sipping at her wine and trying to put the jumbled thoughts in her head into some kind of order. Draining the glass, she made her way through to the bedroom. She was trying to get her pyjamas on when her phone beeped and she picked it up, expecting it to be Natalie.

When Jack had dropped her at the café, Lila had asked her boss if she could start back at work. Natalie had been reluctant, but had relented upon hearing her money worries. The crutches would limit what work Lila could do though and Natalie had promised to give it some thought.

The notification wasn't from Natalie though, instead it was a Facebook friend request.

Lila clicked into her account, viewed the request, taken aback to see the name Aaron Gruger. She had met Richard Gruger's son for five minutes, not even that. Why would he track her down on Facebook and send her a friend request? It was odd. Her finger hovered over the "confirm" and "delete" buttons. Richard Gruger may have saved her life, but did she really want to become friends with his son? Why would he want to anyway? She was several years older than Aaron and they had nothing in common. It made no sense.

As she was debating, another notification popped up. Clicking on it, Lila saw Aaron had sent her a message. She hesitated for a brief second before opening it.

. . .

Hi Lila. Sorry to be contacting u on here. I'm not stalking u, I promise, LOL, but I wasn't sure how else to get in touch. I'm so embarrassed at how my mother acted today. My parents have always been private people, but never rude, and I really don't know y she acted the way she did. Please, she's not normally like that and I'm so sorry. U asked me to say thanks to my dad and I will. Maybe he will invite u to the house some time. Oh, sent you a friend request as not sure u c messages if we're not friends. Aaron.

OKAY, so the message made the friend request less creepy. Aaron felt bad about what had happened and wanted to apologise again. Lila didn't like that he had tracked her down on Facebook though and was still unsure what to do about his friend request.

Instead she stalked his profile, learnt from that he was eighteen and a popular kid. Like Stephanie Whitman, he had several friends, and his posts – which contained a lot of what she guessed he hoped were "mean and moody" selfies – had attracted a lot of likes and comments, especially from girls.

Deciding that for now she would leave the request pending, Lila finished getting into her pyjamas and went through to the living room to wait for Elliot.

'GILES, ARE YOU COMING TO BED?'

'Yes, in five minutes. Promise.'

Giles Buchanan fobbed Alyssa off for the third time, knew she was getting impatient. He needed a few more minutes, couldn't she understand that?

Of course she didn't know what he was doing. He had lied to her, telling her it was work, because he didn't want her to know he was looking into Lila Amberson.

The woman was hiding something, of that Giles was sure. He

had already done his homework on her after the accident, would have been inclined to leave it, but then she had shown up at Stephanie's funeral and he had smelt a rat.

The woman was an opportunist and it seemed he was the only one able to see it.

She wasn't financially stable, propping up her little photography hobby with waitressing work. This car crash was just an excuse for her to cash in.

It had been an accident, Giles did believe that, but Lila Amberson was the sole survivor and, despite Henry's determination to prove Lila's boyfriend, Mark Sutherland, had caused the crash, there was no evidence to back him up. The Whitmans were rich and Lila was aware of that. Why would she have shown up at Stephanie's funeral if she hadn't wanted something?

Lila wanted money and Giles was determined she wasn't going to get a penny. This was his family, his future, and he intended to protect it, by any means necessary.

6

Having spent the past five days brooding and feeling like a jerk for how he had treated Lila Amberson, and deciding he needed to apologise, Jack Foley concluded that Nat's Hideaway would be the logical place to try to track her down.

Yes, she probably shouldn't have shown up at Stephanie's funeral and his anger could easily be put down to emotions running high on the day, but still he had overreacted and, while he might have a quick temper, he would always hold his hands up if he believed he was in the wrong. If he apologised, perhaps Lila Amberson would stop weighing on his mind and he would finally be able to break through the block he had been experiencing over the last few days.

It should have been plain sailing. The edits on his latest book were complete and with his publisher, Tiffany had headed back to London, and his schedule was clear. He had a new plot he had been working on for some time and was keen to crack on with, but the words weren't coming, and those he had forced out were crap.

He wasn't short-sighted enough to believe it was solely down to Lila Amberson. Stephanie's death had left him devastated.

Despite the seventeen-year age gap, she had been the closest to him of his half-siblings and the loss was raw. It was only natural it would affect his writing. Plus her death had him questioning the direction of his own life.

Work was good, great even. Not many people got the chance to do their dream job and be paid handsomely for it. His relationship with Tiffany niggled at him though. They had been dating for almost two years, having met on the set of a BBC adaptation of his first book. Tiffany Pendleton-Shay had been the assistant make-up artist on the production and she had suckered him in with her long limbs, throaty laugh and impulsive attitude. They'd had fun; plenty of drunken nights out, some wild dinner parties with interesting guests, and lots of hot sex. It had started off as a no-strings-attached good time for both of them and they had slowly drifted into something more serious. And that was where the differences between them became more apparent.

Tiff was a Chelsea girl through and through and had no intention of leaving London. Jack had tired of the fast life, wanted to set up home on the North Norfolk coast, get a dog. For the past year they had been making their relationship work long distance, neither of them thinking too far into the future. Stephanie's death had made him re-evaluate everything. He was thirty-four and life wasn't slowing down. He loved Tiff, and God, she was beautiful, all long, tanned legs and dark blonde hair, with crystal eyes that could go from hot to ice in less than a second. But was he in love with her?

Maybe he was feeling like this because of Stephanie. Instead of acting rashly he needed to allow time for his emotions to settle, wait until he was thinking clearly again. Give it a few weeks and maybe he would realise that Tiffany was the right fit. At which point perhaps it was time to take things to the next level and propose. The living arrangements stuff would figure itself out. Either she would relent and move to Norfolk or he would have to consider selling the house and moving to London.

For now, he pushed thoughts of Tiff to one side and focussed on the task at hand. By righting the wrong with Lila, he hoped to start getting his life back on track.

Although he had never been inside Nat's Hideaway, he had driven past it countless times, knew it was a popular place with both locals and tourists.

No doubt Lila had told her work colleagues that he'd been a dick to her, so he didn't expect a warm reception. Hopefully they would realise his apology was sincere though and put him in contact with her.

He found a space in the next street along, parked up, and strolled down to the little café where he had dropped Lila five days earlier. On the day of Stephanie's funeral it had been grey skies and heavy rain. Today was dry and warmer, teasing a promise of summer, and tourists were already out in droves, ambling past the art and craft shops, queuing for ice cream, and sitting along the wall that overlooked the beach as they ate chips from polystyrene trays and tried to avoid the swooping seagulls.

He pushed open the door to the café, charmed at the quirky little bell that chimed, announcing his arrival, and glanced around. The place was small, with only a handful of booths and tables, most of which were occupied. As he made his way to the counter, he sidestepped to let two women pass, glanced casually at the woman serving then did a double take, just as her eyes met his.

Lila.

She wore a pale yellow uniform, her hair tied back, and for a moment she looked shocked, though quickly recovered.

'What are you doing here?' she hissed, voice low so as not to disturb the customers.

Jack didn't answer, instead throwing the same question back at her. 'More like what are *you* doing here?' When her scowl deepened he elaborated, 'Shouldn't you be at home recovering?'

'Since when did you become my doctor?'

She was sassier than when they'd first met. Then she had been contrite, mortified, sympathetic, and he had thrown all of her apologies back in her face. She'd obviously had time to think about that and realise how badly he had behaved towards her.

He ignored the gibe. 'Can we talk for a minute?'

Lila raised her eyebrows at that. 'You want to talk? I thought you never wanted to see me again. What were your words? You wanted me to *stay the hell out of your life*.'

'I overreacted. I didn't mean what I said.'

'You didn't mean it?' she repeated, a hint of sarcasm in her tone.

'That's what I said.'

'Oh, right. So now you've changed your mind and you didn't mean to be rude to me, and I'm supposed to be okay with that?'

'I had just put my sister in the ground. Jesus, give me a break!' The words came out harsher than he'd intended, but he saw the flicker of uncertainty in her eyes as she wavered, her scowl softening as she considered his words. 'I'm sorry, I didn't mean to snap at you, I... can we please talk somewhere private? Five minutes, that's all I ask, then you can tell me to go to hell if you want.'

'Is everything okay out here?' A dark-haired woman came through from the kitchen. She was wearing the same yellow uniform as Lila, her look wary as she eyed Jack.

'I'm fine, Natalie.' Lila hesitated. 'Actually, do you mind if I take my break?'

'Of course.' Natalie's eyes were still on Jack, full of questions, though she didn't ask them. 'I'll get Beth to cover.'

'Thanks, Nat.' Lila turned to Jack. 'There's a park area across the road.'

'Okay.'

He waited for her to get her crutches, stepped ahead to hold the door open for her then followed her over to the park. Not so much a park than an area of grass flanked on three sides by houses, with a boating lake that looked like it hadn't been used in a while, and a handful of benches and tables. There were a few people milling about, but it was quieter than on the esplanade. Lila picked an empty bench, propped her crutches against a nearby table and sat down. They hadn't spoken since leaving the café and the air between them was tense. Jack guessed he couldn't blame her for her hostility. He wasn't proud of how he had treated her on their last encounter.

'Stephanie used to like coming here. She loved the beach, loved all of this coastline.'

When Lila simply stared at him, fingers laced, waiting for him to continue, Jack slipped into the seat facing her.

'There's a whole brood of us, Foleys, Whitmans. When my parents split up, I didn't think Tom and I would be getting any more siblings, but then Mum married Henry and had Alyssa, Oliver and Stephanie. I was seventeen when Steph was born, already finished with school and studying for my A levels. She was the baby of the bunch and I guess I felt more protective towards her. She didn't always see eye to eye with Henry; she could be headstrong and he's a tough old bastard at the best of times. They would fight and she would come to me. I always had her back. Except this time I didn't. She was only seventeen. Her whole life was still ahead of her.'

When Jack paused, needing a moment, the image of his bright, bold, vivacious sister clear in his head, Lila spoke.

'It was an accident, an awful accident. I know you're angry, I know you're grieving, but two people lost their lives that night and no-one is to blame. It was nobody's fault.'

Jack snapped back to the present, looked at her. Her tone had been firm, but her dark eyes were filled with compassion.

'I know that. I know what I said at the funeral, but it was a tough day and I wasn't thinking clearly. Yes it was an accident, but it shocked me when you showed up. What I just told you, I said it because I wanted you to know Stephanie, to understand what she meant to me, so maybe you will realise why I overreacted. I'm not trying to condone my actions. The way I treated you was wrong and I'm sorry.'

Lila was silent for a moment. 'I understand. It hasn't been a breeze for me either. Don't get me wrong, I know I'm lucky, I survived and I will recover from my injuries. It's going to take time. Every day though I ask myself, why me? Why was I the lucky one? I feel guilty as hell knowing that a seventeen-year-old girl died, while I got to live. I'm grateful to be here, but I still feel guilty.'

'Do you remember much about the accident?'

'I don't remember anything.' When Jack arched a brow, she continued. 'I'd been out on a date with Mark. You called him my boyfriend. He wasn't. I'd never met him before that night. A friend had fixed us up and I remember being nervous.'

'About meeting him?'

'I don't do that kind of thing.'

'Date?'

'Not in a while.' She looked uncomfortable, a little embarrassed even. 'I'm too busy with work. Besides, this was a blind date. I definitely don't do *that* kind of thing.'

'So why did you go?'

'My friend bullied me into it. I agreed to shut her up. Then it was too late to back out. I knew within ten seconds of meeting Mark that we weren't going to get along.'

'How so?'

'Because he was arrogant and condescending, and it was obvious he thought he was better than me. I wanted to stay local, go to a pub in Norwich, but he insisted on driving out to the coast. I don't remember much of the evening, but I know I hadn't enjoyed it, that I couldn't wait to get home.' She shrugged. 'And that's pretty much it. Then I woke in hospital.'

'You don't remember anything about the ride home?'

'I've had a couple of flashbacks since coming out of a coma, but they've been brief. We were parked in the woods and I was in the car alone. Mark had disappeared, but I didn't know where.'

'Okay.'

'And then we were in the car. Something was wrong, but he wouldn't tell me.'

'Was that after you were parked in the woods?'

'I don't know. I keep trying to remember, to get it clear in my head, but I can't.'

'Have you told your doctor?'

'Yes, apparently it's common. The memories will probably come back, but there's no timescale. I know it was an accident, but I feel there's something I should be remembering about that night. Something important.'

Lila huffed out a sigh, the frustration clear on her face as she ran her fingers up through her fringe, pushing it away from her forehead, and Jack spotted the bruising where she must have hit her head in the accident.

Noticing he was staring at her, she self-consciously pulled her fringe back into place, sat up straighter. 'Filby is a distance from Cley. How come your sister was out that way?'

'We're not sure. She'd been fighting with Henry a lot the last few weeks. My mum and sister say she had been moody and withdrawn. I didn't see her in those last couple of weeks. I'd been away. She texted a few times, asked if she could come stay for a bit when I got back. It never happened. I was on my way home when I heard about the accident.'

Lila's eyes met his. 'I can't even begin to imagine how it felt hearing that news.'

It had been hell: shock, disbelief, numbness followed by waves of anger, despair and grief. The numbness had been the worst, that and having to watch everyone going about their lives as if this terrible thing hadn't happened. He didn't say it though.

'She liked to drive. She only passed her test six months ago. Henry bought her a car and she loved it. Whenever she needed to get away, blow off some steam, she would go for a drive. We think that's probably what she was doing the night it happened.'

For another moment, he was lost in thoughts of his sister, thinking of the paths of fate that had led her to the wrong place at the wrong time. A warm hand on top of his, gently squeezing in comfort, had him pulling sharply back to the present. He must have stared at Lila in shock, because she looked mortified, quickly withdrawing her hand as colour crept into her cheeks.

'I'm sorry. I shouldn't have done that. It was inappropriate.'

She wrung her hands together, sat straight backed when he continued to stare at her.

Lila Amberson was certainly nothing like he had imagined when he had read about her after the accident. For starters the picture they had used in the press did her few favours, but it was more than that; she radiated warmth. He barely knew her, had met her just twice, but she had reached out to him when he hadn't deserved it, and his instincts told him she was both kind and genuine.

'I... I should get back to work.' She pulled her hands off the table, shoved them in her pockets, and her expression changed to one of recollection. 'The locket.' She pulled a silver chain from her pocket, dangled it in front of him.

'What's that?'

'It was with my belongings when I came home from the hospital, but it's not mine. I believe it belongs to your sister.'

Jack frowned, opening it, not recognising either the locket or the picture of the woman inside. 'Are you sure?'

'It has the initial S on it.' Lila held it in her palm so he could see. 'It has to be Stephanie's. They brought us in together and must have got our things muddled up. I was going to post it, but you're here, so...'

'Okay, thanks.' Jack took the locket, slipped it in his jeans pocket. So he didn't recognise it. He didn't know every piece of jewellery Stephanie had owned. Maybe it was something Henry had given to her and the photo was of one of his relatives.

He got to his feet, picked up Lila's crutches in one hand, held out the other to help her up from the bench. She hesitated, looked a little embarrassed again before taking it.

'I APPRECIATE you giving me five minutes,' he told her as they walked back to the road. 'And I'm sorry again for everything.'

Her smile was fleeting, though her eyes remained warm. 'It's okay. I understand why you reacted how you did. I should have stayed away from the funeral. I'm sorry about your sister though. Please know that.'

'I know.' There was a moment of awkward silence. They had cleared the air and it was unlikely their paths would cross again. 'Okay, well, my car's back this way.' Jack hooked his thumb over his shoulder in the opposite direction to the café. 'Take care of yourself, Lila Amberson.'

He offered his hand and she briefly shook it. 'You too, Jack Foley.'

And then she was stumbling away on her crutches and out of his life. Jack watched her for a second, saw her disappear into a crowd of tourists, and he turned to walk back to his car.

He had barely gone ten yards when he heard the slam of brakes and the screaming, and his head shot round in time to see Lila lying in the road in front of a bus before the sea of people gathering around her blocked his view.

7

Lila stared up at the group of people surrounding her, blinked a couple of times. She must have blacked out, though for the briefest of seconds.

She was aware of the noise, the chatter around her, people asking if she was okay, the sound of a baby crying, someone barking out instructions to call an ambulance. She tried to find her voice, to tell them she was fine, that she didn't need one. She had just stumbled, lost her footing while crossing the road.

But that made no sense. She hadn't been crossing the road. She had said goodbye to Jack, was making her way through a crowd of people, someone had knocked into her.

Not knocked into her, they had pushed her into the path of the bus.

Jeans, dark hoodie, walking closely beside her: she recalled him because she'd thought it odd he had his hood up on a warm day. He had started to pass her, but turned into her at the last moment, elbowing her hard in the ribs, making her lose her footing.

She tried to sit up, was aware of hands pushing her back down.

'You mustn't move, love. You need to stay still until the ambulance gets here.'

'She stepped in front of me!' An angry male voice, the bus driver, Lila presumed. 'It was her fault. There was nothing I could have done.'

Lila glanced up at the bus looming over her. It had hit her, but he must've braked sharply. One of her crutches had caught beneath the front wheel, the metal pole grotesquely twisted. She stared at it numbly; aware it could have been her.

'Let me through.' Another raised voice, but this one she recognised.

Jack Foley.

And then he was in front of her, crouching down, concern on his face.

'Lila, what the hell happened? Are you okay?'

She found her voice. 'I was pushed.'

'What?'

'Someone pushed me.' This time she spoke louder, more urgently, heard a few murmurs in the crowd. 'He was wearing a dark hoodie. I remember him. I wondered why he had his hood up on a hot day. He didn't want me to see his face.'

Jack's eyes narrowed as he took in her words then he was on his feet, scanning the crowd. 'I see him. Hey?'

'Jack!'

It was too late. He had already gone.

'Get them to send the police as well.' A blonde woman was barking orders at a man wearing a Norwich City shirt, who had a phone to his ear.

THE PARAMEDICS ARRIVED FIRST, checking her over and wanting to take her to hospital. Lila insisted she was fine, knew it was likely the adrenaline making her feel that way, but really not wanting to go back to hospital. They made her promise to visit her doctor the following day.

By the time the police car arrived, she was back in Nat's Hideaway, sitting in a booth drinking tea and being fussed over by Beth and Natalie as a baby-faced constable took her statement. Lila had just signed it when Jack burst through the door, looking a little out of breath.

'Ooh, hello.' Beth winked at Lila, earning herself a scowl.

'Did you get him?' Lila demanded.

Jack shook his head, dropped into the seat opposite them. 'I lost him down one of the side roads.'

PC Wallace pulled his pocket book and pen out, paying attention. 'Sir, I'm going to need to ask you a few questions.'

Jack shrugged, sat back as Natalie brought over a glass of Coke, setting it down in front of him. He thanked her before she returned to the counter to serve a waiting customer and he turned his attention back to the constable. 'Okay, go for it.'

'Can I take your name?'

'Jack Foley.'

'As in the author?' That was from Beth, whose eyes had widened in anticipation.

Jack glanced at her, snapped out an impatient 'yes' before looking pointedly at Wallace.

The young constable also looked impressed. 'I've read all of your books,' he told Jack excitedly, as Beth nudged Lila, seeming annoyed because Lila hadn't disclosed this titbit of information to her.

Which was of course because she hadn't known.

Not that it mattered. So Jack was some hotshot author. It made no difference to her.

Beth and PC Wallace were viewing him through new eyes though, positively gushing while Jack looked a little bored, as though he had gone through this scenario a hundred times before.

'You said you had some questions,' he reminded Wallace.

'Err, yes. I did.' Wallace studied the page in his notebook as though seeking inspiration. 'Yes, Mr Foley...'

'Jack.'

'Okay, Mr Foley... Jack. You pursued the suspect. Did you see him push Miss Amberson?'

'No. I was walking back to my car and I heard the bus slam on its brakes and people screaming. When I turned back, Lila was lying in the road. She saw who pushed her.'

Lila hugged her arms around her, recalling the moment. She sipped at her tea, annoyed when her hand shook, rattling the cup against the saucer as she set it down.

'Yes.' PC Wallace glanced over the statement Lila had signed. 'Dark hoodie, jeans, and he was wearing the hood up.'

'Correct,' Jack confirmed.

'And you saw him running away?'

'No, I saw him standing on the edge of the crowd, watching. I guessed it was him because of the hood then he must have seen me looking at him because he bolted.'

'Did you see his face?'

'Nope. He kept the hood up, face down. He didn't want anyone recognising him.'

'How about his height and build?'

Jack shrugged. 'Maybe a couple of inches shorter than me, five-nine, five-ten perhaps, slim build... I guess that doesn't help much.'

'Everything helps, Mr Foley... Jack.'

'He was a runner.'

'Sorry?'

'He was fast. I'm not exactly out of shape, but I chased after him for at least five minutes, maybe longer, and he didn't flag. He picked up pace when he needed to, was able to lose me.'

PC Wallace nodded, jotted that down, before going through a

few more questions, asking them to contact the station if they remembered anything else.

Jack got up to shake the constable's hand, see him out, and Lila took another sip of her drink, sloshing tea over the side of the cup.

Beth's eyes narrowed. 'You're shaking.'

'So would you be if a bus hit you,' Natalie pointed out dryly, returning to the table for the constable's empty glass.

'I'm fine.'

'She needs something sugary,' Jack told them, coming back to the booth. 'It's the adrenaline rush.' He pushed his glass of Coke in front of her. 'Here, drink this.'

'I'm fine,' Lila repeated, embarrassed at all the fuss. 'Honestly, it's all a bit of a shock, but I'm okay.'

'You want me to call Elliot?' Beth asked.

'No, he's at work. Give me another fifteen minutes and I'll be fine to go back behind the counter.'

Natalie was horrified. 'You're kidding, right? I'm sending you home.'

Lila sipped at the Coke, willing the shaking to stop. 'But I'm fine.'

'No "buts", Lila. This isn't up for negotiation. Beth can drive you home. I can cope by myself until she gets back.'

'I'll take her.'

Jack's offer had all three women looking at him.

'You will? I mean…' Lila stammered. 'You don't have to do that.'

'It's fine.'

'But I live in Norwich. It's over twenty miles away.'

'I know how far it is. I've been there plenty of times before.' He smiled at Lila, looking amused, and she was suddenly reminded of the Facebook photo with him and his sister. He had looked happy then. This was the first time she had seen him smile since she'd met him. Guilt gnawed at her, remembering that she had snooped on a private memory.

'I have to say, if you could it would really help us out,' Natalie told him. 'I'm happy to cover, but it's a warm day and we're busy. It's easier if Beth can stay here.'

'I agree,' Beth chipped in. 'We don't want to leave Natalie in the lurch, do we.'

She gave Lila a knowing look that had nothing to do with not wanting to leave Natalie in the lurch, which had Lila's cheeks heating.

Jack didn't seem to notice, already sliding out of the booth. 'I'll go get the car.'

So that was it, yet another decision had been made for her. Frustrated, Lila sipped her Coke.

'So,' Beth turned to her the second Jack had gone. 'The bloke at the funeral, the dead girl's brother, I think you skimmed over a few of the details there, Lila.'

'There was nothing more to tell.'

'*Nothing more to tell*, Lila, are you blind? He's hot, he's into you, and he's Jack freaking Foley, the author.'

'I've never heard of Jack *freaking* Foley, the author,' Lila pointed out. 'Besides, he's not into me. He stopped by to apologise for the whole funeral thing. He's only being nice to me because I got hit by a bus.'

'I know you've just had the whole bus thing, but I want to slap you, Lila. You've been single for so long you don't even recognise the signs when a bloke is interested.'

'There are no signs. Seriously, stop trying to fix me up with everyone I meet.'

THEY WERE STILL ARGUING five minutes later when Jack returned to the café.

'You never said if you thought he was hot,' Beth whispered slyly, before sliding out of the booth.

'You ready to go?'

Lila shot Beth a look, stared up at Jack, a little flustered.

'Sure.' She looked around. 'I need my crutches though.'

'You only had one with you when the paramedics brought you in,' Natalie reminded her, bringing it over.

'Of course.' Lila recalled seeing her crutch under the bus wheel. It would be useless. 'The other one got crushed.'

'We can stop by the hospital. Get you another one.'

'You don't have to…' Lila reminded herself she didn't have a choice. She stopped, made the effort to smile at Jack. 'Okay, thanks.'

She slid out of the booth, considering how best to use the crutch Natalie held out to her. As Lila balanced it under her left arm, Jack slipped his arm under her free one and, snaking it around her waist, took the bulk of her weight.

'Hold on to my shoulder,' he instructed.

Given his lean build, he was stronger, harder than he looked, and Lila was very much aware of the warmth of his body through the cotton of his T-shirt, could smell the subtle scents of soap and washing powder.

She snuck a glance at Beth, annoyed to see her friend staring back, a broad grin on her face, knowing she wasn't going to live this down.

'No work for the rest of this week,' Natalie ordered. 'You go see your doctor tomorrow as the paramedics told you and get plenty of rest.'

'I may be okay tomorrow.'

'Not happening, Lila. I know you need the money and I'll try to help you with that as much as I can, but you also need to take care of yourself. You're taking the rest of the week off and that's final. Now let Jack take you home and you get some rest, okay?'

Lila pouted a little, but managed to turn it into a smile. Natalie had been nothing but good to her and it wasn't fair to be mad at her for the situation she was in. 'Okay. Thank you.'

'Take care of her, Jack,' Beth called after them, a smugness to her tone, as Jack helped Lila out of the café.

'I THINK your friend is reading more into this than there is.' He didn't seem embarrassed or annoyed. More amused.

'I'm so sorry, she does this all the time; she tries to fix me up with all of our suppliers. One is in his seventies and doesn't even have teeth.'

Lila's comment had Jack laughing, which in turn made her less tense. She was still a little shaky after being pushed, but the Coke had helped. Feeling easier in his company, she relaxed into him, letting him help her to his car.

It was a weird situation. She had only met him a couple of times and he had initially been hostile, rude and angry. Now he was going out of his way to help her.

It was guilt, she reminded herself. He was beating himself up for how he had treated her and was trying to make amends. Had she not been pushed in front of the bus, Jack would already be out of her life and on his way back to Cley or wherever he lived. Instead he had stayed and was trying his best to help her.

IT WAS close to an hour's drive back to Norwich, plus of course they had to stop off at the hospital, and Lila expected conversation to be stilted. They had said all that needed to be said while sitting in the park and she didn't imagine they had much in common. Jack Foley moved in different circles to her, plus the memory lingered of her last uncomfortable car journey with him, so she was surprised at how chatty he was this time, the conversation easy, and the time passing quickly.

He stopped at the hospital, parking as close as possible to the physiotherapy department, helping Lila inside the building then proving charmingly persuasive with the receptionist in getting Lila seen quickly. She recognised a couple of the nurses from her stay at the hospital, was pleased when they remembered her too, both of them greeting her warmly, expressing concern over her latest accident.

'THEY'RE FIGURING you have seven lives left,' Jack commented wryly, as they made their way back to the car.

'Sorry?'

'Like a cat? Nine lives?'

'Oh, Jesus, I don't want seven more accidents.'

Jack sobered. 'What happened today wasn't an accident, Lila.' He held open the passenger door for her, taking the crutches and helping her into the seat.

'I know. I just hope the police catch him before he does it to someone else.'

Jack climbed into the driver's seat, pulled the door shut. He was silent for a moment; his hand stilled on the ignition key as he turned to face her. 'Okay, I don't want you to freak out, but what if it wasn't a random attack.'

'What are you saying?' A chill ran down Lila's spine. It was a redundant question, as she knew exactly what he was implying.

'What if you were the target all along?'

'Why would someone want to hurt me?'

'I don't know. Have you pissed anyone off lately?'

'Aside from you?'

Jack's lips twisted. 'Touché. I deserved that. Seriously though, you need to think about it. If it wasn't a random attack it's possible you may be targeted again.'

It was a scary thought, but one she had to consider. Lila gave Jack her postcode, settling back in the seat as he typed it into the satnav, letting his words sink in, annoyed that she was shaking again.

Did she have an enemy? Was there someone out there who wished her harm?

8

Lila was quiet on the ride home from the hospital. Jack could tell she was mulling over his words, considering them, and while he knew he had probably frightened her a little, if there was a chance that someone was intentionally trying to hurt her, she needed to be on her guard.

The satnav took him to a quiet street half a mile from the city centre.

'It's here on the left.'

Lila directed him to the one house in the street of large Victorian terraces that actually looked as if someone really cared about it, the long front courtyard garden filled with summer flowers and hanging baskets and a cobbled pathway leading to a bright red front door that, along with the white window frames, looked recently painted. She hesitated for a moment. 'Would you like to come in for coffee?'

'Don't you want to rest? You did just get–'

'Hit by a bus. Yeah, everyone keeps reminding me of that.' She smiled. 'You drove me all the way home. The least I can do is make you a coffee before you drive back.'

'Okay, sure.' Seeing that she got safely inside probably wasn't a bad idea. 'You like gardening?' he asked, following her as she hobbled her way up the front path.

'Oh this? It's not mine. The house belongs to my landlady. She rents me the ground floor flat.'

Jack mentally slapped himself. He had assumed the house belonged to Lila, forgetting that she was a part-time waitress and photographer, and, according to the comment from her boss, relied on every penny. Properties in the centre of Norwich had skyrocketed in recent years and houses like this would be worth a premium, likely well out of her price range.

She leant on one crutch as she fished for the keys in her bag, opened the door and led him into a bright spacious hallway, stopping before another door and turning the key in the lock. 'It's through here.'

The flat wasn't huge, but the high ceilings and wide sash windows gave it a bright and airy feel while the ornamental ceiling rose, fireplace, and restored floorboards were in good order, suggesting the house – like the garden – had been well cared for over the years. Painted in warm rich colours, Lila's personality was all over the place, from the quirky wind chimes and ornaments to the photography on the walls.

'Sit down,' she ordered, pointing to an old sofa covered in a patchwork throw and scattered with cushions. 'I'll go put the kettle on.'

'Why don't I do that since you had the whole bus thing?'

Lila shot him a look. 'Everything's working. I can still make coffee. Sit.'

She had been shaky after the accident and he knew that had pissed her off. Her adrenaline was still spiked though and the aches and pains from that day's incident hadn't hit her yet. Lila Amberson valued her independence, he could see that, knew that she didn't like having to ask for or accept help.

He didn't argue the point, leaving her to go to make the coffee, but he didn't sit either, instead studying the photos she had adorned the walls with, recognising many local places. There was no denying her talent, taking an ordinary scene and bringing out the extraordinary; from the forest at Holkham with the shaft of light falling through the pine trees bathing the forest floor with an ethereal glow to a young child running away from the camera down a rainy cobbled street, the only colour in the picture coming from the child's bright yellow rain mac.

'Do you want milk, sugar?'

'Neither, thanks.' Jack turned to study the opposite wall, eyes immediately drawn to a striking canvas of boats moored at Burnham Overy Staithe, a scene he knew well. The shot had been taken at sunset; the sky filled with hues of pink and orange, the water a dark inky blue.

'Your photos are great. You take all of these yourself?'

'Yeah.'

She sounded distracted and he stepped through into the tiny kitchen to see her struggling with full mugs of coffee and crutches.

'Here.' He took both mugs before she could object, caught her look that was somewhere between annoyed and grateful, carrying them through to the living room.

She hobbled behind him, took a seat on the sofa, set her crutches down, and accepted the mug of coffee he passed her.

'Thank you.'

Jack remained standing, studying the rest of the pictures. There were a few more scenic shots of the county, others that were taken abroad: a Parisian street, what looked like a Greek tavern with strings of lights winding around olive trees. He turned back to the photo of the kid in the yellow mac.

'Was this a random lucky shot?'

'That's my friend, Natalie's son, Joe. It's about fifteen years old and one of the first pictures I took. We were out in the rain and he looked so cute splashing in the puddles I got my camera out, snapped a couple of dozen shots. This was the winning one.'

'Your photos are good.'

'Thank you. I got the arty streak and my brother is the academic.'

'Is it just the two of you?'

For a moment, Lila looked wistful before a frown knotted her brow. 'For as long as I can remember.'

'What about your parents?'

'My dad died not long after Elliot was born. Mum married again within a year, mostly for the security. She wasn't around much after I turned sixteen and was old enough to keep an eye on Elliot. She's off living it up on honeymoon with husband number four.' She gave a dismissive shrug, like it didn't matter, when it clearly did.

Jack dropped into the armchair facing her, stretched his legs out, and took a sip of his coffee, studying her. He had been so angry when Lila had shown up at Stephanie's funeral, only able to see what he had lost and the future that had been taken away from his sister. He had initially blamed Lila, knowing that, although the accident hadn't been her fault, had she not been there at that precise time, his sister would still be alive. He had been too short-sighted to see that Lila had been a victim too, that she deserved to live as much as Stephanie. She had a life and a talent, and people whose lives would have been just as affected had she been in Stephanie's place.

'So you're some hotshot author then.' Her words broke through his thoughts.

'I'm not sure I would use the word "hotshot", but yeah, I write.'

'Beth and PC Wallace seemed impressed. I thought they were going to ask for your autograph.' Lila looked amused and he heard the teasing in her tone, understood that she wanted to turn the subject away from her mother, and that was okay. 'What sort of books do you write?'

'Fiction. Thrillers. You a reader?'

'I am when I have the time. I like thrillers. So how did you get into doing that?' She paused, as if seeking the right words. 'It's something you always wanted to do, right... needed to do? I guess like my photography. I've never really wanted to do anything but take pictures, capture moments. But it's not an easy industry to crack.'

She got it; Jack saw that, the burning need to create something, knowing that you would continue to do it even if it never amounted to anything.

'I was a journalist for a while, figured I would follow in my dad's footsteps. After I graduated university, I moved to London, managed to get a junior job at one of the tabloids and worked my way up. It was never enough though. I had always written, tried to get published, but with no success. I focussed on my career for a while, but the writing bug never went away. A few things happened, made me re-evaluate everything.' He paused, decided not to elaborate. Lila Amberson didn't need his life story. 'I ended up quitting my job, travelling, and while I was away I wrote a book, pitched it to a few agents when I got back, got lucky with one, then the rest is history.

'I'd like to say it was that easy for everyone. I know it's not. I did get lucky. I had a good team working with me who believed in me and they got my book in front of the right people. It sold massively, became a bestseller, and more books, plus a generous deal, followed. Now I get to write full-time, do the thing I love the most, and I wouldn't change that for the world.'

He'd been caught in the moment, drew himself back to find Lila studying him. She pulled her one good leg up onto the sofa, dark eyes understanding.

'I get why you love it.' There was no teasing in her tone. 'I'm glad you get to do what makes you happy.'

Silence lingered between them for a moment then the sound of a key in the latch, the door barging open and a pile of papers slipping to the floor. The guy who had dropped them let out a curse; still oblivious to the fact Jack and Lila were sitting in the living room.

'Elliot? You're early.'

The man jumped, eyes darting up and spotting them both. Jack got up, retrieved the papers from the floor, handing them to him.

'Um, thanks.' Elliot looked confused as he studied Jack, blinked owlishly behind his glasses.

'Elliot, this is Jack Foley, Stephanie Whitman's brother. I had an accident at work and he gave me a lift home. Jack, in case you haven't guessed, this is my brother.'

'Oh.' Elliot looked at Jack again, realisation dawning. 'Oh.'

He regarded the hand Jack offered with suspicion before shaking it briefly then wheeled on Lila, as the rest of her words registered.

'Accident? What accident?'

Lila put her leg down, sat up straight. 'Okay, now I don't want to stress you out, but someone pushed me in front of a bus.'

'What?' Elliot was looking like he was about to hyperventilate.

'It's okay, I wasn't hurt and the police know. Jack was there and he gave me a ride home.'

'Why don't you sit down,' Jack suggested. Elliot had gone white and looked like he might lose his lunch. He was younger than Lila, Jack guessed by about ten years, and awkwardly geeky, though he could see similarities. They shared the same dark hair, dark almond-shaped eyes and stubborn chin.

As Elliot sat looking dumbstruck and Lila started to explain what had happened, Jack slipped into the kitchen, put on the kettle, and fished in the cupboard for a mug.

Lila had an eclectic mix, most of them chipped, and he selected the closest half-decent one, emblazoned with a picture of a sunglasses-wearing polar bear and the words "Daddy Cool", considered how Elliot might take his coffee and, taking a chance, dumped both milk and sugar in the cup.

'HE INTENTIONALLY PUSHED YOU?' Elliot was questioning as Jack returned. 'You're sure?'

'He pushed me,' Lila insisted. 'He even hid his face so he wouldn't be seen.'

Jack held out the mug. 'Here you go, buddy.'

'Thank you.'

Elliot took the mug without question, barely taking notice of it. He continued to stare at Lila as Jack took a seat beside her on the sofa.

'If he did this… if he really did what you said, what if he's done it before?'

'What do you mean?'

Elliot absently took a sip of the coffee, immediately choking and spitting it back into the cup. 'Yuck, sugar!' He pulled a face, set the cup to one side.

'What do you mean, if he's done it before?' Lila repeated.

Elliot nudged his glasses up his nose and sniffed. 'I told you that when you were in the hospital, I found someone in your room.'

Jack narrowed his eyes. Lila had mentioned nothing about that.

'I remember,' Lila told him, her tone a little brisk. 'What is it, Elliot?'

Elliot glanced hesitantly at Jack, seemed to take his measure then obviously decided he could trust him. 'He was wearing a hood.'

Elliot licked his lips nervously and Jack felt the tension in Lila as she froze beside him.

'You were attacked at the hospital?' he demanded, annoyed that he was only just finding this out.

Lila didn't answer, instead stared at Elliot.

'I'm sorry, Lila, I know I said I overreacted, but what if I was wrong. What if the person who did this is the same man who tried to hurt you before?'

9

R ichard Gruger pulled into the long driveway that led up to the family home, head pounding, eyes tired, keen to have a hot shower and a glass of his favourite whisky.

It was not far off nine thirty and the pretty sunset he had enjoyed, the sky aflame with burning shades of orange, as he had driven along the bypass, had almost faded into darkness.

Richard appreciated pretty things; from sunsets to the neatly tended rhododendron bushes in full flower that flanked the winding driveway, to the company he had kept over the past few days. He pulled his Jag to a halt beside his wife's Toyota, grabbed his suitcase from the boot, and hauled it to the front door where Judith stood dutifully waiting, clearly having heard his arrival.

'Welcome home. Did you have a good conference?'

She offered her cheek and he brushed his lips against it briefly, irritation already swirling in the pit of his stomach. Yes, he appreciated pretty things, but Judith wasn't one of them.

He guessed he must have found her attractive enough when she was younger, but she hadn't aged well, didn't take enough care with her appearance, preferring instead to focus her efforts on looking after her family. Richard didn't love her, hadn't done in a long while. Wondered if he ever really had. A lesser man would have walked away, but his parents had instilled values in him, taught him that divorce was for the weak. Plus of course it helped that Judith came from money, stood to inherit a fortune when her parents died. Richard had a good job and a decent income, but it wasn't in the same league. Judith's inheritance was going to set him up for life.

'It was fine,' he said, pushing past her into the hallway. Of course there had been no teaching conference, but she didn't know that, was gullible enough to believe everything he told her, her loyalty and unwavering belief in him making it easy for him to play her as a fool. He pushed the door closed, shrugging her off as she fussed around him, trying to help him with his jacket.

'I kept dinner in the oven for you. I know you said you would eat on the way home, but… I thought you might still be hungry. It's shepherd's pie, your favourite.' She wrung her hands together. 'I could make you up a plate.'

Richard loosened his tie, turned his back on her and skulked into the lounge. 'I just want a whisky,' he grumbled, amazed at how a couple of minutes in her company could crank up his irritation levels.

'Here, honey, let me pour it for you. You must be exhausted.'

When Judith tried to wrestle the whisky bottle from him, his temper snapped.

'God, woman, will you stop fussing, for crying out loud?'

She flinched at his tone. 'I'm sorry, Rich. I was only trying to help.'

'You can help me by giving me a little breathing space.'

'Is there a problem here?'

Richard glanced at his son who had slunk into the room. He was still only eighteen, but Aaron already matched him in build and height. He had his mother's colouring; dark hair and eyes, though mercifully hadn't inherited her dozy personality.

'There's no problem, Aaron. How is your studying going?'

'Fine. How was your teaching conference?'

Richard could see the disapproval in his eyes, hear it in his tone. Aaron knew he hadn't been at a teaching conference.

He wouldn't say anything to Judith though, Aaron understood that if his mother ever found out the truth about his father it would break her.

'Good.' Richard poured his drink, took a sip of whisky. 'In fact, I'm beat. Why don't you keep your mother company. I'm going upstairs for a shower and an early night.'

'You had a visitor while you were away.' Aaron's voice was teasing almost.

'Aaron!' Judith scolded in a hushed whisper. 'You promised.'

Richard's back stiffened, hand tightening on his glass. 'Who? Another reporter?'

He didn't welcome company, liked the privacy his home gave him, and hadn't appreciated the intrusion into his personal life after he had pulled that wretched girl from the broad. He was more than aware that when people started looking too closely, they sometimes found things they weren't supposed to.

'No, this visitor was better than a reporter.'

'Aaron, please...' Judith sounded panicky, her expression contrite when Richard spun round. 'I wasn't going to say anything. I knew you wouldn't be happy.'

'Who was here, Judith?' Richard dropped his voice to a silky whisper, one he knew his wife and son recognised as a warning they were treading on dangerous ground.

While Judith quaked, seeming afraid to say, Aaron smiled slyly, not backing down. 'Lila Amberson stopped by. She wanted to thank the man who saved her life.'

Richard bristled. He had known she might come looking for him, had hoped she wouldn't. 'So you were going to keep this from me?' he demanded of Judith, the easiest target for his anger. 'You were going to lie to my face?'

'I didn't want to worry you. I made her go. I told her she wasn't welcome.'

'You lied to me!'

'I didn't lie. Please, Rich, you have to understand. I did what I thought was best.'

When Judith reached for his hand, he pulled away, hurling his whisky glass against the wall in rage.

'Dad!'

'I am the head of this household. I make the decisions of what is best for this family.'

'Rich, I'm sorry, please don't be mad.'

'How am I supposed to be? I have a wife who is a liar, who is conspiring behind my back to keep things from me.'

When the pathetic woman sobbed, he twisted the knife deeper. 'This is the kind of homecoming I get? I come back tired from my trip and all I wanted to do was relax and have a drink, but oh no, you had to go and ruin that for me.'

'Richard, please.'

'You're an arsehole.'

Richard scowled at Aaron. 'You watch your mouth or you'll be sorry.'

His son glowered back, but was smart enough to keep his mouth shut.

'I'm going upstairs for my shower. I suggest you have this mess cleaned up by the time I get back down.' He stormed from the room, away from Judith's pathetic wails and Aaron's attempts to console her.

THE SHOWER DID little to ease Richard's tension, the night of Lila Amberson's accident replaying in his mind. He had been the first car on the scene, had already been in the water when a second vehicle had stopped on the bridge, and there had been no escaping the questions, first from the police then later from the press.

So far his lies of where he had been that night had held up, but it only took one person to dig too deep, and the truth would be exposed.

How he wished his and Lila's paths hadn't crossed.

And now she wanted to thank him for saving her life.

If she came here looking for him again, he would have to find a way to deal with her.

10

'Okay. Please keep me updated.' Lila ended the call with PC Wallace before muttering, 'And thanks for nothing.'

Frustrated, she hurled the phone across the room as Elliot walked in. He ducked as it whizzed past his ear.

'Jesus, Lila, do you mind?' He sniffed indignantly, bending to retrieve the phone and handing it to her. 'I didn't have to lend you this, you know. You should be more respectful of other people's property.'

'Sorry… I'm sorry.' Lila slipped the phone in her pocket. 'I was just talking to the police.'

'What did they say? Have they managed to find him?'

'No, and I don't think they're looking very hard.'

'Why?' Elliot dropped into the chair facing her, looking annoyed. 'This man pushed you in front of a bus. And he might have tried to hurt you before. Why would they not take that seriously?'

'Because they don't think he meant to push me. They think it was an accident.'

'What? That's crazy. People saw him do it.'

'But that's just it, they didn't. They've spoken with everyone and they all say the same thing; that they saw me fall in front of the bus. No-one actually saw me get pushed. Not even the bus driver.'

'But he ran away. Jack chased him.'

'PC Wallace thinks he was probably in a hurry and nudged me to get past, that I lost my footing, then when he realised what had happened, he panicked and ran.'

'That's bullshit.'

'I know that, but I don't think they believe me. Don't get me wrong; they're still trying to find him, but I don't think it's a priority. And they definitely don't think it's related to what you say happened in the hospital.'

Elliot's expression hardened. 'I know what I saw. You believe me, don't you?'

'Of course.'

At least Lila believed that Elliot thought he had seen someone in her hospital room trying to hurt her. After her conversation with Wallace, she was beginning to even doubt herself, and she couldn't know for sure what had happened while she had been in a coma.

'It's not too late to cancel my trip. I can stay here if you want me to.'

'Oh, Elliot, you don't have to do that.'

Her brother had his annual geekfest break planned with his friends: this year in Scotland where the six of them had hired a cottage in the Highlands for five days of comics, role playing and board games, and they were due to depart that weekend. Lila knew how much he was looking forward to it and would never make him miss it, despite it meaning she would be alone for most of the week.

'My leg's getting better by the day. I really don't need you to keep babysitting me.'

'But what if this bloke's really trying to hurt you?'

'Then I'll keep the doors and windows locked and stay safe

indoors.' Lila forced a bright smile. Although the reaction from the police had pissed her off, she was relishing having her flat to herself for a few days. 'I'm going to lie down for a bit, I have a banging headache. You wanna order takeout again for dinner?'

Elliot, who had less enthusiasm for the kitchen than Lila, immediately perked up at the idea of not having to cook. 'Pizza?'

'Fine with me,' Lila agreed, reaching for her crutches.

'Oh, I almost forgot. I have some good news. I've got your sim card.' Elliot reached into his pocket. 'Dave managed to get it working for you.'

'Really?'

'You can load it into my old phone and get all of your contacts and pictures back.'

'That's not just good news, that's great news, thank you,' Lila told him, genuinely pleased. 'Tell Dave I owe him a drink.'

She made her way through to her bedroom, sat down on the bed and picked up her phone. There were two texts, one from Natalie checking she was okay, the other from Beth asking if anything had happened with Jack. Lila smiled as she replied to both, thanking Natalie for her concern, and telling Beth in no uncertain terms that nothing had happened with Jack, that nothing was going to happen with Jack, and she was off the mark with this one.

But would you want something to happen with Jack?

Clyde, who had been snoozing on the chair she used as a clotheshorse, stretched lazily and yawned before sauntering over for a head bop. Lila scratched him under the chin, annoyed she was actually considering the question.

Jack Foley had been horrible to her the first time they'd met and it was difficult to get past how he had initially treated her. Or at least it would be if he hadn't gone above and beyond to try to make things right. Not many people would give a stranger a lift while attending a family member's funeral. And he had sought her out to apologise for his behaviour, even sticking around to help her after the second accident.

There was no denying he was gorgeous, those light blue eyes that seemed to look right through her and that scruffy golden brown hair giving him a dishevelled charm. He was out of her league though, moved in completely different circles. Beth was barking up the wrong tree.

Still she looked Jack up again on Facebook, annoyed that his profile gave nothing away. Instead she turned to Google, typed his name in the search engine. He was a novelist so there was bound to be some articles about him.

She found his website, read a little about his books, intrigued to know more about them. Clicking on to Amazon, she downloaded the first one onto her Kindle.

Back to Google and she read through a few more articles, both surprised and annoyed at the stab of jealousy when she came across a picture of him with his arm around a stunningly pretty blonde. Tiffany Pendleton-Shay.

Girlfriend? The article didn't say.

Irritated by her reaction, Lila inserted the sim card Elliot had given her into his old phone, waited for it to load. Although he hadn't said it, she got the impression PC Wallace thought she was a little paranoid after all she had been through, and the truth was she was unsettled knowing she only had fragments of memory from the night of the accident.

Perhaps he was right and she was trying to create something sinister out of what had been nothing more than an unexpected tragedy. And as for what Elliot thought he had seen, well, her brother had always had an overactive imagination. Too much time spent with zombies and Marvel superheroes probably had him reading too much into an innocent situation.

It wasn't in Lila's nature to be dramatic or jump to conclusions. She was a pragmatist. If she could just fill in the blanks from the night of the accident, it would help put her mind at ease.

She scrolled through her contacts; pleased to see they were all back. While she had managed to get hold of a handful of numbers, there were many she had been missing. Clicking into photos, she was relieved they had all saved and made a mental note to back them up before she lost them again. She really did owe Dave a drink.

She clicked through the first half a dozen, not remembering taking them, before spotting the date and realising they were all stamped the night of the accident.

Curious, she studied them closely.

They had been taken in the dark, all similar shots of the moon casting a glow over water. Filby Broad, she realised; the place where they had crashed.

Suddenly she was back there, standing on the bridge, snapping away, trying to get the perfect shot. Although there was no footpath, the usually busy road was quiet due to the lateness of the night. It was peaceful, atmospheric and ever so slightly spooky.

Lila glanced back towards the trees on the other side of the road and the little footpath that led to the car park in the woods.

Mark had left her in the car muttering to himself about needing to pee. It should have taken him two minutes, not ten, and Lila guessed he was sulking, trying to punish her for rejecting his advances when he had pulled off the road, clearly expecting they were going to have a post-date sex session before he took her home. The argument that had followed would ensure it was an uncomfortable ride back to Norwich.

Waiting alone in the car had been both boring and creepy, and eventually Lila had decided she'd had enough. Mark hadn't replied when she had called him and she had been reluctant to venture too far into the woods. Instead she followed the little path that led to the road, unable to resist photographing the scene she found before her.

While she didn't particularly relish the idea of going back to the empty car, she also didn't want to risk Mark returning and leaving without her, and she made her way back, figuring she would give him another few minutes before calling Beth and asking her friend to come and pick her up.

Beth wouldn't be happy about turning out at that time of night, but it was her fault Lila was in the situation in the first place. She should have stuck to her guns and her happy single status and not let herself be bullied into going on a blind date. It was the last time she planned on taking Beth's advice.

Huffing to herself, she made her way along the path, cursing as brambles scraped against her bare legs. She was beginning to need the loo herself, the two bottles of lager and glass of wine she'd had in the pub making its way through her. The idea of squatting down in the dark woods didn't appeal though and she swore again when she arrived back at the car to find Mark still hadn't returned.

Where the bloody hell was he?

She peered into the darkness, trying to pluck up courage to go find him, but part of her worried this was some sick game he was playing with her.

She should call Beth.

As she reached into her bag for her phone, a noise came from the woods. Heavy footsteps snapping against twigs, the sound of panting. Startled, Lila swung around as Mark appeared in the clearing. He was out of breath but didn't stop as he pushed past her to the driver's door.

'Where the bloody hell have you–?'

'Get in the car!'

'What the hell–'

'Get in the car, now!'

He was already behind the wheel, fumbling with his keys in

the ignition, looking ready to drive off if she didn't comply. Mad as she was, he was also scaring her and Lila didn't want to be left behind, so she quickly climbed in the passenger seat, reaching for her seat belt as he hurtled out of the car park, heading back into Filby.

'Damn it, Mark. Slow down. You're going the wrong way. What the hell's going on?'

He looked at her then and the wide-eyed fear on his face chilled her.

'What's wrong with you?' she whispered.

He started to answer, then snapped back, just as the car bumped against the verge and he fought to stay in control as it skidded across the road.

Lila screamed as the car swung around, flinging her against the door and they came to a halt facing the opposite direction.

THERE WAS silence and the thump of her heart pounding. 'I don't know what's wrong with you,' she demanded as he slid the car back into gear. 'But I want out, now!'

She reached for the door handle but wasn't quick enough as Mark floored the accelerator, heading back towards the bridge.

'Mark! Stop the car!'

He was driving too fast and as they approached the bridge, he turned again and looked at her, his face pale and sheened with sweat. 'I can't. We have to go.'

Lila saw the fear, her stomach dropping as the car flew over the bridge, and caught the glare of oncoming headlights. Close, too close.

She reached for the steering wheel. 'Mark! Watch out!'

AND THEN THE flashback was over and she was in her room, sitting on the bed, her chest tight, her palms damp and her limbs like jelly. She clutched the phone in her hand, needing a moment to pull herself together.

Just what had happened the night of the accident?

KATE WHITMAN GLANCED at her eldest son as she folded laundry, the briefest hint of a smile on her face. 'So I know you didn't stop by to check up on me. You and Tom have been taking turns and he was here this morning.'

Jack opened his mouth to protest and she forced the smile up a notch. 'I'm your mother, Jack. Trust me. I know how you work.'

She said the words with confidence, even though it still cut deep that she hadn't been able to figure out her youngest daughter. If only Stephanie had talked to her instead of getting behind the wheel whenever she needed to think or to cool off, maybe she would still be here. At times the sadness threatened to pull her under and she had to remind herself that she still had four other children – albeit adult children – who needed her. She would be strong for them.

'So, tell me. What's on your mind?'

They had been drinking tea in the kitchen, as Kate kept her hands busy. Henry had always insisted on employing a maid, but Kate had never been afraid of housework and, finding it therapeutic in helping with the grieving process, she had given Maria the week off. Her talented son who usually had no trouble with words was brooding before her, a frown on his handsome face as he tried to figure out a way to say whatever it was he had come here for.

'I met with Lila Amberson.'

There it was, off with the Band-Aid. Kate remained silent, her expression neutral. She knew the woman had been at Stephanie's funeral, though only after the event when Giles had conveniently let it slip before urging her not to tell Jack. Kate had no allegiance to Giles though, was fully aware that Alyssa's boyfriend worked to his own agenda. Still, she didn't share what she knew, curious to hear what Jack had to say.

'She showed up at the church and I lost my temper with her. I went to see her to apologise.'

That was Jack; hot-headed at times, but always willing to put things right if he realised he was in the wrong.

Kate wasn't sure how she would have reacted if she had seen Lila Amberson at the funeral. She was level-headed enough to know the woman wasn't to blame, that she too had been a victim in the accident, but emotions had been running high, particularly on that day, and it was likely neither her presence nor her condolences would have been welcomed. 'Why are you telling me this now, Jack?'

'I wasn't going to tell you. In fact, I thought it was better you didn't know. But then Lila gave me this.' He reached into his pocket, held up a chain. 'She thinks it was Stephanie's and accidentally got put with her things at the hospital.'

Kate frowned at the chain, not recognising it. 'I don't think so.'

'It's got the initial S on it, so it makes sense, and there's a picture. No-one I recognise, but I thought maybe Henry's mother? Perhaps he gave it to Steph as a keepsake?'

Jack opened the silver locket and Kate took it from him, studied the picture. Henry's mother had passed away before Stephanie was born and Jack had never met her, so Kate understood his train of thought. She had known Beatrice Whitman though and she was definitely not the woman in the photograph.

'I'm sorry, Jack, but that's not her. This locket definitely isn't Stephanie's.'

'Okay, so the owner is a mystery.' He looked thoughtful as he took the chain again, slipped it back in his pocket. No doubt that writer mind of his was going into overdrive. 'I'll let Lila know it's not Steph's and we'll try to figure it out.'

'What's she like?'

'Lila?'

'Yes, Lila.'

Jack shrugged nonchalantly as he toyed with his mug, though took time choosing his words. 'Kind, occasionally misguided, but she means well. And I know she feels guilty about Steph.'

'It wasn't her fault.'

'She knows that.' Jack glanced up, eyes that same sharp blue as his father's. 'But she survived.'

Kate reached over, squeezed his hand, understanding. 'She did.'

THE CONVERSATION STAYED with Kate after Jack had left and she turned up the radio, needing the company. She hadn't missed the familiarity with how he spoke about Lila Amberson and wondered if he was even aware of it himself.

Things with Tiffany seemed to have stalled with the pair of them only seeing each other a couple of times a month and Kate knew he had been upset that Tiff hadn't been there for Stephanie's service. Their relationship had been running out of steam for quite a while, though neither of them seemed ready to call it a day. Would Lila Amberson's presence be the death knell?

As Kate loaded the dishwasher, humming along to Lionel Richie, she considered whether to mention Jack's visit and the locket to Henry, deciding almost immediately it would be a bad idea, as it would invite too many questions. Henry was still angry and bitter about Stephanie's death, looking for someone to blame. If he found out Lila was in Jack's life, her husband would likely blow a gasket. Given his already volatile relationship with his eldest stepson, it was best to keep quiet, at least for now.

The song finished and cut to the news. The same old doom and gloom stories dominating the headlines: politics, energy companies hiking their prices, a proposed airline strike and two missing schoolgirls from Lincolnshire. The girls had been missing over a month and although the police were still treating it as a missing persons case, suspicion was being cast on Phoebe Kendall's uncle, suggesting it could soon become a murder inquiry.

Kate thought of Stephanie again. It had been hard enough losing a child to an accident. How would you cope knowing someone had intentionally taken her life?

She sighed in bitter understanding. Perhaps it was true that there was always someone worse off than you.

JACK GOT up from his writing desk, stretched languidly and scrubbed his hands over his face. Two thousand words were better than none, but still they felt forced, the story not flowing naturally. He picked up his mug, drained the last few mouthfuls of coffee, and moved to stand in front of the wide first-floor window that overlooked the harbour, watching a couple of teenagers attempting to paddleboard.

The window was one of the reasons why he had bought the house. The place was too big for one man, but the uninterrupted view of the quayside with its pretty bobbing little boats and the creeks that wound their way through the desolate marshland down to the sand dunes had sucked him in, had him rationalising that the extra space would be great for when he had guests. And he had been right on that front with his extended family soon making themselves at home and taking over the spare bedrooms for their frequent visits.

He glanced at his watch, saw it was late afternoon, knew he should slug on with the book, but he was restless. He raked his fingers back through his hair, absently thinking that it was getting too long, already touching his collar, and he should go have it cut. He was surprised his mother hadn't commented as such, but then he guessed she had other things occupying her mind. Stephanie had always liked his hair a little longer though, so fuck it.

He remembered how she had joked about beach hair being apt for her beach bum brother when he had first bought the house two summers earlier.

A pitiful whine came from behind him and he turned to see Cooper, his black and white spaniel, who had been fast asleep on the floor, looking up at him expectantly.

'You wanna go for a walk?'

Cooper didn't need to be asked twice, charging off in search of his lead.

WALKING DOWN BY THE CREEK, Jack's head was full of memories from that first weekend in the house, with Tom, Steph, Alyssa and Oliver all staying over for a marathon housewarming with barbecues, too much alcohol and games of rounders and volley-ball on the beach. When he arrived back at the house, he sat back down at his laptop, closed his manuscript and logged into Face-book. Stephanie's account was still live though hopefully not for much longer, as the family had requested it be deleted. It had been something they had argued about. Alyssa, Giles and Oliver wanting it made into a memorial, while Jack, along with Tom, their mother and Henry, felt it should be closed.

Jack didn't give a flying fuck what Giles wanted, couldn't even believe he thought he was entitled to a say, but he respected the opinions of his younger brother and sister, even if he did disagree with them. Ultimately it was Henry and his mother's decision and it was strange to for once be in agreement with his stepfather.

They all had memories of Stephanie. Private memories. The last thing Jack wanted to see when he was logging into Facebook was a public social media shrine to his sister.

Still, after he had gone through her photos, found the album with the beach housewarming pictures and saved them to his laptop, he found himself reading through the messages her friends had posted on her wall.

Some of the names he recognised, a few of the messages touched him, though many others were so over the top they had him scowling at the screen. One from a girl called Ruby Howard caught his attention.

SLEEP SAFE, hun. At least that creep can't get to u anymore. Xxx

JACK REREAD THE POST, frowning. He had never heard of Ruby Howard, though a quick browse through her profile told him she had gone to school with Stephanie. He hadn't been aware of any creeps in Steph's life. Maybe another student had been picking on her. It seemed unlikely. Stephanie had always been able to handle herself.

She had been withdrawn in the weeks before her death though and something had been bothering her.

Jack remembered the texts, how she had wanted to come and stay. She had needed him and he hadn't been there.

Impulsively, he typed a message to Ruby Howard.

THIS IS STEPH'S BROTHER, Jack. I need to talk to you.

HE HIT SEND, logged out of Facebook and switched off his laptop, too fired up to write. The locket was still in his pocket; the one that his mother insisted hadn't belonged to Stephanie.

He would wait to hear from Ruby and then he would return the locket to Lila.

L ila opened the door, surprised, but not disappointed to find Jack standing on the other side. Each time she saw him she figured it would be the last, though the more she got to know him the less she wanted that to be the case.

'Come in,' she invited, not even bothering to ask why he was there this time.

'I have the locket,' he said, without preamble, following her into the small kitchen. 'It isn't Steph's.'

That stopped Lila, had her turning to face him. 'It's not?'

'I spoke to my mother. She confirmed it wasn't Stephanie's.'

'Okay.' Lila processed that bit of news, leaning awkwardly on her crutches as she filled the kettle. 'And she's sure?'

'I believe her.'

'I know.' Lila had been so certain the locket had belonged to Stephanie. The initial S, the fact it had been with her things. If Jack said it wasn't hers though she believed him.

He seemed agitated, there was something weighing on his mind. 'Are you okay?'

She went to touch him, thought better of it, remembering the last time she had tried that.

'Yes… No. One of Stephanie's friends posted something on Facebook.'

He looked so worked up she wanted to hug him, tell him everything would be okay, but instead she gave him a smile. 'I'll make coffee and you can tell me what's happened.'

This time she let him carry the cups, too exhausted to argue. She was still shaken from her latest flashback and had barely slept. She would tell Jack about it, but it wasn't the right time.

Once they were sat down, she sipped at her coffee, wincing as it burnt her mouth. She set it down on the side table, leant back against the cushions on the sofa. 'So what did Stephanie's friend say?' Lila asked.

Instead of answering, Jack got up and paced the living room, rubbing at the nape of his neck in frustration.

'Jack? What did she say?' Lila kept her tone calm.

He stopped pacing, turned to face her. 'She said "at least that creep can't get to you anymore". What the hell did she mean by that? Who was she talking about?'

Lila briefly considered the words. 'Sit down,' she ordered when he started pacing again. When he ignored her, she spoke more sharply. 'Jack! Sit down.' This time she got his attention. When he stared at her, she patted the empty seat beside her. 'Sit.'

He hesitated briefly before doing as instructed, scrubbing his hands over his face and pushing his hair back, and she could see the lines of frustration around those clear blue eyes. When he brought his hands down, she took hold of them in hers, her grip firm. Although he looked a little surprised, he didn't attempt to pull away.

'Okay, so we'll figure this out. Do you know who she could have been referring to?'

'No… God, no.'

'Think, Jack. There was no-one Stephanie had mentioned? Nobody she was going out of her way to avoid?'

He thought for a moment, a scowl on his face. 'No, there was no-one.'

'No-one you know about.'

When Jack glared at Lila, her insinuation that his sister may have kept secrets from him hitting harder than intended, the anger in his eyes outweighed only by the hurt, Lila tried to soften her words with a smile. 'She was a teenage girl. Every teenage girl has secrets. Trust me, I did.'

'Not Steph.'

'You said yourself that she had been moody and withdrawn. I know you loved your sister, but it's possible she didn't tell you everything.'

He wrestled with that for a moment, still looking annoyed, but this time Lila believed it was because he knew deep down that she was probably right.

'Okay... let's, just for a moment, say she did have secrets, what now?'

'We contact Stephanie's friend. Ask her what she meant.'

'I already did. I sent her a Facebook message before I came here.' Jack pulled his hands free, reached in his pocket for his phone, frowning at the screen. 'She replied, but when I pressed her on what she meant she said she couldn't talk about it and then she blocked me. She's deleted the post on Steph's page too.'

Lila reached for her own phone. 'What's her name?' she asked, logging into Facebook.

'Ruby. Ruby Howard.'

Not an unusual name. There would be several of those, Lila figured, and she was right. She showed the list to Jack. 'Do you recognise which one she is?'

He frowned at the list. 'Third from top. You have a mutual friend.'

'We do?' Lila grabbed her phone back and glanced at Ruby's profile. The mutual friend was Joe Mcardle. 'It's Natalie's son.'

When Jack's eyes narrowed questioningly, she elaborated. 'My boss, Natalie... remember, the little boy in the yellow raincoat.'

Jack nodded. 'Can you get him to talk to Ruby? Tell her how important it is she talks to me?'

'I can try.' Lila pulled up Joe's number, and pressed "call". He answered almost immediately and after exchanging pleasantries, she kept the conversation brief, saying she needed to get hold of Ruby and noticed Joe was a mutual friend, so was wondering if he was able to put them in touch. She was careful to keep Jack's name out of the conversation, not wanting to spook the girl. Joe promised he would speak with Ruby and would get back to Lila.

'If she agrees to talk to me then we go see her.' Lila suggested to Jack after she ended the call. 'It might be easier to get her to open up face to face.'

'We?' Jack stared at her, eyebrows raised, and heat crept up Lila's neck. There was an uncomfortable moment of silence before he added, 'You'd do that?'

His surprise bolstered her confidence. 'Of course. She's a young girl and might be intimidated if it's just you. It will help if I'm with you.'

He considered that and Lila thought he was going to protest for a second, but instead he nodded. 'I guess. Anyway, here.' Jack reached into his pocket. 'I didn't actually come here to unburden on you. I came to give this back.'

Lila held up the locket he passed her, thoughtful as she studied it. Small, simple, plain, probably not expensive, but it must be important to someone.

'I can't think who else it could belong to. It's not mine, not Stephanie's. It surely wouldn't have been Mark's. Someone must be missing it.'

'Have you thought about contacting the hospital?'

'I will do, now I know it wasn't Stephanie's.' Lila was quiet for a moment, her mind replaying the lead up to the crash. 'I had another flashback.'

'You did?'

'I saw it happen.'

'The accident?' For a brief moment, those blue eyes hardened and Lila wondered if he was mad at her because she hadn't told him sooner, but then his look softened. 'You're shaking.'

'Am I?' Lila hadn't noticed, but now Jack had pointed it out she made a conscious effort to still her hands, thrusting them together and placing them in her lap.

'Can you tell me what happened?'

'I was in the car park in the woods by Filby Broad; there's a little one just past the bridge. Mark was supposed to take me home, but he had stopped there, thought he'd try his luck.' Lila rolled her eyes, tried to make a joke of it. 'We argued and I remember he was sulky, got out of the car, saying he had to pee, and he went off into the woods. I waited and I waited, but he didn't come back.' She shuddered, the memory of being alone, bored and a little anxious in that dark car park, unsure what to do, clear in her mind.

Jack didn't push her, listening patiently as she recounted what had happened, how Mark had eventually returned to the car, out of breath and panicky, telling Lila they needed to leave, how he had been so agitated he had driven the wrong way, losing control of the car before heading back to the bridge.

As she spoke, she was right back there in the car, filled with panic and confusion as she tried to reason with Mark, her heart thumping hard, the absolute fear that cloaked her when she spotted the approaching headlights. 'He was going too fast. I begged him to slow down. I saw her coming, but it was too…'

Lila struggled with the last sentence, couldn't quite finish it, the shock fresh in her mind all over again. For a moment, she was alone in the room, emotions of grief, fear, guilt and utter despair threatening to pull her under and she fought to keep control. Slowly, Jack swam back into focus and she saw he was battling his own demons, knew her words would have only brought fresh hurt, that she had twisted the knife that little bit deeper. His mouth was set in a grim line, the pain in his eyes a stark reminder of what he had lost, and she swallowed hard, ordered herself to get her shit together.

'I'm sorry, Jack.'

He didn't react until she took hold of his hand again. Like Lila, he had been lost for a moment, probably hadn't heard her words, but the physical contact brought him back, had him staring at her.

'I'm so sorry.'

He gave the slightest nod, his fingers tightening around hers. 'I know.'

'IN HERE?'

'Yes, just on the left before the bridge.'

Jack indicated, slowing as they approached the entrance to the car park and pulled into the wooded clearing, and Lila wondered what thoughts were going through his mind.

She had been reluctant about returning to the scene of the accident, but Jack had been insistent, suddenly having an over-whelming urge to see the place where his sister had died. Lila had tried to talk him out of it, but his mind was set and she knew he was going with or without her. She couldn't let him go alone.

It was already dusk, the car park shrouded in darkness when Jack killed the headlights. He sat in silence for a while before pulling the keys from the ignition and turning to Lila. 'You can wait here if you want.'

'No thanks.' Lila shook her head. 'I'm not being left alone in this car park again.'

The faintest hint of a smile touched Jack's lips. 'Fair enough.'

Lila followed after him along the path that led to the bridge, trying her best to negotiate her crutches in the low light while keeping up pace with him.

Jack reached the bridge several seconds ahead of her and she paused beside him on the path, following his line of vision, knew he was looking at the spot where the accident had happened. The flowers that had been left were still there, though most now looked dead. It would probably only be a matter of days before they would be removed, along with the memories of Mark and Stephanie, and life would return to normal for the residents of Filby.

There was nothing Lila could say to comfort Jack, so she stood in silence beside him on the bridge, the night of the accident replaying in her mind with every car that passed.

FOR A LONG TIME, he was lost in his own thoughts and Lila was again questioning whether this had been a good idea, but then he turned to look at her. His face was partially hidden in the shadows, but the strain of the grief he had been carrying seemed to have eased, the light blue of his eyes more vivid in the darkness, his look intense as he stared right into her as if seeing her for the first time that day, and Lila's belly gave an involuntary flip. She mentally kicked herself; annoyed at her reaction and how inappropriate it was in the moment.

'Thank you for coming with me. I know this wasn't easy for you either.'

'It's okay.' It hadn't been easy, but Jack had needed this, so it was okay with her.

He kept pace with her on the return walk back into the woods, though neither of them spoke until they reached the car park. Lila waited for him to unlock the car, but instead he glanced in the direction of the footpath that led further into the woods.

'What do you think happened to Mark?'

'I don't know. Look around you, we're in the middle of nowhere. If anything had happened I would have heard it.'

'You said he was sulking when he went into the woods, but he was agitated when he returned. That he seemed scared.'

'He was.'

'How long was he gone for?'

'Ten, maybe fifteen minutes.'

'It takes thirty seconds to pee. Even if he purposely took longer to piss you off, we're talking five minutes at most. Something happened while he was gone. Something spooked him.'

'But what?'

Lila had considered this. Mark had been hell bent on getting out of Filby the moment he'd returned to the car. If someone or something had been chasing him though, she would have heard them, would have seen them.

'He took this path, right?'

'Yes.' Lila leant on her crutches, wishing she had brought a jacket. The air was turning cooler as night fell. She let out a sigh of relief when Jack finally strode back towards her and clicked his key at the car. She'd had enough of traipsing around in the woods for one night.

Before she could get to the car, he had the passenger door open and was reaching in the glovebox. Her heart sank again when he produced a torch, flashed it towards the pathway. 'We're not going home yet, are we.'

12

'You okay?'

Jack glanced back at Lila, shone the torch on her, checking she was keeping up. He knew that dragging her on a night-time expedition through the woods while on crutches wasn't wise, but he could hardly leave her in the car, knew she wouldn't agree to it after what had happened with Mark, and Jack would never do that to her anyway. But equally he couldn't leave without first seeing where the path led. He needed to do this.

Something had happened that night in the woods before the crash and he was fairly certain it wasn't just his writer's brain going into overdrive.

'I'm fine,' Lila assured him, sounding more like she was trying to convince herself. She was out of breath and he knew she hadn't wanted to do this, even though she had gamely tried to keep up and hadn't complained once.

That was who she was he was coming to realise. She was humble and honest and kind, and she always put others first, and he didn't want to be someone who took advantage of her good nature.

He would make this up to her, he promised himself.

THEY HAD BEEN WALKING for about five minutes, albeit slowly so Lila could keep up, and the woods were dark, leaving them reliant on the torch to guide them along the path.

Had Mark Sutherland ventured this far into the woods? He would have only had the benefit of his phone to light the way. Jack tried to put himself into Mark's shoes. What would he have done?

It was a difficult question to answer because he wouldn't have been the shithead who had taken his blind date to the woods in the hope of copping a feel in the first place.

RIP to the bloke and everything, but he sounded like he had been a bit of a dick.

Jack tried to visualise him as a character he was writing. The arrogant player who thought a few drinks bought him sex in a backwoods car park. That guy would be annoyed with Lila. He had invested time and money in the date, had even driven. He would expect a return for that investment. Mark had sulked, he had left her in the car alone, and wandered off into the woods. If he had genuinely only wanted to pee, he could have just disappeared behind a tree. No, Mark had wanted to get her back for rejecting his advances and he probably thought it would be fun to watch her panicking about where he was and whether he was coming back.

That was all good and well, but the scenario suggested that he would have stayed close. That he would have wanted to see Lila's reaction. And if he had been that close and something had happened to spook him, Lila would have heard. No, something lured him further into the woods, but what? He'd been out of breath when he returned to the car, so he had to have ventured along the path. What had spooked him?

Caught up in his thoughts, Jack had momentarily forgotten

about Lila and he turned to check on her again, saw the grimace on her face as she grappled with her crutches, and in that moment he felt like a prize arsehole.

He shouldn't have dragged her out in the woods. 'You're struggling. We're going back.'

Lila put up her hand to protest, to tell him she was fine, and took a wobbly step forward. As she lost her footing, Jack dropped the torch, lurching forward to catch her as her chin bashed his chest.

Although she was breathless, sweating from the exertion of trying to keep up with him, she was freezing, and he noticed for the first time that she had no jacket on.

'I'm sorry,' she managed between breaths.

And now she's the one apologising. Nice going, Jack, you dickhead.

'We'll go back,' he told her. 'I'm the one who's sorry. I shouldn't have made you come out here.'

'This was important to you.'

With the torch on the ground, he couldn't see her face, but he heard her sigh, heard the frustration in her voice, and realised she was annoyed with herself for not being able to keep up. Steadying her back on her feet, he rubbed his palms up and down her arms, trying to warm her up.

'Not so important it can't wait a couple of days. You're freezing.'

He took off his jacket, helped Lila slip her arms into it then zipped it up for her.

'Thank you.'

The torch was still working, casting an eerie glow along the floor of the wooded path, and he retrieved it, held it up so he could see her face. She blinked at the light, looking slightly ridiculous in the oversized jacket.

'Are you going to be okay to walk back to the car park?'

'I'll be fine.'

That's what she had said coming out here, yet she wasn't.

Fuck it.

'Can you hold on to your crutches if I give you a piggyback?'

'You don't need to do that.'

'Lila, you can barely walk.'

'I'll be okay. I just need to take it slow.'

Jack considered her argument, dismissed it. It was his fault she was out there in the first place and it was his responsibility to get her safely back to the car.

'You'll need to hold the torch too,' he told her, pushing it in her hand and turning round, leaning down so she could climb on his back.

'You really don't need to carry me to the car. I can walk.' She sounded mortified at the idea and he knew it was because she hated having to rely on someone else.

'Damn it, Lila, will you stop being so stubborn and let me help you.'

She hesitated and he heard her huff loudly before she did as she was told, nearly punching him in the face with the crutches as he caught hold of her under the thighs and hoisted her up.

'Jesus, be careful with those things.'

'Sorry.' She didn't sound sorry.

'Point the torch ahead, okay? I need to see where I'm going,' he grumbled, slowly making his way back along the path, keeping his pace steady. Although Lila had her arms around his neck, she was trying to hold on to both the crutches and the torch and didn't have a tight grip. He couldn't risk dropping her.

The crutches didn't make things easy and he was tempted to tell her to leave them, either jog back for them once they reached the car or say to hell with them and get her another pair. He grunted as one bashed against his right knee for the third time, part of him wondering if she was doing it on purpose.

'It would have been quicker if I'd walked,' she remarked dryly in his ear. 'Probably safer too.'

Jack ignored the comment, as he was trying to ignore that her breasts were mashed up against his shoulders. He could smell her scent; a light spicy fragrance tinged with something fruity, was aware of her warm breath on his neck.

He glanced around the dark woods, trying to get his bearings and figure out how much further they had to go to get back to the car park. In the distance he spotted a flash of light, a sliver of yellow through the trees.

'Hey, you see that?'

'See what?'

'There's a house out here. I can see the light on in the window.' Jack turned so Lila was facing the property. 'Look straight ahead.'

'I see it. I think the Grugers have the only place out here.'

'That's what I thought,' Jack muttered, mostly to himself, as he stepped off the path towards the house.

'What are you doing?' Lila demanded, her tone slightly alarmed. When he ignored her, she bashed her elbow against his shoulder. 'Jack! Where are you going?'

'For a closer look.'

'You said we were going back to the car.'

'We are. This will only take a couple of minutes.'

'Jack, I don't want to go back there. Richard Gruger's wife told me she didn't want to see me again.'

'You won't have to see her. They don't have to know we're there.'

'I don't care. I don't want to go back.'

'You'll be fine.'

Jack picked up pace as she continued to argue and when it was clear he wasn't going to back down, she settled into a sulky silence.

As they neared the house the trees became sparse. There was no border between the woods and the sprawling lawn that led up to the wide patio that ran the length of the back of the house. The light he had spotted was still on and he could see that it was the kitchen. A figure flittered back and forth in front of the window; a woman, and it looked like she was clearing away dishes. Judith Gruger, he guessed.

Jack knew little about the family, only what he had read in the news. Lila had told him about her visit to thank Richard Gruger though and the hostile reaction from his wife, which had piqued Jack's interest. Perhaps they were a private family who didn't welcome the press intrusion, but theirs was the only property near the woods. Maybe they would have answers to what Mark Sutherland had been running from on the night of his death.

'Can you put me down, please.'

When Jack ignored her, Lila kicked him with her good foot. 'Jack, put me down!'

'You can barely walk.'

'I don't care. Just put me down.'

'Suit yourself.' He lowered her to the ground, waited until she had steadied herself on her crutches; avoiding the glare she gave him.

'I told you I didn't want to come back here. You've seen the house, now can we go please before she sees us?'

A rustling noise in the brush behind them had Lila jumping. Jack turned to see a small terrier charging out of the woods and onto the lawn. It circled back, yipping at them.

'Lila? Is that you?'

A male voice, sounding surprised, pleased even.

Jack gave the kid who paused to join them on the edge of the lawn a glance over. Maybe late teens, wearing jeans and a dark hoodie: he had to be the Gruger kid. Aaron, he recalled Lila saying. The one she said had been messaging her on Facebook.

'Hi.' Lila looked mortified to see him, like she would rather be anywhere else.

'It's Aaron, right?' Jack said.

'Yes, yes it is. What are you doing here?'

Lila glanced at Jack for help. Aaron also looked at him, as though noticing him for the first time, his expression curious.

'Umm, this is Jack. He's...' She tapered off, seeming unsure how to explain exactly who he was.

'Jack Foley. I'm a friend of Lila's.' Jack kept it simple, offering his hand.

Aaron shook it warily, his gaze flittering between them, looking like he had a dozen questions he wanted to ask. He opened his mouth, but before any words came out, a light flooded on, illuminating the whole back garden, and a patio door opened.

'Aaron, who are you talking to?'

The dog yapped again and made a beeline for the door and the woman holding it open.

'You'll never guess who I ran into in the woods, Mum.' Aaron stepped forward, the dog lead swinging from his hand.

Jack caught Lila's eye, didn't miss her warning scowl.

'Don't even think about it,' she hissed.

He gave her a challenging look, as he took a step after Aaron. They both knew she needed him to get back to the car.

'Jack, please.'

'Five minutes,' he promised. 'Come on.'

Judith Gruger had looked curious, but her expression tightened when she spotted Jack, darkening further when Lila appeared.

'You. I already told you to stay away. You're not welcome here.'

'Judith? What the bloody hell's going on?' A male voice, sharp and irritated.

'Richard?' Suddenly she sounded concerned, looking worriedly over her shoulder. 'You're home.'

Richard Gruger appeared in the doorway, a frown on his face

as he glanced at Jack and Lila standing on his back lawn. 'I know you.'

'I ran into Lila and Jack in the woods while walking Toby,' Aaron announced to his father, stepping forward. 'You remember Lila Amberson don't you, Dad? The girl you pulled out of the broad? I know she wanted to thank you for saving her life, so I invited them back to the house. I hope that's okay.'

There was something challenging in his tone, mocking even, in the way he emphasised 'Dad'.

Jack shot Lila a brief look. If she hadn't had the crutches, he was pretty certain she would have bolted for the woods. He knew she wasn't happy about being there, but she would have to be patient just a little while longer. The Gruger family dynamics were fascinating and Jack had only met them a minute earlier. He was curious to know what made them all tick.

Richard Gruger's expression had gone from annoyed to uncertain, as he glanced between his son and Lila. Aaron had wrong footed him and he was deciding how best to play it. Jack took the opportunity to step forward, offering his hand. 'Jack Foley. It's good to meet you, Mr Gruger.'

'Jack Foley, as in the author?'

'The one and only,' Jack confirmed with a wide smile. If Gruger knew who he was, he intended to use it to his advantage. He wondered whether the man knew that Stephanie had been his sister. There had been some press coverage, but Henry had mostly dominated the headlines meaning Jack had been left blessedly alone.

Gruger glanced hesitantly at Lila again, a smile creeping onto his face as if he decided to go for genial. He pumped Jack's hand. 'It's good to meet you, Mr Foley. I've read a couple of your books. Very enjoyable.'

'Thank you, and it's Jack, please.'

'And Miss Amberson, it's nice to finally make your acquaintance. Please both of you, come in.'

Lila smiled politely, though didn't speak, her eyes on Judith Gruger who stood rigidly by the door, watching the whole exchange. Jack couldn't get a read on the woman. It was obvious she didn't want them there, but there was something else. Was it a fear of her husband?

She disappeared into the house, followed by the dog then her husband.

Jack glanced at Lila again. 'Just for a few minutes then I promise I'll take you home.'

The smile he attempted to charm her with was met by a scowl.

'You can hold on to my arm and I can take your crutches if you want,' Aaron offered.

'I've got it, thank you,' she told him stiffly, tottering towards Jack and the house.

13

'Tea, coffee, or something stronger perhaps?' Richard Gruger offered, leading them through into a spacious lounge.

The place was traditionally yet tastefully furnished with wide beige sofas and lots of lacquered wood, the lighting from two chandeliers was soft and cosy, and the wall art very middle of the road, though expensively framed. In the corner of the room sat a grand piano. Everything was too neat though, too clean. Every surface gleamed, the scent of pine furniture polish clinging to the air. On the centre of the mantle of the wide fireplace sat a carriage clock, its tick loud and methodical. The cushions on the sofas were perfectly plumped. Nothing was out of place.

Did the family actually use this room? Did they ever put their feet up on the sofas, leave magazines on the floor, spend time together either watching TV or just hanging out? Lila didn't think so. From what she could gather, their dog wasn't even allowed in there; probably confined to a bed somewhere less plush, the kitchen most likely.

She glanced down at her crutches, suddenly fearful the bottoms of them were dirty. Richard Gruger had asked them to remove their shoes in the kitchen and Jack had helped her get her boot off her good foot, but of course she was reliant on the crutches. She edged one forward relieved it had left no more than a slight indent in the plush pale carpet.

'Just coffee for me, thanks,' Jack answered.

'Miss Amberson?'

Lila looked up, met the man's dark eyes. He was the man who had rescued her from drowning, the man who had saved her life. Why did she feel so uncomfortable around him? 'Umm, coffee would be great. Thank you, Mr Gruger.'

He didn't ask her to call him Richard, seemed quite happy that she had addressed him that way. Lila had read he was a headmaster, guessed he was used to being called Mr Gruger. She realised that she hadn't actually thanked him properly yet for pulling her from the broad. The man might be a little intimidating, but she would never be able to fully repay him for what he had done. If he hadn't been there that night, she would have died along with Mark and Stephanie.

'I'm glad I finally got the chance to meet you,' she told him, trying to pick the right words. What exactly was the correct etiquette for thanking someone for saving your life? 'I don't know how I will ever be able to repay you for what you did the night of the accident.'

Gruger shrugged. It seemed more dismissive than modest. 'Nonsense. I did what anyone else would have done. It's really no big deal.'

'It is to me, so thank you.'

He smiled briefly at her before throwing a look in his wife's direction.

She was standing in the doorway again, wringing her hands together. 'I'll, um… I'll go put the kettle on.' She cast her eyes downward and disappeared.

'Please sit,' Gruger gestured to one of the perfectly plumped sofas.

Lila glanced at it reluctantly, not wanting to be the one to crease it.

She didn't have to though as Jack was quick to take a seat, making himself at home. She guessed he had grown up with money, probably in a house similar to this, so it was all quite normal to him. It had to be the money and the lavishness of the house that was making her uncomfortable. Not wishing to appear rude, she took a seat beside Jack on the sofa, not too close because she was still pissed off with him, but close enough for reassurance.

Aaron loitered by the piano while Gruger took a seat on the sofa opposite. He had a commanding presence and it felt like this was an interview.

'So what brought you back to Filby, Miss Amberson?' Gruger addressed Lila directly, eyes on hers, as if deliberately trying to cut Jack out of the conversation.

Jack either didn't notice or didn't care, answering for her. 'She came at my request. I wanted to see the place where my sister died.'

There was a moment of uncomfortable silence as Gruger looked at Jack, visibly taken aback by the words. Jack's eyes never left his, as he waited for a reaction.

Lila was aware of Aaron pulling out the stool to the grand piano and dropping down on it, looking on with interest, as she chewed her bottom lip, heart thumping uncomfortably, and waited.

Eventually Gruger's eyes narrowed. 'The girl in the other car, the one who died, she was your sister?'

'Stephanie Whitman, she was seventeen.'

Gruger recovered quickly. 'I'm sorry, Mr Foley... Jack. I had no idea. Please accept my condolences. I can't imagine what you must be going through. If I could have saved your sister too I would have.'

Jack knew that, but his grief was still raw and Lila saw a

muscle in his cheek twitch.

Part of her wanted to reach out to him, but she wasn't yet ready to forgive him for dragging her there, plus she didn't want Gruger overanalysing her connection to Jack and trying to figure out if there was something between them. Of course there wasn't, but it was still none of Gruger's business.

'Now, where's that coffee. Judith?' Gruger smiled apologetically at them, getting up from the sofa. 'Let me go see where she is. Make yourselves comfortable. I'll be back in a moment.'

He left the room and Jack exchanged a glance with Lila. He caught her hand, gave it a discreet reassuring squeeze. 'We'll go after we've had coffee,' he told her in a low voice.

'We'd better.'

The clang of piano keys made Lila jump and she looked up, yanking her hand away from Jack's. Aaron had been sitting so quietly at the piano that she had forgotten they weren't alone.

He was looking directly at her, smiled when he had her attention. 'Oops, sorry, I didn't mean to make you jump.' He ran his fingers down to the higher keys, played the first few notes of *The Twilight Zone* theme, then laughed.

'You play much?' Jack asked, getting up from the sofa and ambling over, hands shoved in the pockets of his jeans.

'Not as often or as well as my father would like, but I can play a bit. My mum is the real talent. She could have probably played professionally if he had let her pursue it.'

If he had let her, suggesting that Richard Gruger was in charge of his wife's decisions.

Lila wished again she hadn't come there, that Jack hadn't made her.

Everything about the house and family made her feel uncomfortable and it annoyed her that she couldn't figure out why.

'Can I use your loo, please?'

Aaron looked at her, shrugged. 'Sure. There's a cloakroom

next to the kitchen. Head back out the way you came in, last door on the left.'

Lila excused herself, making her way out into the wide hallway, her pace slow as she manoeuvred her crutches on the polished wooden floor.

As she neared the kitchen, she heard voices. Richard Gruger angrily berating his wife. His tone was hushed enough that she couldn't hear what he was saying, but his posture suggested he was furious with her. Judith Gruger meanwhile stood and took his vehemence, her head bowed and shoulders drooped, as he continued to put her down.

The man was so quick to appear welcoming and friendly to Jack and Lila's faces, but was this who he really was? Did he beat his wife or was it solely psychological abuse? Lila stood and watched a moment longer, knowing she should go into the cloakroom, but transfixed by the scene in front of her, as she re-evaluated what little she knew about these people, now realising that the woman she had found as rude and intimidating was probably just scared. When Richard Gruger turned, as though suddenly aware she was standing behind them, it made her jump.

'Miss Amberson?' His tone was surprised and for the briefest moment he appeared off guard. 'Can we help you with something?' There was an edge, a warning in the question.

'I... I was looking for the cloakroom.'

'The door immediately to your left.' Gruger's mouth was a thin line, his eyes never leaving hers as she opened the door and quickly shuffled inside.

Lila's heart was thumping. She'd been caught snooping, witnessing a domestic scene she was never supposed to see. Would Richard Gruger call her on it when she returned to the lounge?

She took her time peeing and washing her hands, annoyed when she caught her reflection in the mirror above the sink and saw how tired she looked, the inky smudges dark beneath her eyes, the bruising on her forehead still not completely healed. She rearranged her fringe, tried her best to make herself look presentable, like she fit into this world. Her thoughts went to the girl she had seen in the photograph with Jack: all sunshine hair, bronzed skin and vibrancy. No, Lila Amberson was never going to fit into this world.

AS SHE LEFT THE CLOAKROOM, readying herself to rejoin the group, Aaron appeared from the shadows. 'You found it okay?'

'What? Yes, yes, thank you.'

She started to walk past him, flinching when he reached out, put a hand on her arm.

'I messaged you… on Facebook. I wanted to explain.'

Lila played dumb. 'Did you?'

Aaron gave her a look that warned he wasn't stupid, though he didn't call her on it. 'My mum, the way she was that day you stopped by the house. It wasn't her. It's not who she is.'

'It's fine, honestly. I'm sure she was just busy, had a lot on her mind.'

'No, it's not that. I'm scared for her. I worry that one day he will go too far. He's not the man he pretends to be.' Aaron's tone was urgent, his grip tightening on her arm.

Lila wrenched it free, gave him a shaky smile. She glanced over her shoulder to the kitchen, saw it was empty, and the light off. 'I'm not sure I'm the person you should be telling this to.'

As she made her way back along the hallway to the lounge, Aaron fell in step beside her. 'I know you saw them,' he hissed.

Lila ignored him, stepped into the lounge to find Jack deep in conversation with Richard Gruger, while his wife sat meekly on the sofa not joining in. She looked downtrodden, beaten.

Gruger glanced up at Lila, all smiles: his mask firmly back in place. 'Miss Amberson, come and join us. Jack was just telling us you're getting some of your memories back from the night of the accident. That's great news.'

Lila took her seat again next to Jack, picked up the cup Gruger pushed towards her, trying to stop it rattling against the saucer as her hand shook. In the corner of the room, Aaron had returned to the piano stool and he sat with his eyes on her, watching, waiting for her reaction.

'I've remembered some of what happened. Not everything. The doctors said it will take time.'

'These things often do,' Gruger agreed. He was back to being friendly. No hint of the man she had seen in the kitchen.

Judith Gruger looked up, met Lila's eyes for the briefest moment, the look in them unreadable. Judith no longer seemed angry that Lila was in her home. Was she embarrassed about what she had witnessed?

She had assumed the woman was in her mid to late fifties, but looking at her, Lila realised she was probably much younger. The way she wore her hair in a dated layered look did her no favours, neither did the loose ill-fitting clothes she wore.

Lila felt a pang of guilt for the woman. She looked like she was once pretty, probably vibrant. Had Gruger stamped all of that out of her, taken away her spark?

'Lila remembers Mark going into the woods before the car crash. Something spooked him, but she's not sure what.' Jack threw that out there, fishing for reactions. When he didn't get any, he jokingly added, 'You haven't got a resident ghost haunting them, have you?'

'That'd liven things up around here,' Aaron muttered sardonically, casting a scowl in his father's direction.

'Maybe he was spooked by a squirrel,' Gruger suggested. 'They can be noisy little buggers.'

'Yours is the only house out this way, right?'

'Correct.'

'You get many people using these woods?'

'I guess a fair few. Some dog walkers, others visiting the broad. It's a popular area.'

'Not too many visitors or dog walkers after dark though.'

The smile slipped from Gruger's face as he set his cup down. 'Where exactly are you going with this, Jack?'

'Nowhere in particular; I'm just trying to figure out what happened with Mark that night.'

'The crime writer turned true detective. I thought for a moment we were research for your next novel.' Gruger gave a humourless laugh. 'Perhaps Miss Amberson is confused with what she thinks she saw. The mind is a funny thing, especially if you have a head injury, and sometimes we think we remember things, but not quite how they really happened.'

He looked at Lila, eyes cool. 'I would encourage you to focus on your recovery, my dear. We wouldn't want you to have any setbacks now, would we?'

14

'You haven't said a word in nearly twenty minutes. Are you going to give me the silent treatment all the way home?'

Lila was aware of Jack glancing in her direction and she slipped down in the passenger seat, burrowing herself in his jacket. It smelt of him, that same comforting mix of fabric conditioner, aftershave, soap and light sweat that had filled her senses when he had given her a piggyback ride in the woods. She was tired, she was still a little shaken by what she had witnessed, and it was tempting to stay quiet, let him drop her off home and crawl into bed.

She knew she wouldn't sleep though. Her head was too full of the evening's events and she needed to share. Of course she could tell Elliot. He would listen, but he hadn't been there. Jack had.

'You shouldn't have made me go to the house. You knew I didn't want to.' She started on the defensive, figuring she would work her way down to reasonable.

'I know. I'd say I'm sorry, but I'm not. I'm sorry I made you do something you didn't want to do, but I'm not sorry we went. Hold that against me if you want, but I'm being honest with you so I hope that you won't.' He gave her a persuasive smile, one she suspected he had used before when trying to wheedle his way out of trouble and damn him, but she thawed a little.

'So are you going to tell me what happened? I know you were uncomfortable when we arrived, but you were downright skittish when you came back from the loo.'

She had been, and to his credit, Jack had picked up on her vibes, discreetly placing a comforting hand at the small of her back.

'I saw them in the kitchen, Mr and Mrs Gruger. I couldn't hear what he was saying, but he was giving her hell about something. He caught me watching them.'

'And how did he react to that?'

'He didn't say anything, but he knew what I'd seen and wasn't happy. Then when I came out of the loo, Aaron was there. He told me not to believe a word his father says and he suggested that things are pretty bad for his mum.'

Jack was silent and Lila waited for a reaction. She studied his profile; furrowed brow, straight nose, strong chin, determined mouth. Only a couple of weeks earlier they had been strangers, probably still should be, but the accident had somehow pulled them together and, despite the fact they came from different worlds, it was scary how easily he was slotting into her life and how right it felt having him there.

'I wondered that,' he said eventually. 'When we first arrived, there was something off. I suspect Gruger runs the show and has his wife chasing around after him, probably the kid too at one point, but the dynamics are changing. Aaron is big enough to clout his father if things ever got physical. He doesn't like how his mother is treated and he's testing boundaries, seeing how far his father can be pushed.'

Jack had noticed a lot and Lila suspected his theory was spot on. She remembered him telling her he had been a reporter before he became an author, guessed he was probably good at reading people.

· · ·

ELLIOT'S CAR was already parked out front by the time they arrived back. His boot would be loaded up with his luggage, ready to head off with his mates in the morning. Lila had told him not to bother staying that night, but he had insisted.

'You want to come in?'

Jack glanced at the clock on the dashboard, hesitated briefly. 'Okay, sure.'

Elliot was sprawled on the sofa, eyes shut and glasses slipping down his nose, the TV blasting an episode of *The Walking Dead*. Lila picked the remote up from his belly, muted the sound, and he rose immediately, shoving his glasses back in place and sniffing indignantly.

'Hey, I was watching that.'

'With your eyes closed?'

'I was resting them for a second.'

'I told you not to have the TV turned up so loud, you'll disturb Primrose.'

'In case you hadn't noticed, Lila, your landlady is almost deaf. I doubt she'd be disturbed if you had a horde of zombies actually in your living room.'

'Aren't zombies mostly silent? Apart from the groaning,' Jack questioned, earning a glare from Elliot.

'I'm sure if there were enough of them in here you would hear them,' he huffed. 'Where have you two been anyway?'

'Just out and about.' Lila kept her tone light and breezy, knowing Elliot would fret if she told him she'd been back to Filby again. 'I'm going to put the kettle on. Do you want a cup of tea?'

Elliot glanced down at his glass of Coke. 'I'm good, thanks.'

Lila hopped through to the kitchen, started making drinks, leaving Jack in the living room, making small talk with her brother. She could hear them talking about *The Walking Dead* and knew Jack would never be able to shut Elliot up if he got him too excited. As the kettle boiled her mind wandered back to the Grugers and the uncomfortable evening at their house.

When she had first learnt what had happened she had been so eager to meet Richard Gruger, knowing she was indebted to him. Somehow in her mind she had managed to convince herself that they would share some kind of bond and instantly connect. She hadn't expected to feel intimidated by him, and she certainly hadn't thought she would dislike him or find him creepy.

As she balanced on one crutch and reached into the cupboard for mugs, a hand on her shoulder made her jump and she swung around in the small space, losing her footing and falling forward, finding herself face to chest with Jack.

'Jesus, I didn't hear you over the kettle.'

'Apparently not.' He grinned, setting his phone down on the counter and retrieving the mug that had landed between them, while using his other hand to help steady her back on her feet. 'You know that's the second time you've thrown yourself at me tonight.'

He was teasing, but Lila swallowed hard, aware he was still standing in her personal space and making no attempt to move. As she took the mug from him, set it down on the counter, she attempted a joke back. 'Ha, you should be so lucky.'

Those intense blue eyes locked on hers and Lila swore the temperature in the room suddenly rose several degrees.

'I should,' he agreed, his tone sobering.

'What?'

The look he gave her became heated as his gaze dropped to her mouth and Lila's heartbeat quickened as he tenderly tucked a strand of hair behind her ear, leaning in closer. 'I said I should be so lucky.' His voice was little more than a whisper, a caress against her skin.

She wanted him to kiss her. The anticipation of it made her tingle.

'On second thoughts, maybe I will have a cup of tea.'

Lila's head shot up, as her brother appeared in the doorway, his empty glass in his hand. His eyes went saucer wide, his cheeks reddening. 'Shit, sorry. I didn't mean to interrupt anything.'

'You didn't.' The moment killed, Jack stepped back, rubbing at the nape of his neck and looking downright uncomfortable. 'You didn't interrupt anything. In fact, it's getting late. I should probably pass on coffee and get back home.'

Love her brother she might, but if she had a bat, Lila was pretty sure she would wallop him with it. It was not at all how she had imagined that moment would be.

'I'll just use the loo.' Jack disappeared into the hallway as Lila glowered at Elliot.

'I'm sorry,' he protested in a loud whisper. 'How was I supposed to know you two were in here having a moment?'

Lila clenched her fists in frustration. 'Do you have any idea how long it's been since I've had sex, how long since I met someone I actually want to have sex with,' she fumed.

'That's enough information.' Elliot covered his ears, looking mortified. 'I really don't want to know about my sister's sex life.'

'Lack of, you mean. And not likely to change any time soon, thanks to you.'

She was careful to keep her voice hushed, because the only thing that could possibly be worse than what had just happened would be for Jack to overhear her lamenting about her dry spell. Her really long dry spell.

At least, that's what she thought could be the worst.

As if on cue, Jack's phone vibrated, bouncing around on the kitchen worktop.

Elliot and Lila both stopped bickering long enough to glance at it, to spot the name of the caller.

Tiff.

Lila thought back to the Google picture of Jack and the leggy tanned blonde and sickness coiled in her belly. She had convinced herself that the woman wasn't of any significance in

Jack's life. After all, why would he be knocking around with Lila if he had a stunning girlfriend waiting for him at home? He had never mentioned being in a relationship, certainly hadn't acted as if he was, at least not in the last few moments.

She tried to convince herself that there had to be an explanation for Tiff. Maybe she was just a friend. An old friend who had his number and who just happened to be calling him up at quarter to eleven on a Friday night.

'Who's Tiff?' Elliot asked, regarding Lila with suspicion.

She was saved from answering as Jack returned to the kitchen, looking like he couldn't wait to get out of the flat.

'You just had a missed call.' Lila picked up the phone, passed it to him. She couldn't let him leave without knowing the truth. 'Someone called Tiff.'

For the briefest moment, he frowned then as if remembering, put his hand to his forehead. 'Shit! I forgot she was coming up tonight.'

'Who's Tiff?' Elliot repeated, this time to Jack.

Lila was glad he had asked the question, as she wasn't sure she could muster the words. Jack locked eyes with her for a brief moment and something passed over his face. Not guilt. Regret.

'She's my girlfriend.'

Fuck.

The thread of hope Lila had been clinging to dissipated.

'Best you get back to her then,' she said tightly, wanting him gone.

Lila closed the door behind him, her chest physically hurting. It was exactly why she had backed away from dating; from getting involved with men on any level. They always ended up disappointing her.

'Probably for the best that I interrupted you, eh.'

If she'd had a cushion at hand it would have gone flying at Elliot's head, but then he smiled sympathetically and she realised she had misread her brother's attempt at dry humour.

He stepped forward, slipping his arm around her and pressing his lips against her temple. 'I'm sorry, Lila. I know you liked him.'

Lila forced a smile. 'At least I found out now.'

Elliot pointed towards the other side of the room. 'Want to eat ice cream and drink wine? I've got chocolate chip in the freezer.'

'That sounds like a plan.'

15

Elliot set off for his Scottish jaunt just after eight on Saturday morning. He made enough noise to wake the dead, including Lila, who was sporting a monster hangover. Head throbbing, too much going on in her mind to attempt sleep again, she threw back the duvet, grabbed her crutches and hopped through to the kitchen to put on the kettle.

Jack hadn't called or texted. Why did that disappoint her? She tried to put things into perspective, reminding herself that they had only met a handful of times and that when they had it had always been about the night of the accident and his sister's death. Why would he call or text her? He owed her nothing, had done nothing wrong.

Except nearly kiss her.

But then had she misread that moment in the kitchen? It had been so long since she had kissed anyone; maybe he was being friendly, nothing more.

Irritated that she was overanalysing everything, Lila downed two paracetamol with a glass of water and dumped a spoonful of coffee in her favourite mug. As she waited for the kettle to boil, she leant on the crutches and rummaged in the fridge, finding bacon and eggs, and heated a pan. It was Saturday, she had a hangover, the day stretched out ahead of her with no visitors, and she needed to perk herself up. Food was the way forward.

BY NINE THIRTY she had eaten her fry-up, drank two cups of coffee, and was climbing the walls.

Fetching her camera, she made her way out into the garden, loving the warmth of the sun on her back as she snapped pictures of Primrose's colourful tulips and bluebells.

STILL, Lila was itching to get out and by lunchtime she was on a bus heading up to Cromer. It was a gorgeous day and she figured she would find a bench to sit down on and try to get a few tourist shots before heading over to Nat's Hideaway. Beth was on a day off, but Natalie would be working and Joe had mentioned he was back at the weekend and would be helping cover. Lila would see if Ruby had been in touch.

Not that it really mattered much anymore, how things were with Jack.

THE PLACE WAS PACKED when she finally pushed open the door just after two in the afternoon. Natalie was working the counter, Joe clearing tables. He gave Lila a wide grin. 'Hey, I was going to call you when I was on my break. I heard back from Ruby.'

'You did?'

'She was a little hesitant, but I told her you're a good friend, so she agreed I could give you her number.'

'Joe, you're a star. Thank you.'

'Wait until I've sorted this lot and I'll get it for you.'

'Thank you.' Lila set down her crutches and settled into a booth, wondering what the hell she was going to say to Ruby.

Was it even worth still calling her? Joe had gone to the effort of getting in touch with her though and Jack did still need answers. She would speak to the girl and try not to spook her then maybe fire a brief text off to Jack. As she debated how best to gain Ruby's trust, Joe came over with a pot of tea and a slab of chocolate cake, which he set down before her.

He grinned when Lila reached for her purse. 'Mum says it's on the house. I've just texted you Ruby's number.'

'Thank you.'

She waited until Joe had gone back to the kitchen before pulling out her phone and looking at the text, storing Ruby's number on her memory card.

Once again she wondered what on earth she was going to say to the girl. Throwing caution to the wind, deciding she was going to have to make it up as she went along, she pressed "call", and waited, her heart thumping.

For a long moment it continued to ring and Lila thought it would go to voicemail, but then a wary voice answered. 'Hello?'

'Ruby? This is Joe's friend, Lila.'

'Yes?'

'I really need to speak with you, in person if possible.'

'What's this about?' The wariness was still there.

'You were friends with Stephanie Whitman.'

There was silence and Lila wondered if Ruby had hung up. 'Ruby? Are you still there?'

'Are you a friend of her brother's?'

'Jack just–'

'I can't talk about it. I have to go.'

'Please, Ruby. Please don't hang up. This is really important.'

There was silence down the line, but the call was still live. Ruby didn't speak again. Instead waited, presumably to hear what Lila had to say.

'I know you were Stephanie's friend. I know you cared about

her. If something bad happened to her before she died you have to let us know. She deserves that, doesn't she?'

The silence continued.

'Please, Ruby.'

'I shouldn't have put what I did on her Facebook page.'

'But you did and now Jack is in even more turmoil. It's killing him not knowing. You can help. You need to talk to him. Please.'

It took another five minutes of cajoling, but eventually Ruby agreed to consider Lila's request to meet. Whatever it was, it was clear the guilt of keeping Stephanie's secret was weighing heavily. She promised Lila she would be in touch.

Lila hoped she was telling the truth, wondered if she should message Jack and let him know they had spoken. If Ruby agreed to meet, would he still want Lila to go with him? It would be bloody uncomfortable.

She picked up her phone, started to write a text. *Hey, Jack. I have some news about Ruby...* then hesitated, deleting the message.

After a moment's deliberation, she logged into Facebook, clicked on to his profile, but his settings were still tight and gave nothing away. Was Tiffany on Facebook? Lila wanted to know, but didn't want to know. She would be a fool to even look.

She tapped the table impatiently, glanced round the almost-empty café, before typing Tiffany Pendleton-Shay into the search engine, feeling sick when Jack's bombshell blonde girlfriend beamed back at her. Jack was in her profile picture, his arm around her, and they looked perfect together. Lila knew she should click off Facebook, but the masochist in her couldn't resist clicking through the handful of public photos Tiffany had posted. Jack was in most of them, smiling and gorgeous, those cool blue eyes of his staring straight at her, while Tiffany possessively held on to him. She was also smiling, but her expression clearly spoke, "He's mine".

Jack was Tiffany's boyfriend and Lila was no relationship

wrecker. It was for the best that she didn't see him again. But would Ruby agree to meet him if she wasn't there?

And she had to tell him about Ruby. She knew how important this was to him.

Just text him. Send a simple text saying that you've spoken to Ruby. If he doesn't reply then you know he wants you to butt out.

Lila argued with herself for another five minutes, over-analysing everything, getting annoyed because she wasn't usually so indecisive. Finally she wrote a message, kept it simple. *I've spoken to Ruby. She's a little freaked out about meeting, but said she will think about it. I'll let you know what she says.*

Brief, friendly, but non-committal. She had opened up a line of dialogue and the ball was now in Jack's court whether to reply.

JACK WAS out for a run when Lila's text came through, needing to clear his head after a late night of drinking and soul-searching, the events of the previous evening still replaying in his head.

Bored of waiting at the station where he was supposed to have picked her up, Tiff had put herself in a black cab. The lights had all been on when he'd arrived home, but then that was Tiff. Screw the electricity bill. He was a terrible boyfriend, she had told him and Jack supposed it was true. Not just because he had forgotten to pick her up, but also because he had almost kissed Lila.

Correction: would have kissed Lila if Elliot hadn't interrupted them.

It wasn't like Jack had planned it, but he would be a liar, as well as a terrible boyfriend, if he didn't admit he had wanted to kiss her. Yes, he had wanted to kiss her, had for a moment forgotten he already had a girlfriend, and now Tiff was pissed off with him and Lila disappointed in him. Knowing that had eaten at him all the way home, gnawing at his temper, and by the time he found Tiffany in the kitchen, topping up her glass of wine, he had been ready for a fight.

'Nice of you to finally show up,' she had snarled as she turned to face him.

'Nice of you to light up the house like it's the bloody Blackpool Illuminations,' Jack growled back, throwing his keys down.

From his bed in the corner of the room, Cooper whined.

Tiffany glared at the dog before turning her attention back to Jack. 'You owe me ninety quid for the taxi.'

'You paid ninety quid, are you kidding me?'

Leaving her in the kitchen, too annoyed to look at her, Jack had gone from room to room, switching off the lights he was certain she had turned on to goad him.

Tiffany followed, her high heels clacking on the wooden floors, the sound irritating him as she followed him upstairs. 'Where were you?'

'Out.'

'Out where?'

'It doesn't matter.'

'It bloody well does to me. I want to know where you were that was so important that you forgot you were picking me up from the fucking station.'

Things had gone downhill fast from there. Tiffany didn't understand why Jack would want to visit Filby Broad or why he was still struggling with Stephanie's death.

He bitterly recalled her words. 'She's gone, Jack. It's time to move on and you need to focus on those of us who are still here.'

'Time to move on?' He had questioned incredulously, pacing the landing. 'She only fucking died six weeks ago.'

'I'm aware of that, but wallowing about it isn't going to do you any good.'

'Stop! Just fucking stop talking before you dig yourself any deeper, please.'

Tiffany's mouth had been a thin painted line as she scowled at him, one regal eyebrow arched. She was beautiful even when she was angry, but it was all manufactured, from her threaded eyebrows to her manicured nails to her golden tan. He realised he wasn't even sure he had ever seen what the real Tiffany Pendleton-Shay looked like and that realisation had been followed by a slamming revelation.

He didn't love her.

TIFFANY HADN'T TAKEN the break-up well and after a difficult night of temper tantrums, sulking and tears, Jack had endured a frosty ride back to the station to drop her off.

He had brooded during the ride home, remembering the good times, part of him doleful at the finality of the relationship, but also relieved he had ended things.

PUTTING IN EARPHONES, he lost himself for an hour, running a coastal route to Holkham and back, Cooper keeping pace, trying to push Tiffany, Lila, and the still-raw grief over Stephanie out of his mind. As they closed in on the final half-mile stretch he felt his phone vibrate in his pocket, guessed it was probably Alyssa reminding him not to be late for the dinner thing she was hosting that night, and wondered how best to break it to her that she needed to set one less place as Tiff wouldn't be there.

Approaching the quayside, he slowed his pace, backhanding sweat from his face and chugging water from the bottle he carried with him. Capping the bottle, he reached in his pocket for his phone, stopping to a walk when he saw the message was from Lila.

It was brief, nothing about what had happened the previous night, instead telling him she had spoken to Ruby Howard and the girl was considering meeting with him. *I'll let you know what she says*, the text ended, non-committedly.

Jack hesitated then typed a message back. *Can I call you in a bit?*

He had reached the back porch of his house, was fishing for his keys when her reply came back. It was just one word. *Okay.*

Yes, she was still pissed off with him and he guessed he couldn't blame her. He had nearly kissed her and then seconds later, she had found out he had a girlfriend.

He was a bloody fool. Why had he tried to make things personal between them? The previous night had been a huge mistake.

He would have a shower and give her a call in a bit, keep things to the point and find out what Ruby said, try to redress the balance between them.

As THE BUS pulled into Norwich, Lila glanced at her phone. No new calls or text messages.

Jack had said he was going to call her, but she hadn't heard anything more from him. She had done the right thing, telling him about her conversation with Ruby and there was nothing more to really be said until Ruby got back to her.

Saturday evening loomed ahead of Lila and she had no plans, no company. Usually it wouldn't bother her. Lila enjoyed her own company, liked having her independence. It was the frustration of having the cast on her leg, hindering everything. Typically on a Saturday evening with no plans, she would get in the car, head out on an adventure with her camera, but of course she couldn't drive, so was effectively tied to the flat.

Netflix, takeaway, and a couple of glasses of wine, she decided, with Clyde for company, assuming he wasn't upstairs with Primrose or planning on hitting the tiles. The thought that her landlady's cat currently had a better social life than her brought a smile to Lila's face, briefly lightening her mood.

She got off the bus, started the ten-minute walk – which took her twenty with the crutches – to her flat, stopping off at the local Spar shop for a bottle of wine. The plastic bag it was in bashed awkwardly against her crutch as she cut across the park that led to the end of her street. Aside from a couple of dog walkers in the distance, the park was empty. Although the day had been bright and warm, storms now threatened, the sky darkened to a moody grey, the sun blocked out by cloud, despite there being another hour of daylight left. Luckily it was still dry and Lila hoped she would make it home before the rain started.

She paused briefly to rest, adjusting the bottle bag to her other arm. The exertion of walking on crutches didn't get any easier and she had already built up a light sweat. As she caught her breath, a rustling noise came from the bushes behind her and her head swung around.

There was no-one there and she shrugged it off, knowing it was probably just a bird or a squirrel. She was about to continue on her way when her phone rang. Balancing both crutches in one hand, she reached into her pocket for Elliot's borrowed mobile, heartbeat quickening when she saw Jack's name.

Still she hesitated for a second, not wanting to seem too desperate to speak to him. He had said he was going to call her hours earlier.

Eventually she clicked answer, tried to keep her tone nonchalant. 'Hello?'

'Lila, it's Jack.'

'Hey.'

'You okay?'

That was a loaded question given everything that had happened the previous night. 'I'm fine,' she told him stiffly. This conversation was proving to be more difficult than she had anticipated. She didn't bother to ask how he was. The more impersonal she kept this the better.

'I'm sorry I didn't call you earlier. Something came up.'

'Not a problem. You didn't have to call. I felt I should tell you about Ruby.'

'Okay, thank you. I appreciate that.'

'When I hear–'

Another rustling in the bushes had Lila stopping. She glanced over her shoulder again, for the briefest second thought she saw a figure, but then they, it, disappeared. It was probably a trick of the light. There was no-one there and she was being skittish.

'Lila?'

'I'm here. Sorry, I thought I heard… it doesn't matter.'

'Where are you?'

'Walking home. In fact I'm almost there, so I should go. I'll let you know when I hear from Ruby, okay?' Jack started to speak, but she cut him off. 'I really have to go now. Take care.'

She ended the call, annoyed when she swallowed and found a lump in her throat. She barely knew Jack and nothing had technically happened between them. It was ridiculous he was having such an effect on her. Time to snap out of it and move on.

Glancing hesitantly at the bushes again, convinced that her imagination had been playing tricks on her, she slipped the phone back in her pocket and started walking again. Neither of the dog walkers were in sight, probably already gone, but she was halfway across the park, only a few short minutes from her flat.

She would order takeaway as soon as she was home, indulge in a bubble bath with a glass of wine while she waited for the delivery. Pyjamas, cuddles with Clyde, maybe check out the new horror film she had seen advertised on Netflix, and she would feel much better. Jack Foley had managed to get into her head quickly enough, so it should be just as easy to get him back out again.

'Lila.'

Her name was spoken softly, barely a whisper, though drawn out in a singsong tone.

Lila froze, swung round. No-one was behind her.

Wind rustled through the bushes. Had she imagined it? Was her brain really that frazzled that she was hearing and seeing things?

There was no-one hiding. She was being paranoid.

But as she stared at the thicket, the whisper came again. This time there was no pretending it was the wind or her imagination playing tricks on her, the breathy voice so taunting in tone.

'Lie–laaa.'

A shiver ran down her spine as she took a tentative step back, part of her fearful that if she made a quick movement, something might come rushing out of the bushes at her.

She was alone in the park and, although the safety of her flat was a few minutes away, she felt vulnerable.

For a moment, there was silence, then a sudden rush of wind rustled the leaves of the trees, making her jump. She turned on shaking legs, stumbling her way on her crutches as fast as she could, focussing on the entrance to the park in the distance, and not daring to look back.

With the sound of the wind picking up, the noise of her crutches and her harsh breathing, she couldn't hear anything else… at first. But then it was there, distinctive footsteps and they sounded as if they were gaining pace on the pathway behind her. She tried to move faster, almost lost her footing, the shaky sigh of relief when she finally reached the entrance shuddering through her body.

She still wasn't home safe, but at least she had the security of houses on either side of the street, could see the comforting glow of the chip shop at the end of the road, the group of loitering teenagers she would usually find irritating, a welcoming sight.

She could no longer hear footsteps behind her, risked a brief glance over her shoulder, saw nothing. Was she actually losing her mind?

No, the sound had been real. The voice coming from the thicket had been real.

HER LEGS WERE STILL SHAKING when she reached the house, fumbling in her bag for her door keys, annoyed when her trembling fingers struggled to get them in the lock.

Eventually she managed to get the main door open, gave the street another cursory glance before closing and bolting herself inside. She looked at the stairs, knew Primrose was up there, no doubt watching TV, and some of the fear ebbed away. Still Lila didn't feel completely safe until she had opened the door to her flat and locked herself inside.

For tonight at least, she was safe.

J ack was the last one to arrive, irritation pricking at the back of his neck as he saw Giles throw open the front door of the cobbled cottage he and Alyssa owned in the market town of Aylsham, obviously having heard the sound of Jack's engine.

The man was wearing a suit and tie as per usual, hair slicked down, a glass of what looked like whisky in his hand and a snaky smile on his face.

'Jack, glad you could make it,' he called as Jack killed the engine, opened the door. 'We've been waiting for you.'

Jack ignored him, grabbing the wine he'd brought with him – a bottle of his sister's favourite Rioja Gran Reserva – and the dog biscuits from the passenger seat, catching hold of Cooper's lead as the spaniel bounded over his lap and out of the car.

The smile fell from Giles's face. 'What is he doing here?'

Jack closed the door with his elbow, clicked his key at the car, and grinned broadly at Giles. 'Look, Cooper, it's Uncle Giles.'

He had purposely brought Cooper with him, knowing Giles hated dogs.

Cooper let out a loud gleeful bark that had Giles taking a step back and Jack loosened his lead to allow the dog enough manoeuvre room to jump up at his sister's odious boyfriend.

'Get down, goddammit!' Giles snapped, taking another step back as whisky sloshed out of his glass.

'He just wants to say hi to his favourite uncle,' Jack goaded.

'You're not bringing him in the house. He can stay in the car.'

Blatantly ignoring the order, Jack followed Cooper into the house, stopping briefly to give the seething Giles a condescending slap on the shoulder. 'He'll be fine.'

'Jack, is that you?'

Alyssa rushed forward, concern and questions ready for him after he'd vaguely replied to her earlier texts about Tiffany, not in the mood for dissecting his relationship with his one remaining sister. Her expression changed as she spotted the dog. 'Ooh, you've brought Cooper.'

Cooper jumped up again, his tail wagging and licked her hand as Alyssa tickled under his floppy ears. She grinned at Jack. 'This is a nice surprise.'

She stopped fussing the dog long enough to give Jack a hug and a kiss on the cheek, accepting the bottle of Rioja he handed her. 'Giles, go pour Jack a glass of wine.'

'No wine for me, I'm going to drive back.'

'But, Jack…'

Jack held up a hand. 'I've got a lot on my mind. I'd rather keep a clear head tonight.'

Alyssa nodded. 'We need to talk about what happened with Tiffany.'

'Not right now, Lys, but maybe later, okay? Where are the others?'

'They're through in the dining room. Let's go see them, Cooper.'

'The dog stays out here, Alyssa,' Giles argued. 'The dining room is no place for him.'

Alyssa shot Giles a brief look before overruling him. 'He'll be fine. Come on, Cooper.'

Jack gave Giles a broad grin and followed his sister down the hallway.

As Jack had suspected, everyone else was pleased to see Cooper, who lapped up the fuss from Tom, his wife Imogen, Oliver and his partner Simon, before settling himself under Imogen's chair. He ignored the bowl of biscuits that Alyssa set down for him, but happily wolfed the titbits Imogen kept passing to him, much to Giles's annoyance.

Jack nursed his one beer, part of him tempted to say 'fuck it' and join his siblings and their partners in getting drunk, and catch a taxi home. He refrained though, knowing he would be making a mistake.

The break-up with Tiff was still raw and despite his best intentions to try to forget her, Lila was weighing heavily on his mind. She had been cool when he had spoken to her earlier and a little terse. He knew she was pissed off about what had happened, but he had also heard the hurt in her voice and he hated knowing he had caused that. What with Tiffany, Lila, and this stupid dinner party Alyssa had insisted on throwing to raise a glass to Stephanie, who had barely been put in the ground, drinking would only sour his mood, probably loosen his tongue and make him say things he might later regret. It was safer to stay sober and ride it out.

He glanced discreetly at his watch, figuring it was going to be a long night.

Mercifully there were few questions about Tiff, the others picking up that he wasn't ready to discuss the break-up. Giles was the only one who mentioned her and Jack knew full well it was retribution for bringing Cooper. Tiffany he was prepared for, he had already accepted her name would come up, but mention of Lila's name caught him off guard.

'Your friend, Miss Amberson, is proving to be an interesting character.' Giles dropped the comment casually as Alyssa served seafood paella.

The conversation had sobered over the past half hour with talk turning to the accident that had claimed Stephanie's life, and the mood was melancholy, making Jack glad he had refrained from drinking. He was pleased he had his wits about him, as Giles was obviously in the mood for one of his mind games.

'I'm sure she is.' Jack kept his tone light, almost disinterested; aware Giles was watching him for a reaction.

'I've had a buddy of mine look into her... you know, her finances, her business, her past relationships.'

'Why would you do that?' Although his tone was still calm, inside, Jack was seething.

'I already told you; I don't trust her. There was no reasonable motive for her showing up to Stephanie's funeral.'

'Other than to pay her respects.'

'She was at Steph's funeral?' That was from Oliver, who was eyeing Jack curiously.

Tom was also watching him, though more to see how this was going to play out, Jack thought, aware he would need to pick the right moment if he was going to step in to back up his brother. He was the only one who knew Jack had seen more of Lila than just at the funeral.

'Did you know she has been bankrupt? That the partner of her first business went to jail for money laundering? Seems to me that Lila Amberson has seen an opportunity with the Whitman family.'

Jack didn't know that, but he also knew Lila. Couldn't believe for one second that she would be involved in anything illegal. He was holding on to his temper by a thread when he spoke. 'You know nothing about Lila Amberson and you have no right to dig into her private life. She was a victim in the car accident that killed my sister. There's nothing sinister about her motives.'

'I have every right,' Giles snarled. 'I care about this family and I won't let this woman try to manipulate us.'

'Us? You're *not* part of this bloody family, Giles. You have no right. No fucking right!'

That had Giles reddening with rage, his tiny eyes bulging as he got to his feet. 'I have every right,' he repeated. 'I'm going to be part of this family whether you like it or not. What hold has this woman got over you, Jack?'

Under the table, Cooper woofed, followed by a low ominous growl. Oliver sat open mouthed, looking ready to fire a dozen questions, while his boyfriend, Simon, seemed intrigued, and Imogen studied the table, looking downright uncomfortable.

'That's enough, Giles.'

Giles scowled at Tom, annoyed at the interruption, before wheeling on Jack again. 'You're supposed to be a crime writer; you were an investigative journalist for fuck's sake. Yet you're so bloody stupid, man, you can't see when you're being duped!'

'That's enough!' Alyssa snapped, also getting to her feet. 'Giles, you need to ease up on the whisky. What is that, your fifth or sixth double? And don't you ever dare call my brother stupid again.'

Giles's eyes bulged further, as he yanked to loosen the tie around his chubby neck. 'That's just typical, Alyssa, take your family's side over mine.'

'You're out of order, Giles.' Jack was angry, angry on behalf of Lila and livid that Giles had tried to destroy the evening Alyssa had wanted so desperately to honour Stephanie. He might not have agreed with this whole memorial dinner thing, feeling it was far too soon, but he had at least respected her wishes, unlike her prick of a boyfriend. 'Lila is kind and considerate, and she puts everyone else before her. I couldn't tell you about her past, but I do know that you have her completely wrong and she's a hell of a better person than you will ever be.'

'So you know her pretty well then,' Oliver breathed, his expression unreadable.

Jack glanced at his youngest brother. This wasn't the time to try to explain his connection to Lila. Oliver had questions, but they would have to wait.

'Sit down and eat your dinner, Giles. Your food's getting cold.'

Instead of doing as ordered, Giles pouted at Alyssa. 'I insult your brother and World War Three kicks off; he insults me and you're okay with that?'

'You need to cool the hell down.'

Giles sneered his nose up at her then glanced with contempt at the rest of the group. 'You people are all the same. You think you're so bloody special, but you're all just one big joke.'

'Giles!'

'I need some air.' Giles threw down his napkin, stormed from the room.

MOMENTS later the front door slammed shut followed by the sound of an engine revving.

Panic crossed Alyssa's face. 'He's shitfaced and he's taking the car.'

Jack was already on his feet, followed by Tom, Oliver, Simon and Cooper.

By the time they reached the front door, the taillights of Giles's Porsche were fading in the distance.

'Should we call the police?' Simon asked.

Tears filled Alyssa's eyes. 'They'll arrest him. I know he's a jerk and he was out of order, but I love him. Please don't call them,' she begged.

Jack slipped his arm around her, led her back through to the dining room. Cooper followed close behind them, whining softly. God knows where Giles had gone. Jack loved his sister, but if Giles caused an accident, like what had happened to Steph...

Jack clenched his fist, thought of his youngest sister, and wished to hell he had never agreed to come here tonight.

THE MOVIE ENDED and Lila switched off the TV, ruing her decision to watch a horror film. Yes she had enjoyed it, but now it was over and her flat was silent, the dark rooms filled with shadows, she kept thinking back to the incident in the park and how she had been convinced someone had been following her, how scared she had been at the time.

Over the course of the evening, her belly full of Chinese, the half-bottle of wine she had drunk comfortably mellowing her mood, she had tried to rationalise what she thought she had heard. It made no sense. There was no way that someone would be hiding in the park, knowing that she was going to walk past at that exact moment. It was a ridiculous idea. Much more plausible to believe she had mistaken the rustling of the breeze against the leaves to be a spooky voice.

With the flat dark and silent, the creepy film still playing in her head, she was questioning everything all over again and her initial fears seemed more plausible.

Telling herself to stop being an idiot, she undressed and cleaned her teeth, started to go through to her bedroom, but doubted herself, going back to once again recheck the front door was locked, that all of the windows were shut.

Eventually satisfied that she was safe, she turned off the lights and crawled into bed, switched on the night lamp. It was still early – just gone ten thirty – and although she was tired, her overactive imagination was working overtime. She picked up her Kindle, figured reading for a short while might refocus her mind. Jack's book, *Something Wicked*, sat top of the list – her most recent download. She didn't want anything scary though, plus she needed to take her mind off Jack, not be thinking about him.

Instead she opted for a sweet looking rom-com, something light to chill her addled brain.

She read the first couple of chapters then, exhausted, set the book down, turned off the light and settled back against the pillows, closing her eyes.

SHE HAD NOT LONG DOZED off when a creaking noise awoke her.

That was her first coherent thought, pulling her from her dream world back to reality with an unwelcome bump. There was a creaking noise, like the sound of a foot treading on that uneven floorboard in her room, the one she kept meaning to get fixed.

Lila cranked one eye open, the room initially black, but as her vision adjusted, she spotted the window, the light of the moon shining through, the hooded figure that slowly moved across in front of the window. And she almost stopped breathing.

Someone was in her bedroom.

Suddenly her brain was fully awake, though physically she dare not move, other than the violent trembling she tried to so hard to control, her breath coming fast and shallow after she had initially tried to hold it.

Whoever it was had his back to her, but Lila knew it was only momentarily, that he would turn again, and then what? What was his motive? Did he intend to rob her, rape her or maybe kill her? The thought of the last two things made her convulse, a violent shudder rippling through her body.

She couldn't afford to panic. One shot. She had one shot.

As she was thinking about how to use that one shot, the figure started to turn and the panic she was trying not to give into came automatically. In blind fear, she grabbed for the nearest possible weapon, her crutch, and swung it hard at the intruder. He saw her at the last second, putting his arms up to shield himself and trying to move out of the way. The crutch smashed into his arms and she heard a satisfying grunt before she realised he had hold of her weapon, easily managing to wrestle it from her.

It was at that point she finally found her voice, let out a piercing scream.

The man glanced around. In the dark, with the hood up, he was little more than a shadow, and she couldn't make out his features. He seemed to be debating his next move. Lila knew if he tried to attack her that her broken leg would prevent her from getting away. She was trapped, had only her voice, so she used it, screaming again, this time louder and for longer.

A timely creak came from the floor above. It wouldn't be Primrose. Lila's landlady struggled with her hearing. The man wouldn't know that though, just as he wouldn't know the old building regularly creaked and groaned. Although Lila couldn't see his face, she was aware of his panic as he realised he might get caught. The crutch dropped suddenly and he turned and fled from her bedroom. She heard his footsteps in the hall then a grunt and a crunch of gravel. He was outside.

She reached across, flicked the night lamp switch on with shaking fingers. Her crutch lay on the floor where he had dropped it, her bedroom door wide open. He was gone, but he had managed to get into her flat somehow and she needed to find out where.

Easing herself out of bed, heart still hammering, she reached for her crutches, made her way to the bedroom door on trembling legs that threatened to buckle. She was aware she was wearing just a skimpy vest and knickers, but although her state of undress left her feeling vulnerable and exposed, finding out how he had managed to get into her flat was more important.

She flicked switches as she moved, flooding each room with light, needing the comfort and wanting to be sure there was nothing hiding in the shadows. In the bathroom, the window was wide open, the handle lying on the floor. A partial muddy boot print on the toilet seat confirmed this was where he had entered and exited her flat. Lila pulled the window shut as best as she could. He must've broken it when he got in. Why had he been there? What had he wanted?

She had to call the police, report what had happened.

BACK IN HER BEDROOM, she made the call, glancing at the spot where the man had stood a few moments before as she waited for the operator to connect her. If she hadn't awoken, if he hadn't stepped on the creaky floorboard, what would have happened?

She swallowed down the sob that was rising in her throat as her call was connected, surprising herself at how calm she sounded as she explained what had happened. As she waited for the police to arrive, she pondered calling Elliot, knew it wasn't fair to ruin his holiday.

Instead she tried Beth, frustrated when her friend's phone went to voicemail. She didn't leave a message, instead fired off a brief text. *Someone broke into my flat. Police are on their way. Can you call me when you get this? I really don't want to be alone tonight.*

She stared at her phone, willing Beth to call. As she waited, she became aware again of her state of undress. The police were on their way and she couldn't answer the door to them as she was. She slipped on her pyjama bottoms and robe, knotting it around her waist, checked her phone again. Although she had turned down the volume, she hadn't left the room so would have heard it if Beth had called, but still she wanted to be sure.

Nothing. Her friend must be busy.

She tapped the screen impatiently, annoyed that she was thinking about texting Jack.

He would be with his girlfriend. Lila had no right to get in contact with him about this.

'Come on, Beth. Please call me.'

· · ·

FIVE LONG MINUTES ticked by and still her phone didn't ring.

She guessed she could try Natalie, though Joe was home for the weekend. It wasn't fair to drag her out. Instead Lila opened up a new text message, typed in Jack's name. She didn't expect anything back from him, she would just send a text, let him know what had happened.

Someone broke into my flat. Police on way.

She pressed send before she could reconsider, telling herself she was an idiot the second the message left her phone. She shouldn't involve him in this, especially after she had promised herself she would cut contact with him.

A loud rap on the front door made her jump. The police were already there. It was too late to worry about messaging Jack. She needed to get this over with. Dropping the phone on her bed again, she grabbed her crutches and went to answer the door.

GILES HADN'T RETURNED and Alyssa's dinner party, which had already been a morose affair, became gloomier as the evening ticked on. She kept apologising to everyone for Giles's behaviour while looking at her watch, noting how long he had been gone. Jack had offered to go and look for him, but she had insisted everyone stay put and finish eating the meal she had made.

Dessert was served, followed by brandy for everyone except Jack, who had coffee. Beneath the table, Cooper had eventually stopped whining and had fallen asleep.

It was almost eleven by the time they helped Alyssa clear up, still no sign of Giles, and Jack was getting ready to make a move. Oliver and Simon were planning on crashing the night, so at least Jack knew his sister wouldn't be alone; and he planned on giving Tom and Imogen a lift home.

As he carried glasses through to the kitchen, Jack felt his phone vibrate in his jeans pocket. He set the glasses down by the dishwasher and reached for his phone, surprised to see Lila's name on the screen. She had pretty much hung up on him earlier, so why was she texting him this late?

He read her message then reread it, his mouth dry. Hitting "call", he strode out of the room, pacing the hallway as her phone rang, swearing when it went to voicemail. Annoyed, he tried again. 'Damn it, Lila, answer your phone.'

'You okay out here?'

Jack glanced at Tom, ignoring him as he hit redial. This time when it went to voicemail he left a message. 'It's me. I just got your text message. Call me back.'

He looked at his brother again. 'I have to go. Lila's in trouble.'

'What kind of trouble?'

'Someone broke into her flat. That's all I know. She's not answering her bloody phone.'

Tom nodded. 'Of course, go. Immy and I will get a cab.'

Tom and Imogen lived up on the coast, a couple of villages away from him. Completely the wrong direction to where he was heading. 'Shit. I'm sorry.'

'It's okay, Jack. Go check on Lila.'

'Lila?' Alyssa asked, joining them in the hall, Cooper at her heels.

'I have to go. Tom'll explain.' Jack already had his car keys in his hand, the front door open.

'You've forgotten Cooper.'

Shit, the dog.

'He can stay here.'

When Alyssa frowned, Jack attempted a brief grin, hurrying back inside to peck her on the cheek. 'Please, Alyssa. It's just for tonight. I'll come back for him in the morning, I promise.'

'Jack! You can't just leave–'

'His biscuits are in the kitchen. I have to go, but I'll be back for him in the morning.'

Ignoring her protests, he got into his car, put his phone on hands-free, dialled Lila's number again as he swung out of the driveway. Still it went to voicemail. Aylsham was twelve miles from Norwich, a twenty-five minute journey. He could do it in twenty if he put his foot down.

'You're sure you've never seen this man before?' Detective Constable Galbraith questioned, tapping his notepad.

'I don't know. I don't think so. It was dark.'

'You said he was wearing a hood. Can you describe him other than that? I know you couldn't see his face, but can you give us an idea of height or build?'

Lila's mug shook in her hands, tea sloshing over the edge and onto her pyjama bottoms, as she tried to recall the man she had seen standing in her room. She had been relatively calm when she had let the officers into her flat and made the drinks, but now she was sat down and trying to recount what had happened she couldn't stop shaking.

Galbraith's partner, DC Jones: a dark-haired woman with kind eyes, smiled gently at her. 'Try taking a few deep breaths, it will help relax you.'

'I'm sorry.'

'Don't apologise, love. You've had a traumatic experience. Anyone would be shaken if they woke to find an intruder in their home.'

Lila nodded, doing as instructed, and sipped at her tea. Tears pricked at the back of her eyes. So far she had kept them at bay, but her emotions were all over the place, and she wasn't sure how much longer she could hold them back.

'I was in bed and it was dark, so it's hard to tell how tall he was. Maybe five eight or nine... I'm sorry, I don't know.'

'How about build?' Galbraith's tone was patient, his greying moustache twitching slightly as he waited for her to answer.

'Average build, not too skinny, not too fat. That's not much help, I know.'

'Everything helps, Miss Amberson.'

'Why do you think he broke in?' Lila whispered the question, knowing it was a stupid one, that the police had only been there twenty minutes and hadn't even started investigating. Still she had to ask, needing some kind of reassurance that the motive hadn't been sinister. 'Do you think it was a burglary?'

Galbraith exchanged a brief look with his partner that only served to deepen her fears. 'You fell into the path of a bus last week. I know it appeared to be an accident, but you said when my colleague spoke to you that you'd been pushed.'

Lila's heartbeat quickened. 'I had.'

'And that the man who pushed you wore a hood.'

Her hands were shaking again and she attempted to set the cup down on the coffee table, spilling more tea as she did. 'You think it was him?'

Another exchanged look.

'You think he wanted to hurt me.' This time it wasn't a question. Lila sucked in a breath, held it, willing the tears not to fall, furious when they did. 'Why?' she demanded, angrily swiping them away. 'Why is he doing this?'

Jones smiled sympathetically. 'We don't know for sure. This incident could be unrelated. At the moment we are theorising and trying to connect dots.'

'Can you think of anyone who might want to hurt you?' Galbraith asked. 'Anyone you've pissed off lately?' It was his attempt at humour; Lila could see that from his half-smile, obviously he was trying to lighten the mood slightly. Unfortunately it wasn't working. Someone had pushed her in front of a bus and it was likely that same person had broken into her flat with the intention of hurting her.

'There's no-one.'

'You're certain?'

'No.' She wracked her brain, frustrated. She was a fairly easy-going person, wasn't she? She tried to be kind to people and didn't have enemies. Sure there were probably people who found her annoying – you couldn't please everyone – but she would like to think that none of them would want to physically hurt her. She thought about the earlier incident in the park, still unsure if it had been her imagination. Given what happened that night maybe it hadn't. 'I thought I was being followed earlier.'

'You did?'

She went over the incident in the park, feeling a little stupid that the details were so scant, guessing the detectives would think she was being paranoid. They didn't though, Galbraith making plenty of notes and asking a lot of questions. It seemed they were taking her suspicions quite seriously, wondering if the intruder had followed her home and waited until he knew she was asleep before breaking in.

'He entered through the window–'

Galbraith was interrupted mid-sentence by a loud banging on the front door. Lila jumped, clutching at the arm of the sofa, as she looked to the two detectives for support.

'I've got it,' Galbraith told her, getting up.

Still she started shaking again as he opened the door to her flat, disappearing momentarily as he unlocked the main door to the house. She heard voices, first the detective constable, his tone calm and rational then another more familiar voice, raised and angry in response.

'Lila?'

Her heartbeat quickened. 'Jack?'

She got up from the sofa, had started to reach for her crutches when he appeared in the doorway.

'Jesus, Lila, I called you a dozen times on the ride over here. You didn't pick up.'

'I was...' Her words were lost as he caught her in an unexpected hard hug.

'You scared me. What the hell happened?'

'There was a man. I woke and...' She couldn't finish the sentence. Jack was warm and comforting and familiar, and she held on to him, needing that for a moment.

Eventually he eased her back, sat her down on the sofa, though took the seat beside her, his arm around her, keeping her close.

'Someone broke in while she was asleep?' he demanded of the detectives.

'Through the bathroom window,' Jones told him. 'We're still trying to establish the motive. You're Miss Amberson's—'

'Friend!' Jack snapped.

She nodded, smiled, as Galbraith jotted that down.

Yes, friend, Lila reminded herself. Jack already had a girlfriend. Clearly an understanding one if she had let him rush over here. It had been wrong of Lila to text him, unfair, but he had come and she really needed the support. She could beat herself up about it in the morning.

'And your name is?'

'Jack Foley.'

Galbraith glanced up from his notebook. 'Stephanie Whitman's brother.' He nodded. 'You were with Miss Amberson that day in Cromer, right, when she was hit by the bus?'

'Correct.'

'Did the two of you know each other before the accident at Filby Broad?'

'Nope.' Jack's tone was tight and Lila caught hold of his hand, squeezed it.

'We met at Stephanie's funeral,' she told the detectives. 'I went to pay my respects.'

Jones nodded again at that, a vague smile on her lips that gave nothing away.

'So Lila and I have become friends,' Jack continued. 'I don't see how that is relevant to what happened here tonight or what happened in Cromer last week. Someone is trying to hurt her. Perhaps that should take precedence?'

Galbraith's moustache twitched again. 'It is, Mr Foley, and as you and Miss Amberson have become such good friends...' He made a brief point of looking at Lila's hand covering Jack's. 'I'm sure you won't mind answering a few questions.'

IT WAS NEARLY an hour later when the police left and Jack's friendship with Lila had been thoroughly dissected. Because of the way they had met, because she had been involved in the car crash that had killed his sister, the police somehow doubted his motives and were questioning how genuine their connection was.

It pissed him off that someone was trying to hurt Lila and they were wasting their time over irrelevant details, instead of trying to catch whoever was responsible. For that night though she was safe. He had insisted on staying, despite her protests. There was no way on hell's earth he was leaving her alone with a broken window, knowing someone out there wanted to hurt her.

After the detectives had left, Lila opened a bottle of wine. It was already gone midnight, but Jack knew sleep wouldn't come easy for her. She sat beside him on the sofa, poured them both a glass, and she looked exhausted, dark circles haunting her eyes.

'You didn't have to drive all the way down here.' She managed a smile, but it was weak and forced.

'Yes I did. We're in this together, remember?' Jack tried his best to coax another smile out of her. Failed. 'I've got your back, Lila.'

She looked so sad, so beaten, and he hated that.

'Why don't you try to get some sleep?' he suggested, reaching out to brush her cheek.

'I don't think...' Her voice cracked and she tried to clear her throat. 'I can't sleep in there...' She took a gulp of wine, struggled to swallow it.

Jack took her glass, setting it down on the table. He wished he could find the person responsible for scaring her.

'You don't have to,' he told her softly, pulling her towards him, feeling the briefest resistance before she leaned into him and choked out a sob. He held her as she cried, stroking her hair and trying to comfort her, wishing there was something he could do or say to ease her pain.

Eventually she fell asleep in his arms and he eased her back on to the sofa, placing a cushion below her head and fetching the duvet from her room, covering her.

Finally she looked peaceful.

He settled into the armchair opposite, watching her until his eyes finally drifted shut.

When Lila awoke it took her a moment to realise where she was, figure out why she was asleep on the sofa and not in her bed, but then the events of the previous night came flooding back; a nightmare that had actually happened.

Someone had broken into her flat.

Icy fear clawed at her throat, as she remembered how she had woken up, seen the hooded man standing in her bedroom. She had always felt safe in her flat. How was she supposed to get that feeling of security back again?

The police had taken her statement and one of their crime scene colleagues had arrived to lift the boot print in the bathroom, but she knew they didn't have any leads. And Jack, he had been there, had gone over and beyond, letting her cry all over him, staying with her until she fell asleep.

She wondered what time he had left, knew he had his own life to get back to.

Rubbing at her sore eyes, she threw back the duvet, climbed off the sofa, grabbing her crutches and made her way down the hallway to the bathroom, wanting to assess the damage to her window.

The handle had come off and was broken on the floor. Priority of the day would be getting the window fixed, though she wasn't sure whom she would find to do that on a Sunday. One thing she knew though, she couldn't stay in the flat that night knowing the window offered an opportunity for the intruder to return.

As she splashed water on her face, trying to relieve the soreness of her tired eyes, her phone beeped. Lila went through to her bedroom to check it, shocked by the number of missed calls and messages.

Most of the missed calls were from Jack and had been last night in response to her text message, but there were a couple from Beth, who had also sent two text messages demanding Lila call her immediately. There was also a text from Ruby Howard, agreeing to meet with Jack, at a service area just outside her hometown in Lincolnshire. She would have her brother with her, and could do later that afternoon.

Lila dealt with Beth first, calling her friend who was furious with her for not phoning sooner. Beth hadn't seen Lila's text message until an hour earlier and Lila knew she felt terrible about it, guilty that she hadn't been there when needed. Lila assured her she was fine, trying to downplay what had happened, admitting Jack had shown up and had stayed with her.

For once there were no smart-arse quips. Beth must have really been feeling bad.

Next Lila texted Ruby, telling her she would speak to Jack and get back to her.

First she needed coffee, and painkillers for the raging pain in her head.

She had made a cup, was taking her first sip, when the door to her flat opened and Jack walked in, a bag in one arm. As he pushed the door shut he glanced up, spotting Lila, and nodded. 'Hey, you're up. I thought you'd still be asleep. You were dead to the world when I left here an hour ago.'

'You were here all night?'

Lila didn't mean to blurt out the words. He had told her last night he intended to stay with her, but she had assumed it was until she fell asleep, that he would need to get home... to Tiff.

'I told you I would stay.'

As she absorbed that information, he headed past her into the hallway, towards the bathroom. 'What's in the bag?'

'A new handle.'

'You went and bought a new handle?'

'You need the window fixed, Lila.'

She followed him down the hallway and into the bathroom, watching as he emptied the contents of the bag onto the toilet seat. Not just a handle. He'd bought the tools necessary for the job. 'I have a screwdriver.'

'I wasn't sure, so I bought one anyway.'

Lila watched as he ripped open the box containing the new handle. He had stayed all night, gone out and bought the tools needed to fix her window, and was now doing the job himself. 'Okay, thank you. You'll have to tell me how much it came to, so I can pay you back,' she told him, suddenly feeling in debt.

Jack glanced over his shoulder, the look he gave her so chastising she actually felt guilty for offering to pay him. 'How about you go put the kettle on while I sort this,' he suggested, keeping his tone neutral. 'I could murder a coffee.'

Lila did as asked, cooking up the rest of the bacon and making butties along with the coffee. It was the least she could do.

She waited until he had fixed the window before telling him about the text from Ruby.

'So she'll meet today?' Jack confirmed through his mouthful.

'I need to text her back and let her know if that's okay.'

'It is. Do you still want to come with me? You were pretty shaken up last night, so I understand if you'd rather not.'

Lila had assumed he wouldn't want her there after what had happened on Friday night, was surprised he did. She wanted to ask where his girlfriend was, knew she was in Norfolk this weekend and couldn't get over how understanding she must be, letting Jack spend so much time with another woman. Did she even know about Lila?

Still she didn't ask, couldn't bring herself to have that uncomfortable conversation, instead trying to rationalise that nothing had happened between her and Jack and that nothing was going to.

'I'll come,' she found herself answering. 'I need something to take my mind off what happened, if I'm honest.' Besides, she had the impression Ruby would be expecting her to be there.

Jack nodded. 'Okay. She's near Sleaford, you said? It'll take a couple of hours to get there. Text Ruby back and tell her we can get there later this afternoon?'

THEY LEFT the flat just after midday. Jack had grabbed a shower at Lila's, but was still tired, his muscles stiff from a night spent sleeping in a chair. He had woken early, watched Lila sleeping for a while before making coffee and heading out, figuring he may as well get a start on clearing up the aftermath of the night before.

She didn't want to be in the flat and he got that, could only guess at how intrusive it felt to have someone break into your home, into your bedroom, while you slept. The least he could do for her was fix the window. He had also paid a visit to her landlady, explained what had happened, and talked her into installing an alarm system. He hadn't told Lila that bit yet, didn't want her thinking he was taking over – which he guessed technically he was – or making decisions without her – which again, he supposed he had. She might not like that he had done it, but it was for her own good. She would be safer, and he wouldn't have to worry about her being in the flat alone.

They had only gone a couple of miles when Jack's phone rang. He answered it on hands-free, wished he hadn't when Alyssa's voice filled the car.

'What has four legs, begins with D, and got left behind at my house when you rushed off to save your new girlfriend last night?' she began, dispensing with any pleasantries.

D. Dog. Fuck! Jack had forgotten all about Cooper.

'She's not my girlfriend, she's fine by the way, and actually in the car with me. Oh, and you're on loud speaker.'

There was a moment of silence. 'You need to come and get your dog, Jack.'

'Okay, here's the thing. I'm heading up to Lincolnshire, so I need you to look after him for a bit longer.'

'Come and get your bloody dog now.'

'You're being unreasonable, Alyssa, it's just a few more hours. You like Cooper. Stop overreacting.'

'I'm not overreacting. Your fucking dog has chewed up Giles's golf shoes. You need to come and get him now!'

Jack struggled to suppress his laugh. 'I can't. We're already on the way.'

'So make a detour.'

'Damn it, Lys!'

'One hour, Jack! If you're not here in one hour, I'm driving him over to yours and leaving him on the porch.'

She hung up before Jack could respond to her threat. He didn't believe for one second she would ditch Cooper, but even so, she'd sounded mad, and he couldn't take the risk.

'You have a dog?' Lila asked.

'Yes… shit, I'm sorry. I need to swing by and get him.'

'It's fine. Where is he?'

'He's at my sister's place in Aylsham. I was there last night when I got your message.'

'I take it your dog doesn't like this Giles person.'

Jack glanced at Lila. She seemed amused by the conversation she had heard. 'It's a long story.'

She shrugged. 'We have plenty of time.'

BY THE TIME he pulled into Alyssa's driveway, Lila knew all about the disastrous dinner party, that Jack thought his sister's boyfriend was a pompous arse, and how Giles had stormed off in a drunken rage halfway through dinner. Jack didn't share that Giles had paid someone to look into her. He was still livid about that himself. Lila didn't need to know.

'It may be best if you wait here,' he suggested, as the door opened and Alyssa appeared on the front step, arms folded, and a scowl on her face.

Lila was happy to oblige, her expression suggesting she was in no hurry to meet Jack's angry sister.

Cooper charged out from behind Alyssa's legs as Jack got out of the car, tail wagging like crazy as he woofed in joy.

'Is Giles back?' Jack asked as Alyssa dumped Cooper's biscuits and lead in Jack's arms.

'Yes, and in a foul mood, thanks to you and your dog.' She peered over Jack's shoulder, trying to get a glimpse of Lila.

'Hey, don't blame Cooper. Dogs are supposed to be a good judge of character. If Cooper doesn't like Giles's shoes then maybe you should be questioning why.'

Alyssa turned her attention to her brother, her frown deepening as she stepped back inside in the cottage and slammed the door in his face.

He glanced at the dog. 'So, that went well.'

Cooper grinned up at him, barked again.

Alyssa had always been so feisty, never taking any crap from anyone. It annoyed the hell out of Jack that she had a weak spot when it came to Giles Buchanan and couldn't see him for the tosser he was.

'You wanna go for a car ride?'

Another woof.

Back in the car and Cooper was delighted to meet Lila, leaning through the gap between the front seats and covering her in wet sloppy kisses. She didn't seem to mind, rubbing his ears and making a fuss of him.

Jack left them to get acquainted as he reset the satnav, pulled out of the driveway.

He'd had reservations about bringing Lila with him after the awkward moment in her flat on Friday night, had decided that if Ruby agreed to meet him, he should go alone, but Lila had been so shaken by the break-in, he had been reluctant to leave her, wondering if the distraction might do her good.

And it had been the right decision. Not only did she seem to be a calming influence on Cooper, she was also in better spirits by the time they crossed the county line, with colour back in her cheeks, some of the light back in her eyes, and she kept Jack distracted, so he couldn't keep mulling over the meeting with Ruby.

As the dog snored on the back seat, they had fought over the radio station and kept the conversation light: trading family stories, arguing over whether fried eggs and anchovies belonged on pizza, discussed favourite bands, learning they had similar taste and had seen several of the same acts live, found out they shared a mutual dislike for reality TV, but loved Hitchcock movies, that they both found the occult fascinating, though were on the fence when it came to believing in ghosts.

Lila learnt that Jack had a scar next to his naval after getting glassed while trying to break up a pub fight when he was in his early twenties, that despite travelling across five continents on book tours, he had a fear of flying, and that he had been sent some strange gifts from some of his female fans, including an engraved "I love U" butcher's knife and a framed photo of one reader posing in stockings and suspenders, a copy of one of his books covering her modesty.

Meanwhile Jack discovered Lila had once got a peanut stuck up her left nostril following a dare from Beth that she couldn't snort it and make it come out of her mouth, (she couldn't, resulting in a visit to A&E), that she was freaked out by clowns, that her singing was painful (proven when she attempted to sing along to a Scissor Sisters track on the radio, which had Jack threatening to stop the car), and – despite working in Cromer – she had never eaten crab.

He made a promise to himself that at some point he would take her to a little restaurant in Wells that he knew sold some of the best crab salads on the North Norfolk coast.

As they neared Sleaford, conversation skirted around relationships, with both sharing their most embarrassing dating stories: Jack's when he had drank a bellyful of alcohol aged seventeen, vomiting all over his date's shoes, while Lila recounted the time she had gone on a date with a boy she had crushed on for ages, only to fall flat on her face as she showed up to meet him.

Jack was careful to avoid the subject of Tiffany, not wanting to make things awkward. He hadn't mentioned to Lila they had broken up, figured it was safer to keep that barrier between them. He would be a liar if he didn't admit to having feelings for her, but ultimately she was helping him get answers about Stephanie and that had to take precedence. They had become friends, and that was fine, but it was better, safer, for both of them if it stayed that way.

As the satnav announced they were five minutes from their destination, anxiety gnawed at his gut.

At least that creep can't get to u anymore.

Ruby's words suggested someone had been harassing Stephanie. Who?

The girl lived with her family in the village of Navenby, having moved there after she had finished high school according to Lila's friend, Joe, and she attended college in Lincoln, while Stephanie had stayed on at school to do her A levels.

Stephanie and Ruby had obviously still been in touch though, and it bothered Jack that Ruby seemed to know more about his sister's life than he did.

Who was the creep trying to get at Stephanie? Was it someone at sixth form or someone closer to home? At Henry's insistence, she had spent holidays helping out in the Whitman Homes head office. Henry employed a large staff. Was one of them the creep Ruby referred to?

'It's going to be okay,' Lila told him, picking up on his unease.

He glanced at her, saw the warmth and compassion in her dark wide-set eyes, finding her accuracy at reading what was going on in his head at times both comforting and a little unnerving. Lila Amberson really was like no-one else he had ever met.

She was make-up free, the dark circles of her late and traumatic night still evident under her eyes, and her hair was plaited into two messy braids, while the demure neckline and shapeless style of the candy-pink gypsy dress she wore ended mid-thigh, leaving her legs on show all the way down to her plaster cast and one scuffed cowboy boot.

She really didn't care what anyone else thought, marched to her own beat, and everything about her was quirky and mismatched, yet somehow effortlessly sexy.

And yet again he realised she had distracted him from thinking about what Ruby might say.

Because you're thinking about what's under that dress.

He dismissed the goading little voice in his head, concentrated on the road, reminding himself yet again that things with Lila were platonic and should stay that way.

THE CAR PARK to the service area off Holdingham roundabout was busy and as Jack drove slowly up and down the lanes looking for a space, he glanced at the KFC restaurant where Ruby and her brother were supposed to be meeting them. On the back seat, Cooper stirred, sitting up straight and yawning. He let out a woof of excitement, tail thumping furiously as Jack pulled into a space and killed the engine.

'You ready?' Lila asked.

Jack nodded. 'As I'll ever be.'

'I'm right here with you, Jack.'

Knowing that she was, glad he had brought her along, he got out of the car, ready to face whatever Ruby Howard had to say.

The KFC restaurant had outside seating, which meant they didn't have an issue about what to do with Cooper. Lila sat down at one of the tables, keeping a firm grip on the dog lead, while Jack went inside. Cooper initially whined a little as he tried to go after him, before giving up and settling down under the table. Despite the fact it was a bright warm day, there was no-one else sitting outside and only a handful of people were in the restaurant from what she could see. Her view was partially blocked by a missing poster in the window of the restaurant. It looked several weeks old and Lila knew that Phoebe Kendall and Shona McNamara still hadn't been found, that the missing person's enquiry had since turned into a murder investigation, centring around one of the girl's uncles.

Lila had studied Ruby's picture before they had left and was fairly certain she wasn't there yet; that Lila would have recognised her if she was.

She was glad she had come, was grateful for the distraction. If Jack had gone without her, she would have stayed home in the flat, kept replaying that horrible moment where her eyes had fluttered open and she had seen the hooded figure standing over her bed. It was still in her head, she saw the image every time she allowed her mind to wander, but the banter in the car with Jack, learning more about him and his life, had mostly kept her occupied, made her feel normal again.

Still, there was a dread that later that night she would have to go back to the flat, would have to try to sleep in her bedroom again. Jack had fixed the window, but it hadn't been broken before the intruder got in. And that made her feel vulnerable, knowing that he could return. She kept that dread quashed down, figured she would deal with it when she returned home.

For now it was about Jack and finding out what Ruby might know about Stephanie, and Lila sensed he needed her as much as she had needed him the previous night.

He returned with two coffees, set them down on the table then briefly disappeared again, coming back with a bowl of water for Cooper.

'They're not here yet.'

As he sat, Lila noticed lines of strain on his face. She glanced at her watch. They had already been ten minutes late when they arrived, but Ruby knew how important this was. She didn't believe they would have left already. 'We're meeting a teenage girl,' she downplayed. 'They don't run on time. I know I didn't.'

Jack gave a half-smile, though didn't look convinced.

Cooper, who had looked disinterested when Jack set down the water bowl, decided to slurp from it. Jack glanced down at him, ruffling the fur behind his ears, and Lila could feel the anxiety rolling off him.

'It's okay, Jack.' She reached across, caught his free hand.

He didn't react, other than to look at her with those clear blue eyes, his expression unreadable.

Remembering he had a girlfriend, Lila let go.

Last night he did more than hold your hand.

The previous night had been different she reminded herself,

but still it niggled her how apparently understanding Tiff was to let her boyfriend spend so much time with another woman.

Maybe she doesn't know.

Lila shrugged the thought away.

'I think this is them.'

Jack was glancing over her shoulder and Lila turned, spotting a young couple heading towards the restaurant. Jack was already on his feet.

The girl looked nervous, hands stuffed in her jacket pockets, while the boy with her appeared more confident, though still seemed wary.

'Ruby Howard?'

Lila recognised her from her picture: slim, petite with long straight brown hair.

'Jack Foley?' That was from Ruby's brother. He glanced briefly at Lila. 'You're Joe's friend.'

It wasn't a question.

As far as meetings went, this one was awkward. Ruby and her brother, who introduced himself as Matthew, took a seat at the bench, both declining Jack's offer of a drink. Ruby made a fuss of Cooper, who lapped up the attention, and she seemed uncomfortable with meeting Jack's eyes.

'You knew my sister, Steph?'

'We went to school together.' Still no eye contact, as Ruby continued to focus on the dog. 'I haven't seen her since last year.'

'I was sorry to hear about what happened,' Matthew offered.

Jack ignored him, focussing on Ruby. 'You stayed in touch with her?'

'Just through Facebook and text.'

'But you were in touch enough to know someone was bothering her.'

This time Ruby looked up, hesitantly met his eyes.

'I saw what you wrote on Facebook. *At least that creep can't get to you anymore.*'

When she didn't answer, instead exchanged a look with her brother, Jack pressed on. 'I need to know what you meant, who you meant.'

Ruby must have given this some thought before coming there, must have known what Jack was going to ask, but still she seemed reluctant to answer.

'Who was the creep, Ruby? Who was harassing my sister?' Jack's tone was heated, his frustration clear, and Lila could see Ruby shrinking away.

'Easy, Jack, give her a moment,' Lila urged, finding a smile for the girl when she looked her way. 'I know it can't be easy for you coming here today. Stephanie was your friend.'

'She was.'

'How long had you known each other? Since you were both little, I bet.'

Jack opened his mouth to cut in; shut it again when Lila shot him a warning look.

'We were in primary school together. She was my oldest friend.' Ruby twisted a chunky silver ring on her middle finger. 'I missed her so much after we moved away. We kept in touch through messenger and text, but it wasn't the same.'

'She confided in you.'

'We confided in each other.'

'Did you know someone was upsetting her before you moved away?'

'No.' Ruby twisted the ring harder. 'Something happened at Christmas. She wouldn't tell me what, but she was in a bad way. She texted me on Boxing Day, said she needed to talk, that something had happened and she didn't know what to do, who to tell. I was away with my family and didn't have a good enough signal. I didn't get her text until a couple of days later and when I tried to call her, she didn't answer. I texted her loads, I was so worried about her, but it was over a week before she got back to me, and by then she was brushing it off, pretending it had been nothing and she had overreacted.'

'Did she ever tell you what had happened?' Lila asked gently.

'No. But I knew something was wrong. She seemed different after that and it was like she didn't want to know me.'

Lila was making headway, but she was aware of Jack looking agitated, knew he had been waiting for answers. He was going to have to be patient for a little longer.

'Did she confide in you again?' she pressed.

'A few weeks before she...' Ruby glanced guiltily at Jack. 'Before she... you know. Before it happened.'

'What did she tell you, Ruby?' Lila silently urged the girl to focus.

'She was struggling at school and she was panicking because she wasn't ready for her exams. Steph had always been smart and she worked hard, but whatever had happened at Christmas had thrown her and I think it was eating away at her. She told me she had been drinking, stealing from her dad's drinks cabinet. She admitted she was out of control. Told me she was worried she was going to fail her exams.'

'What happened next?'

'She said there was someone who could help her pass. She'd heard about him from one of the other students. He was very selective with who he helped and he charged a lot of money, but he had a copy of the test answers and could guarantee she would pass her A levels.'

'The money she wanted to borrow.'

Lila glanced at Jack; saw the distraught look on his face.

'She told me it was for an after-exam holiday with her friends,' Jack explained. 'Henry was being a tight ass and wouldn't lend it to her, so she came to me.'

'Did you give it to her?'

Jack shook his head. 'I was going to. She never got back to me.'

'She didn't need the money.' Ruby was looking at them both, midnight blue eyes wide in her pale face. 'This man who had the test answers, he agreed to help her, but he didn't want her money.'

'What did he want?' Lila barely dared ask the question, suspecting she wasn't going to like the answer.

Ruby shot another brief look at Jack before studying her hands intently, twisting her ring again. 'She told me he wanted sex.'

'What?' Jack's tone was thunderously low.

'She said no of course. Steph wasn't like that. But this man, he told her if she didn't go along with it, he would expose her, that he would leak their conversations to her dad and the head-mistress at her school, that everyone would know she had tried to cheat.' Ruby let out a shaky sigh. 'That's why she got in touch with me. She was in a panic and didn't know what to do.'

'Who was it?'

Ruby looked at Jack, her eyes widening even further. 'I... I don't know.'

'She never gave you a name? She didn't tell you anything about him or who he was?'

'No.'

'Fuck!' Jack got up without warning, skulked away from the table and into the car park. Cooper was on his feet staring after him and tried to pull on his lead, whining when he realised he couldn't follow.

Lila couldn't begin to imagine what it was all doing to Jack. She wasn't sure what she had expected Ruby to say, but it certainly wasn't this.

Matthew was watching him warily, while Ruby continued to twist her ring, looking as if she would rather be anywhere but there.

'What happened next?' Lila tried her best to keep her tone

soft, patient, knowing she had to get the rest of the details out of the girl before she bolted. 'Can you tell me?'

Ruby watched Jack pacing for a moment then refocussed on Lila. 'We only spoke one more time after that. It was the night before she died. I had told her to go to her dad, admit the truth, but she said the situation was in hand, that she knew what she was doing.'

'Do you know what she meant by that?'

'I don't. I suspect, but she never actually confirmed it.' Ruby lowered her voice to a whisper. 'I think she was planning on going through with it.'

20

Jack barely spoke on the drive home. Lila attempted to talk to him a couple of times before giving up, knowing that he was trying to process what he had learnt. She remembered he had told her that Stephanie had contacted him before she died, that she had wanted to come and stay, but he had been out of town, and Lila knew Jack well enough to know that it would be eating him up, wondering if it would have made a difference if he had been home, that it would be killing him that he hadn't been able to protect his baby sister.

Lila didn't tell him the last thing that Ruby had said; that she suspected Stephanie had planned to have sex with her black-mailer, fearing it would push Jack over the edge.

If they had an identity for this man it would be different and Lila would happily accompany Jack and cheer him on while he beat the shit out of the lowlife piece of scum. Without a target for his fists though, the rage would be building up inside of him. She couldn't add to that, especially when Ruby was speculating and didn't know for sure.

.   .   .

THEY HAD NOT LONG CROSSED the Norfolk border when Jack pulled off the road into a pub car park.

'It's getting late,' he told Lila when she looked at him. 'We haven't eaten.'

He was right, they hadn't, and her belly was grumbling. 'Cooper?'

Jack switched off the ignition. 'It's dog friendly.'

She tried to keep pace as she stumbled after him across the car park, dog in tow. The evening was still light, the sky a pretty colour of oranges and yellows as the sun started to set, and it was still warm out. Through a slatted fence, she could see the beer garden was full. She followed Jack into the pub as he grabbed a couple of menus, headed for a corner table, and they perused in silence for a couple of minutes, while Cooper settled himself down on the floor, before a waitress came over, took their orders. Although hungry, Lila wasn't sure how much food she could stomach. She opted for a chicken, bacon and avocado salad, while Jack went for a burger, and ordered a bowl of sausages from the "doggy section" for Cooper.

'Are we going to talk about what Ruby said?' she asked quietly, as the waitress left.

'I'm not sure what you want me to say?' Jack huffed out a sigh that sounded both exasperated and defeated.

'It's a lot to take in, I get that, I really do. We have to find him though.'

'And how do you propose we do that?' He arched a brow. 'Ruby couldn't even give us his name.'

'We'll figure it out.'

'Ever the optimist.' His words were laced with sarcasm.

Lila chose to ignore the comment, knew he was lashing out.

They ate mostly in silence, the limited conversation between them banal, neither of them mentioning Ruby again.

. . .

As they returned to the car, the sick feeling resumed as Lila realised she would soon have to conquer her demons and go back to her flat alone.

Jack wouldn't stay with her that night. She had felt him withdrawing ever since Ruby's revelation, knew it was understandable, but hating that it hurt all the same.

It was getting dark as he pulled onto the road and Lila let her tired eyes drop shut, aware this could be the last chance of sleep she had that night.

When she reopened them they were on a narrow country lane and she had no idea where she was.

She blinked and refocussed, spotting a sign ahead for Burnham Market, realised they were heading in the wrong direction.

'Where are you going? You've missed the turn off for Norwich.'

Jack was quiet for a moment. 'We're not going back to Norwich.'

Lila was now wide awake. 'What do you mean we're not going back?'

Silence.

'Jack?'

He looked at her then, face immersed in shadows. 'We're going to my place. I'm tired and I really can't be arsed with all the driving. You can stay with me tonight.'

'You're telling me this now?'

'I am. You have a problem with that?'

Yes she had a problem with it. He couldn't spring it on her without any warning. She had no overnight bag and couldn't remember if she'd left Clyde locked in her flat. She was sure he had been snoozing in her bedroom when they left.

'Yes. For starters I have nothing with me.'

'You can cope for tonight. I managed last night.'

The gibe hit its target, reminding her that he had dropped everything to stay with her.

'And I think Clyde, my landlady's cat, might be locked in my flat.'

'So why don't you text Primrose? She'll have a key to your place. She can nip downstairs and get him.'

'Primrose?' Lila's jaw gaped. She had never mentioned the name to him. 'How do you know my landlady, Jack?'

There was another moment of silence. 'We talked this morning.'

'About?'

'I told her about your break-in. Recommended getting some security for the house.'

'You did what?'

Jack shot her a cool look. 'She actually agreed with me. The second I told her what had happened, she wanted to step up the security, install an alarm system. I might have recommended someone.'

Lila wanted to be angry with him for going to Primrose behind her back, though a nagging voice reminded her he had done it with the best of intentions. And it seemed he had an answer for all of her excuses, which when peeled away, left the real reason why she was in a panic about going to his house.

She was going to have to meet Tiff. The thought filled Lila with nearly as much fear as going home to her flat and trying to spend the night there alone.

'You had no right to go to Primrose behind my back,' Lila grumbled, aware how ungrateful she must sound after everything Jack had done for her, but wishing to hell he wasn't putting her in this uncomfortable position.

When he ignored her and continued driving, his jaw stubbornly set, making her realise that he wasn't going to change his mind, she knew she was going to have to come clean about why she really didn't want to go back with him.

She tried to find a diplomatic way to broach the subject, decided there wasn't one.

'How's your girlfriend going to feel about this? Is she really going to welcome having me in the house?'

Lila waited for a reaction, her face on fire. Tiffany had been a strictly taboo subject since Friday night. Jack didn't answer her, but she noticed a muscle clench in his cheek.

'I'm not comfortable with this, Jack,' Lila pressed. 'I don't want to meet her.'

There, she had been brutally honest with him, bared her soul and lost a little bit of her dignity in the process. Hopefully though he would understand why she had such an issue about going home with him.

Jack eased to a halt as they approached a T-junction, remained stationary even though there was no traffic on the road, and turned to face her.

'You won't have to meet her. We broke up. She went back to London.'

Of all the things he could have said, Lila wasn't expecting that, and her brain scrambled to process his words. Tiffany was gone, she wouldn't have to meet her, but why hadn't he mentioned anything about that before? They'd spent pretty much the last twenty-four hours together.

'You broke up?' she repeated numbly, still a little shocked.

'That's what I said. So can you shut up now and stop making such a big deal about staying at my place? It's one night and you won't run into Tiffany. I'm not looking for a rebound fuck, Lila. I have three spare bedrooms and you can take your pick. I'm tired and I want to go home. Okay?'

He stared at her, the scowl on his face warning that the matter wasn't up for further discussion, and Lila wasn't quite sure how she was supposed to respond to that.

'Okay,' she agreed quietly, the sting of his words still reverberating in her ears. She had never seen him this closed off or angry before and knew anything she said wouldn't get through to him. She wasn't sure she even wanted to try. After she had been honest with him, admitting she had a problem with meeting Tiffany, the reason why being fairly obvious even though she hadn't spelt it out, he had bluntly told her in no uncertain times that sex wasn't on the cards, acting as if she had offered to throw herself on the floor and be his pity fuck.

He was lashing out, she got that, and she understood why, but he had just humiliated her in the process, and if he hadn't been so good to her in the past twenty-four hours, if she didn't know the way he was behaving was out of character, she would be getting out of his car and finding her own way home, even if she had to hobble all the way on her crutches.

As they rode the remainder of the journey in silence, it occurred to her that she didn't even know where he lived. She had guessed it was somewhere in North Norfolk, assumed it was close to Cley next the Sea, so she was surprised when they entered the village of Burnham Overy Staithe and he pulled off the main coast road.

Lila knew the place well, had photographed the sun rising and setting over the creek on many occasions, was fairly certain she had photos of the very house Jack pulled into the driveway of.

'You live here?' She breathed out the words as she got out of the car, temporarily forgetting that she was mad at him; in awe of the large house with its wide windows and balconies that she knew would offer amazing views of the quayside. She had known Jack came from an affluent family, that he had a successful writing career, but she hadn't figured it was on this kind of level. To her, he was just someone she had met under unusual circumstances and had developed a friendship with, had slowly fallen for. He never acted like he thought he was better than her, never showed any airs or graces. It was easy to treat him as an equal when they were in her flat or roaming around the woods at Filby, but here was different. Here knocked it firmly home that he lived in a completely different world to her, one she would never fit into. Tiffany Pendleton-Shay fitted in here, Lila Amberson didn't.

Jack didn't answer her, had already strode towards the front door, Cooper charging after him. The dog glanced back at Lila and woofed, as if to say, 'So are you coming?', and grabbing her crutches, she reluctantly followed.

INSIDE WAS A LITTLE LESS DAUNTING, the wide-open spaces and high ceilings were light, bright and welcoming, the furniture comfortable and homely, not showy as she had expected. There were plenty of plants about and art on the walls, some of it looked expensive and gallery bought, but other pieces were generic store photos and paintings. The walls were neutral, their tones subtle, but warm, and colour was added through the long curtains hanging at the patio doors, the rugs on the wooden floors and the various cushions scattered across the two huge sofas. Either Jack had a great eye for interior design or he'd had some help (sisters or girlfriend, Lila guessed) in furnishing the place.

She had a ton of questions but knew he wasn't in the mood to answer them, so instead she followed him through into an impressive sleek white kitchen, aware of the noise her crutches were making on the uncarpeted floors, unsure what to do with herself and feeling a lot like an unwanted guest. She stood by the counter, watched as Jack fished inside an enormous fridge, pulling out a beer. He glanced up at Lila, seeming for a moment as if he'd forgotten she was there. 'Help yourself to whatever you want. There's water, juice, lager and white wine in the fridge. If you prefer red, there's some over there.' He indicated towards a chrome wine rack on the opposite counter. 'Glasses are in the cupboard above. Tea, coffee, it's all there. Whatever you want.'

Lila nodded, though didn't move.

He opened his beer, gulped down half of it, setting the bottle on the counter. 'I need to take Cooper out. He's been stuck in the back of the car all day. Make yourself at home. Go pick a room, doesn't matter which one. They're all en suite. I have someone come in every Saturday, so towels and sheets are all clean. I'll drive you home in the morning.'

That was it. He had played the genial host, she was dismissed. She remained by the counter, watched him leash Cooper and unlock the kitchen patio door. The dog glanced back as if to ask why she wasn't coming, Jack didn't, and then they were both gone.

Feeling on edge, Lila found a wine glass in the cupboard and glanced over the wine rack. No screw tops. All of the bottles looked expensive and she didn't like to touch them. She pulled open the door to the well-stocked fridge. A bottle of white wine sat in the door, already open. She poured a generous glass of that instead, replaced the cork, shut the fridge door then leant against the counter as she drank it in large sips, partly to calm her nerves, but also because she was frightened of trying to carry it with her through to the lounge in case she spilt it on the undoubtedly expensive rug.

Jack had told her to make herself at home, but still she felt she was trespassing as she slowly made her way around the big lounge, balancing on her crutches as she glanced over his bookshelves, studied the collage frame filled with pictures of Jack and his extended family. In one of the pictures, she spied Tiffany. They had only just broken up so it was inevitable her presence would still be in the house. Lila recognised one picture, it was the same one she had seen on Facebook of Jack and Stephanie fooling around on the beach.

Aware she was snooping, she stepped away, decided to head upstairs. Jack had made it obvious he didn't really want her around and that he would prefer to be alone with his own thoughts. She would pick a bedroom before he got back with Cooper and try to get herself settled, stay out of his way.

As luck would have it, the first door she opened led into his bedroom, a space that was not far off the size of her entire flat, dominated by a large sturdy-looking oak bed, the walls and bedding in a soft grey. One bedside table was bare, except for a slim slate-coloured lamp, while the other held a matching lamp, a well-worn paperback and an empty water glass. On the opposite wall to the bed, in front of a floor-to-ceiling window, sat a slim desk with a laptop on it, the lid up, though the screen blank, a pot of pens and a couple of hardback notepads. Jack's black bomber jacket hung over the back of the desk chair.

Feeling guilty for intruding in his private space, Lila closed the door, checked out the other three bedrooms, picking one at the far end of the landing, furthest away from Jack's room, a more feminine space decorated in shades of lemon and cream, with balcony doors that looked out over the marshes. As it was a warm evening, she pushed open the doors, enjoying the salt air breeze that gently billowed the long cream curtains as she set down her crutches and flopped back on the bed.

She thought back over the meeting with Ruby and the revelation that someone had tried to blackmail Stephanie. They needed to find out whom, but how were they going to do that? Stephanie hadn't even confided a name in Ruby. And then there was the incident Ruby had mentioned that happened at Christmas. Just what had been going on in Stephanie's life in the lead up to her death?

Lila needed to sleep, hoped it would clear her head, help her to think straight, but first she needed water. Her mouth was so dry. Reaching for her crutches, she made her way downstairs again. Jack was obviously back from his walk with Cooper as the dog padded over as soon as she entered the kitchen. Jack though wasn't around, so must be staying out of her way. She reached in the cupboard for a tumbler, filled it with water and downed the glass before rinsing it under the tap. Cooper tried to follow as she headed back towards the stairs, whimpering in protest when she told him no. Although he slunk back into the kitchen, Lila suspected he was planning on sneaking upstairs when he thought the coast was clear.

As she passed Jack's bedroom, she noticed the door was open. The light was off, but she could see him standing in front of the picture window, looking deep in thought.

Something must have alerted him to her presence because he glanced back over his shoulder, stared at her for a moment, his expression unreadable.

'You find everything you need?'

'Yes… thank you.'

He nodded, turned back to his view, dismissing her.

'Goodnight, Jack.'

He didn't answer.

RICHARD WAS AWAY on another weekend conference; at least that was what he told her.

Judith had long suspected the conferences and meetings he attended were cover stories and didn't really exist, but she chose to go along with the lies, terrified it would fracture her family if she tried to find out the truth, so when she came across receipts for motel rooms in different areas to where his "conferences" were held, knew, in truth, that he seldom left the county, she turned a blind eye. Whatever he was up to, she had convinced herself it was better if she didn't know.

That was her job, to be the glue that kept them together.

Certainly they had their ups and downs, like any other family, and yes, maybe Richard didn't treat her as well as he should do at times, but she took her marriage vows seriously, and would stick by him for better or for worse. Sometimes, when it all became too much, she would lock herself in the bathroom and cry, let all of the emotion and frustration out, but then she would dry her eyes and pull herself together.

Her husband appreciated an orderly home and she went out of her way to give him just that, keeping the floors sparkling clean, every surface free of dust. She always made sure the kitchen cupboards and fridge freezer were fully stocked, that there was a hot meal on the table every night.

If there were any problems, she took care of them, so as not to burden him. Like when the boiler had packed up as they had entered that cold spell back in February. Richard had been travelling home from one of his alleged conferences and would be expecting a warm house. By pure miracle, she had managed to get a plumber out at the last moment. Her husband hadn't been troubled and he had never known any different. She dreaded to think what might have happened if she hadn't managed to solve the problem before he returned.

Aaron knew how hard she worked to keep his father happy and she knew it frustrated him listening to Richard's lies. He didn't seem to understand that Judith didn't mind, as long as she kept her family together, and she so wished Aaron wouldn't keep testing Richard's patience.

He didn't seem to understand that if he kept goading his father, things could turn very bad for them both, very bad indeed.

Jack awoke from a pleasant dream involving Lila, her demure pink gypsy dress, and her cowboy boots (in his dream she hadn't worn the cast), and enjoyed approximately twelve seconds of post-fantasy bliss before reality kicked him in the balls, souring his mood, reminding him of the meeting with Ruby Howard, how he had learnt that some nameless man had harassed his sister in the lead up to her death and tried to black-mail her into having sex.

Almost as a guilty afterthought Jack remembered that Lila was staying in one of the spare bedrooms and that he had taken all of his frustration out on her the previous night, acting like a complete dickhead. He cringed as he recalled the look on her face, her utter mortification when he had harshly told her he wasn't looking for a rebound fuck, knew he deserved a slap for that, and how he had then dragged her here instead of taking her home, leaving her alone in the big house and making her feel unwelcome instead of putting her at ease.

If his mother knew how he had treated her she would be appalled, but no more than he was with himself.

He searched for some kind of brownie point, reminding

himself that the true reason he had brought Lila home with him was because he didn't like the idea of leaving her alone in her flat. Of course he hadn't told her that. No, the previous night he had been trying to push her buttons and it had been far easier to let her believe his motives had been entirely selfish.

Throwing back the duvet, he climbed out of bed, too annoyed to try to get back to sleep, heard a yowl as he stepped on fur and a startled Cooper shot to his feet.

'When the hell did you sneak up here?'

Cooper sat obediently still and grinned, his tail thumping back and forth at a dizzying pace. The dog was a law onto himself.

'Stay here,' Jack ordered, shaking his head and disappearing into the bathroom.

AFTER SHOWERING, Jack shrugged on jeans and an old T-shirt, rubbing at his tired eyes. He had slept eventually, but it hadn't come easy and, until the pleasant Lila dream, he had tossed and turned, the previous day's events never far from his mind.

Yet to decide what he was going to do with the information he had learnt, one thing was for certain, he had no intention of telling his mother the truth. It would destroy her.

He padded downstairs, the dog behind him, and filled the coffee machine, left it to filter while he slipped his bare feet into trainers, and grabbed Cooper's lead.

IT WAS BEFORE seven on a Monday morning and the quayside was quiet with only one other dog walker further along the creek who raised a friendly hand in greeting. Jack waved back, enjoying the peace and solitude. He watched Cooper frolic in the water, finding the time alone outside therapeutic.

Eventually he whistled the dog, headed back to the house,

spending a couple of minutes rubbing him down with an old towel.

While Cooper chomped on a bowlful of biscuits, Jack poured himself a coffee, turned on the TV in the kitchen for background noise to take the edge off the silence, grabbed one of the many notepads and pens he kept in various locations around the house and sat down at the kitchen table.

He began by jotting down what Ruby had told them. Starting with the incident at Christmas. He had seen Stephanie on Christmas Day, but Ruby said Steph had texted her on Boxing Day. He needed to find out where his sister had been, what might have caused her to become upset. And the exam fixer; was he a teacher at Steph's school?

Jack was sipping at his coffee, deep in thought, when he heard Lila's crutches on the stairs. 'There's coffee in the machine,' he told her, focussed on the words on his pad.

He would wait for her to get a drink and join him before figuring out how the hell he was going to apologise for the previous night.

When she didn't answer him, he glanced up, immediately zoning in on the pretty silk kimono robe she wore, the cream-coloured material covered in colourful butterflies. He had seen that robe so many times before, remembered picking it out himself.

'What are you wearing?' He snapped out the words more harshly than intended.

Lila reached the bottom step, frowned as she glanced down. 'This? It was hanging on the back of the bedroom door.'

Blood thumped to Jack's head, so many memories rushing back. His sister had loved butterflies, had adored her birthday present, and she had practically lived in the robe whenever she stayed over.

'Jack?'

'It was Stephanie's. You're wearing her robe.' He said the words tightly, with more control than he felt. 'Take it off.'

'I didn't know it was Stephanie's,' Lila pointed out quietly. 'I haven't got anything with me and you told me to make myself comfortable.' When he continued to scowl at her, she shook her head wearily. 'It's fine. I'll go take it off, but then I want to go home.'

A FRESH START, that's what she had told herself.

Jack had been hurting the previous night, had said some spiteful things. He hadn't meant them for Lila, but she had been there and had been a convenient target. She had lain awake trying to convince herself until sleep had finally pulled her under that the next day would be a fresh start for them both.

How wrong she had been.

The robe was distinctive, she got that, and so pretty too. Which is why she had slipped it on while she headed downstairs for coffee. She only intended to wear it until she had showered and dressed. It had been hanging on the back of the bedroom door and Jack *had* told her to make herself at home.

Furious, she slammed the bedroom door shut, pulled off the robe and threw it on the bed. Screw coffee. She would shower and get dressed then insist he drive her home.

Her sympathy well had dried up and she was done with Jack Foley and his Jekyll-and-Hyde mood swings.

HER RESOLVE LASTED until she got back downstairs; saw him still sitting at the table. He hadn't moved since she had gone up to shower and dress twenty minutes earlier, head down and hands pushed back in his hair, and he looked utterly broken.

As she stopped beside him, he glanced up at her, eyes damp

and full of pain. They were a lighter shade than normal; navy rims around crystal blue irises that were flecked with silver, staring straight into her and sucker punching her right in the gut.

'Don't go.' He caught hold of her arm. 'I'm sorry for last night. I'm sorry for overreacting just now. I didn't know how hard this was going to be... losing someone, finding out things you didn't know about them. I'm trying to work my way through this and sometimes it gets too much and I do the wrong thing. I was mean to you. After everything you've done, how you've been there, I pushed you away and I was mean to you. I'm so, so sorry.'

'Jack... I–'

'I need you, Lila. Please.'

He looked so crushed, his words desperate and sincere, she couldn't help but react, setting one crutch against the table and reaching out to place a comforting hand on his shoulder.

One moment she was standing beside him, the next he had turned his head, had buried his face against her belly. As he gave a shaky jagged sigh, she stroked her hand over his hair, holding him close.

She stood like that for a couple of minutes and at first it really was purely about comfort, but then something shifted and Lila gradually became oh so conscious of where Jack's mouth was, could feel the warmth of his breath against her belly.

Startled by her reaction, she attempted to ease away, was prevented from doing so when his arms unexpectedly locked around her, holding her firmly in place, and, before she could respond, his hands were caressing her back, the touch warm and teasing, dipping lower to the top of her buttocks, his thumbs boldly working their way over the edge of her knickers through the fabric of her dress. She caught her breath as heat spread inside her.

Picking up on her reaction, his grip tightened and without warning his mouth dipped and he nipped gently at the tender flesh just below her naval. Lila let out an involuntary shudder as the remaining crutch clattered to the floor, caught hold of his other shoulder to steady herself as he started sucking, nibbling and tormenting her through the flimsy material of her dress, his mouth hot and wet. Digging her fingertips into his shoulders, she released a trembling sigh.

Jack eased his head back, glanced up at her. Those eyes that had been so pained and so sincere now held a feral glint, his intentions clear, and with a sudden tug she found herself straddling his lap. He didn't give her time to protest, his mouth covering hers and taking greedily.

Every fibre in her body was on fire, the touch of him, the taste of him, the scent of him proving too difficult a combination to resist, so she didn't, told herself not to overthink it, that it might be rebound sex, but she wanted him as much as he seemed to want her. She would beat herself up about it later.

As she returned his kisses, her own hands running over the taut muscles of his back, up into his hair, he moaned in her mouth, the sound guttural, and his hands worked their way down under her bum, pulling her legs around him, lifting her and sitting her up on the table. He broke the kiss, the look he gave her purely carnal as he used his hips to spread her legs, his arms still linked around her, fingertips tracing patterns against her back.

'I had a very dirty dream about you wearing this dress last night,' he told her, his voice low and throaty.

'You did?' The words came out so breathily, Lila barely recognised them as hers. Her skin was on fire with every touch, the need for more aching deep inside her. 'What happened?'

The crooked smile he gave her was wickedly seductive as he gently pushed her back on the table, his hands skimming over her breasts and down the length of her body to her thighs, his touch light and tormenting. 'Let me show you.'

22

S ex hadn't been on his list of morning tasks. Walking the dog, apologising to Lila and brooding some more about Steph's blackmailer had, but not sex. But then Lila had been there offering comfort and she had been warm and soft and smelt so good and, remembering the dream he had awoken from, his dick had reacted.

Talk about screwing up an apology.

The sex had been both memorable and satisfying, and Lila had been a more-than-willing participant, but of course she was going to think this was the rebound thing he had thrown in her face the previous night. He had just fucked her on his kitchen table – not exactly his finest moment – why would she possibly think otherwise?

He hadn't been lying to her that morning when he said that he needed her. He did need her, more than he had realised, had actually reached that conclusion only after he had very nearly messed everything up. He had told himself he had ended things with Tiffany because they had grown apart, that the relationship was already dying. It had been the truth, but what he had conveniently been ignoring was he had also ended things because she wasn't Lila.

Spontaneous sex was great and he planned, hoped, to have plenty more of it with Lila, but it was hardly the way to convince her she meant more to him than that. Given that it had been their first time and he hadn't even told her how he really felt about her, he knew she deserved better than what had happened that morning and added it to the list he was keeping in his head of things he needed to make up to her.

Luckily she had agreed to stick around and wasn't insisting on going straight home. After dissecting the meeting with Ruby, something Jack felt able to do with a cooler head, he left Lila musing over his notepad scribbles while he took a call from his agent about his new book.

WHEN HE RETURNED to the kitchen twenty minutes later, she still had the pen in her hand, but her attention was focussed on the TV and her face drained of colour.

Jack touched her shoulder. 'Lila?'

Startled, she looked at him blankly for a moment.

'What's wrong?'

'I've been watching the news while you were talking.'

'Yes, I can see.'

'You know the two missing girls in Lincolnshire?'

He nodded, couldn't recall their names but was certainly familiar with the story. It had been national news for weeks. 'What about them?'

'They were interviewing Shona McNamara's grandmother.'

'And?'

'Jack, I think it's her picture in the locket.'

187

WITHIN AN HOUR, they were in Jack's car and heading back to Norwich.

Although Jack had seemed dubious of Lila's claim that it was Shona McNamara's grandmother in the picture, he'd given Lila the benefit of the doubt, agreeing to at least let her check.

It occurred to her that he was going out of his way to keep her happy since they'd had sex, but given that she'd been berating herself for giving into him so easily, wished she'd put up a little more resistance (though she couldn't bring herself to regret it had happened), she doubted she had that amount of allure over him. Jesus, she hadn't been with anyone in nearly five years, had been woefully out of practice.

No, it was more likely he was still feeling guilty for how he had treated her after the meeting with Ruby.

Lila tried not to analyse anything too much. Jack had made it clear that anything after Tiff would be a rebound fuck. Lila had known exactly where she stood when she'd had sex with him.

CLYDE WAS on welcoming duty as she unlocked the main door to the house, circling Lila's legs then Jack's, purring his head off. Lila bent to stroke his ears, spent a few seconds making a fuss of him, but as she opened the door to her flat, expecting him to follow them inside, he turned and ran upstairs to Primrose.

Lila left Jack to put the kettle on while she went through to her bedroom, tried not to think about the hooded man who had stood there two nights earlier, as she retrieved the locket from the little trinket dish she kept on her dressing table. She glanced at the picture inside. Although black and white, the image of the woman was clear and she was certain it was the same woman she had seen on the TV screen a couple of hours earlier.

She carried the locket through to the living room, almost colliding with Jack as he carried mugs of tea out of the kitchen, and they shared a brief awkward moment where neither of them seemed sure how to react. Lila stepped back, leaning on her crutches as she let him go ahead, and considered for the first time that sleeping with him might ruin the easy friendship they had built. She followed him into the living room and made a point of sitting on the chair instead of the sofa next to him.

'It's her,' she told him without preamble, handing the locket across. As Jack clicked it open to study the picture, she picked up her mug, took a sip of the tea that was still a little too hot.

He frowned, pulled out his phone.

'You don't believe me.'

'I never said I didn't believe, but you saw the woman on a TV screen. I want to check.'

Frustrated that he seemed to be doubting her, she waited impatiently while he googled for information, studying his intense expression, the way he shoved his hair back off his face, looking annoyed when it fell forward again, remembering how he had tasted, the touch of his hands and his mouth against her skin making every nerve end tingle, how it had felt to have him inside her. She wasn't ready to let go of that.

'Okay, I've found a photo.' He held up the locket, comparing it to his screen, nodded slowly.

'It's her?' Lila breathed. 'I told you.'

He didn't confirm either way, instead closed the locket and slipped it into his pocket, laying his phone down on the coffee table.

'We'll drop it in at the police station.' He met her eyes, his expression sober. 'I want you to come back to Burnham with me, stay for a few days.'

'Jack, I–'

'I won't leave you alone here after what happened. I'd stay here with you, but I have Cooper to consider.'

'But all my stuff is here.'

'You can bring whatever you need over to mine. It's not like I don't have the space.'

'And Primrose, what if she needs me?'

'She's your landlady, Lila, not your mother. She'll be fine. And I'm sure she wants you to be safe.'

She would, Lila knew that, just as she knew how much she was dreading being back in her flat alone. Going into her bedroom to fetch the locket had made her anxious, so she knew she would be a nervous wreck by nightfall.

Still she wavered, wondering in what capacity Jack wanted her as a houseguest. Was he purely looking out for her as a friend or did he want more? She wasn't sure she could spend another restless night in the guest bedroom knowing he was across the landing, especially not after that morning.

'If you refuse to come with me I'll have to put Cooper in kennels and come stay here.'

'You wouldn't.'

Jack nodded solemnly. 'I will if you leave me no choice. He's only ever been in kennels once and he hated it. I promised I would never do that to him again. You'd really make him go back?'

The corner of his mouth twitched, confirming he was winding her up, but it knocked it home that her being in the flat alone was almost as big a deal to him as it was to her.

'Okay, I'll come back with you, but just for a few days.'

He seemed satisfied with that. 'Deal. Now go get your stuff together.'

Lila carefully made her way upstairs to speak to Primrose before they left; although she was only the woman's tenant, they had always had a close relationship and she knew Primrose relied on her sometimes to run the odd errand or help her out with things around the apartment. Lila felt guilty leaving her to fend for herself.

When Primrose opened the door, Clyde purring in her arms, a smile lit up her face. 'Lila, dear, how are you? I've been thinking about you after what happened on Saturday night. Such a terrible shock for you.'

'I'm okay, thanks. Still a little shaken up, but I guess that's to be expected.'

Lila had exchanged a couple of texts with her landlady, but they hadn't actually seen each other since the break-in.

'I'm not surprised. I hope Jack's been looking after you. I know he was so worried.'

'He has been.' Lila didn't miss the familiarity with how Primrose spoke about Jack. Amazing how quickly he could charm his way in when he put his mind to it. 'And thank you for nipping down to rescue Clyde last night. I shouldn't have left him locked in my flat all day. I'm sorry I couldn't get back to let him out myself.'

'It's no trouble, dear. I was wondering where the rascal was.'

'Jack wants me to go and stay with him for a few days. I don't like to leave you in the lurch though. If there's anything you want me to do or need me to fetch for you while I'm gone, you have my number and I can always try to pop back during the day.'

Primrose waved her away. 'Lila, you worry too much. I'm a tough old bird and I'm more mobile than you at the moment. I can cope by myself for a few days. I managed before you moved in and when you were in hospital. Jack's right. I don't think you should be in your flat alone until the new alarm system is installed.'

'Thank you... and about that... he told me he had spoken to you about it. Really, Primrose, you don't have to do that because of what happened. Jack fixed the window. He was overreacting about the alarm and he shouldn't have come and spoken to you.'

Her landlady smiled. 'Really, I'm glad he did. He was right about making the house more secure. It's an old building and Saturday night proved we're not as safe as we like to think we are. Plus he's been so good sorting it all out for me. His friend is stopping by later this week to install the system.'

'I can't let you pay for all of this. It was my flat that was broken into, so at least let me contribute.'

Lila wasn't sure what she could afford, but she had to at least offer.

Primrose frowned slightly, ran an affectionate hand down the snoozing Clyde's back. 'You don't need to pay anything, dear. Didn't Jack tell you he's taking care of it all?'

Lila's mouth dropped open and she was quick to close it when Primrose's eyes narrowed.

'He didn't tell you, did he.'

Lila forced a smile. 'I guess it must have slipped his mind.'

She left her landlady and the cat, head filled with questions. Part of her was annoyed with Jack for footing the alarm bill behind her back. He knew she would have never agreed to it. She was reluctant to say anything though, the soft irrational part of her that seemed to have fallen for him, flattered that he had cared enough about her to want to keep her safe.

The previous night he had told her that anything that happened between them would be a rebound thing, yet he had rushed to be by her side after the break-in, had gone out of his way to make the flat safer.

She brooded as they got in the car, not at all sure where she stood with Jack Foley or what he wanted from her.

They stopped at Norwich Police Station before heading back up to the coast and handed in the locket. The desk clerk didn't give much away, but promised it would be passed on to the relevant department. Lila figured that between the car accident, getting pushed in front of a bus, her flat being broken into, and being in possession of a dead girl's locket, the police probably had a special file on her that recommended 'Avoid'.

'Let them figure it out,' Jack told her as they drove back to Burnham. 'It's their job.'

'I know. I just don't understand how a missing girl's locket could get mixed up with my stuff.'

'There are any number of ways. For starters we're assuming it belongs to Shona McNamara.' When Lila started to protest, he held up a hand. 'Let me finish. Yes, I think it's likely it does belong to her, but we could still be mistaken. If it is hers, it's possible she lost it a long time ago or maybe someone stole it. Hell, maybe she sold it. We don't know, Lila. There are any number of ways it could have gotten mixed up with your stuff.'

'Do you think it's possible Stephanie knew her?'

'Possible, but I think it's unlikely. They lived in different counties. I looked through Steph's Facebook friends while we were in the police station. I couldn't see any connection to Shona McNamara. Definitely can't see why my sister would have had her locket. Maybe Mark knew her.'

'Maybe.'

Lila was thoughtful for a moment, before she looked at Jack.

'All of those possibilities are plausible, I get that, but what if she didn't lose her locket, it wasn't stolen and she didn't sell it? What if it got mixed up with my things because she was in Filby?'

'You know they've arrested her friend's uncle, right? They wouldn't do that unless they had some kind of evidence implicating him.'

'I know. But you're a writer, Jack.' She looked at him, made a point of ensuring she had his attention. 'Surely you still have to ask, what if?'

23

J ack seemed distracted by the time they arrived back at his house. Unsure where he was expecting her to sleep, Lila left her bag in the hallway, figured she would try to work it out later. Instead she settled herself on one of the large sofas with a cup of tea while Jack disappeared upstairs. She called her boss, Natalie, told her she was ready to come back to work. As she suspected, Nat knew about Saturday night, Beth having filled her in on all the details. Lila reassured her she was fine to come back, told her the distraction of work would be more of a benefit than a setback. Eventually Natalie agreed she could return the following day.

Feeling a little more satisfied, Lila turned to her iPad, the locket still bothering her. She read what articles she could find online, learning that Shona and Phoebe had disappeared on a Saturday morning, telling their parents they were going into Lincoln, as they often did at the weekend. It wasn't unusual for them to meet up with friends, end up staying out into the evening. Shona's parents had become worried when she hadn't returned home by ten, wasn't answering her phone. They contacted friends, put up a Facebook post, asking people to share. When she hadn't returned home by Sunday morning, they had contacted the police.

It took a moment for Lila to register the date the girls had disappeared. Saturday the seventh of April. The car crash that had killed Mark and Stephanie had occurred five days later. Lila chewed over that information, her imagination running riot by the time Jack finally reappeared.

'Phoebe Kendall and Shona McNamara disappeared exactly five days before the car accident. Did you know that?'

Jack shrugged, seeming disinterested. 'What about it?'

'Don't you find that odd?'

'Not especially. Where are you going with this, Lila?'

'Shona's locket was with my things. Something spooked Mark when he went into the woods. What if there's a connection?'

'What do you mean a connection?'

'What if Mark was the one with the locket?'

'You think he killed Shona? How did he manage that when he was on a date with you?'

'No.' Lila shook her head impatiently. 'I'm not suggesting he killed her, but what if he saw her that night?'

'In the woods?'

'Yes, Jack, in the woods.'

He perched on the arm of the sofa beside her, as he ingested her theory.

'The locket turned up in Norfolk, right where the crash happened,' Lila pushed. 'Is it really that big a stretch?' As far-fetched as it sounded, she knew her theory held some weight. She recalled Mark's face that night. He looked like he had seen a ghost. 'We need to figure out what happened with Mark, find out what he saw.'

'He's dead, Lila. How are we supposed to do that? We already went back to the woods. The police have the locket. Let them look into it.'

He still seemed distracted and for the first time, Lila noticed he was wearing his jacket, had his keys in his hand.

'You off out somewhere?'

'I'm going over to Queen's House School. Steph's head-mistress has agreed to meet with me.'

Of course, the revelations about Stephanie were still weighing heavily on his mind. It was understandable that they took precedence. Lila set down her iPad, reached for her crutches. 'I'll come with you.'

'There's no need. I'll be back in a couple of hours.'

Was he closing her out again? She changed tack. 'Okay... I'd like to come with you.' She forced a smile. 'We're in this together, remember?'

Jack stared at her for a moment, looking a little annoyed at having his own words thrown back at him. 'Okay,' he relented. 'But come on. We're going to be late.'

HE WAS quiet on the drive over to the school, seemed preoccupied with how the meeting was going to go and whether he would get the answers he so desperately wanted. Lila let him brood, understood him well enough to know that he was stubborn and wouldn't open up until he was ready. She was here with him, would be there for him, if and when he did need her. For now that had to be enough.

The school was just outside Holt. She knew it was private and suspected that the parents paid a hefty fee to send their little darlings there. She still found it daunting when Jack took the turn off between two large stone pillars into a long driveway flanked by tall neatly trimmed conifers. She had attended a purpose-built state school that no way resembled the large old ivy-covered house they were approaching. This building was more like a stately home than a place of education with its wide sash windows and huge black front door, above which hung a brass sign welcoming them to Queen's House Private School. Lila spied a couple of pupils heading around the far side of the house wearing the smart green uniform and felt inadequately dressed.

'Did you go to school here too?' she asked as Jack found a space in the car park to the side of the main house.

'What? No, this is an all-girls' school. But no, I didn't go anywhere private like this.'

She thought for a moment he was going to leave it there, given the monosyllabic answers she had mostly gotten during the journey, so he surprised her by elaborating. 'Henry has deep pockets. My dad was – is – a journalist. Used to do some quite cutting-edge stuff. He has always been a firm believer that you have to earn your way in life. We moved around a bit. Cambridge, London, eventually Norfolk. All state schools though. He wanted Tom and me to have opportunities rather than hand everything to us on a plate. I think my mum would have done the same for Alyssa, Oliver and Steph, but Henry could afford it, so insisted on them having the best.'

Lila suspected there was no love lost between Jack and his stepfather. He seldom mentioned his own father though. 'Does your dad still live in Norfolk?' she asked.

His lips curved at the question. 'Two minutes from here with wife number three, who is exactly six months and thirteen days older than me. He sold out cutting-edge journalism for cosy life-style columns in the local press and pretends to be working on his first fiction book, which we both know he will never finish. You want to stop by for afternoon tea after we're done here? I can't promise he won't hit on you though.'

Lila could tell from the amusement in his eyes that the question was rhetorical, so chose to ignore it. 'He sounds like quite a character.'

'He has his plus points.' Jack switched off the ignition. 'Come on.'

She stored the information away as she climbed out of the car, fascinated at the snippets she was gradually learning about Jack's life. He wasn't a closed book, but likewise he didn't give information away freely. The more she got to know him, the more intriguing she found him, and the more intriguing she found him, the harder she fell.

JACK MAY NOT HAVE GONE to a private school, but he seemed comfortable enough in finding his way around. Lila followed him across to the main entrance, into the wide high-ceilinged reception and along the corridor, struggling to keep up with his brisk pace. The hallways were quiet, pupils in lessons, the only sound coming from the pair's footsteps and Lila's crutches as they hit the hardwood floor. She had a hospital appointment in a couple of weeks and would be glad to finally have her leg out of plaster and be rid of the things.

As they entered a small reception area, a blonde lady glanced up from her computer and smiled warmly. A gold name plaque on the desk identified her as Mrs Rosemary Vale.

'Good afternoon, may I help you?'

'I have an appointment with Mrs Crawford. Jack Foley.'

Rosemary clicked her mouse, glanced at the screen and nodded. 'Yes, please take a seat. Mrs Crawford is with someone at the moment, but she shouldn't be too long. I'll let her know you're here. Can I get either of you a drink? Coffee, tea, water?'

Jack asked for coffee, while Lila opted for water. Her throat was a little dry; nerves she guessed. This place was like a different world to her; the wall behind the reception desk adorned with expensively framed certificates and photographs of pupils graduating. A glass cabinet stood centre of the wall, lit up to display numerous trophies. Lila and Jack sat on the Chesterfield sofa as Rosemary fetched their drinks before going to knock on the headmistress's door, slipping inside to let her know they had arrived.

'Have you ever met this Mrs Crawford before?' Lila asked Jack quietly.

'Nope.'

'So how are you going to approach this?' When Jack shot her a hard look, she elaborated. 'She may not take kindly to being told someone in her school is leaking exam answers.'

'Leave the questions to me, okay?'

Lila liked being right as much as the next person, but on this occasion she would have preferred that she wasn't.

Mrs Crawford (no indication of a first name on her desk plaque) was slight in build, softly spoken and had the mannerisms of a small bird. At first, Lila was shocked that this docile-seeming woman held such a high position of authority. She quickly learnt that first impressions were deceiving and the headmistress was a formidable force, more than ready to stand her ground against Jack.

She had politely welcomed them into her office, giving Lila a brief questioning look, clearly curious as to whom she was. Pleasantries and condolences dispensed with, Jack got straight to the point of why they were there, the accusation that someone at the school was selling test answers and blackmailing pupils hanging in the air as Crawford's smile froze, the look in her eyes when she addressed him, pure steel.

'We are an all-girls school, Mr Foley.'

'I'm aware of that.'

'So you're insinuating that a member of my teaching staff has been engaging in criminal activities and sexual encounters with the pupils?'

'Not insinuating. Telling you this happened to my sister.'

'What happened to your sister was a tragedy, nothing more, nothing less. Creating vicious rumours isn't going to bring her back.'

'I'm not–'

Mrs Crawford held up a hand, cutting him off. 'Stephanie was a spirited girl, smart when she applied herself, but often too caught up in the drama of life. She also had a fanciful imagination and given that she was struggling in classes in the last few months, it doesn't surprise me that she was looking for an excuse.'

'My sister did not make this up.'

Lila glanced at Jack, aware how tightly coiled he was, knew he was barely hanging on to his temper. 'Mrs Crawford,' she tried to reason, keeping her tone neutral, friendly. 'Stephanie confided in a friend. She was scared and worried. I don't see what she would have to gain by making this up.'

The headmistress pulled off her glasses, gave Lila a cool glance, as she set them back in her perfectly coiffed chestnut bob. 'With all due respect, this has nothing to do with you, Miss Anderson.'

'Amberson.'

Lila's correction was lost, as Crawford had already dismissed her, returning her attention to Jack.

'It's amazing how the mind can react when you are backed into a corner. It wouldn't be the first time Stephanie had created a story to get herself out of trouble.' Crawford gave a thin smile. 'I guess fiction must run in the family.'

That was it; Jack was on his feet, rage flushing his cheeks. 'Just so I'm clear, I've come here today to warn you that a member of your staff may be behaving inappropriately with your pupils and engaging in criminal activity, and you're choosing to ignore me? Instead you're telling me my sister was a troublemaker and a liar, and you have no intention of doing jack shit about any of this?'

Crawford also stood, a full foot shorter than Jack, but her fists clenched on her desk, her chin set at a determined angle as she scowled up at him.

'We are an elite group of schools, Mr Foley, and we only accept the best. All of our members of staff are thoroughly vetted before we employ them and only the head teachers have access to exam papers. Now I am truly sorry about Stephanie, but reputation is key and I do not appreciate you coming into my school and questioning the ethics of my teachers.'

With that they were dismissed.

Lila caught the almost-sympathetic look that the receptionist gave her as she tried to keep up with Jack who had stormed off ahead, guessed she must have heard the raised voices. She didn't envy Rosemary having to work for Mrs Crawford. The woman was a dragon.

Jack had threatened that he would go to the police, but it was a bluff. They all knew that there was not enough proof for the police to investigate anything.

JACK WAS OUTSIDE, appeared to be waiting for her, as Lila pushed open the heavy entrance door. As she approached him, feeling his frustration and wishing she could magic up the answers he needed, a tall blonde girl strode confidently towards him, spoke a couple of words to him then embraced him in a hug he was quick to return.

The girl was a pupil, wearing the regulation green uniform, though looked older than her years. Put her in a bar and Lila guessed she could pass for twenty-two. Way too young for Jack, but she was pretty and long-limbed, and the way she was touching his arm with one hand while playing with a long strand of hair with the other was pure flirtation and had something stirring in Lila's belly. She recognised it as jealousy and, irritated by her reaction, poked it down as she hopped her way across to join them.

'Everything okay?' she asked brightly as the girl pouted, looking a little annoyed that Lila had interrupted.

'This is Jessica,' Jack told her. 'She was a friend of Steph's.'

Jessica studied Lila briefly before turning her full attention back to Jack. 'So as I was saying, if there's anything I can do to help, and I mean anything, you just have to ask. I'll never forget all the good times and memories we shared, the beach parties and staying over at your house. Oh, Jack. I miss her so much.' Tears welled in the girl's eyes and she flapped a hand in front of her face as if that would somehow control them, as Jack put a comforting arm around her.

Lila managed to resist rolling her eyes, noting a little bitchily that none of the tears actually fell. She didn't doubt that Jessica missed her friend, but suspected the over theatrics were purely for Jack's attention.

'Actually, there is something you can do to help.'

Jessica glanced at Lila as if she was a bug she'd just wiped off her shoe; her eyes suddenly dry and filled with annoyance at having her moment interrupted. 'There is?'

It wasn't Lila's place to ask, but Jack had had no luck with the headmistress. Lila couldn't leave without at least trying to get him answers.

'We need information about someone at the school. A teacher.' Jack shot Lila a look, warning her to tread carefully. Obviously he didn't want everyone finding out about what had happened to Stephanie. Lila got that. 'Before Stephanie died, she mentioned there was someone selling exam answers.'

'She did?' Jessica's tone turned wary as she cautiously looked from Lila to Jack. 'Is that why you're here?'

'Do you have any idea who she was talking about?'

'No I don't. No idea at all. Sorry.'

She was lying. Lila debated on whether to call her on it, didn't have to as Jack spoke.

'This is important, Jess, please. I promised Steph I would check it out. Now she's gone I feel like I would be letting her down if I don't.'

The girl wavered, reluctant to reveal what she knew, but seeming desperate to please Jack. And damn him if he didn't pick up on that, played on it, stepping in close and personal, and fixing

Jessica with a look that most women would find hard to resist as he lightly ran his fingers over the back of her hand. 'Please, Jess. I need this. I miss her too, so much. You have to help me. You're my only hope.' His voice was no more than a silky whisper, but it broke her.

She caught hold of his hand, squeezing tightly. 'I only know a little.'

'Tell me.'

'Steph was right. There's this guy – they call him The Bishop – and he can help with test answers.'

'Who is he?'

'I'm sorry, I don't know, Jack. I've only heard his name mentioned. He's very careful not to be found out.'

'But he has to be a teacher at this school, right? How many male teachers are there? You must have your suspicions who it is.'

Jessica shook her head. 'I don't think he's at this school. I've heard he's helped students over at King's House in Cambridge too. If you want to get hold of him you have to go through the right source, but he won't meet with you until he's thoroughly checked you out, knows you're genuine and not going to rat on him.'

'So give me the name of the right source who can put me in touch with him.'

'I'm sorry; it doesn't work that way. If you want to get in touch with him you have to follow an Instagram page: Beat The Bishop–'

'Beat The Bishop? Seriously?'

Jessica shot Lila a look, annoyed at the interruption, probably not even understanding what the saying meant.

'Go on,' Jack urged, narrowing his eyes at Lila when she added under her breath, 'Classy.'

'So you go on to the page and it's full of movie pictures. There's one from *The Godfather* and you have to like the post and comment, 'I'm going to make him an offer he can't refuse.'

'What then?'

'Then you wait. The Bishop checks you out, makes sure you're legit and if he thinks you are, he gets in touch. It's all on his terms though and you have to pay. If he agrees to help you then it's not cheap.'

'I know,' Jack said tightly. 'Listen, I want you to make contact with him for me.'

'I can't.'

'Please, Jess. I just need you to make the initial contact.'

'He won't pick me, Jack.' Jessica looked genuinely apologetic. 'I'm a straight-A student and top of my class. He checks this stuff out. He'll know I don't need his help. I'm sorry.'

Although he seemed initially annoyed, the information Jessica had provided still gave plenty to think about, and Jack was in a brighter mood on the way back to Burnham than when he had left the headmistress's office.

'Thank God we ran into Jess,' he told Lila as he pulled out of the long driveway and back onto the main road. 'At least this wasn't a completely wasted journey.'

'Thank God she had a crush on you,' Lila added dryly. 'I don't think we'd have gotten anything if you hadn't flirted it out of her.'

Jack glanced in Lila's direction, his sharp blue eyes not missing a beat. 'You sound jealous.'

'Ha, Not jealous. I was fascinated. You turned on the charm and she was putty in your hands. It worked. You *were* flirting with her though.'

'I've known her since she was twelve. Steph used to sometimes bring her over for the weekend. And yes, she might have a crush, but she's barely eighteen, still a kid. I don't think of her that way.' He was silent for a moment, before adding with a grin. 'I would have charmed the pants off Mrs Crawford if I'd have thought it would get me answers.'

His comment made Lila giggle as she tried to imagine it. 'I think you'd need to do more than flutter your baby blues at that lady. She was evil.'

'The White Witch, Mrs Danvers and Nurse Ratched all rolled into one.'

Another moment of silence passed. Jack took one hand off the wheel, reached across and squeezed Lila's hand. 'Thanks for coming with me. I might have really lost it if you hadn't been there.'

His words had her chest tightening, but she found a smile, tried to keep it casual, not read too much into them. 'Any time.'

'We're getting closer to finding him, Lila. I'm gonna get this bastard for what he did to Steph.'

Lila believed him, knew that Jack wouldn't give up until he had answers. She only hoped those answers didn't come at too high a price.

24

Jack didn't have an Instagram account. 'Do you have one?' he wanted to know as soon as they arrived back at the house. Cooper was going nuts to see them, running circles around Jack as he headed straight through to the kitchen, grabbing his iPad from the counter. 'In a minute, Coop,' he told the dog, distracted.

'I do. I set a page up for my photography last year.'

Lila fetched her own iPad, clicked on the Instagram icon and handed it over.

'Want me to show you how it works?' she offered.

Jack rolled his eyes as he sat down on the sofa. 'I'm not a technophobe,' he told her, his frown deepening as he tapped at the screen.

Eventually he conceded, glancing up with a contrite smile. 'Yes please.'

Lila sat down beside him, leant in to show him how to navigate the site. This close she couldn't avoid her leg and hip pressing against his, was aware of the warmth of his breath on her neck as she tapped on the screen, and she was conscious it would take just the slightest of moves to have her lips pressed against his. The thought made her tingle inside, distracting her, made her wonder if Jack was thinking the same.

'Okay, I've got it.' He pulled the iPad away from her, leaning back on the sofa and breaking the contact, and she realised he wasn't. He was solely focussed on finding out who had tried to blackmail his sister and not remotely interested in anything else. Lila got that, she really did, though it still disappointed.

It was just rebound sex, Lila. Get used to it.

'This is the account. Beat The Bishop.' Jack gave a wry smile. 'As you said earlier, classy.'

'Let me see.' Despite telling herself to play it cool, Lila scooted forward and found she was once again pressed close to Jack as they scrolled through the pictures. This time though she tried to keep her mind on The Bishop, wanting to find out more about him. 'There it is. The Brando pic.' She tapped the screen, blew up the iconic image of the moody actor in his tuxedo.

There were several comments and Jack scrolled through the most recent, stopping when Stephanie's name appeared.

'We find these kids,' he told her. 'Speak to them. One of them will give us the bastard's name.'

'No they won't, Jack. For starters, just because they've quoted the line doesn't mean they got help. Jessica said this Bishop person is picky. For all we know he only helped a handful of them. Plus the kids paid a lot of money for his help. If they were desperate enough to cheat they won't want anyone finding out what they did.'

He considered that, clearly not liking her answer. On the floor beside them, Cooper whined.

'I need to take him out.' Jack got to his feet, and an excited Cooper charged ahead of him into the kitchen, feet slipping on the hardwood floor.

Lila remained on the sofa, watching them leave, wishing she could have gone with them, but knowing the crutches would only hold them back.

She had realised after they had met with Ruby just how vulnerable and affected by Stephanie's death Jack was. Lila desperately wanted to help him, would continue to try to, as long as he didn't shut her out. Picking up her iPad again, she logged back into Instagram and on to the Beat The Bishop page. The posts were all movie quotes and there was nothing personal to give a clue about the owner of the page.

Maybe if they contacted Instagram they could find out the account holder details.

Unlikely though. It was a huge American company and she doubted they would be interested in helping.

She clicked on the Brando pic again. *The Godfather* wasn't a recent film, which suggested someone older managed the page; though that was a sweeping assumption. Lila was a huge Hitchcock fan and many of her favourite films had been released before she was born.

On a whim, she gave the page a follow, added a comment to the Brando photo. 'I'm gonna make him an offer he can't refuse.'

It was stupid. The Bishop was easily going to suss that Lila wasn't a school kid, but maybe it would give him pause for thought, make him consider that someone might be onto him.

She checked her e-mail, uploaded a couple of archive photos on to her Facebook page and Instagram account, aware she had to keep her social media presence active, even if she wasn't able to get out and about with her camera, and was still debating the stupidity of her decision to post on The Bishop's page when Jack and Cooper returned.

It was too late to delete the comment without alerting Jack to what she had done, so she kept quiet, hoped he wouldn't find out, unsure how he would react.

Cooper leapt onto the sofa before Jack could stop him and Lila laughed, could feel from the dampness of his fur that he had been in the water. Still she hugged him back, unable to resist his sloppy kisses.

'For fuck's sake, Cooper! Lila, don't encourage him.'

Jack stood by, watching them in exasperation, a towel in his hands. He looked so frustrated, so adorably angry, his sun-streaked brown hair a scruffy mess, light blue eyes full of annoyance as he failed to control both her and the dog, and Lila's heart lurched, making her question her decision to come back to the house with him. She gave herself a sharp reminder that she was going to have to be careful around him, knew she had to reel herself in, as it was likely he was going to break her heart.

That had always been her problem with men. She tended to wear her heart on her sleeve, try to put others first, and take everyone at face value. It had been her downfall more than once and was the reason she was so reluctant to get involved with anyone. She had resigned herself to having terrible judgement when it came to dating, knew it was safer to stay solo. Somehow though Jack Foley had snuck around the walls she had built and the more time she spent around him, the harder she was falling.

Why couldn't she just come at things from a male perspective? Good sex and no strings attached, no feelings involved. It would be so much easier for everyone.

She released Cooper, urged him back towards Jack, watching them together for a moment as Jack wrestled him to the ground, attacked him with the towel, getting annoyed when Cooper kept trying to wriggle away. It was all good-natured though and Lila knew that despite Jack's protests, he adored the dog, just as Lila was starting to. This wasn't good. She had fallen for Cooper and she was falling for Jack, and with him just days out of a long-term relationship, it had disaster written all over it.

'I was thinking while I was out about what to do next.' Jack gave Cooper a final rub before releasing him and sitting back on his haunches, the damp towel still in his hands. 'I'm going to head over to my mother and Henry's place tomorrow, have a snoop round in Steph's room. She may have kept a diary or something.'

'Are you going to tell your mum the truth?'

Jack hesitated, shook his head. 'Not yet. I need to know more before I can tell her… if I ever tell her. This will break her. Thing is, I need to do this next bit by myself. My mum understands you weren't responsible for the accident, but you were still part of it. And Henry…' Jack tapered off.

'It's okay, Jack. I get it.'

She did get it, but still it stung. She was falling in love with a man she had no right to be with. What would Stephanie think if she knew her brother had been intimate with the woman involved in the car crash that killed her? It was ridiculous to believe that any of Jack's family would ever accept her. No, the accident was not her fault, but her face would forever be a reminder of what they had lost.

She forced a smile for him, knew it was important that he understood she was okay with it. 'I'm not going to be about tomorrow anyway.'

'You're not?'

'I spoke with Natalie earlier and she's agreed I can go back to work in the morning.'

Jack frowned. 'Sure you're ready for that?'

'Completely. I can't keep putting it off. The bills aren't going to pay themselves.'

He hesitated, looked like he was going to say something then changed his mind. Dropping the towel, he got up, came to sit on the sofa beside her. 'Don't go back unless you feel ready. We can work something out.'

'It's fine. I'm ready,' she insisted, keeping her tone light.

Work something out? Lila wasn't quite sure what he meant by that, but she suspected it would involve him helping her financially. Something she couldn't and wouldn't accept, not after everything he had already done.

'You paid for the alarm system that's being fitted at the house.' She didn't mean to blurt it out, hadn't planned on even mentioning it, but there it was, she'd said it.

'You know about that?' he said, meeting her eyes.

'Primrose told me. Why wouldn't you tell me though?'

'Because I knew you wouldn't let me.'

'But why though, Jack? You don't owe me anything.'

'No, I don't.' He reached out, tugged gently on a strand of her hair. 'Maybe I wasn't doing it for you though.'

As he held her gaze, Lila caught her breath.

They were silent until Jack broke the tension, easing back, getting to his feet. 'Come on, I need your help in the kitchen.'

'You do?' Part of her curious, the other part reluctant, she took hold of the hand he held out, let him pull her to her feet. 'What kind of help?' she asked dubiously, as she reached for her crutches.

'You want to eat tonight, right?'

'Maybe. It depends what I have to do to earn the food.'

Jack grinned. 'You really hate cooking that much? Doesn't part of your job at the café include preparing food?'

She shrugged. 'It's different when it's work.'

He pulled out a stool for her to sit on. 'Not this, this will be fun. Come on.'

HE WAS RIGHT. It was fun. They spent the next forty minutes chopping and sautéing onions, peppers and chicken, the mood back to being light-hearted as they laughed and bickered, Jack learning Lila was not actually as bad in the kitchen as she pretended to be, Lila discovering his hidden talent for cooking. Well, she called it a talent; the curry they had prepared looked and smelt good, but she had yet to taste it. He was easy to be around when she wasn't thinking about the sex and the attraction bit – which admittedly wasn't often – and she let her guard down, appreciating his dry humour, the similarities in their personalities, how she got every single movie quote or reference he threw her way and vice versa, and in doing so she fell further down the rabbit hole.

Leaving the pot to simmer on a low heat, Jack retrieved her bag from the hallway, taking it upstairs. Lila reached for her crutches and followed, glad to be unburdened of the decision of where she would be sleeping, part relieved, part nervous, when he headed straight to his bedroom, dropping the bag on the floor. It was so stupid how she had been overanalysing this. They'd had sex on his kitchen table that morning and now she was being prudish, wondering where he expected her to sleep. Still that prudish part of her hadn't wanted to assume and was making her uncharacteristically shy and a little awkward as she followed him into the room.

What had happened that morning had been spontaneous and for her, so out of character. She didn't regret it, had wanted it to happen, but one-night stands and sexual encounters just for the hell of it were a first for her. She could count her past partners on one hand, had only ever had sex in steady relationships, and she was still trying to figure out the protocol of how fuck buddies were supposed to behave around each other.

Because that's what they now were, right? Jack wanted her to sleep in his bed, so he obviously planned on having sex with her again.

Annoyed for overthinking things, she focussed on the view from the floor-to-ceiling window, amazed by the sensational sunset. The sky was ablaze with amber, smeared with little bursts of pink, the anchored boats just silhouettes against the glistening water that snaked a path through the dark marshes out towards the sea.

She had photographed the sunset from the quayside on countless occasions, but she had never viewed it from this window. Jack possessed many material things she would never be able to afford and for the most part none of it bothered her. But she was envious of the window, of the view.

'This is stunning. I wish I had my camera.'

'The view is why I bought the house.'

'It is?' Lila turned briefly to look at him. He was sitting on the edge of the bed, kicking off his shoes.

'I remember coming back for a second viewing. It was early evening and I got to witness the most gorgeous sunset I've ever seen. I knew then that this was home.'

As he spoke, he shrugged off his T-shirt, and for a moment she found herself caught up in an entirely different view: broad shoulders and a defined chest, his stomach taut, toned and tanned, dusted with a light smattering of hair.

'It really is beautiful,' she murmured, blushing when he gave her a sly smile, not sure herself what view she had been referring to.

He pulled off his socks, stood and yawned, scratching at his belly, before losing his jeans. 'I need to shower,' he muttered, as Lila gaped, distracted from the sunset. With that he disappeared into the en suite bathroom, leaving his clothes in a heap on the bedroom floor.

Lila fought the urge to give him his privacy and leave the room, reminding herself that it had seemed to matter little to him when he was stripping off. Instead she watched the sunset for a few moments longer before realising she wasn't really focussing and instead turned her attention to the bag she had brought with her.

It seemed bold and presumptuous to hang her clothes, even though there were only a few garments. They would crease though if she left them in the bag. Feeling almost guilty, her movements hampered by the crutches, she opened the large wardrobe, pulled some of the hangers out then, finished with her clothes, put her toiletries bag on the chest of drawers.

She hadn't expected to feel as uncomfortable as this, given that it was what she had been desperately wanting all day. She wasn't quite sure what the level of intimacy rules were supposed to be after one brief lust-driven encounter.

SHE WAS STILL FUSSING over her stuff when Jack emerged from the bathroom in a cloud of steam, just a towel wrapped around his waist.

He offered her a clean towel. 'Do you want to freshen up?'

'Thanks.' She snatched the towel, attempting to go for casual and relaxed; instead her voice came out squeakily high-pitched, sounding uptight and nervous.

Cursing under her breath, she ignored the bemused look on Jack's face, and grabbing a hairband and the plastic bag she used to tie over her cast, she fled – make that hobbled – into the bathroom.

Dear God! Could she make this any more awkward?

She took her time in the shower, partly because she needed it, but also because working with a broken leg hindered her movements.

WHEN SHE EVENTUALLY STEPPED BACK INTO the bedroom, towel wrapped around her, she expected to find it empty, assuming Jack would have gone downstairs, so was a little taken aback to see him sitting on the bed. He was dressed in jeans and a clean T-shirt, though barefoot, a frown on his handsome face, as he studied his iPad.

Hearing her, he glanced up. 'Everything okay?'

Lila flushed again, aware she was only wearing a towel. 'I'm fine.'

His eyes were on her, watching as she awkwardly crossed the room, trying to keep her towel around her while holding on to her crutches, pulling clean underwear from her bag and taking one of her dresses off its hanger. Self-consciously, she took her clothes back into the bathroom to get dressed.

HE WAS STILL on the bed when she returned, though had shifted to sit on the edge of the mattress, and he was no longer looking at the iPad, his full focus on her.

'Come here a moment.' He patted the duvet beside him.

Lila hesitated before doing as he asked. As she leant the crutches against the bed and sat down beside him, she was aware of the scent from his shower and the freshly laundered smell of his T-shirt. It was familiar and comforting, yet somehow unnerving at the same time.

'What's up?' she asked, trying to keep her tone light.

'This is making you uncomfortable, isn't it?' When she didn't answer, Jack caught hold of her hand, held on firmly when she attempted to pull away. 'What happened this morning,' he clarified, though Lila knew exactly what he meant.

'I'm fine,' she repeated, even managed a smile for him this time in an attempt to convince him she was. 'I'm a big girl, Jack. It was just sex, right? I know that. You already made that perfectly clear last night.'

She tried to sound casual about it all, hated that the words stuck in her throat.

For a moment he looked at her confused, eyes slightly narrowed as he tried to make sense of what she was saying then the penny dropped and he let go of her hand, fingers raking back through his damp hair. 'Christ, don't listen to anything I said last night. I was acting like a twat.'

'You were?' Lila's tone was wary, her words part question, part agreement.

He gave her a testing look, eyes narrowing further. 'You know I was.'

'Yes, you were, but you had–'

He silenced her with a finger over her lips. 'No "but"; there's no excuse for how I treated you last night or for what happened this morning. You deserve better, I know that.'

'Okay.'

'I got caught up in the moment. Of course that was your fault for seducing me.'

When Lila gaped at him, started to protest, he grinned, mischief clear in his eyes, and realising he was teasing, she relaxed a little. 'My fault, huh?'

'Entirely.' The air hung thick between them as Jack caught her chin between his thumb and forefinger, raised it slightly, his gaze dropping briefly to her mouth, before he met her eyes again. This time his expression was sober, his words when he spoke sounding sincere. 'Trust me, Lila. There is nothing rebound about you.'

Her heart hammered as he cupped her face in both hands and leaned in to kiss her, this time slow, soft and passionate, and her awkwardness melted away, wrapping her arms around him, pulling him closer as he deepened the kiss, his tongue probing and exploring as one hand slid back into her hair, his fist tightening around the loose knot she had pinned it up in, the other running down the length of her spine. He slowly guided her back on to the bed, settling himself on top of her then broke the kiss, easing back onto one elbow to study her face, pulling the hairband loose and freeing the knot, smoothing her hair around her shoulders.

'Better,' he told her, leaning forward to trail feather-light kisses down the side of her neck.

Lila wriggled beneath him, arms tightening around his neck, fingertips digging into his shoulders, as his mouth moved lower to explore the deep v neckline of her dress. She let out a gasp, tried to draw him closer, frustrated when instead he eased himself back again, looked down at her, a sly smile on his face.

He reached for the top button on her dress, popped it open,

kept his eyes locked on hers as his fingers deftly worked lower, until the dress was open down to her waist exposing her bra and belly, dipped his head to softly kiss the flesh just above the silk cups, easing one hand inside the dress, warm and gentle, caressing bare skin and making her tingle in anticipation.

Need and urgency taking over, Lila reached up, slipping her hands under his T-shirt, her fingers finding hot flesh and hard muscle. She ran her palms over his shoulders, pulling him towards her, annoyed when he resisted. Instead she tried to free him of the T-shirt, eager hands trying to pull it over his head, frustration burning through her when he stopped her, catching hold of her wrists, gently pushing them down by her sides. Holding them there, he shook his head. 'Uh-uh. Not yet.'

When she responded with a protest, he cut her off with a deep kiss that was hot and heavy and had her insides melting. His lips curved against hers as she let out a moan, and he eased his head back. 'This time we take things slower, okay?'

He waited until she nodded before letting go of her wrists, returning his attention to the dress and slowly working the rest of the buttons open, taking his time as he stopped to nibble, kiss and tease each newly exposed bit of flesh.

Lila squirmed, her breathing heavy as heat spread through her.

'Is this from the accident?'

She raised her head slightly, looked down at the bruising that ran from her left breast down across her belly. It was healing, wasn't as ugly as it had been, but the marks were still there and would take time to fully go.

'Seat belt,' she told him as his eyes met hers.

Jack nodded, gently kissing the marks on her belly before unhooking her bra. As he eased her out of it, threw it on the floor, Lila realised he had already discarded her dress and that she was naked apart from her knickers.

'I know you said take things slow–' She gasped as he cupped her breasts, rubbed his thumbs over her nipples.

'I did.'

'But I'm the only one naked.'

Jack dipped his head to kiss the bruising on her left breast. 'That's the plan.'

'The plan?'

He gave her a devilish smile, fingertips skimming down over her belly, stopping short of where she wanted them, gently caressing and teasing. 'For what I said last night and what happened this morning. I'm going to make it up to you.'

25

Aaron watched as the two detectives showed his parents pictures of the missing schoolgirls. They sat around the kitchen table, the cups of tea his mother had made them still untouched, probably because his mother wasn't good at making tea, never leaving the teabag in for long enough. Despite Aaron repeatedly showing her, she seemed to think people liked their tea a milky white colour.

His father frowned, made a point of studying the pictures before shaking his head. 'No, I've never seen them around here. You said some evidence was found near the accident site?'

'We did, sir,' the red-haired detective told him. She didn't elaborate.

'I'm sorry, I can't help you.' Gruger gave an almost bored sigh as he handed the photos to Aaron's mother.

She studied them briefly. 'Sorry, I've never seen them… other than on the television.' She put a hand to her chest, looking pained. 'Their poor parents; I can't even begin to imagine what kind of hell they're going through.'

Neither detective missed the look Gruger gave Aaron's mother, rolling his eyes as though she was being melodramatic.

Aaron bit down on his temper. Even in front of company, his father had to belittle his mother.

'Can I see?' Aaron asked, stepping forward as the female detective started to slip the photos back in a folder.

'What's the point in that? You're not going to recognise them.'

Aaron scowled at his father. 'You don't know that. I might do.' He glanced at the detective. 'It's worth me at least looking, right?'

'It certainly is,' she agreed with a half-smile, handing him both pictures.

He recalled her saying they had driven down from Lincolnshire and were part of the Major Investigation Team and he guessed neither detective wanted this to be a wasted trip.

Aaron studied the photos carefully, first the picture of the dark-haired girl with the curly hair then the blonde. Despite having a shorter more boyish haircut, her fringe flopping in her eyes, the blonde was prettier; her wide grey-green eyes and freckled nose softer than the dark-haired girl, who had a harder pinched look about her. He had seen both of them on the television, the coverage becoming more extensive the longer they were missing, especially when Phoebe Kendall's uncle was arrested on suspicion of murder.

Aaron hadn't seen these photos though. They looked like they had come out of family albums, possibly even frames that were displayed around the house. It felt a little voyeuristic to be studying the memories of two grieving families, but it was intriguing all the same. Plus of course it vexed his father, who was not going to be happy about this police visit at all, and that just about made Aaron's day.

LILA PLANNED on catching the bus into work, but Jack insisted on taking her, promised to be back to collect her at the end of her shift. As she unlocked her seat belt, he leaned across, drawing her in for an unexpected lingering hot kiss that made her pulse race and had her cheeks flushing.

'I'll pick you up at three thirty, okay?'

'Okay,' she managed breathlessly as he ran the pad of his thumb across her cheek, kissing her again before releasing her.

She waved him goodbye before turning to go into the café, struggling with her crutches on shaky legs, a little annoyed when she realised Beth had been standing at the front window and, judging from her grin, had seen everything.

'You have a nice healthy glow about you,' she commented dryly. 'Looks like we have a lot of catching up to do.' Before Lila could respond, Beth sauntered back towards the kitchen.

Lila reluctantly followed, not sure she wanted Beth dissecting her relationship with Jack. Not that it was a relationship. They'd had sex three times and, yes, it had been really good sex, and okay, he had made it clear that he wanted it to be more than just sex, but it was still early days and there were too many hurdles in the way of it ever becoming serious. She didn't want to think about those hurdles, couldn't bear the thought of not having Jack in her life, so, for now, she was choosing to ignore them.

'Good morning,' Natalie greeted her brightly, looking up from the ice cream she was churning. 'How are you?'

'Glad to be back,' Lila told her, setting down her bag. 'I've missed work.'

'Crazy girl, though I guess it gets boring sitting around.'

'Oh, I don't think Lila's been bored,' Beth chipped in. When Lila shot her a warning look, she added innocently, 'I didn't recognise the car that dropped you off this morning. Did you stay with a friend last night?'

That caught Natalie's attention. 'Have I missed something?' she asked, eyes darting from Beth to Lila.

Lila's cheeks flamed. 'No-one has missed anything. I stayed with Jack last night and Beth is trying to make it into a bigger deal than it is.'

'Bollocks. That kiss looked like a big deal.'

'Kiss?'

'Jack just dropped Lila off for work and the kiss he gave her before she got out of the car had the windows steaming up.'

'If they steamed up, I'm surprised you were able to see anything,' Lila retorted sarcastically.

'I saw enough. Have you slept with him? That kiss suggested you have.'

'I...'

Lila's pause was confirmation enough for Beth, who clapped her hands in delight. 'You bloody well have. What was it like?'

Hungry, intense, passionate, emotional, easily the best sex she'd ever had: Lila didn't say any of those things, certainly didn't let on that she had fallen hard for Jack, so hard it actually frightened her, instead she smiled demurely. 'It was just sex. As I said, no big deal.'

Beth's expression suggested she didn't believe her, but with the café due to open, there was no time to grill Lila further. As Lila helped Natalie finish preparing the counter food, Beth went out front to stock the cabinets.

'Oh, while I remember. You had a visitor yesterday.'

Lila glanced up at Natalie. 'I did? Who?'

'He didn't leave a name, popped in as we were closing, and seemed to think you'd be working. Obviously we didn't give him any personal details, but he said he'd call back, that he needed to speak to you.'

Lila's heartbeat quickened as both intrigue and apprehension niggled at her gut. After questioning Natalie further, she was able to rule out the police, who for starters would not have been cagy about who they were, and it wasn't Richard or Aaron Gruger, given that the visitor was somewhere around the thirty age mark.

Two possibilities lingered in her mind and she didn't particularly like either of them. It could be the man who had attacked her, pushing her in front of the bus then breaking into her home.

It sounded incredulous that he would be bold enough to waltz into her workplace, but he clearly wished her harm and with the hood down, Lila would never recognise him. Maybe it was some kind of mind game.

The other possibility both unnerved and excited her. What if it was The Bishop?

The timing was close – she had posted the comment around four in the afternoon and Nat's Hideaway closed a couple of hours later. He would have had to have seen her message and reacted almost immediately, but it was possible, wasn't it?

Her initial instinct was to let Jack know, but then she remembered she hadn't told him about the post she had left on the Instagram page. She needed to hold fire, wait and see who had wanted to speak with her, hope they would return that day.

THOUGHTS of the visitor played on her mind for much of the morning and she tried to work out what the hell she would say if it were The Bishop, as she prepared the lunchtime salads and scrubbed jacket potatoes.

Would he really risk coming there? He would know Lila wasn't a student, didn't really need his help. The only reason he might approach her would be to warn her off, but this was a public place and her territory. He wouldn't get away with making any threats there.

Her phone vibrated in her pocket and she wiped her hands on a tea towel, pulled it out to see she had a text from Jack. She swiped the screen to open it, the message making her smile and blush to her roots as she read in detail exactly what he planned to do to her when they got back to his house. Damn, the man definitely had a way with words.

Heat warming through her, her smile breaking into a grin, she fired an equally dirty text back, glanced at the time on her phone, realising it was going to be a painfully long and frustrating afternoon.

JACK LINGERED on her mind for the next couple of hours, mostly distracting her from thoughts of her mystery visitor, and Lila was counting down the last hour of her shift, eager to see him, when the bell sounded and a stocky man of about thirty entered the café. He stood out from the tourists, dressed like he was off to a bank meeting in an expensive-looking suit and conservative tie. Lila was serving at the time and gave him a smile. The lunchtime crowd had died down and only two couples remained inside.

'Hi there, may I help you?'

'Lila Amberson?' It was phrased as a question, but she suspected the man knew exactly who she was. He gave her a slick smile that didn't touch his eyes. 'My name is Giles Buchanan.'

The name meant nothing to her, but it didn't mean he wasn't The Bishop. He offered his hand and she took it, unimpressed with his weak handshake.

'How can I help you, Mr Buchanan?'

'Could we talk in private?'

Lila made a show of looking around her. 'I'm sorry, but as you can see I'm at work. I can't just down tools.'

His lips thinned as he peered over her shoulder towards the kitchen. 'I'm sure one of your colleagues will cover for you.'

'I'm not due a break.' True, though Lila knew Natalie would give her five minutes.

She had no intention of going off alone with this man though. 'Could you tell me what this is about please?'

He hesitated, seeming annoyed that she wouldn't do as he asked. Lila got the impression he was used to getting his own way. She smiled pleasantly and waited.

Realising that she wasn't going to budge, he leaned forward, lowering his voice.

'I'm here on behalf of the Whitman family.'

Lila's chest tightened at the mention of the name. Giles Buchanan. Hadn't Jack mentioned his sister's boyfriend, the one whose shoes Cooper had chewed, was a Giles?

'You're Jack's sister's boyfriend.'

Small close-set eyes narrowed suspiciously. 'You know who I am. Good.'

'Why are you here, Mr Buchanan?'

'I want you to leave the family alone. I don't know what kind of game you're playing, but they've been through enough and they don't need a troublemaker like you trying to manipulate them.'

Lila swallowed hard, her heart hammering. 'I haven't done anything to the Whitmans and I haven't tried to manipulate anyone. Did they send you?'

'They want you to leave them alone,' Giles said more forcefully. 'And they want you to leave Jack alone too. I've done some digging, Miss Amberson, hired a friend to look into you. I know all about your past and I bloody well intend to make sure you don't get your hands on a penny of their money.'

'What?' Lila shook her head, disbelieving what she was hearing. 'I'm not after anyone's money. You have this all wrong.' She could feel herself shaking, couldn't believe what she was hearing. 'I want you to leave.'

'I will, once we're clear. Do you understand, Miss Amberson? You don't want to take me on. I will break you.'

'Get out!' When Giles flinched, but remained where he was, Lila yelled the words again.

Natalie and Beth came running through from the kitchen, suspicious eyes on Giles.

'What's wrong? Lila?'

Lila ignored Natalie. 'I told you to get out. Now!'

'Do we have an agreement, Miss Amberson?' Giles pushed, angry.

'Who the hell are you?' That was from Beth.

'This is Jack's sister's boyfriend,' Lila told her, her voice shaky. 'He stopped by to tell me to leave the family alone. Apparently I'm a troublemaker who's after their money. Isn't that right, Mr Buchanan.'

'Get the hell out of my café.' Natalie's tone was low, but her words held a threat.

When Giles hesitated, she added. 'I'm going to count to five then I'm going to call the police. One... two...'

Giles's face deepened to a dark purple, a scowl on his face. 'You've been warned,' he snarled at Lila.

'Three... four...'

'Okay, okay. I'm going.' He smoothed a hand over his hair, took a step back, trying to retain his dignity. 'Crazy bitches,' he hissed at them as he turned.

The door slammed behind him, the customers in the café watching him go. All four of them had been discreetly listening in.

'Lila, go back in the kitchen,' Natalie ordered, taking charge. 'Ladies and gentlemen, I'm sorry you had to witness that. Beth will sort you all with a free drink.'

Hurt followed shock and was swiftly replaced with anger, as Lila tried to process what had just happened. She lowered herself onto one of the two kitchen stools, annoyed that her legs were shaking, tried to draw a few deep breaths to calm down.

With hindsight, she thought of a dozen things she should have said to Giles Buchanan, wished she had been angrier with him, showed him she wasn't prepared to take any crap. Hindsight was a wonderful thing though and truth was he had blindsided her. She had been relaxed and happier than she had been in a while, counting down the last hour of her shift, desperate to see Jack. Her guard had been down and she hadn't been expecting the attack.

Who the hell did Giles think he was, making threats to her to stay away from the Whitmans, and from Jack?

He knew about her past, had hired someone to look into her.

A sliver of dread snaked through Lila's belly. She had worked hard to bury what had happened, was terrified though it would one day come back to haunt her. Her skin was burning, her chest tight, as a wave of nausea washed over her. She grabbed her crutches, pushed past Natalie who was coming to check on her.

'I need to get some air.'

Outside the café, Lila leant against the wall, greedily sucking in mouthfuls of the salty sea air, knew that Giles had backed her into a corner.

She had no choice. She would have to deal with her past.

26

Jack spent a productive morning with his new book, pleased with the word flow and putting his reinvigorated writing juices down to good sex. Stephanie and The Bishop were still weighing heavily on his mind, and that afternoon he intended to delve further into his sister's past, but Lila had offered a pleasant escape from that, and the previous night, for a few hours at least, he had managed to lose himself in her, push the other stuff to the back of his mind.

She really was like no-one else he had met. When he looked back at past women he had been involved with, Tiffany included, they all fitted a mould: beautiful to look at, confident, a little hard around the edges and, dare he say it, spoilt.

Not Lila. Everything about her was a contradiction. She wasn't stunning in an obvious way like Tiff. Lila was shorter, curvier, darker (until then he'd always had a thing for blondes), quirkier in the way she dressed, but she had a quiet beauty that radiated from within, those wide eyes so expressive, her full upper lip hitting a solid ten on his sexy radar.

She was kind and compassionate, though not a pushover, wore her heart on her sleeve – whether she was happy, sad or angry, he knew it, and despite seeming comfortable in herself, at times she showed a vulnerability that tugged on his heartstrings. He had seen that side of her the previous night, realised how much she had read into the words he'd thrown at her on Sunday. Someone harder like Tiffany would have shaken the words off, but not Lila. She had taken them at face value and he'd learnt he couldn't treat her like that, had taken his time making things right, because it mattered. She mattered.

And that was the other thing about Lila. There was chemistry. Hot smouldering chemistry. She was open and so responsive, and when he was with her he felt everything.

He spent a few pleasant moments reminiscing about the previous night, aware he was due to pick her up in a few hours. His imagination working overtime, he grabbed his phone and sent her an explicit text, telling her what he intended to do to her when he had her back behind closed doors.

Shutting down his laptop, he reached for his jacket. Time to pull his mind out of the gutter and head over to see his mother. He grabbed his phone, heard a text ping back from Lila before he'd even slipped it in his pocket. He read it, grin spreading, his mind crawling right back into the gutter.

HE TOOK Cooper along for the ride, knew his mother adored the dog and would likely be distracted enough to leave him alone while he went through Stephanie's room. Purposely keeping his mind off Lila, he tried to focus on his sister and The Bishop, not wanting to show up at the family home with a hard-on.

Why would his bright beautiful baby sister resort to cheating? Had she been placed in that desperate a situation? It was killing him that he hadn't been home when she had wanted to come stay. If he had been, maybe she would have opened up to him, wouldn't have driven out to Filby that night.

He thought back over the conversation with Ruby, remembered her saying there had been an incident at Christmas, that something had upset Steph. What had happened? What was he missing?

HE WAS STILL BROODING over things when he pulled into his mother's driveway twenty minutes later. The house was sprawling, set in the countryside just outside of Cley village in grounds that ran over several acres. It was a new build back in the nineties that Henry had designed himself. Mock Tudor with a fountain out front and a swimming pool out back. After the divorce, his parents were given joint custody of their children and, along with his brother, he had spent four nights a week in the house. That seemed a lifetime ago.

He heard his mother call through from the kitchen as he opened the front door. 'Jack, is that you?'

'Yep, and I've brought company.'

Delicious smells wafted down the hallway as he went to find her, Cooper scrambling ahead, his nose already excited by the scent.

'Hello, this is a nice surprise.' Kate Whitman looked delighted as the bounding bundle of black and white fur skidded to a halt in front of her legs, letting out a woof in greeting.

Jack watched with a smile as she made a fuss of Cooper, who greedily lapped up the attention.

As she stood, he leaned down to kiss her cheek. 'Sausage rolls?'

She reached up to give his cheek an affectionate pat. 'I thought we could have lunch together as you're over. I find the cooking therapeutic.'

Although she smiled, the strain was there in her eyes, and she looked older. Losing a child would do that to you. Henry had thrown himself into work and when he wasn't working he spent his days protesting for justice, still angry at Stephanie's death, but his mother had dealt with things more quietly, wanting time to grieve and attempt to come to terms with what she had lost. She needed her other children more than ever at that point. Oliver was the only one still living at home, but the rest of them tried to call in on her regularly and Jack made a point of phoning her every day.

'I'd like that,' he told her, watching as she slipped on oven gloves and reached into the double oven for the tray of sausage rolls. He had a couple of hours before he had to leave to go pick up Lila and could have lunch with his mother before he did what he'd come there to do.

She knew the purpose of his visit was to spend some time in his sister's room. He had been honest with his mother at least on that point. Of course she believed it was for therapeutic reasons, that he needed time alone with his sister's things to grieve and process her death. He couldn't tell her the truth was he intended to snoop through Stephanie's things. That would bring with it questions, some of which he had answers to, others he was still trying to figure out, and a whole new level of hurt he couldn't expose her to, at least not for now. She had suffered enough.

THEY ATE ON THE PATIO, enjoying the warmth of the late May afternoon, as Cooper charged around the garden and leapt into the pool, working off some of his spaniel energy.

'Have you spoken to Tiffany at all since she went back to London?' his mother wanted to know.

'Just a few texts.' Jack didn't point out that he hadn't replied to them. Truth was he had been too preoccupied to give Tiffany much thought at all since dropping her off at the station. 'It was the right decision. We'd grown apart.'

Kate nodded, seemed lost in thought for a moment. 'How about Lila? How is she?'

'We're still in contact.' Jack picked his words carefully. He knew his mother held no grudge against Lila, but was unsure how she would react if she found out Lila was staying with him, sleeping in his bed. It was early days and too soon to be having that conversation. 'How is Henry holding up?'

There was no love lost between Jack and his stepfather, but the topic was safer and guided his mother away from Lila. He listened as Kate told him the doctor had upped Henry's blood pressure tablets, that she worried he was working too hard, before conversation turned to Jack's younger half-brother, Oliver, who was due to turn twenty-one later in the week.

'It's going to be hard for him not having Stephanie here.'

'Hopefully the surprise will help take his mind off things.'

The family had decided to forego the kind of lavish party they generally threw for big birthdays and planned to gather for a low-key meal. They had clubbed together to pay for a trip to New York, a place Oliver was desperate to visit, and they intended to surprise him with the tickets at the meal on Friday night.

JACK AND KATE continued to chat for another hour before Jack discreetly looked at his watch, saw he only had about forty minutes left before he would have to leave to pick up Lila. He excused himself, left his mother sitting in the garden with Cooper.

She caught hold of his hand as he brushed past her, gave it a comforting squeeze, her smile sad, but encouraging, wanting him to find the answers he was looking for.

Jack quashed down the feeling of guilt that he was about to snoop through his sister's things, took the stairs to the first floor, hesitated before opening the door to Stephanie's room, finding it harder to go in than he had expected.

The bed was neatly made, the lemon duvet on a white wrought-iron bedframe that was cluttered with cushions, the walls papered with a butterfly print. The wall to the right was filled with built-in wardrobes, while on the other side of the bed stood a tallboy chest of drawers and a dressing table. That was where Jack started.

Trying to push all personal feelings aside, he sat down on the dresser stool, glancing over the trinket boxes, tea-light holders, and the white wooden picture frame that held a photo of the five siblings, taken the previous summer at his beach house, felt his heart squeeze. He looked at the mirror with a string of rose fairy lights wound around the frame. There were more pictures tacked to the edge: Stephanie with her friends, smiling and carefree in every photo. He recognised Jessica in one shot, Ruby in another.

He took a moment before forcing himself to open the drawers of the dresser. It was mostly make-up in the left drawer, while the other held a mishmash of more jewellery and cosmetics, tissues, half-eaten packets of chewing gum, a few receipts and a box of matches. He went through the receipts, noting they were all for clothing stores.

Finding nothing of significance, he moved on to the tallboy and pulled open drawers, quickly closing the top one that contained underwear. He had no intention of rooting through his sister's bras and knickers. The other drawers held clothing. Nothing there.

He performed the same checks on the two bedside tables, had more luck when he came across Steph's tablet. He pulled it out, switched it on; annoyed to find it had a passcode protecting it. He tried a couple of codes without luck, set the tablet down on the bed, figuring he would come back to it.

The wardrobes provided the most interesting find. They were packed with clothes and shoes – Stephanie had been obsessed with shopping – and at first Jack thought he wasn't going to find anything of interest, but then he spied the gift boxes, tucked away in the bottom corner, looking like they had been intentionally hidden behind some of the longer dresses. He pulled them out, noting each box was brightly coloured and that they varied in size. Opening a smaller one first, he read the plain handwritten card lying on top of the black tissue paper.

An apology for what happened at Xmas. Remember it's our secret xxx

Jack's heartbeat quickened. He pulled back the tissue paper to reveal a pair of silver diamond studs, stared at them for a moment before seeing red and ripping the lids off the other boxes, finding in them a silk scarf, perfume, a Gucci key ring, underwear in raunchy red. Each box had a handwritten card; the message in the other boxes simply saying: *our secret xxx*.

Who the hell had sent this stuff to Stephanie? She dated, but only with boys her age, and they wouldn't have been able to afford these things. The message bothered him. *Our secret xxx*, written in a loopy, almost flamboyant, scrawl. It was someone who didn't want to be found out. Had she been having an affair? She was only seventeen, damn it.

He stared at the boxes, drew a deep breath and tried to think more rationally, taking solace that all of the items looked unused. The scarf and underwear had tags on, the key ring and earrings were still in their cases and the perfume was sealed. Stephanie had hidden these gifts away, hadn't used any of them, suggesting perhaps they had been unwanted.

But who had sent them and why?

The Bishop was trying to blackmail her. Why would he send her gifts?

Not wanting to risk his mother walking in and finding the boxes, Jack pulled out his phone, took photos of all the gifts and slipped the first handwritten card into his wallet, before placing everything back in the wardrobe as he'd found it.

He glanced at the tablet on the bed, suspecting it held answers – if he could only figure out how to get into it. Slipping off his jacket and hiding the tablet underneath it, he let himself out of Stephanie's bedroom and closed the door.

. . .

HE FOUND his mother in the kitchen with Cooper, sneaking him a sausage roll. She looked up guiltily as she heard Jack enter. 'I hope you don't mind. He could smell them and kept whining. I think he's hungry.'

Jack forced a smile for her. 'That dog's always hungry.'

'Did it help, spending time in Stephanie's room?'

'It was weird being up there, knowing she's not coming back, but yeah, I think it helped a little. Thank you.'

Kate nodded, her eyes so sad. 'We all have to find our own way to deal with the grief, Jack. I don't think there is a set pattern to follow.'

'I need to go now, Mum. I have to be somewhere. But I'll call you tomorrow, okay?'

He whistled to Cooper who was avidly watching the counter with the remaining sausage rolls.

Kate bent down to rub the dog's ears as he turned to look at Jack, gave him a kiss on the head. 'You come back and see me soon, Cooper, okay?' She smiled up at Jack. 'You too. And thank you for staying for lunch today. It was nice.'

He returned her smile, gave her a kiss on the cheek. 'Yes, it was.'

Jack waited until she had closed the front door before setting the tablet down on the passenger seat. He felt guilty as hell about taking it, but he needed to find answers to what had been going on with his sister and suspected the tablet would provide them.

HE PULLED up outside Nat's Hideaway, glanced at the clock seeing he was five minutes late, though Lila wasn't waiting outside. Sticking on his hazards, cranking the window open a few inches and leaving Cooper in the car, he stepped inside and headed straight to the counter. Lila's friend, Beth, was serving, had just finished handing change to a young mother who'd bought ice cream for her toddler.

Beth glanced up at Jack as the woman fussed with her purse before slipping it back in her bag. 'Oh, it's you.'

'Is Lila ready? Can you tell her I'm parked out front?'

'She's not around.'

Beth's tone was cool to the point of unfriendly and Jack narrowed his eyes.

'What's going on?'

'Giles is what's going on. Your sister's boyfriend, I believe. I don't know who you people think you are, but what the hell did he think gave him the right to come in here and threaten her like that?'

'What? Slow down.' Jack's temper was simmering. 'Giles was here, today?'

'Yes,' Beth answered stiffly.

'Do you have...?' Natalie tapered off as she stepped through from the kitchen, clocking Jack. 'Oh, you.'

He rolled his eyes impatiently. 'Yes, me! Will someone please tell me what the hell happened. Giles came in here and threatened Lila. Threatened her how?'

'He said he has information on her, that he knows she's trying to cause trouble for your family. He warned her to stay away from you all, said he had your family's blessing. Told her if she didn't he would come after her.' Natalie paused, studying Jack, could obviously see the shock on his face. 'You didn't know.'

'Of course I didn't bloody know and no, he doesn't have anyone's blessing.' Jack shook his head, barely able to comprehend what he was being told, rage rising inside of him. 'I'm gonna fucking kill him.'

'Join the queue,' Beth muttered sarcastically.

'Where's Lila? I need to talk to her.'

When Natalie and Beth exchanged a glance, he called out her name, pushed past them into the kitchen. He found her getting her things together, saw both anger and hurt in her expression when she looked up.

'I can't do this, Jack.'

He went to her, frustrated when he put a hand on her arm and she shook him off. Rage was still burning inside him, but that was for Giles, and he drew a breath, tried to clear his head, needing to think straight. Pulling up one of the two stools, he sat down. 'Come here and talk to me for a minute.' When he saw her waver, he added, 'Please.'

She actually huffed at him, but did as asked, setting down her crutches and taking a seat on the other stool, though refusing to look at him.

'Listen to me.' He caught hold of her hands, held on when she tried to pull away. 'Just listen to me, okay?' He sounded calmer than he felt, tried to keep his voice even. 'Firstly, there's something I need to know. Lila?' He paused, waited for her to react. 'Lila, look at me.' He waited until she did, hating the guarded look in her eyes.

'What happened today, you know that I had nothing to do with that, right?'

She didn't respond immediately, her expression resigned.

'Of course I know,' she said eventually. 'It doesn't change anything though. This isn't going to work. Your family hate me. They're never going to accept me after what happened with Stephanie.'

'That's not true, my family don't even know you, and I can promise you they will be as mortified as I am when they find out what Giles did today.' Jack released one of Lila's hands, reached up to smooth his fingers through her hair. 'My mother knows I've been seeing you.'

That had Lila's attention. She looked up again, her guards dropping a little. 'She does?'

'Yes, she does.' Jack mustered up a grin for her. 'Admittedly she doesn't know I'm sleeping with you, but yeah, she knows you're in my life.'

'And how does she feel about that?'

'She's fine with it. In fact she even asked after you today.'

Lila narrowed her eyes slightly, searching his face for the sign of a lie. 'She did?'

'Yes, Lila, she really did. It's early days, but I promise you this can work, will work.'

'But Giles–'

'Isn't even a part of our family,' Jack said firmly, his temper rising at the mention of the man's name.

'He had someone look into my past. He knows things, Jack. Things I haven't told you.'

'And you don't have to tell me. As long as you're not some psycho bunny-boiling serial killer, I really don't care about your past.' He had attempted to make a joke about it, but didn't get the smile he was hoping for. 'Listen. I'm going to kick Giles's arse for what he did to you today and then I'm hoping Alyssa is going to kick him out of the house. The man is a twat and I've never been able to figure out why she's with him anyway. Please don't punish me, us, for what he did. That means he wins.'

He saw her bottom lip wobble.

'He is a twat,' she agreed.

'A slimy lowlife twat,' Jack cupped her chin in his hand, looked into her eyes, knew her resolve was weakening. 'Come home with me, Lila. Cooper's in the car and he's going to be devastated if you don't come back with us; he's already bonded with you, is used to having you around.'

'You're trying to blackmail me with a dog?'

'Is it working?'

The corner of her mouth twitched. 'Maybe.'

27

Jack updated her on his visit to the family home on the ride back to Burnham, telling her about the boxes hidden in Stephanie's wardrobe and that he had taken her tablet.

Lila knew he felt guilty about taking it, tried to reassure him he had done it for the right reasons, knew as well as he did that if Stephanie had left any clues they would likely find them there.

The whole Giles incident still rankled her and although she knew Jack wasn't to blame, she couldn't help but sulk a little over it. She had been shocked when it had first happened, but as the afternoon wore on she was plain pissed off.

Still she was thinking clearly enough when Jack revealed his intention to drop her and Cooper off at the house then head straight over to Aylsham, knew he was currently too hot-headed to act rationally in a confrontation. She managed to talk him down – actually threatened him that she would go back to her flat if he left the house – persuading him that Giles could wait. Jack wasn't happy about it, though seemed more worried she might actually act on her threat if he left her alone, so he reluctantly agreed to stay put.

While she had stopped him from leaving the house, Lila

couldn't prevent him using his phone and within five minutes of arriving back at the house, after being unable to get hold of Giles, he had called Alyssa, taking all of his rage out on her.

Lila tried to keep her head down, letting Cooper out of the French doors, staying in the kitchen to make a cup of tea, wincing a little at the side of the conversation she could hear. Jack was furious and his poor sister was getting it both barrels. In fairness to Alyssa, she sounded like she was holding her own, seemed as fiery as her older brother, and the conversation ended with Jack hanging up on her, throwing his phone on the sofa in frustration.

Mad as she was at Giles, Lila hated that she was coming between them. She reminded herself that it wasn't her fault and it was Giles who had caused this, but still she felt guilty.

'Do you feel better for that?' she asked, making her way through from the kitchen.

Jack shot a glance in her direction. 'No.'

'I didn't think so.'

She watched him pace for a moment before he picked up Stephanie's tablet. He dropped onto the sofa, spent a few frustrated minutes trying to work out the passcode.

'Date of birth?'

'Tried it.'

'Pin number?'

'Only she would have known it.'

'Another memorable date?'

'None I can think of. And before you ask I've tried all the obvious one, two, three, four bullshit.'

'I didn't,' Lila bristled.

He glanced up at her again, looking contrite. 'Sorry.'

Putting the tablet down, he got up. 'I'm gonna take Cooper out, work off some energy since you won't let me go beat the shit out of my sister's slimeball boyfriend.' The last few words were said with a part smirk, telling her his anger was ebbing. He paused beside her and hooked his hand around her waist, giving her a quick kiss on the lips. 'Thank you.'

'For what?'

'For coming back here with me and for stopping me going over there tonight.'

Lila smiled tightly. Although she was still riled by what had happened, under the annoyance, guilt bubbled. Giles was right that she did have a history, one she was embarrassed of and had worked hard to keep buried. She hated that the odious man was forcing it to the surface. Jack may say he didn't care about her past, but still she was ashamed in keeping it from him.

'Go take Cooper out,' she told him lightly. 'We'll talk when you get back.'

WHILE THEY WERE GONE, she settled down onto the sofa and read her Kindle for a while. Finding it difficult to concentrate, the day's events still weighing heavily, she switched off her book after a couple of chapters, logged into Facebook, glancing through her newsfeed, liking a handful of posts then clicking on to her photography page. There were a number of new notifications, most of them likes for the various archive sunset pictures she had been trying to share daily. She had three new private messages. One was from a man enquiring where he could purchase her work; the other two were wedding enquiries.

She replied to the first, telling the man who was interested in her photography he could either purchase from one of the bespoke shops that stocked her work or she could sort something for him directly, before replying to the two wedding e-mails, one directly from a bride, and the other from a mother of the bride. Lila already had a handful of weddings in the diary for the following year, but she desperately needed more work. The accident had set her back and she'd had to tighten her purse strings to make allowances, which scared the hell out of her. Natalie had tried to help her out with sick pay, but there was a limit to how much she could do.

She had responses back almost immediately from the man wanting to buy her work, asking if he could deal with her directly, while the mother of the bride wanted to know about dates. Replying to the man first, Lila asked him if there was a specific picture he was interested in, before confirming to the mother of the bride she was free on the date the woman was looking for. She was logging off her iPad when Jack and Cooper returned.

She looked up, couldn't resist a smile as Cooper circled Jack, entranced by the ball in his hand. Jack put it to one side, bent down to rub the dog behind the ears, equally engrossed in Cooper as he spoke to him, fed him a few treats he'd stashed away in the pocket of his jeans, and Lila's heart flipped. He really did love his dog.

'You two have fun out there? I'm beginning to feel like three's a crowd.'

Jack grinned. 'We had a good talk. Coop helped work me down.'

Lila nodded. 'That's good.' She turned back to her iPad, saw she had another message from Veronica Crowther, the mother of the bride, and rolled her eyes. 'Christ, lady, you're keen.' It was the fourth message she'd had in fifteen minutes and she really wasn't in the mood.

'Everything okay?'

'Yes, I have a potential wedding booking and the mother of the bride keeps messaging me.' Lila read the message asking to meet. It wasn't an unusual request. Photography was a big part of the day and most brides wanted to meet beforehand to discuss details of the pre-wedding shoot that usually took place a month or two before the wedding. She wrote a message back as Jack sat down beside her, slipping his arm around her and pulling her close as he leant in to nibble on her neck. Distracted, she told

Veronica she would check her diary and be in touch. 'I'm always a little wary when the mother is running the show. They can be control freaks. Not my favourite kind of job.'

'So turn it down,' Jack murmured against her ear.

It was so easy for him; he never had to worry about money, about paying the bills. It must be nice to be able to pick and choose, not worry about having to pay the rent, or in his case, mortgage. Though did he even have one of those?

She pushed him away, annoyed. 'Beggars can't be choosers, Jack. Some of us are reliant on work and we have to take whatever jobs we can get.'

'Whoa, hold up. You know I wasn't trying to belittle what you do,' he told her as she set her iPad down. 'Things aren't as easy for you, I get that, and I know you don't have as many choices. I'm sorry.'

She drew in a breath, aware she had overreacted, knew it was because she was dreading what came next. 'No, I'm sorry. I didn't mean to throw that in your face.'

She was tired, irritable and a little cranky because she had been looking forward to hot sex, and Giles Buchanan with his little piggy eyes and self-righteous attitude had ruined that.

'Jack, I know you said you don't want to know what happened before, but–'

'I already told you I don't give a shit about your past.'

'But I do. I didn't want to have this conversation, but now I realise it's necessary. I'll be blunt; you're loaded, I'm broke. Hell, I'm so broke sometimes I have baked beans on toast for dinner.'

'That's a nutritious meal.'

Lila scowled, warning him she wasn't in the mood for jokes. 'Not if you're eating it every night of the week. Okay, how about your bank account? Do you ever dread looking at it? I'll bet you never even give it a second thought. I do, I'm scared to look at it every single day. Most of my clothes are second-hand, the only reason I have an iPad is because my brother was kind enough to give me his old one when he upgraded, I only buy wine when it's on offer, can't remember the last time I went on holiday, and every taxi ride, every meal out, every unexpected expense I have to budget for, I have to consider if it's really necessary. Hell, I saved for over a year before I could buy my last camera.'

'What's your point, Lila? You want me to feel guilty because I have money and you don't?'

'No, of course not.' She was getting flustered, wanting him to understand where she was coming from. 'My point is I want to make you realise how different we are.' Her voice cracked. 'I'm no Tiffany, Jack.'

'I don't want Tiffany. Why the hell do you think I ended the relationship?'

That had Lila pausing. For some reason in her head, she had seen Tiffany as the one who had finished things. 'You did that because of me?' Lila whispered.

When he gave the slightest of nods, his eyes not leaving her face, her heart surged and she had to force herself to regroup and press on.

'You paid for the alarm and I let that slide because I knew I couldn't afford it and if you didn't pay for it, Primrose would have to. You can't do that though. I know it's just money to you, but it's a huge bloody deal to me.'

'I need to know you're safe. Trust me, Lila, I did it for me, not for you.' His tone was a little heated and again she paused for thought.

'Okay, so here's the thing. You need to know this because it's important. I was declared bankrupt five years ago.' When he arched a brow, stared at her, she continued. 'I had a business, I had a boyfriend, Charlie, and things went horribly wrong.'

'I know.'

'What?' Incredulous, her jaw dropped.

'Giles already told me. I told him to go to hell.'

'You knew?' Lila wasn't sure if she wanted to punch Jack or kiss him.

'You were bankrupt, your partner – I admit I didn't realise he was your boyfriend – ended up in jail for money laundering.'

'And you didn't think it was relevant to tell me you knew this?'

'No, because it wasn't.'

Everything was so straightforward to him. 'Why does this not matter to you? How do you know you can trust me, that I wasn't involved?'

'Were you?'

'Of course not!'

'So, it's irrelevant.'

'I might not have been involved, Jack, but I was gullible enough to trust him with my finances. I was starting out with my photography business when we began dating and I was doing okay, building up a reputation, particularly in the wedding market. I was never very good at dealing with the money side of things, couldn't afford to pay an accountant. Charlie, he had some finance background, offered to take care of things for me. We had gotten serious and it was easy to let him take charge of that side while I concentrated on taking pictures. I trusted him. I didn't know he was using my account to fund his little business on the side for his friends. They needed someone to stash their drug money and Charlie was more than happy to oblige for a fee. It was nearly two years before the police sussed out what was going on then another year of hell as Charlie tried to drag me down with him. They went through every one of my transactions, froze my accounts, trying to figure out if I had been in on it or if I had just been that stupid. Luckily for me they decided on the latter, but I lost everything. I had no money and had to declare myself bankrupt. I lost my business, my reputation, and of course I realised I had been duped, that Charlie had just used me for a means to an end. So yes, I may not have been guilty, but I sure as hell had mug written on my forehead.'

'And that's why you stopped dating.'

Lila gave a hollow laugh. 'It's true what they say, once bitten and all that. I wised up after Charlie went to jail, gradually got my life together and now I keep my circle close. I've learnt it pays to be shrewd. So, although Giles is a slimy piece of work and I quite like the idea of you punching him in the face, you can understand why he doesn't trust me, might doubt my motives. Hell, if I were him, I know I would.'

'Don't make excuses for Giles, Lila. You weren't guilty. You were the victim and the police cleared you of any wrongdoing.'

'Maybe, but when you've been under suspicion, investigated, even after you are cleared, the stigma is still there. People wonder if deep down they can really trust you, whether perhaps the police got it wrong and you are guilty.'

'I don't think that and let's be honest, mine is the only opinion that counts.'

'Is that so?' He was teasing her and despite herself, she smiled. She had been dreading this conversation, knew it had to happen and couldn't believe how little a deal it was to him.

Beside her, she heard Cooper whine. While Lila had been getting serious with Jack, the spaniel had managed to work his ball off the worktop, sat with it in his mouth, tail thumping, as he urged her to throw it for him.

'How did you get that?'

Tail thumping harder, Cooper dropped the ball, seemed as if he couldn't decide whether he should be pleased with himself or worried.

'Coop, you're too smart for your own good.' Jack got up from the sofa, picked up the slimy ball and with the dog following went over to the French doors, throwing the ball out onto the decking. Without a moment of hesitation, Cooper charged after it. 'So if you've finished showing me your skeletons, I have something I want to show you.'

'You do?'

He pulled his phone from his pocket, dropped down on the sofa beside her again. 'I took pictures of the boxes I found in the back of Steph's wardrobe.'

He handed over the phone and Lila studied the images. 'Those are expensive gifts.'

'I know. Steph had a boyfriend, but it was a while back and he wouldn't have been able to afford this.' Jack reached in his pocket again, pulled out a card. 'This was in the box with the earrings. There were messages in all the boxes that just said "Our secret xxx".'

'Our secret,' Lila repeated, reading the words aloud, feeling a little sick. 'Jack, I know you don't want to hear this, but the gifts, the fact it was a secret, it suggests she was having an–'

'Affair. I know.'

'Do you think that's why she was in Filby that night?'

'I honestly don't know at this point. If you had asked me that question a week ago, I would have said no. Now though, I'm not sure of anything.'

It had to be so hard for him, finding out that Stephanie had kept secrets. Lila scooted in closer, leaning against his shoulder as she studied the pictures again.

'These gifts look unused,' she pointed out.

'They are. That's the one thing that's keeping me sane. If they were wanted gifts they would be used.'

'Agreed.'

'She never even opened the perfume to smell it.'

Lila tilted her head to look up at him. 'Do you think The Bishop sent them?'

'I considered that.' Jack frowned. 'He was blackmailing her though. Why would he send her gifts? Besides, the first card referred to Christmas. She didn't contact The Bishop until much later. She had never struggled at school before. Something happened at Christmas that made her lose focus and these gifts were part of it. I just wish we could figure out how to get into her tablet.'

'Dave!' Lila exclaimed, sitting up straight.

'The passcode is four numbers, not four letters.'

'No, you idiot, I mean Dave can help us.'

'Who's Dave?'

'He's a mate of Elliot's, my brother, and a really lovely bloke. If anyone can help us, he can.'

'Should I be jealous?'

'He has a mullet and goes to *Star Trek* conventions and battle re-enactments. Do you think you should be jealous?'

Jack grinned. 'Depends if that's your thing.'

'Seriously, Dave is a top bloke. He managed to recover the information on my sim card after the accident.'

'And you think he could get us into Steph's tablet?'

'It's worth asking. He's been on holiday with Elliot, but they're due back late tomorrow.'

'Okay, we'll speak to him.'

Jack put his phone down, pulled her close again, and she rested her head against his chest, finding the warmth of his body and the steady beat of his heart comforting as his fingertips traced a pattern on her bare arm.

They sat like that for a few minutes, neither of them talking, Lila's mind still working overtime trying to figure out the puzzles of Stephanie's life.

Jessica had told them she didn't think The Bishop was part of Queen's House School, that he had helped pupils at a school in Cambridge too. Was there a connection between the two places? She thought back to the meeting with Mrs Crawford. She had mentioned they were an elite group of schools, not school.

'What was the name of the Cambridge school Jessica mentioned?'

'King's House.'

She sat back up again, the lightning bolt hitting.

'King's House, Queen's House: they're sister schools, Jack.'

He looked amused. 'I know. Have you only just figured that out?'

'You know?'

'Queen's House is all female and King's House is all male. My mum and stepdad toyed with sending Oliver there to board.' Lila must have looked crestfallen because he added as encouragement, 'Keep thinking though.'

'So if King's House is the all-male school, The Bishop has to be there.'

'That's what I'm thinking, but we'll never narrow it down without extra help, which is why we need to get into Steph's tablet. That's the key.'

'Is there a website though? We should at least look.'

'I already glanced through the staff page and there weren't any names that stuck out. We need more to go on to be able to narrow it down, but if you want to look, knock yourself out.'

Jack was right. They would never narrow it down, but stubbornly, Lila picked up her iPad anyway, did a Google search for the school. She scrolled through the staff page, the names meaning nothing. There were several male teachers and any one of them could have been Steph's blackmailer. Frustrated, she clicked on the history link, reading about the origins of the school, the information surprising her. Still, she was a little more reserved this time when she spoke. 'I'm guessing you know there are two other schools in the group.'

'There are?' Jack sat up, snatched the iPad from her.

'According to this there's a Knight's House in Nottinghamshire and Bishop's House in Suffolk.'

He brooded on that briefly. 'Bishop's House.' She saw the moment that the penny dropped. 'The Bishop. Damn it, Lila. We're looking at the wrong school.'

She watched over his shoulder as he clicked on to the Bishop's House website, another all-male school located just outside the town of Bungay. As with the King's House School, the home page contained a welcome message from the headmaster.

She skim read it as Jack scrolled down the page, her mouth dry, heartbeat quickening as she reached the end, saw the sign-off on the greeting, recognised the photograph.

Richard Gruger.

28

Had Richard Gruger been the one blackmailing Stephanie? It was logical to assume that The Bishop would come from Bishop's House School, and they knew Stephanie had been in contact with him, plus it was one hell of a coincidence that she had been in Filby on the night of the accident, several miles from home, yet just a few metres from Gruger's doorstep. Was Gruger The Bishop?

The man was arrogant enough; had been a reluctant hero saving Lila, preferring to keep his head down, out of the media spotlight. Something he would do if he had secrets he needed to keep hidden. Plus there was the whole control thing with his wife and kid, the way he spoke down to them, not treating them as equals. He certainly had all the signs of a sociopath.

Jack had no proof though; nothing of any worth that he could go to the police with. If Elliot's friend could get them into Steph's tablet, Jack was certain they would find the answers they needed. He was going to pick Lila up when her shift finished at six and they planned to head over to Norwich to meet with Dave. Hopefully he was as good as Lila said he was and would be able to help them.

. . .

UNABLE TO FOCUS on his book, Jack spent an hour googling Gruger, trying to find everything he could about him. There was frustratingly little. The man really was private. He grew up in Oxfordshire, had remained local, marrying Judith Winter when they were both still young. Aaron was their only child. From what Jack could see, Judith came from a wealthy family: her father owning a chain of jewellery stores. The family had stayed in Oxfordshire for several years before leaving for East Anglia. The move appeared to be abrupt. In one article, Gruger was talking about his plans for the future at the school where he was headmaster then just six weeks later, he was announced as the new headmaster at Bishop's House School. Had he wanted a change or had something happened to pre-empt the decision? From what Jack could find on Judith Gruger, family was everything to her. Why would they up sticks and move to somewhere where they knew no-one?

With plenty to ponder on, Jack found it difficult to concentrate on his manuscript. He forced a few words out then decided, fuck it, and went downstairs to grab Cooper's lead, figuring that a long walk might get his brain into a better gear. He had just locked up when his phone rang. Ignoring an impatient Cooper he glanced at the screen, seeing Lila's name, and hoped Giles hadn't shown up again.

'Hey, everything okay?'

'Yes, no… I think so.'

'Giles hasn't–'

'No, he hasn't come back.'

Thank God. Jack was still trying to confront him about what happened with Lila, but Giles – who had obviously been warned by Alyssa that her brother was baying for his blood – was conveniently avoiding his calls. If he hadn't manned up by the weekend, Jack intended to drive over to the house and have it out with him. Lila might have calmed down some, but he wasn't prepared to let what had happened slide.

'Listen, Jack. Do you mind if we go to see Dave a little bit later?'

'Why, what's up?'

'Veronica Crowther is who's up.'

'Who?'

'Remember the mother of the bride, the job I was unsure about? She wants to meet and she's insisting it has to be today as she's about to go on holiday. She only lives half a mile down the road from the café so I figured I could call in after work, get it over and done with. Beth said she would drop me off and I was hoping you could pick me up from her house.'

'If you're sure you really want this job. She sounds a pain in the arse.'

'I need the work, Jack. I can't afford to turn wedding gigs away.'

'Okay, how long do you think you'll need?'

'Probably an hour. I'll text you the address. If you pick me up about seven.'

Her text came through after they ended the call. Jack glanced at the address, slipped his phone back in his pocket before unleashing Cooper and throwing his favourite ball.

JACK SPENT a pleasant couple of hours walking down to the sea, letting the dog frolic in the waves, thinking that once Lila had her cast off he would bring her down here one evening and they could sit together on the beach and watch the sun set over the sea, share a bottle of wine, maybe more if there was no-one else around.

BACK AT THE HOUSE, Jack finally found his mojo, fingers burning on the keyboard, and for a blessed couple of hours, he lost himself in the book, thoughts of Stephanie, Richard Gruger and the odious Giles pushed to the back of his mind.

When Jack finally came up for air, he glanced at the time, saw it was five thirty. Saving his manuscript, he stretched at the knots in his shoulders, figured he had time for a shower and to feed Cooper before heading over to this Veronica Crowther's place to pick up Lila.

Lying on the bedroom floor, exhausted from his walk, Cooper's ears pricked up, large brown eyes glancing up expectantly at Jack. The bloody dog was telepathic, he swore.

He pulled out his phone, checked the address again that Lila had sent him, put it in Google. His satnav would tell him where he was going, but still he was curious to see where the woman lived. The house was huge and secluded, less than a mile from the centre of Cromer, surrounded by a high hedgerow and a long narrow driveway. Veronica Crowther had money and he hoped she would make it worth Lila's while and not mess her around.

On a whim he clicked on to Facebook, looked up Lila for the first time, figuring since they were sleeping together, he should ping her a friend request. After doing so, he clicked onto her photography page, spent a few minutes looking through her photos. She really was talented and some of her pictures of the North Norfolk coastline were breathtaking. He spotted one, a golden sunset over the sea, the waves glistening in the dying light as they crashed against the beach. It would go well downstairs on the wall behind the sofa. Maybe he would speak to Lila about buying it.

She had albums of the weddings she had shot. Jack preferred the scenic stuff, guessed she did too, but understood that this was where she made money. He clicked through a handful of pictures, was about to logout when he spotted Veronica Crowther's name in the comments below. She popped up on a handful of the pictures with mostly generic comments, such as, 'This is lovely', or 'Simply beautiful'. She didn't sound like that much of a pain in the arse.

He clicked on to Veronica's profile. The privacy settings were high and it didn't give much away. One profile picture of a smartly dressed redhead, her hair swept up under a hat, sipping bubbly. Her friend list was hidden and there were no comments or likes on the picture. He clicked on photos, saw there was just one more: Veronica with a younger woman, probably the daughter due to get married.

There was nothing to see; nothing to tell him what Veronica Crowther was really like. Scrubbing his hands over his face, he logged off Facebook, went downstairs to feed Cooper then left the dog eating while he had a shower.

As he stood under the hot spray, something niggled in the back of his brain, something that didn't feel quite right, and it annoyed him he couldn't figure out what it was.

Back in the bedroom, he threw on jeans and a T-shirt, scrubbed a towel over his hair then pushed the damp mess out of his eyes. Cooper had snuck his way back upstairs and was lying at the foot of the bed. He gave Jack a grin and thumped his tail.

'Something's off, Coop.'

He sat back down at his desk again, pulled up Facebook. This time he didn't logon to Veronica Crowther's profile via Lila's photography page, he typed her name in the search box, blinked sharply when he saw the two top listed women with that name shared the same profile picture. He clicked on the top Veronica. It was the profile he had looked at before he showered. Just two pictures and, according to Facebook, both uploaded a day earlier.

He scrolled down her timeline, past the two photos, trepidation knotting his gut when he spotted the date Veronica Crowther had joined Facebook. The day before.

Furiously, he clicked back to the list, looked at the identical profile below. This one was far more detailed. Tons of friends, comments and photos, some recognisable local shots but the most recent were posted from Australia – the previous day. The real Veronica Crowther holding a koala.

He had to warn Lila.

DESPITE TELLING Beth to drop her at the end of the driveway of the Crowther residence, her friend insisted on taking her up to the house, and Lila was glad when she realised how long and winding the driveway was. This house really was secluded.

She hoped Jack wouldn't have a problem finding it, as she and Beth had struggled, driving past the entrance twice.

The family had to be loaded to afford a place like this and Lila hoped Veronica wasn't going to be one of those rich but incredibly tight women that she so often encountered. It had never failed to amaze her that sometimes the people with the most to give held on to it meanly while those who counted on every penny were unfailingly generous.

She thanked Beth for the lift, waved her goodbye. Her friend hadn't let Jack off the hook yet for what Giles had done. Although she had warmed up to being coolly polite to him, she was having her doubts whether he was right for Lila, convinced he was going to break her heart.

Lila didn't point out to her that it was already too late for that.

As the car disappeared around a bend, she glanced around her, aware of how quiet it was out in the countryside. She couldn't even hear the sound of any traffic once Beth's car was far enough away. Feeling an unexplained shiver come over her, Lila headed to the front door, eager to get this visit over with.

The doorbell announced her arrival, the sound reverberating into the heart of the house. She waited patiently, half expecting a maid to answer the door.

Seconds ticked into minutes and reluctantly, she pushed the bell again. The thing made such a racket it would be impossible to not hear and she didn't want to piss off a potential client by seeming too impatient.

While she waited, she glanced around again. There were no cars in the driveway, just a white van parked by the garage. Of course Veronica's car would most likely be something posh and shiny and would be locked in the garage, away from the elements.

Lila waited on the doorstep, couldn't help the ominous feeling rising in her gut. The woman had insisted on meeting her here this evening. Okay, Lila was a few minutes early, but still, why wouldn't Veronica be here? It made no sense. Something was off and Lila couldn't quite figure out what.

For a moment, she wished she had asked Beth to stay, told herself she was being stupid and overreacting. Given everything that had happened in the last couple of weeks though it was understandable that she was jumping to conclusions.

A rustling came from the trees behind the van and Lila thought she heard footsteps. Maybe Veronica had gone for a walk. She had told Lila six o'clock and that was still ten minutes away.

'Hello?'

Lila was met by silence.

'Hello? Is anyone there?' She sounded a little less confident this time, which annoyed her, as she hesitantly hopped towards the van, convinced she was overreacting and it was nothing. Still her legs shook as she neared. She cautiously stepped past the van; saw no-one was there or hiding in the trees. She must have imagined it.

Feeling a little stupid, she turned to go back to the house, paused when she heard her phone ringing in her bag.

It was Jack. She noted with concern she had already had two missed calls from him. Hoped he was okay.

'Hey.'

'Lila, don't go to meet Veronica Crowther.'

'I'm already here, Jack.'

'Are you with her?'

'No. No-one's answering the door.'

'Listen to me. She's not who she says she is; the real Veronica Crowther is on holiday in Australia. Someone lured you there.'

'What?' Lila tried to digest his words. 'But her daughter's getting married. She seemed so genuine. Are you sure?'

'I'm sure. Where are you? Are you still outside the house?'

'Yes.'

'I want you to walk down the driveway. Get away from the house and back to the road.'

'Jack, you're scaring me.'

'You're going to be fine. I've called the police and I'm on my way. Just get to the road. Promise me you will.'

'You called the police?'

'Yes! The road, Lila, go now.'

'I–'

Lila heard the footsteps behind her, but barely had time to react as something heavy hit her hard between the shoulder blades. She dropped her phone and both the crutches, fell to her knees as pain blasted through her, followed swiftly by a wave of nausea.

Her hands hit gravel and she was aware of the sting, her head swimming as she tried to take on board what was happening.

As HER VISION swam back into focus, everything went black.

Someone had hold of her and the blackness was suffocating, smelt old and stale. To her horror, she realised she had a hood over her head.

Survival instinct took over as she kicked and fought, her screams muffled by the hood. She recalled being pushed in front of the bus, the man standing over her in her bedroom. Whoever had orchestrated this elaborate set up meant to kill her, she was certain.

Her foot connected with bone and she heard a grunt, felt her attacker's grip loosen.

She tried to clamber to her feet, pain shooting through her broken leg, and she cried out, falling forward.

The man had hold of her again, was trying to wrench her arms behind her back. She heard yelling then the weight was gone and she was alone on the ground.

Through the thickness of the hood, she heard the faint shuffle of footsteps crunch against the gravel, the sound of an engine being floored. She yanked at the hood with shaking hands. It had some kind of drawstring that had tightened around her neck and she scrambled to find it, panicking when hands touched her, screaming again and lashing out.

'It's okay, love, it's okay. You're safe.'

The hood loosened and was pulled from her head. Lila blinked, her heart racing, as she stared at a man before her. Middle-aged, ruddy faced, kind eyes. She noticed the van was gone, but a Range Rover was in its place. This man, had he saved her? She tried to speak, found it a struggle.

'I was coming down the driveway, saw him sat on top of you.' The man looked shaken himself, as though what had happened was only starting to sink in. 'I... I should call the police, love.'

Lila heard the sirens in the distance, forced herself to take another deep breath.

Her voice shook badly when she spoke. 'They're already on their way.'

29

Frustratingly, Ted Crowther was unable to give the police much information about Lila's attacker, but what he could confirm was the man had been wearing a hood, leaving little doubt it was the same person who had pushed her in front of the bus and who had broken into her flat on the Saturday night. Jack was pleased the police were starting to take Elliot Amberson's claim that someone had attacked her at the hospital more seriously, accepting that someone was trying to hurt her and this time had gone to elaborate lengths to do so, might have succeeded if Veronica's brother hadn't stopped by to water her plants.

They already had more to work with, a description of the van and the fake Facebook profile. Whoever the man was, he had to somehow be connected to the real Veronica, the lady who owned the house Lila had been lured to, in order to know she was away.

After the paramedics had checked Lila over, the police agreed to Jack's request to take her home, telling him they would stop by to talk with her the following morning. She was badly shaken, just about holding it together, and didn't protest when he helped her into the car, fastened her seat belt for her.

'Do you mind if we go straight back to yours? I know you want to meet with Dave, but I'm not sure I'm up for it tonight.'

JACK STARED at her in shock, his hand pausing on the ignition key. Meeting with Dave was the furthest thing from his mind and the twenty minutes driving over there after Lila had been cut off while talking to him was the most scared he had ever been. Seeing her sitting in the back of the ambulance, knowing that she was safe, the relief had been immeasurable. 'I *am* taking you home. There's no way we're going to meet Dave tonight. You frightened the crap out of me, Lila.'

'He meant to kill me. If...' She trailed off, bottom lip trembling.

As much for his own comfort as well as hers, Jack reached across, placing his free hand over hers and squeezed tightly. 'He didn't and he's not going to. I'm not going to let you out of my sight until the police have caught him. No more going off to meet clients, okay? No more going anywhere alone until this is over. Promise me.'

She drew in a shaky breath. Nodded. 'I have to tell you something.'

'Okay.' He waited for her to continue.

'It might not be the same person who broke into my flat.'

'I think it's pretty obvious that–'

'I did something really stupid, Jack.'

His heartbeat quickened. 'What did you do, Lila?'

'The Bishop – I commented on his Instagram page.'

'What? Why the hell would you do that?'

'I wasn't thinking. I just did it. I wanted to try to lure him out.' Her voice lowered to a whisper. 'What if it was The Bishop who attacked me tonight?'

Frustration and anxiety knotted in Jack's gut, though he pushed them down. She was safe and that was the most important thing. Okay, so she had done something stupid, really bloody stupid, but she was okay. He couldn't bring himself to be mad at her.

BACK HOME, Jack went out onto the deck, leaving Lila on the sofa, arm around Cooper, the TV playing a cheesy movie. He had put it on more as a distraction for her, suspected she wasn't really paying much attention. The spaniel refused to leave her side, his doggy intuition picking up that something was wrong the second they had walked through the door.

Elliot Amberson sounded in a panic as soon as he heard Jack's voice. 'Where's my sister? Is she okay?'

Jack explained what had happened, didn't sugar coat it, wanting to be sure Elliot understood the gravity of the situation, would know to be on alert if he was alone with Lila, and he could hear the kid hyperventilating. 'Oh my God, Jesus, I can't believe this happened. Where's Lila? Can I talk to her?'

'She's asleep.' She wasn't, but Jack figured it was only a white lie, knew she wasn't up for talking to anyone. 'The paramedics have checked her over and she's going to be fine. She's just badly shaken up. I'll bring her over tomorrow to see you.'

'She's staying with you?' It sounded almost as much an accusation as a question.

Lila obviously hadn't told her brother about her current living arrangements when she had texted him to arrange the meeting with Dave.

'I didn't want her staying alone after the break-in,' Jack answered, his tone neutral, realising when Elliot let out a gasp that he didn't know about that either.

'Break-in? Where was there a break-in? At Lila's flat?'

Jack tried to remain patient as he briefly explained, suspected from the reaction coming from the other end of the phone that

Elliot wouldn't be getting much sleep himself that night. Jack asked him to apologise to Dave, to try to reschedule a meeting, promising to bring Lila back to Norwich to see her brother the following day.

The next call was to Natalie. Lila didn't know about that one, but as he suspected she was stubborn enough to try to go into work the next day, he had taken Natalie's number from her contact list when he took Elliot's, intended to ensure it didn't happen.

As it turned out, Natalie was in complete agreement with him, told Jack he had her blessing to use whatever means necessary to keep her home and safe for the next few days. He promised to keep her updated, figured if it came down to it he would hide Lila's crutches.

Leaving both phones on the kitchen counter, he went through to the lounge where Lila was still on the sofa holding onto Cooper. She looked broken.

'Scoot over,' he told her, easing the dog out of the way and sitting down beside her when she moved to make room for him. He slipped his arm around her, realised she was still trembling from the attack, and pulled her close. Shifting her weight, he eased them both back down onto the sofa so she was lying partly on top of him, and when her body jolted against his, he rubbed his hand up and down her back, trying to soothe her, tenderly touching the spot where she had been hit (an iron bar or similar, both the police and paramedics suspected). She tightened her arms around his neck, burying her face into his shoulder and he felt her tears dampen his T-shirt. Turning slightly, he pressed a kiss against her temple.

'I won't let him hurt you again, I promise,' he murmured against her ear, meant it.

Stephanie's blackmailer had been his top priority, was still high on his list, along with finding out who had sent her the gifts he had found hidden in her wardrobe. He had been so obsessed with trying to seek justice for his dead sister though he hadn't fully realised those priorities had shifted and what mattered most was right there in front of him. Someone was trying to hurt Lila. Scrub that. Someone was trying to kill her. And he intended to do everything in his power to ensure they didn't succeed.

But who was posing the danger? Was it the hooded man who had attacked her in Cromer then broken into her flat or had she foolishly managed to lure The Bishop out of his hiding place and that night suffered the consequences?

It niggled him that Richard Gruger was the headmaster of Bishop's House, that he had connections to Stephanie by the accident alone. And he was also connected to Lila, had been from the night he had saved her. Before the hooded man started his campaign to try to kill her. Give life with one hand and take with the other.

Were the hooded man and The Bishop one and the same person?

RICHARD STILL WASN'T HOME and Judith was beginning to worry. It was stupid of course, as she had been there so many times before, but this felt different.

She tried so hard to ignore the lies, knew she had to be the glue to keep the family together. They had made promises to each other when they had first moved to Norfolk, knew that Aaron needed them, that family had to come first, but it seemed she was the only one making the effort.

The police visit had rattled him, she had seen it on his face and sitting there, watching him as he studied the photographs of the two missing girls, a sliver of fear had snaked through her belly. Did he know?

She had promised herself she would turn a blind eye to his indiscretions, but as she returned home from her club, found the driveway empty yet again, she couldn't help, but question, 'Where is he?'

30

When Lila awoke she found she was alone in Jack's bed. Her head pounded, her mouth was dry and her eyes stung as she tried to adjust to the light coming through the half-opened curtains. Gradually, piece by painful piece, everything flooded back to her: how she had been visiting Veronica Crowther when Jack called to tell her it was a trap, the fear of his words before she was attacked. She rubbed gingerly at her neck, remembering the thump as something heavy had hit her between the shoulder blades, the raw fear as the hood had been forced over her head, and she was annoyed when she started to shake again.

The previous night she had been an emotional wreck, and although she was holding it together, the truth was she was still a mess. Someone wanted her dead and they had gone to elaborate lengths to try to make it happen. The knowledge of that terrified her.

She wondered where Jack was, aware she had gone to pieces on him twice in less than a week, and hating herself for that. She wasn't normally so emotional, but guessed having someone wanting you dead would have that effect. Hard as it was, she threw back the duvet, climbed out of bed, knowing she had to somehow pull herself together, as crying and hiding away wasn't going to solve anything.

She wanted to shrug off the attack, pretend she wasn't scared, but she could feel the toll it had taken on her physically. She turned slightly, studying her naked back in the reflection of the mirror, lifting her hair and wincing when she spotted the large ugly bruise that had already started to form.

Jack's wristwatch sat beside the sink and she glanced at it, taken aback to see the time read nine fifty-four. She should have been in work nearly an hour and a half earlier.

She had to call Natalie and apologise. But where was her phone?

She vaguely remembered Jack borrowing it to get Elliot's number. Knew he had phoned her brother to explain what had happened when she had been too exhausted to make the call herself. It had to be downstairs.

She grabbed her robe, knotting the belt around her before negotiating the landing with her crutches. As she neared the top of the stairs, she heard voices: Jack's and at least two others, a man and a woman, and she froze momentarily, before pushing herself to go downstairs with a sharp reminder that she needed to call Nat.

Jack sat in the lounge with his brother, Tom, and a blonde lady. Lila guessed she was Tom's wife, Imogen. Cooper was lying under the coffee table. Immediately her gut twisted, the desire to flee back to the safety of the bedroom paramount in her mind. She hadn't expected company, looked like shit, and was naked under the robe. It was too late though, as Cooper had spotted her, tail wagging as he got to his feet, fetching his favourite ball to take to her, and she realised all three of them were looking in her direction.

'You're awake,' Jack said, getting up and coming to her, pulling her in for a kiss that made no secret of their relationship. His mouth was close to her ear as he murmured, 'Come on, there's someone I want you to meet.'

It was too soon and this certainly wasn't the right day, but Lila didn't have a choice.

'This is my brother, Tom, and his wife, Imogen.'

After the encounter with Giles, she readied herself for hostility, so was surprised by the warmth in Tom's eyes and Imogen's smile.

'It's nice to meet you, Lila,' Tom told her, sounding like he genuinely meant it.

'Jack was telling us about what happened last night.' Imogen's face was etched with concern. 'What a horrifying ordeal for you. Are you in much pain?'

'It's better than it was last night,' Lila downplayed. Truth was her upper back was throbbing, the ache reaching up her neck and into her head, and the area where she had taken the blow was painfully tender. Tom and Imogen didn't need to be bored with the details though. Lila managed a smile for them. 'It's nice to meet you both too.'

Jack guided her to one of the sofas. 'Sit down. I'll get you a coffee.'

'Wait, I need my phone. I have to call Natalie. She'll be wondering where I am.'

'No need, I already spoke to her last night.'

'You did?'

'She's not expecting you back this week.'

Lila saw the lines of strain on his face. Knew what had happened to her had scared him too. She wanted to be annoyed with him for contacting Natalie and making the decision on her behalf of whether or not she was okay to go to work, but knew it had been the right call. She had overslept, would have let Natalie down, plus Jack was right; she couldn't work. She was in too much pain and still trying to come to terms with what had happened.

Doing as told, she sat down as he disappeared into the kitchen, a little self-conscious that he had left her alone with Tom and Imogen, who she had nothing in common with other than the fact she had been in the car crash that had killed Tom's sister. They both seemed comfortable around Lila though and their conversation was easy, their concern seeming genuine.

'Immy's a nurse,' Tom told Lila as Jack returned from the kitchen. 'You should let her take a look.'

Lila liked him, she decided. He was softer than Jack. There was less of an edge, and he seemed kind and steady, and there was definitely a family resemblance, same straight nose, crooked smile and long lashed slightly downturned eyes, though Tom's were brown. His hair was lighter too, and he wore it shorter and neater than Jack's scruffy mop.

'That's kind, but you really don't have to worry. The paramedics checked me over last night.'

Jack set a mug of coffee down on the coffee table, along with a plate of slices of buttered toast. 'Eat,' he ordered.

Lila glanced at the food, aware she hadn't eaten in nearly twenty-four hours. Still she wasn't sure she could muster an appetite. Instead she sipped at her coffee, felt it burn her hollow stomach.

'It's really no trouble for me to take a look.'

'Immy's right,' Jack agreed, sitting down beside Lila and scooping her hair back into a ponytail in his hand, holding it to one side. 'Jesus, Lila, this is nasty.' He tenderly touched the spot where she had been hit and she flinched at the contact.

Imogen got up to look for herself. 'Ouch, honey, that has to hurt.' As Jack moved aside, she gently examined the bruising. 'Have you been sick at all?'

Lila had felt sick with shock, but she hadn't actually thrown up. 'No.'

'Dizziness?'

'No dizziness, but I have a cracking headache.'

'You have any paracetamol?' Imogen asked Jack.

He nodded, went to fetch them.

'Take it easy, okay? I can't stress that enough, and no work, definitely not this week. Take the paracetamol every four hours. They'll help with your headache. Unfortunately you're going to feel a bit battered for a while.'

'Okay, thank you.'

Jack returned with a glass of water and two tablets, which Lila gratefully took, before making an effort to nibble at a piece of toast and finishing her coffee.

HER HEAD WAS STILL BANGING, but the pain had eased by the time Tom and Imogen went to leave.

'Don't forget Oliver's card, Jack.' Imogen reminded him of the reason they'd stopped by, pecking him on the cheek. 'You're the last one to sign it, so we're relying on you bringing it along on Friday night.'

'I've got it covered.' At her raised eyebrows, he gave an easy grin. 'You can trust me.'

'That's what I'm worried about.' Imogen shook her head before embracing Lila warmly, though careful to avoid where she had been hit. 'It's been lovely to meet you. Jack will give you my number. If you need anything, give me a call.'

'I will. Thank you.'

Lila received a goodbye kiss from Tom, watched Jack seeing them out of the door, thinking the encounter had gone better than expected. Tom and Imogen seemed like genuinely nice people and there was no bitterness towards her. Hope bubbled inside her. Maybe Jack was right and this could work. She quickly quashed it down though, suspecting that the Whitman family might not share the same sentiments.

She tried to take Imogen's advice, to rest and take things easy, as well as her own, that she needed to accept what had happened and deal with it, move on, but then Detective Constables Galbraith and Jones showed up for a follow-up interview on her attack at Veronica Crowther's house and by the time they left, her mood had plummeted.

WHILE JACK PUT in a few hours with his book, Lila curled up on the sofa and checked her phone. There was a text message from Elliot, saying he had spoken to Jack and hoped she was feeling okay, and another from Beth, who had learnt the news from Natalie. Not in the mood to talk to anyone, Lila replied briefly to both before switching her phone off.

She alternated between sleeping and watching crappy daytime TV, while Cooper kept her company, wanting to be positive but instead feeling pathetically sorry for herself.

JACK PICKED up on her mood when he came down for coffee, spent a few minutes trying to tease her out of it before disappearing again. He reappeared about half an hour later, sounded busy in the kitchen, before coming through to where she still lay on the sofa. 'Come on, get up, we're going out to get some fresh air.'

Lila wasn't in the mood. 'I don't want to. I'm fine here.'

'You're wallowing.'

'I'm not wallowing.' She was aware she sounded a little testy. Couldn't help it. 'I'm resting, just like your sister-in-law advised.'

'She told you to take it easy, not spend all day on the sofa feeling sorry for yourself. It's a gorgeous day. Getting out of the house will do you good.' He held out his hand. 'Come on.'

'No.'

'Lila, stop being so bloody stubborn!'

'I just want to–' She didn't get to finish the sentence, caught off guard when Jack grabbed hold of her. One moment he was pulling her up from the sofa, the next she was in the air as he hoisted her over his shoulder. As she kicked out her legs, squealed in shock, her heartbeat quickening and arms thrashing out, trying to find something to hold on to, convinced he was going to drop her, but he gripped her arm with one hand, the other clamping over the back of her bare legs.

'Jack, what the hell are you doing? Put me down!'

When he ignored her, heading purposefully towards the stairs, Lila pummelled at his back with her free hand as she wriggled to get free. 'Put me down. I'm injured. I mean it, Jack!'

He was on a mission though, marching her up the stairs, into the bedroom and through into the bathroom as her protests fell on deaf ears. Cooper charged behind them, excited by the new game, looking positively delighted when Jack dumped Lila on her bum in the shower, turning on the spray and blasting her before she had time to react. She squealed, cursing at him as she got a face full of cool water, the powerful spray slicking her hair to her head, soaking through her robe.

'You bastard!'

He grinned at her as he blocked her exit, looking far too pleased with himself, which only annoyed her further.

'It's not funny, Jack.'

She had been attacked. Someone had hurt her, tried to kill her. It wasn't the time for pranks. So what if she was feeling sorry for herself? Anyone would be in her situation. She didn't deserve to get thrown in the shower and dunked in cold water like that.

Okay, he hadn't exactly thrown her in the shower. He had sat her in the shower, and, she noticed, he had managed to keep her leg with the cast on out of the spray. And he may have manhandled her a little, but he'd been careful not to hurt her. The only thing he had slightly bruised was her ego. As the water warmed, she slowly thawed, and despite her best attempts to glower at him, not ready to let him off the hook, when he openly laughed at her, she struggled to suppress her smile.

He didn't miss it, reached down to cup a hand under her chin, brushing his thumb over her bottom lip. 'That's better. Don't let this creep beat you, Lila.'

She considered Jack's words, knew he was right.

'I'm still mad at you,' she told him stubbornly, though the anger had gone and her threat sounded unconvincing.

'I know.' He let his hand linger for a moment. 'Get showered and dressed, and I'll make it up to you, I promise.'

Dave was already in the pub when they arrived, his laptop set up on the table and over halfway through a pint, having snagged a table towards the back of the bar. Lila made the introductions then sat down at the table while Jack went to order a round of drinks. He spotted Elliot arriving while he was still at the bar. 'What are you drinking?'

'Umm, just a Coke please.'

Elliot scuttled off to find Lila and Dave while Jack paid for the drinks, grabbed the tray, joining the three of them a couple of minutes later. He handed Elliot his Coke, Dave another pint of bitter and Lila a large glass of Rioja.

'I think you've earned it,' Jack told her when she raised her eyebrows. He glanced at Dave, who was studying Stephanie's tablet. 'So do you think you can get it unlocked?'

'Yeah.' Dave frowned, his face deep in concentration. 'Yeah, I should be able to get in. Give me twenty minutes.'

While he played around with the tablet and his laptop, Lila asked Elliot about his holiday. She seemed distracted as he talked, taking a couple of large sips of her wine, and Jack knew that the attack was still weighing on her mind. He had taken her to

Holkham for a picnic to get her out of the house, but although her mood had lifted, she was still shaken by the events of the previous night.

He caught her free hand under the table and gave it a squeeze as he listened to Elliot talking animatedly about a marathon *Star Wars* viewing and how he had been victorious on the final games night.

'Poker?'

Elliot and Dave both shot him a look.

Jack shrugged. 'What?'

'Give us a little credit.' Elliot sounded insulted. 'Pandemic, Risk, Dungeons & Dragons...'

'You played board games?'

'They're not just board games.'

'So what, do you dress up like wizards and stuff?' When he received a scathing look, Jack held up his hands. 'Hey, I'm only asking.'

He immediately wished he hadn't when Elliot launched into a passionate rant about the world of gaming, the skill and patience involved, and how, as a community, gamers deserved more credit. Jack wasn't mocking him. Gaming had never been his thing and he knew little about it, but he did know that Elliot was a smart kid, even if he did take himself a little too seriously at times. Lila caught his eye, lips curving, and Jack guessed she had heard this all before. At least she was smiling again.

'Okay, you're in.'

'Really?' Jack snatched the tablet from Dave, as Elliot sat back in his chair with a huff, annoyed at the interruption.

Lila reached across the table and squeezed Dave's arm. 'Thanks for doing this, Dave. It means a lot.'

'Yes, thank you.' Jack echoed Lila's words, remembering his manners. He shook Dave's hand. 'What do I owe you?'

'Nothing, don't be silly, you're a friend of Lila's.' Dave gave a toothy grin. 'I'm happy I could help.'

'Can I buy you another pint?'

'Thank you, but I have to head off. I'm on the early shift tomorrow.'

'Okay, well, thank you again. I really appreciate it.'

Jack had hoped Elliot was going to disappear with Dave and give him and Lila some privacy so they could go through Stephanie's tablet together, but he seemed intent on sticking around, waving goodbye to his friend before settling back in his seat. He'd only drunk a third of his Coke, which suggested he was here for the long haul and intended to go back to Lila's flat. Not that there was any need for Elliot to stay over at Lila's. She had already told him she would be going back to Jack's place and the alarm was installed, meaning the place was secure. For some reason Elliot, with his gangly frame and nervy disposition, seemed to believe he added an extra level of protection.

As Lila chatted with her brother, Elliot keen to tell them both more about his week away, Jack zoned out. He was distracted by the tablet and couldn't stop himself from logging into Stephanie's Instagram account, keen to check her private messages.

The Bishop had made contact with her just two days after she had commented on his *Godfather* post, simply asking for her e-mail address. Stephanie had replied, giving it, and there was no further contact between the two of them. Jack clicked on to her e-mail account, grateful that all of her social media accounts were automatically logged in.

He felt a little guilty as he scrolled through her inbox, had to remind himself he wasn't snooping and that he only wanted answers about what had happened to her.

'What exactly is it you're trying to find?'

Elliot's voice broke his concentration and he glanced up, aware Lila's younger brother was staring at him, his brown eyes curious behind his Jarvis Cocker glasses.

'Trying to tie up some loose ends.' Jack kept his tone light. Although Elliot was Lila's brother and had put him in touch with

Dave, he was keen to protect Stephanie and had no intention of letting anyone else find out what had been happening in the weeks leading up to her death.

'It's easier for Jack and his family to deal with everything that needs to be done if they can access her accounts,' Lila told Elliot when his eyes narrowed in suspicion.

Elliot sniffed, appearing to accept that, and Jack shot her a grateful look as the conversation turned back to the holiday. He tried to focus on what he was looking for, skimming past e-mails from Amazon, eBay and a number of clothing stores (how much crap did Steph buy?), statements from her bank and mobile supplier, many of which had come in since she had died. There were a couple of messages from friends. He ignored those, figuring he would come back to them only if it was absolutely necessary. Stephanie might be gone, but he wouldn't infringe on her privacy unless he had to.

He found the e-mail trail with The Bishop easily. Whoever her tormentor was he was keen to keep his identity a secret, his e-mail address giving no clue as to who he was. The first message urged Stephanie to reveal what it was she wanted. She had told him, had been upfront about her fears of failing her A levels, pleading for his help and telling him she could get her hands on the three-grand payment. The Bishop had replied telling her his fees had doubled, that the money he had been asking was no longer worth the risk.

The bastard had been playing her. Steph couldn't get her hands on that kind of money without raising suspicion – hell, she'd asked Jack for over two grand and although he had intended to give it to her, he'd initially questioned the extravagance of what was supposed to be a graduation holiday. The Bishop knew she wouldn't be able to get the money, as did Steph, but it didn't stop her begging. When he'd refused to budge on his fee, she agreed in desperation she would somehow figure a way, and then he had tightened the noose, giving her an impossible twenty-four-hour window.

'You find anything?'

Jack glanced up at Lila's question; saw Elliot was no longer at the table, though half a glass of flat Coke remained.

'She was e-mailing him,' he told her, keeping his voice low, not wanting anyone to overhear the conversation. 'Where's Elliot?'

'Loo.' Lila leant in close, resting her chin on Jack's shoulder as she read the e-mail trail. 'Bastard.' She murmured the word, though her tone had heat. 'He set her up.'

'I know.'

Jack clicked on the next e-mail, read The Bishop's compromise, sickness swirling in his gut. Lila snaked her arm around his waist, and God he needed that connection, as together they read his proposal. The arsehole had known Stephanie would be desperate by that point, was counting on it.

Even though Ruby had told them what had happened, what The Bishop had demanded, it didn't make the words any easier to read. Anger followed the sickness as Jack realised how dark a place his sister had been pushed to.

It was a one-time offer. Stephanie was to meet The Bishop the following night at a car park in Great Yarmouth. Once she had given him what he wanted, he would send her the test answers. If she didn't agree he would expose her. Jack noted the date, realised she was supposed to meet him the night before she died.

There were more e-mails on the morning of her death.

She had gone to the car park, but to Jack's relief had chickened out at the last minute.

That relief was short-lived though as he read three frantic e-mails from his sister, admitting she had panicked when The Bishop had wanted her to get in his car and let him drive her to an undisclosed location. She was begging for a second chance.

It was mid-afternoon before The Bishop replied, his response brief and angry, saying she had blown her opportunity and there were no second chances, and it cut Jack when Steph had e-mailed back immediately promising if he helped her she would do anything he asked.

The Bishop hadn't replied to that and the final e-mail was from Stephanie, her tone desperate, but her words more revealing than the rest of the trail.

I KNOW WHO YOU ARE. *You tried to keep your face hidden under your hood, but I remember you from the French trip, and I haven't forgotten what happened. I know you were angry with me and that's why you're doing this, to get back at me.*

PLEASE, *I need you to give me another chance. I promise I won't bottle it again. My dad can't find out. It will destroy him. One more chance and I will do anything, I mean ANYTHING, you want. I need to pass. PLEASE. You are my only hope.*

'SHE KNEW HIM.' Lila's voice was barely more than a whisper. 'That means we can find out who he is. If something happened between them, people will remember. When did she go to France?'

Jack cast his mind back. He was fairly certain it had been her final year of high school. 'I think it was the summer before last. I remember she was excited because she'd nearly finished school.'

'So we speak with her friends, find out what happened. We're going to figure out who he is, Jack, and I promise we will make him pay for what he's been doing.'

Lila's dark eyes sparked with passion and Jack knew she really believed that, made him want to believe it too. She was right; they were getting closer to finding out The Bishop's identity.

Still, Jack's tone was sober when he spoke. She had skim read the e-mail trail and had missed one important detail.

'Steph said he was wearing a hood, Lila.'

He saw the fear then, knew she had joined the dots and was reliving her attack. 'Oh God, it *was* him. We need to tell the police.'

'Tell them what? That someone tried to blackmail my sister and he might be the same person who attacked you because he was wearing a hood?'

'But Stephanie's e-mail proves–'

'Nothing. At least it proves nothing they can use as evidence. We need something substantial before we can take this to the police. The Bishop has been clever enough to avoid getting caught so far. He's smart and calculating. We need more rope to hang him.'

'I guess we'd better start looking.'

Elliot dropped back down onto his chair, picked up his flat Coke and took a sip. 'Looking for what?'

'Nothing,' Lila told him absently. She was distracted, Jack could see that, and he wished he'd kept his big mouth shut, at least until they were home.

'Listen, Elliot, Jack and I need to get back.'

'Already? But we only got here an hour ago.'

'I know, but I have a headache and I feel crappy. I need to rest. The paramedics said I shouldn't overdo things.'

When Elliot pouted, Jack offered a compromise. 'I'm out tomorrow night. Why don't you come over and you can keep Lila company? You're welcome to stay the night.'

He had Oliver's birthday meal and much as he wanted Lila there with him it was too soon. Henry would have a fit if he brought her along and he couldn't be sure how Oliver or Alyssa would react. There was no way he would put her through that. Instead he figured he would give it a few weeks then arrange a casual lunch with his mother. She was already halfway on board and he knew she was the key to getting the rest of his family to give Lila a chance.

Elliot seemed unimpressed by the offer, frowning at his sister. 'Are you ever going home?'

Not exactly the reaction Jack had counted on. Lila had agreed to stay with him for a few days and, in truth, now her brother was home there was no reason she couldn't return to her flat. Jack didn't want that though. He liked having her around and intended to keep her at his place for as long as possible. Neither of them had broached the subject of her going home and he didn't appreciate Elliot suddenly pushing the question to the forefront, wanting a definite timeframe.

'She's safer with me.'

'What about the new alarm system? Isn't that supposed to keep her safe?'

'She's still safer with me!'

'I can stay with her.'

Jack didn't even bother to dignify Elliot's offer with a response. To his relief, Lila didn't seem in a rush to go home either.

'I'll be home in a few days, okay?' Her tone was non-committal, as she downed the last third of her glass of wine and reached for her crutches. 'You should come over tomorrow night though, Elliot. It would be nice to have the company.'

Elliot shrugged. 'Yeah, maybe, I'll let you know.'

ONCE THEY WERE ALONE in Jack's car, Lila immediately perked up. 'Okay, we need a plan. Do you know any of Stephanie's friends who were on the French trip with her? We can try to get hold of them when we get back.'

Jack gave her a sideways glance as he eased the car out of the parking space. 'Headache gone already?' he asked dryly.

'I'll take some painkillers when we get back to yours. Do you think Ruby would have gone? We can ask her.'

'Jessica's probably the best person to ask.'

'You want to go to Barbie?'

Jack ignored the bitchy dig. 'She was close to Steph and she knows me.'

'Are you going to flirt the information out of her again?'

Lila's tone was light and teasing, but Jack sensed the insecurity bubbling underneath. Jessica was just eighteen, still a kid, but for whatever reason Lila felt threatened by her.

'Actually, I thought I'd fuck her this time.'

'Ha, that's cute, Jack.' Although she smiled, it was weak, and Jack caught hold of her hand, brought it to his lips.

'I'm only going to call her, okay? Trust me, Jessica's the one who will be able to give us answers. I know she went on the trip with Steph and the two of them were close. Whatever this thing was that happened in France, she will know. He's still out there and he might try to hurt you again. We need to figure out who he is, Lila. If Jess can give us answers we need to go to her.'

Lila hesitated, huffed a little, partly he suspected because she hated the idea of him talking to Jessica, but mostly because she knew he was right.

'Okay,' she agreed resignedly. 'Call Jessica.'

3 2

While Jack walked Cooper, Lila sat in the middle of his big bed, having snagged one of the jotter pads and a pen from his writing desk, she made a list, her mind working overtime. Everything was connected somehow, she knew it, but she needed to see it in black and white to figure out how.

By the time Jack returned, the page was full and her iPad had provided some interesting revelations she couldn't wait to share with him.

'What are you doing there?' he asked, kicking off his trainers and sitting on the bed beside her, peering over her shoulder.

'Making a list.'

When Jack slipped his arm around her waist, she leant into him, turned the pad so he could read her notes easier. She went through them point by point.

'So we know something happened with Stephanie around Christmas time, something that distracted her from her studies. Someone was sending her gifts, apologising for what had happened at Christmas, and given that the gifts were hidden away and unopened, we already know they were unwanted.'

'Agreed.'

'But the gifts weren't from The Bishop. She turned to him later when she needed help with her exams. He tried to hide his face from her when they met, but she recognised him, realised they had met a couple of years earlier on a school trip to France, so it's logical to assume he was a teacher at her school.'

'Unless the sister schools were part of the trip.'

Lila nodded, agreed that was possible. 'Maybe. She knew him though regardless, because something had happened between them on that trip, and she was convinced he wouldn't help her because of it.'

'I left a voicemail for Jessica. When she gets back to me, we'll know soon enough.'

Lila hated that she tensed slightly at the mention of the girl's name. Yes, Jessica was just a teenager and yes, Lila knew Jack had no interest in her, other than as a link to finding out who had been tormenting Stephanie. It still stung though the way Jessica had looked down her nose at Lila, how she thought she was better, and that Lila was so irrelevant it was okay to flirt with Jack right under her nose.

It was no excuse for her bitchiness earlier though. Lila realised that and regretted it. She tried her best to chew down on her insecurity that she would never really be good enough for Jack. 'Fingers crossed.'

While he had been out with Cooper, Lila had contacted Ruby – at first by calling then, when the girl hadn't answered, by sending her a text. Jack was certain Jessica held all the answers, but it didn't hurt to cast the net wider. If Jessica came back first then great, but if not, at least they had a backup.

'So that's what we know about Stephanie, but we still have to take into consideration how Shona McNamara's locket ended up with my stuff.'

Jack shot Lila a look and she knew he was so caught up with Stephanie he didn't really want to consider that the two missing girls might somehow be involved. It was a truth though he could no longer avoid.

'I think Shona and Phoebe are both dead, Jack. And somehow they are connected to this, to Stephanie.'

He scowled at her, but didn't protest. Like it or not, this thing was bigger than his sister.

'There's something obvious we've been missing.'

'Which is?'

'Phoebe and Shona came from Lincolnshire, right?'

'And?'

'And it's been under our noses this whole time, Jack.' Lila had been busy while he had been out with Cooper, reading through articles again on the missing girls, but this time she wasn't working blindly and knew exactly what she was looking for. The name of the school they had attended. 'They went to Knight's House School, the sister school of Queen's House and Bishop's House. It's just over the county border in Nottinghamshire, near Newark. Don't you see? That's why we didn't connect it to them before.'

'Shit.'

'Wait, there's more.' She picked up her iPad, already logged into Instagram, showed him the comments under the *Godfather* picture on The Bishop's account.

'Lila. We've seen all this.'

'No, Jack, we were so blinkered by Stephanie we missed it.' She showed him the comment from PrincessPheebs.

I'm going to make him an offer he can't refuse.

PrincessPheebs. Phoebe Kendall. Posted almost two weeks before she disappeared.

Jack shook his head. 'Fuck! How did we miss this?'

'It was buried further up the comments and we didn't see it because we weren't looking for it. Besides, she hasn't gone by her full name, so it was easy to miss. The Bishop, Stephanie, Shona,

Phoebe, the car accident; somehow it's all connected. We just need to figure out how the–'

'Lila Amberson, do you have any idea how much I love you right now?' Jack caught her face between his hands, kissed her hard on the mouth.

Heat crept up her neck as she registered his words. He hadn't meant them, had just said them in the moment. Hadn't he?

As he released her, picked up her iPad again, and scooted up the bed to reread Phoebe's comment, she realised he wasn't even aware of what he'd said and she was annoyed at the stab of disappointment in her gut. They were just words and he had said 'love', not 'in love'. Besides, they had only known each other a couple of weeks. It was too soon and she was being ridiculous, reading too much into everything.

Was *she* in love with Jack?

That was a loaded question.

She studied him, how his brows knitted in concentration as he looked at Phoebe Kendall's Instagram profile, the long sweep of his dark lashes hiding eyes that were a pool of blue. His hair was a mess, his jaw covered in day-old stubble where he hadn't bothered to shave. He was hot-headed, stubborn, at times beyond frustrating, but equally he was passionate, kind and he knew how to make her smile when she was down. That mattered.

Beneath it all though, he was vulnerable and it was that vulnerability that had initially sucked her in, seeing how lost he was trying to mourn his sister, wanting... no, needing, to help him.

Her feelings ran deep, but was she in love with him? Certainly she was in lust. Jack made her feel more than anyone had ever done before and she craved being with him, couldn't stop thinking about him when they were apart. Was that love? Was she in love with him?

If she wasn't, she was well on the way, and that scared her a little, knowing that there were so many obstacles for them to overcome and that he had the power to break her.

He glanced up, caught her watching him, that sexy mouth curving as his eyes locked on hers, not missing a trick. 'See something you like?' he teased.

Lila flushed. How did he do that, have this ability to make her blush so easily? Determined not to let him have the upper hand this time, she gave him a demure smile. 'Maybe.'

Boldly, she crawled up the bed, took the iPad from his hand, never breaking eye contact, and sat it down on the duvet as she settled herself in his lap, wrapped her legs around his waist as best she could, though the cast made it difficult, her left leg pointing out at an awkward angle.

His eyes heated as he raised his hands to touch her, looking surprised when she pushed them away.

'No touching.'

He seemed amused. 'Okay.'

Lila traced her finger around the outline of his mouth before leaning forward to kiss him chastely, sweetly, on the lips. When he reacted to the kiss, she eased away, teasing, and trailed feather-light kisses along his jawline and down to his neck as her hands played in his hair, running her fingers through the length, loving that there was enough to tug on. She clenched a handful in one fist, let her other hand trail down his back, her fingertips slipping beneath his T-shirt as she moved her mouth to his earlobe, sucking and nibbling. Jack caught his breath as she playfully nipped a little harder and he let out a growl, his arms locking around her, catching her by surprise, before he flipped her on her back, pinning her to the bed.

'Hey, I said no touching.'

'I don't care.'

His lips curved an inch above hers before he closed his mouth over her protests, kissing her deeply and possessively, his body melding to hers. Lila gave in, melting beneath him, wrapping her good leg around his waist and her arms around his neck, trying to pull him closer as need took over.

Jack had just slipped his hand up her dress when his mobile rang and his head shot up.

'Leave it,' Lila demanded. Whoever it was could wait.

She guided his mouth back to hers, distracted him with another deep kiss, infuriated when the phone rang again and Jack eased himself off her.

'No, Jack.'

'Two minutes, I promise.'

Hot, horny and frustrated, Lila gave an exaggerated sigh, damning the caller to hell for the interruption.

'Jessica, hi. Thanks for calling me back.'

Great, it would be little miss snooty.

'No, it's fine. I know it's late, but you're not interrupting.'

Jack glanced at Lila, sensibly retreating from the bedroom when she shot him daggers. She listened to his side of the phone call as he asked Jessica about the French trip, wanting to know if anything had happened, if there was someone Stephanie had fallen out with or upset.

There was silence for a few moments and Jack paced on the landing. Jessica continued to speak, Jack interrupting with a few terse one-word questions. He sounded agitated, which had Lila sitting up and paying attention.

Eventually the call ended and he came back into the bedroom, barely giving her a glance as he slipped his feet into his trainers.

'What did she say?'

He didn't answer, but Lila could tell it wasn't good from the scowl on his face. He was shutting her out again. She watched as he skulked back to the bedroom door.

'Jack? Look at me.'

He did as told, but his face was an angry mask. 'What?'

'What did Jessica say?'

He seemed to consider that for a second, the frown

deepening.

'It's Gruger. He was on the trip. Something happened – Jessica isn't sure what because Steph refused to talk about it – but she caught them arguing the next day, said Gruger was furious and screaming at her.'

With that, Jack turned and skulked from the bedroom, leaving Lila to deal with the revelation that the man who had pulled her from the accident was her attacker and also The Bishop, that Gruger was the one who had tried to blackmail Stephanie and that he might very well have killed Shona McNamara and Phoebe Kendall.

She heard Jack on the stairs, clambered from the bed, reaching for her crutches, having a bad feeling about what he was about to do.

'Jack?'

He continued to ignore her and she found him in the kitchen hunting for his car keys, growing angry and frustrated when he couldn't find them. Cooper was attempting to run circles around him, agitated and whining when Jack ignored him, pushing him out of the way.

'Jack, what are you thinking of doing? You can't go over there.'

'Get out of my way, Lila.'

'You can't do this. We have to go to the police!'

He found his keys, scowled at Lila when she blocked his path to the front door.

'Move!'

'Please, sit down for five minutes and talk to me about this. Think about what you're doing.'

'Get out of my way now or God help me, Lila. I will move you.'

Lila didn't doubt him. He was bigger, stronger and raging mad, and he wasn't listening to her. She needed a compromise.

'If you insist on driving out there, I'm coming with you.'

'I don't need you with me. I need you to stay here.'

'It's not your decision to make, Jack. We're in this together. If you're going to confront Gruger, I have a right to be there.'

Lila saw the flicker of hesitation.

'He attacked you, he blackmailed my sister, and it's possible he may have killed two girls. You stay here.' This time, Jack pushed past her and out of the front door.

Lila caught hold of it before it could slam in her face, following him awkwardly on her crutches. 'And what if he tries to hurt you?' The fear was real and suddenly foremost in Lila's mind. Gruger had done some terrible things and he wouldn't want the truth to come out. Jack wasn't thinking straight and that made him vulnerable.

'Get back inside the house, Lila.'

'I don't want to stay here alone. What if he's not at home? What if he comes after me again while you're gone? Please don't leave me here alone, Jack. I'm scared.'

It was a lie. Lila knew she was safe in Jack's house. The only thing that terrified her was the thought of Jack confronting Gruger. She was desperate though.

He hesitated, seeming torn, and she knew then that she had him and that he wouldn't leave her behind. 'Okay. Get in the car before I change my mind.'

LILA TRIED to talk him down during the ride out to Filby, but Jack wasn't having any of it, his mouth drawn in a tight line, his focus solely on getting to Gruger. He hadn't said what he intended to do once he had confronted the man, whether he wanted a confession, to use his fists, or do worse, and Lila knew that was because he hadn't thought that far ahead. Which was why this whole thing was such a bad idea.

She toyed with calling the police, but realised that in her rush to stop Jack, she had left the house without her phone or her bag.

Instead she sat helplessly beside him, watching the road ahead as the car ate up the miles, wondering how her evening could have taken such a terrible turn. Damn it, she was supposed to be having hot sex, not on her way to confront a madman and potential murderer. She prayed that Jack would see sense before he reached the Grugers' house.

HE DIDN'T, pulling into their driveway, already out of the car and hammering on the front door before Lila even had her seat belt off. She reached in the back seat for her crutches, in her haste knocking one on the floor. Knowing she had to get to Jack and that time was of the essence, she would manage with just one.

'Gruger! Open the door. I know you're in there and I know what you did to my sister, what you've been doing to Lila Amberson.'

Jack's rage was met with silence. There were two other cars in the driveway and lights were on in the house upstairs, but no-one came to answer.

He banged his fist on the front door again. 'I know you're in there and I'm not going anywhere until you open the door.'

Lila caught hold of his arm, annoyed when he shook her off. 'Please, Jack. Stop. This is a huge mistake.' She glanced at the lounge window with the curtains drawn, saw the flicker of movement and realised they were being watched. 'Let's go home. Please.'

She wished she had her phone with her so she could call for help. Jack wasn't backing down and things could only end badly. The curtain at the lounge window flickered again before fully opening. Richard Gruger stood behind the glass wearing his pyjamas, and he looked furious. Cowering behind him, Lila spotted Judith in a shapeless white nightgown, clearly petrified.

Jesus, they had been in bed asleep and Jack had woken them.

'Mr Foley?'

Jack paused his assault on the front door, storming up to the window when he realised Gruger was speaking to him. 'Get out here now!'

Gruger didn't move, his tone cool and authoritative. 'Mr Foley, I am going to tell you this politely just once. You are trespassing. Please get off our property.'

'You don't get to call the shots. I know what you did to my sister, you perverted piece of shit. She was seventeen. And you attacked Lila with a metal bar, tried to kill her. What the fuck's wrong with you?'

Gruger didn't respond, simply stared at Jack, his expression grim. Lila noticed Aaron slink into the room, his eyes bug wide as he stood behind his father.

Lila stared from Richard Gruger to Jack, not sure how the standoff was going to end. Her mouth was dry, her palms clammy, her heart almost stopping when Gruger turned his attention to her, eyes narrowing and his expression a sneer of disgust.

'Hey! Don't you dare fucking look at her,' Jack raged, moving to stand in front of Lila so he was mostly blocking her view.

She wanted to look away, but could still see Gruger and she couldn't bring herself to break eye contact with the man who had saved her and then tried to kill her. Her attention was off Jack just long enough to miss him picking up the flowerpot, realising too late his intention as it hurled into the lounge window, smashing the glass.

Judith screamed, the shrill sound piercing the air, and Lila heard swearing and scuffling coming from inside the house.

Oh fuck, Jack. What have you done?

The sound of a rattling chain came from inside the front door. Jack was already striding towards it but stopped as Richard Gruger threw it open, the barrel of a shotgun pointed clean at Jack's chest.

'Jack!' Lila stumbled forward, flinching when the shotgun

swung her way. She caught hold of Jack's hand, trying to pull him back from the danger.

Instead he attempted a step forward, wavered when the gun was aimed again in his direction. 'What are you going to do? Shoot me? Is that what you did to Shona McNamara and Phoebe Kendall?'

Gruger's eyes widened slightly, but he gave nothing away. 'I've called the police, Mr Foley. I suggest you and Miss Amberson stay exactly where you are.' When Jack looked like he might ignore that order, Gruger cocked the shotgun. 'I'm a keen huntsman with a good aim. As a homeowner with a frightened family who have been woken up by intruders in the middle of the night, I have a right to defend my home. I strongly urge you not to test my patience.'

For one terrified moment, Lila worried that Gruger was actually going to shoot them. She knew what he was capable of. Also knew that by showing up at his house this way, Jack had given him the perfect alibi. In the distance, a siren wailed and she let out the breath she hadn't realised she was holding, wanted to cry with relief that he hadn't been lying about calling the police.

'You're going to pay for what you've done.'

Jesus, Jack. Stop goading him.

'It might not be tonight, but I'm going to make sure you pay for what you did to Steph, for what you've been doing to Lila. Do you seriously think you're going to get away with it all?'

'Please, Jack. Stop winding him up.'

'My husband has done nothing wrong.' Judith Gruger's voice was shaky, tears streaming down her face. 'I don't know what's wrong with you people. He saved your life,' she spat at Lila. 'Is this how you repay him?'

'Judith, get back to bed, you too, Aaron. I've got this.'

'But, Dad, I–'

'I said bed, both of you!'

There it was, that cold temper Lila had seen flashes of the first time she had met him after the accident.

What did he plan to do once his wife and son had disappeared upstairs? Shoot both her and Jack, pretend to the police it had been in self-defence? She started to shake, her gut churning when Judith Gruger put her arm around her son and led him away from the door.

'Jack?'

He finally seemed to register she was there, slipping his arm around her and pulling her close. Lila repositioned herself so she was between him and the gun and held on tight, terrified Gruger would put a bullet in Jack's chest if he made a sudden move.

'Back away please, Miss Amberson. I want to see your hands in the air.'

Lila glanced at Gruger, still clinging to Jack.

'I won't ask again.'

'It's okay,' Jack whispered against her ear.

Reluctantly she let go of him, took an unsteady step away.

'Both hands in the air,' Gruger repeated.

'Damn it, she's got a broken leg.'

'I don't care. That crutch could be used as a weapon. Both hands, Miss Amberson.'

Careful to keep her movements slow, Lila set down her crutch on the gravel driveway, raised both hands as she tried to keep her weight on her good leg. She was still shaking badly and tried to control her breathing, not wanting to lose her balance.

'You too, Mr Foley.'

Jack hesitated, a scowl on his face as he reluctantly did as told.

Lila glanced in his direction. He was still worked up, that temper of his simmering away, but it seemed like he was finally working his way down to rational, and she only hoped he wouldn't try anything stupid.

The sirens were getting louder, but they weren't there yet. What was Gruger's plan? Did he intend to shoot them and claim self-defence just before the police arrived?

'What are you going to do to us?'

Gruger looked amused at her question. Lila hadn't wanted to ask, but the words had slipped out, and she hated how shaky her voice sounded.

'Well, Miss Amberson, I guess that depends on you. Your boyfriend here has caused me a considerable amount of trouble tonight. As I said earlier, I would be entirely within my rights to defend my family.'

'Please don't do this.'

Gruger frowned, as he seemed to consider her request.

To her relief, Lila heard engines, the wail of the sirens cutting off as headlights swept up the driveway. Gruger glanced in the direction of the two cars as the policemen jumped out, though kept his shotgun pointed at Lila and Jack.

'Sir, I need you to drop your weapon.'

Gruger glanced in the direction of the policeman making the statement, but made no attempt to lower the gun. 'I don't know what took you so long. Bloody police, it's us taxpayers paying your wages. Seems like we have to do your job for you these days too.' When the man frowned at him, he added, 'Mr Foley here broke my window trying to get into the house and he threatened my family.'

'Sir... Mr Gruger? I need you to lower your weapon and then we will talk.'

Gruger let out a huff, but set the gun down on the floor as asked. 'I'm not the bloody criminal here. I was trying to protect my family.'

'You know these people?' the police officer asked, once the weapon had been safely retrieved.

'Unfortunately yes.' Gruger made a point of making eye contact first with Jack then Lila. The look he gave her chilled her. 'And if I see either one of them on my property again, I won't be waiting for the police to arrive.'

3 3

It was gone four in the morning when Jack was finally released from custody. Lila and Tom were waiting for him at the front desk of the police station, having been there for much of the night, Tom quick to thank the family's solicitor who had arrived within an hour of being called.

Richard Gruger had also been taken in for questioning, but had been released. He wasn't interested in taking matters further, just repeating his request to the police that Jack and Lila stay the hell away from his property, and given that Jack had no prior convictions, the police decided the matter wasn't worth pursuing.

Lila had given a statement, told them everything she knew, and if the constable taking notes was as certain as she was that Richard Gruger was guilty of the things she accused him of, he didn't show it. Still he went over everything thoroughly with her before getting her to read through and sign the statement, telling her in a non-committed tone that it would be looked into.

Tom had been the glue that had held her together, first dropping Imogen off in Filby so she could drive Jack's car back to Burnham and look after Cooper then coming straight to the station, arranging for the solicitor to meet them there. Although she knew he was worried about his brother, he remained clear-headed and supportive as they waited for news, not pushing Lila for too much information, which she appreciated. Stephanie had been his sister too and it was Jack's place, not hers, to tell him everything they had uncovered.

He was so different to Jack, steadier and less reckless, and his calming presence and pragmatic approach to the situation helped soothe her frazzled nerves. She was tired and anxious, the realisation that she had come close to losing Jack, that Gruger could so easily have put a bullet in him, hit home hard, but she managed to hold it together thanks to Tom.

Jack was subdued, though still a little cranky on the ride back to Burnham. His temper had mostly dissipated and he was able to be more rational, Lila guessed he could see how badly he had overreacted.

Tom asked a few questions as he drove, had his head bitten off on a couple of occasions, but much of the journey was spent in silence, and Jack didn't attempt to open up until they were back at his house, sat around the kitchen table, Imogen telling them she'd been ready with the kettle as soon as she'd heard the car pull into the driveway.

As she set mugs of strong tea down before them, slipping into the chair beside her husband, Jack placed his hand over Lila's on the table. It was the first real physical contact he had given her since being arrested, having stood stiffly when she'd tried to hug him after he was brought through from the holding cell. She turned her hand, entwining her fingers with his, grateful that he seemed to be coming back to her.

'So are you going to tell us what this is all about?' Tom asked, his tone patient.

Jack exchanged a glance with Lila, gave her hand a tight squeeze before meeting his brother's questioning gaze. 'This could take a while.'

He laid everything out for them in a chronological order, starting from the car accident and meeting Lila, the locket in her possession, and the first visit to the Gruger house. Tom and Imogen already knew about the attacks on Lila, but they were clueless about everything that had happened with Stephanie in the lead up to the accident and Lila could tell they were shocked as they learnt about the hidden gifts and how Stephanie had been blackmailed after trying to cheat on her A levels.

'Why didn't she come to us? We've always been a close family. We would have supported her.' Tom looked dazed by the revelation Stephanie had tried to cheat.

'She was seventeen, honey,' Imogen reminded him. 'It's not easy being a teenager and sometimes things can manifest themselves into a bigger deal than they actually are. Plus you know the pressure Henry puts those kids under to do well.'

Tom looked at his wife, gave the slightest nod, but Lila could tell he was still reeling.

'Do either of you have any idea who could have sent her the gifts?' she asked gently.

Jack might not know, but it was possible Stephanie had confided in Tom or Imogen.

They shook their heads, though Lila noticed Imogen seemed distracted, toying with her mug as she studied the table and she appeared to wrestle over whether to say something. When she finally looked up, Lila made a point of catching her eye, giving her an imploring look. Stephanie was gone. If Imogen had been keeping secrets for her and they could lead to answers to find out who had been harassing her, they needed to know.

'They were expensive gifts,' Tom mused, having seen the photos on Jack's phone. 'And there's no giveaway on her tablet? No e-mails from a boyfriend?'

'Nothing I can see,' Jack told him, 'but I'll have a more thorough look once I've had some sleep.'

'She came to the house on Boxing Day,' Imogen blurted out.

When Tom and Jack's heads shot in her direction, she reddened, looking downright uncomfortable.

'When?' Tom demanded. It was the first time Lila had seen him look annoyed. 'Why didn't you say anything before?'

Jack, who seemed to have burned out all of his anger on Richard Gruger, was for once the calmer of the two, simply staring at Imogen, waiting for her to elaborate. Her eyes flickered again to meet Lila's, and Lila gave her a brief nod of encouragement.

'You had gone over to see your dad,' Imogen began, seeming unsure where to start.

'That was first thing in the morning. Steph was up that early?'

'I was surprised too when I saw her car pull in the drive.'

'Did she say why she was there?'

'Not at first, she came in, made herself a coffee. I was still clearing up from Christmas Day and she helped me load the dishwasher. We chatted for a bit, but I could tell she was agitated.' She glanced at Jack. 'I think she'd gone to you first wanting to talk. The two of you were always so close. She thought she'd catch you before you and Tiffany headed to London.'

'We ended up driving down Christmas Day night. It's why we didn't go to yours. Bloody Tiff wouldn't wait till morning. If she had I would have still been here when Steph showed up.' Jack looked upset that he had failed his sister again, hadn't been there when she had needed him.

'I asked her what was wrong,' Imogen continued. 'At first she was reluctant to say, but then she got tearful, said she'd been a little drunk on Christmas Day night and she'd made a terrible mistake.'

'She didn't come to yours Christmas Day evening?' Jack demanded.

'No, neither Oliver nor her did,' Tom told him. 'Oliver went over to see Simon and Steph said she wasn't feeling great, so she was going to stay home and have an early night. It was just Mum,

Henry, Alyssa and Giles who came in the end, plus Immy's family of course.'

'Did she say what kind of mistake she'd made?' Lila pressed.

'She'd had a visitor, I know that much, but she refused to say who it was. She said she'd had quite a bit to drink and they were flirting a little.' Imogen's voice trailed off as she looked at Tom and Jack. 'Things got out of hand.'

'What do you mean by that?' Jack's tone was steel.

'She wouldn't tell me exactly what happened, but the way she spoke, I thought it was that ex-boyfriend of hers, Dan, the one who cheated on her last summer. I knew he'd been sniffing around her again and she still liked him, but she was trying to be strong and not give in. I did ask her if it was Dan, but she didn't confirm nor deny it. Just said she'd been drunk and made a mistake. I honestly never thought much more of it. But now...' Imogen stared at her hands. 'Dan's a teenager. He wouldn't have sent her expensive gifts.'

'You're just saying this now?' Tom sounded broken.

'She swore me to secrecy. Made me promise I wouldn't say anything. I thought it was Dan, Tom! If I'd thought for one second it wasn't then of course I would have said something.'

'So if it wasn't Dan then who the hell was it?'

Lila didn't know Stephanie and aside from Jack, Tom and Imogen hadn't known any of the people in her life, so it was impossible for her to answer Tom's question. It didn't stop her thinking, figuring there had to be a way to find out who had visited the family home that night. She recalled the security system Natalie had installed at Nat's Hideaway following a spate of vandalism. The Whitmans were rich and would want to guard their assets. 'Would there be any security camera footage?' Lila asked.

Jack exchanged a look with Tom. 'There's a camera above the front door.'

'I'm not sure how long Henry keeps the footage for though. It's stored online so I can check easily enough.'

'Tom's the tech savvy one in the family. Not quite as geeky as Dave...' Jack explained to Lila. 'But he helped install the cameras.' He nodded at his brother. 'You check the camera footage and I'll go speak with Dan. We need to be certain it wasn't him before we rule him out.'

'Meanwhile, what do we do about Richard Gruger?'

'We can't do anything. The police cautioned me to stay away from him. I've told them everything I know, so we have to trust they will follow it up.' Jack shrugged helplessly. He looked exasperated by the whole situation. 'I lost my temper and I messed up. He knows we're onto him though, so hopefully he won't be stupid enough to try anything else with Lila.'

TOM AND IMOGEN didn't leave until after six in the morning, Tom promising to check out the security footage at the Whitman house, while Imogen looked a little subdued. Lila felt sorry for her, knew it wasn't her fault and she shouldn't blame herself for not taking Stephanie more seriously at the time. Lila made a point of thanking them both for everything they had done, knew they had gone above and beyond for her and Jack.

Sleep came easily as she crawled into bed beside Jack, her eyes closed before her head had even hit the pillow, but it was dream fuelled, with memories of the accident merging with what had happened that night.

Richard Gruger was pulling her from the water, but instead of calling an ambulance, he carried her back to his house. She tried to pull free when she spotted two bodies lying side by side in the driveway in front of the door, but Gruger tightened his grip. As they neared, she realised one was Mark and the other was Stephanie. Their hair and clothes were wet, their faces bloated and carrying a horrible greyish hue.

Gruger had laid them out neatly and Lila could tell they were both dead.

As she continued to stare, Stephanie's eyes shot open and she screamed, the sound piercing through the night air. Gruger put Lila down and went to silence Stephanie, thrown off balance when the girl was suddenly on her feet and running away from him, and he chased her into the house.

When Stephanie reappeared, she was at the lounge window, banging frantically on the glass, warning Lila to leave, her voice loud to begin with, but becoming softer to the point where Lila couldn't even make out what she was saying.

She wanted to get up, leave before Gruger returned, but her limbs weren't working. Seeing him walking through the doorway towards her, she tried frantically to scramble to her feet, but then he had hold of her again, was dragging her towards the house.

She glanced at Mark's body, except he was no longer dead. He stood before her, skin sallow and bloated, eyes dark holes in his head. He held his hand out, a look of panic on his face. 'We have to go.'

Lila fought against Gruger, but his grip was tight.

'Lila, come on. Now!'

She glanced back at Mark, except he was no longer Mark. Jack stood in his place, urging her to run to him. Kicking out at Gruger, she managed to wrench herself free from his grip, tried to run to where Jack was waiting for her.

'I told you never to come back!' Gruger roared behind her as he spotted him.

A shot rang through the air; the bang making Lila jump, and then Jack was on the ground, his body twisted at an awkward angle as blood poured from a wound in his chest.

Lila screamed.

Arms grabbed her again and she fought frantically to free herself, heard a grunt as her fist connected with bone.

'Damn it, Lila, wake up!'

Her eyes sprang open. She was in a dark room, though a thin

trail of sunlight cut through from behind the drawn curtains. Jack was leaning over her as he pinned down her wrists. He looked annoyed, worried, tired and very much alive.

'What the hell were you dreaming about?'

He wasn't dead and he was right there with her. Lila yanked her wrists free from his grip, threw her arms around him, hugging him hard. 'You're not dead.'

'Still alive, though no thanks to you,' he grumbled. 'You just punched me in the face.'

'I dreamt he shot you.' She sucked in a hard breath. 'God, Jack, I thought I'd lost you.'

The anger ebbed from him as he pulled her close, rubbing his hands up and down her back. 'Hey, it's okay. I'm sorry I scared you earlier. It was a dream. I'm right here and I promise you I'm not going anywhere.'

He pressed a kiss to her forehead, kept his arms around her when they finally lay back down. Lila's heartbeat slowed, her breathing becoming more settled, as she drew in his scent, felt the steady rise and fall of his chest.

Jack was there and he was with her, and they had both survived a terrible night.

Still though she couldn't shake the ominous feeling that worse was yet to come.

A aron's heart had been in his mouth as he'd watched his father unlock his precious shotgun from the cabinet. What the hell was he planning to do? Was he really going to shoot Lila and her friend?

Jack, that was his name. Aaron did actually know that, had googled him and knew he was some hotshot author. He'd even downloaded and read one of his books, curious to know more about this man in Lila's life, (the book was okay, he guessed, though nothing special), and although he referred to Jack as Lila's friend, he suspected they were more than that, wasn't sure he particularly liked it. Lila was soft and sweet and pretty, too good for the likes of Jack Foley.

Jack was the half-brother of Stephanie Whitman, who had been in the accident with Lila. It was funny how fate had worked, bringing the pair of them together.

Not of course that someone like Aaron would ever have a shot with Lila. She had to be at least ten years older than him. Probably thought of him as a stupid kid, which is why his friend request on Facebook had gone unaccepted.

His parents didn't think he was old enough to understand

love, but Aaron had been there before. His father had called him stupid and reckless at the time, told him he had been an idiot risking his future over a girl. But then his father would think that way. Richard Gruger carefully plotted every move in his life and everything he did was either for financial or personal gain. Meanwhile Aaron's mother foolishly worshipped the ground he walked on and would do anything, literally anything for her family. Did she realise deep down that she was just a pawn in his father's game?

She had lied to the police.

Jack Foley may have been arrested, but it seemed the police were keen to follow up on the allegations he had been making. Not only had Jack accused Aaron's father of blackmailing Stephanie Whitman and terrorising Lila Amberson, even to the point of attacking her, he had also intimated Richard's involvement with the two missing girls from Lincolnshire.

The accusations were intriguing for Aaron to listen to and it was kind of funny to hear his father bluster in outrage when they questioned him. The man was many things and, true, there were times when his absence from the house couldn't be explained, but to think he had been attacking Lila, trying to kill her, after he had saved her life was ridiculous.

Wasn't it?

Aaron's father was cold and calculating, but he wasn't the type of person to break into someone's house, and he sure as hell wasn't savvy on social media. He didn't even know how Facebook worked, so wouldn't have a clue about setting up a fake account. It was laughable really.

While Aaron didn't believe he had gone after Lila, it did bother him that his father's whereabouts couldn't always be verified, so when the police wanted alibis and Aaron's mother was quick to provide them, anxiety had knotted his gut.

The night of the most recent attack on Lila, Richard hadn't been home with Judith. Aaron clearly remembered that she had arrived back from her club and had spent much of the night worrying where the hell his father was. He had his suspicions, was fairly certain Richard was seeing other women, and knew his mother suspected so too.

So why was she covering for him?

If she got caught, if the police found out that it had just been Aaron and his mother in the house, what would happen? Would she be arrested for lying? Go to prison even?

Aaron couldn't deal with that, was so mad at her for taking the risk. His mother was the one constant in his life and she loved him regardless, and he knew, beyond doubt, that she would do anything for him. He couldn't afford to lose her.

She was repeatedly telling Aaron that he was the most important person to her, so why was she now putting his cheating cruel father first, when he really didn't give two hoots about her?

What if his father really had been up to no good and it was found out Aaron's mother had lied? Aaron stewed on that thought for much of the day, too restless to study, too wound up to play computer games, and he finally concluded he wouldn't settle until he found out what his father was really up to.

It was early evening and his mother had gone to the supermarket, while his father was still at school (allegedly), the only one not to rush out of the building to enjoy a warm Friday evening. Aaron knew this scenario well – hell, he lived it most weeks. His mother would spend time in the kitchen preparing dinner, leaving it in the oven as she waited for his father to arrive home. She would alternate between pacing and sitting at the kitchen table looking confused and dejected, and often she would pour herself a generous vodka and tonic, desperate to numb the disappointment. Eventually she would eat alone, though keep Richard's plated, ready to fuss around him when he eventually returned. Invariably these days he got takeout on the way – Aaron thought, often to spite her – and he would reject the food she offered, instead retiring to his study.

That was where Aaron started, figuring if there were clues about his father, Aaron would find them in there. The room was locked – no surprise – and the key would be with his father, on his key ring. There was a spare though and Aaron knew exactly where his father hid it. Aaron found it on the top wide ledge above the door and let himself into the room.

The place was his father's sanctuary and where he spent most of his time; the cherry-red walls neatly filled with various certificates and photographs, though none there of Aaron or his mother. The large mahogany desk in front of the sash window was showy, its surface shiny and neat with a computer, a leather diary, a pot of pens and the one framed photograph finally acknowledging family. It was a shot of Aaron that had been taken at school and was about three years old. There was nothing in the room though to hint Richard had a wife. This was his room, his private space, and Judith Gruger wasn't welcome, not even to clean.

Aaron had been in the room many times when his parents were out, so was familiar with where to find things. Although he had flicked through the diary before, he still sat down at the desk and studied the pages, this time more carefully. They gave nothing away, recording only school activities and a couple of official dinners and conferences that were coming up.

The desk drawers were almost empty, one containing a handful of business cards, half a packet of mints and a couple of jotter pads. They were unused though. There was only one item in the other drawer; a well-thumbed Ian Rankin novel.

Aaron turned his attention to the filing cabinet, his gaze slipping to the small side table that housed two decanters. He knew one contained whisky, the other brandy, having sampled them before, and decided to have a quick sneaky sip from each decanter before he continued his detective work.

The filing cabinet yielded no surprises. Aaron knew it contained school documents, but did a brisk check through to be sure he hadn't missed anything. He glanced at the wall clock, conscious his mother would be home soon.

He took another cheeky swig from the whisky decanter before giving the office a once over, satisfied nothing looked as though it had been disturbed, and closed then locked the door. He replaced the key, frowning as he debated where else his father's secrets might be hidden.

The warm lick of whisky sizzled in his stomach, making him bolder, as he made his way upstairs to his parents' bedroom. He eased open the door, guilt burning with the whisky. While he was happy to snoop through his father's study, the bedroom was off limits. This was his mother's space too and Aaron had no want or need to invade it.

He found what he was looking for in the bottom drawer of a chest that sat facing the bed. The drawer contained mostly scarves, gloves and woollen hats, the kind of items that weren't needed much at that time of the year. The mobile phone that was hidden inside one of the gloves was a cheap model.

Aaron licked his dry lips, switching it on, waited for the screen to load. There were no calls or text messages and there was only one app downloaded. It was for Facebook.

He clicked on the icon, heartbeat quickening as the phone logged straight into an account. Veronica Crowther.

He knew the name, had heard the police mention it to his father when they were questioning him about Lila Amberson. He glanced at the profile, recognised it for the fake that it was. So it was true, his father had been the one going after Lila.

Did his mother have any idea?

Closing Facebook, Aaron clicked into pictures. There were a dozen images, all appeared to be of Lila and taken from a distance. She had no idea she was being photographed.

He scrolled through the pictures, zoomed in on a couple. She really was very pretty, with her soft dark hair and wide expressive eyes, but she was so down to earth and modest, he knew she would never think of herself that way.

The last picture had him gasping out loud and for a moment, he couldn't actually breathe, his vision swimming as he tried to refocus on the screen, understand what he was seeing.

It couldn't be.

How the hell had he missed this?

He was so caught up in his thoughts he almost didn't hear the front door opening.

His mother was home.

Aaron forced himself to move, closing the drawer and slipping the phone into his pocket.

He got to his feet, annoyed to feel his legs shaking.

He needed to go downstairs to his mother and tell her what he had found, and he needed to do it quickly.

Before his father arrived home.

3 5

It was his youngest brother's twenty-first birthday and Jack knew he should want to help Oliver celebrate, but instead he was dragging his heels, spending time with his dog down by the creek, reluctant to go shower and change, even though he was cutting things tight before he had to leave, because he knew he didn't want Lila to be on her own.

Technically she wasn't on her own. Elliot had eventually agreed to come over and the pair of them were currently fighting over what movie they planned to watch on Jack's huge screen TV. Elliot being there made Jack feel a little easier, though he wasn't quite sure what use the kid would be if Gruger made another attempt to get to Lila. Elliot was company though, the house was fitted with a good alarm system, and hopefully Gruger wouldn't be stupid enough to try anything after the previous night's fiasco.

It had been a mistake driving out to Filby, Jack knew that now; the hot-headed temper that he'd inherited from his dad getting him into trouble not for the first time. And Jack had scared the crap out of Lila, regretted it bitterly; hence his reluctance to leave her alone.

She wasn't Tiff, didn't have her hard exterior where she could just shrug things off. Not that it made her weaker. Lila was one of the strongest people Jack had met. Her weakness was that she cared, maybe too much, and unlike Tiffany, Lila wore her heart on her sleeve. The previous night he had hurt her and scared her, almost gotten her shot. If he hadn't gone off half-cocked and determined to make Gruger pay, she wouldn't have had that nightmare, wouldn't have spent all night down the police station with Tom. It was his fault she'd had barely any sleep and was exhausted.

Christ, Jack. You really are a shit.

Maybe someone like Tiffany was better for him. She was more brittle, didn't bruise so easily. And he didn't carry all this guilt when he fucked up with Tiff. Whenever he lost his temper and did something rash, she would cold shoulder him until he apologised and then they would start over. He had never caused her a sleepless night.

She would take him back in a heartbeat, Jack knew that, had five texts and one voicemail on his phone – none of which he'd replied to – since they'd broken up.

Because you don't love Tiffany.

No, so okay he didn't, but there was no denying she was stunning to look at and they'd had fun together. And it wasn't as though he was in love with Lila. It was far too soon for that. They'd barely known each other any time at all, had been thrown together in unusual circumstances.

The sex was good, he wasn't disputing that… okay, it wasn't just good, it was great, and he liked having her around, spending time with her, to the point he didn't want to leave her, knew she would likely be on his mind for much of the evening.

Because you're falling in love with her.

He wasn't. That was ridiculous. They were still getting to know each other.

Bottom line was, he didn't want to hurt her and, hard as it

would be to end things, maybe walking away would be better for her in the long run.

And then who would look out for her? You're worried about leaving her alone tonight?

True, he was, but maybe he was overreacting. She had Elliot and when she returned to her flat it would be fully alarmed. Jack hadn't skimped on the system, wanted to know that Lila would be safe there the next time she was alone.

So one minute you're worried about leaving her alone in the house, the next you're thinking about leaving her permanently. What the fuck is it you want, Jack? Just yesterday you were planning to introduce her to your mother!

Truth was, he didn't know what he wanted. The previous night had shaken everything up and he had no idea why he was suddenly feeling that way when he had been so certain of what he wanted up until that morning.

'You okay in here?'

Jack glanced up, the look of concern on Lila's face making his heart flip and question everything further. He had never been attracted to anyone like her before and the idea of not having her in his life, in his bed, was so unbearable he wasn't sure he could end it, but he had no right to keep on hurting her.

He finished rubbing Cooper down, got to his feet. 'I'm fine. I need to go shower. I'm gonna be late.'

She didn't say anything, watched him go, and Jack didn't look back at her.

As he went through the motions of getting ready, his mood soured further. He wasn't in the right mind space to be around anyone, knew he wasn't going to be good company at his brother's meal.

'I'm off!' he shouted through to where Lila and Elliot were sat on the sofa, heading straight to the front door. 'I won't be late.'

Elliot raised a hand though didn't look up from the TV screen. Jack was expecting Lila to get up, but she surprised him, remaining on the sofa beside her brother. Instead she nodded, gave him a brief smile.

Had she picked up on what he'd been thinking?

He didn't stop to find out, instead let himself out of the house, soothed by the touch of the early evening sun on his skin, relieved to finally be alone.

AS HE WAS BACKING out of the driveway, the front door opened and Lila appeared. She was holding up a card.

Oliver's card with the New York tickets. Jack had nearly bloody forgotten it.

He pulled on the handbrake, got out of the car. 'Thank you.'

Lila held on to the card for a moment. 'Are you okay, Jack? I mean, really okay?'

'I'm fine.' The words rolled off his tongue, the lie smooth and light. 'I'm going to be late though.'

He distracted her with a brief kiss on the lips, took the card. 'Lock the door, okay?'

Lila nodded again, though stayed where she was, watching him as he drove away.

Jack was late for the meal, but it didn't stop him taking a longer route to the restaurant. He wasn't in the mood for company. He was still conflicted over what to do about Lila, irritated also because he had tried to get hold of Stephanie's ex-boyfriend, Dan, only to find out he was away travelling.

WHEN JACK PULLED into the car park twenty minutes later, Alyssa was waiting outside for him, arms crossed and foot tapping in irritation.

'Jack! You're late. Oliver's going to be here any minute.'

Jack scowled at her, handing over the card. 'Best you stop moaning at me then and go inside.'

He didn't wait for her reply, striding ahead of her into the almost-empty restaurant, heard the clip of her heels as she darted along behind him.

Giles and Simon were the only ones sitting at the large corner table the waiter directed Jack to and Giles glanced up sheepishly as he saw Jack heading towards them. He had been avoiding Jack ever since approaching Lila, and Jack was still fuming about the encounter.

'Not tonight, Jack,' Alyssa warned. 'Tonight is about Oliver. Don't ruin it by causing a scene with Giles. Talk to him afterwards if you have to, but not now, not when Oliver is about to get here.'

It was going to be difficult. Jack wanted to throttle her boyfriend, but she was right, if he said anything before the meal it would get ugly fast. 'It's fine. I'm not going to ruin Oliver's meal.' He nodded a hello to Simon then purposely took a seat on the other end of the table to Giles and gave him a glare. 'He's not off the hook though,' he told his sister, making sure Giles realised what he was talking about. For once the pompous arse stayed quiet. 'Anyway, where are Tom and Immy? I thought everyone else was here.'

'They've got a flat tyre. Immy called just before you got here to say they're running late.' Alyssa opened Oliver's card and glanced over it. 'Jack! You haven't signed this.'

'What?'

'For God's sake, Jack, Olly's going to be here any minute.'

Jack looked at the card. With all the drama of the last twenty-four hours, he had forgotten. Still it was only a stupid card, hardly the end of the world. His sister was getting high-pitched though and he couldn't be dealing with that.

'It's no big deal. I'll sign it now.' He took the card from her, realised he didn't have a pen. 'Have you–?'

'Here!' Alyssa had already pulled one from her handbag, was holding it out to him, a glare on her face. 'Hurry,' she fumed.

'All right!' To piss her off, Jack took a moment to read the other messages. The one in the bottom right corner from Giles caught his eye.

Enjoy New York, old chap. Hope you like our surprise. It's been tough keeping it a secret.

A fist clenched Jack's gut, squeezed hard, as he focussed on the word *secret*, recognising the loopy scrawl.

He tried to remain calm and rational despite the heat of blood rushing to his head as he pulled out his wallet, reached inside for the gift tag he had taken from Stephanie's room. The heavy black ink, the wide loopy S, the over exaggerated hook on the bottom of the T. He was no handwriting expert but didn't need to be to know both the card and tag had been written by the same hand.

'Jack! What the hell are you playing at? And what is that?'

Jack looked past Alyssa to Giles, saw his piggy eyes drop to the tag and caught the moment of recognition as his face drained of colour.

'It was you!'

'Jack! What are you talking about?'

Alyssa was still speaking, but Jack wasn't listening, the blood pounding in his head, rage swirling in his gut. He thought of the gifts in Stephanie's wardrobe, about what she had told Imogen happened on Christmas Day, his focus purely on Giles who was suddenly squirming in his chair.

THE NEXT COUPLE of minutes were a blur as Jack was on his feet, closing the distance between him and Giles. Giles was already protesting his innocence, wildly looking around him and trying to get to his feet, seeming keen to make an escape. He was wedged between the table and the wall though, had barely made it out when Jack's fist connected with his jaw.

As Giles stumbled against the table, red wine spilling and glass smashing, Alyssa was screaming at Jack to stop, hanging onto his arm as he grabbed Giles by the collar then Henry's angry voice was booming across the room and Jack glanced up to see him marching towards the table, accompanied by Jack's mother and Oliver, demanding to know what the hell was going on.

Jack ignored him as he took another swing at Giles, heard a satisfying crack. He would have taken a third shot, but hands had hold of him, were pulling him back.

'Are you crazy?' That was from Giles, who was doing his best to look affronted. 'I think you've broken my nose!'

'What the hell, Jack?' Alyssa hissed. 'I told you to drop the whole Lila thing for tonight. What the fuck's wrong with you?'

'This isn't about Lila,' Jack raged in her face. He tried to pull free from the iron grip his stepfather and Oliver had him in, saw Giles flinch and take a step back. He was cupping his hand over his nose, but Jack could see the blood dripping through his fingers. 'Go ahead and tell her what you did to Stephanie, you fucking creep.'

'What's he talking about?'

'I have no idea.' Giles's eyes were wide with shock and his expression had gone from guilty to outrage, as he clearly decided denial was his best way of getting out of the situation. 'Alyssa, darling, you saw what happened. He attacked me for no reason.'

'Jack, I think you'd better go outside and cool down before you completely ruin Oliver's birthday,' Henry barked. 'I don't know what the hell's gotten into you lately.'

Jack ignored him and snarled at Giles. 'Tell them what the fuck you did! Tell them what happened on Christmas Day. Tell Alyssa why you were sending her sister creepy fucking gifts.'

'Please, Jack. I've no idea what you're talking about. You've got it all wrong.'

'Giles was with me all of Christmas Day,' Alyssa's tone was firm. 'I don't know what you're trying to insinuate, but nothing happened with Steph. You're losing the plot, Jack.'

'Not *all* of Christmas Day.'

Jack heard Tom's voice. He sounded angry. As he joined the group, he gave Giles a look of disgust. 'You left ours early Christmas Day night, had a headache if I remember rightly. You didn't go home though, did you.'

'Of course I did! Where the hell else would I have gone?' Giles was looking a little wild, like a cornered animal, though he clung to denial.

'Ten fifteen, that's the time the front door security camera shows you arriving at the house and Steph letting you in. Of course you thought you'd got rid of the footage. I knew something was up when just Christmas Day was missing in the security archives. Only a few of us have access. I guess you didn't know about the backup. Thank God Henry is so bloody paranoid he keeps everything. Took me a while to find it, but there you are arriving at the house.'

'You went to the house? I thought you had a headache!' That was from Henry. 'Why would you go to the house?'

'You lied to me. You told me you'd gone straight home to bed.'

Giles had gone sickly pale. 'I can explain, Alyssa.'

'I didn't know Henry had installed cameras inside,' Tom continued. 'In fact I probably wouldn't have noticed if you hadn't deleted the footage from the hall camera too. But there it was, with a clear view of the lounge, showing exactly what happened that night. Exactly what you did to my sister.'

Jack's heart thudded. He wanted to be sick. The insinuation of Tom's words was clear, but still he had to hear it from Giles. 'What did you do to her?'

'It was all her. She wanted it.'

'What?'

Giles's eyes widened as Alyssa took a menacing step towards him.

'I didn't mean for it to happen. She was drunk and one thing led to another. I'm telling you, she wanted it!'

'Maybe at first she was flirting a little, and yes, she'd been drinking,' Imogen agreed, moving to stand beside Tom and taking his hand. 'But I saw the footage with Tom. She tried to stop you. What you did to her was definitely not consensual.'

'You raped my sister?' Oliver released his grip on Jack's arm and lunged forward.

Giles whimpered. 'Please, it wasn't like that.'

Jack couldn't listen to it anymore, the lies and the denial. Stephanie was no longer there to defend herself, but they had the truth. It didn't make him feel any better though and if he stayed there he was going to go for Giles again, end up being arrested for the second night running. Jack shook off Henry's hand, aware his stepfather had for once been rendered speechless. Learning that Giles, the favoured son-in-law-to-be, had raped his daughter was going to take a while to properly sink in. Beside Henry, Jack's mother looked broken.

'I can't be here right now,' Jack muttered to Imogen, pushing his way past the startled-looking waiters who seemed to be deciding a little too late what course of action they should take.

OUTSIDE IN THE CAR PARK, Jack sat in his car, head in his hands, and attempted to process everything that had happened. The rage was still there, but it had simmered, leaving him feeling hollow and numb. He had failed Stephanie.

Unable to face returning home, needing instead to be alone for a while, he headed to the coast, parking up about a mile from the house. The temptation was there to stop at an off licence, but alcohol mixed with his current frame of mind probably wouldn't be a good idea. Instead he left his car, hiked down to the beach and sat on the sand, watching the waves crash as they hit the shoreline. How had he missed all of this? Why hadn't Steph told him?

He bitterly reminded himself that she had tried, but he hadn't been there.

In his pocket his phone vibrated. As tempting as it was to ignore it, Jack knew he couldn't. There was too much going on. He glanced at the screen; saw it was Tom.

Police had to pull Alyssa off Giles. She's given him two black eyes to match his broken nose. We're at your place. Where the hell are you?

Jack didn't reply, not ready to talk about what had happened that night.

He spotted another text that must have come through earlier in the evening. It was from Tiffany.

Hey stranger. You've not returned any of my messages. I thought you said we'd stay friends?

The corner of his mouth twisted as he closed the message and slipped his phone back in his pocket. It was something people said when they broke up, but they seldom meant it.

He knew Tiffany well enough to realise that it was an excuse.

Still she lingered on his mind for a while as he continued to watch the waves. It was almost a full moon and there was enough natural light to see the water building before it rolled towards the shore, each wave lapping that little bit closer. In the distance there was a flicker of yellow light from a boat. Jack watched it move slowly across the water. Stephanie had always wanted him to get a boat, said it was a waste living right on top of a harbour if he had nothing to put in it.

He remembered Imogen's words, that Stephanie had stopped by his house on Boxing Day, wanting to talk to him, but he had already left for London. Would it have made any difference if he had been there? Would she have opened up about what had happened?

They were questions he would now never know the answer to, but regardless of what the answer would have been, he still felt guilty. He was her big brother and he was supposed to protect her. He had failed.

His phone rang again, jarring him from his thoughts, and he

pulled it from his pocket, heartbeat quickening when he realised it was Lila. Was she in trouble?

He went to answer, stopped himself when he remembered Tom's text, knew it was okay and she wasn't alone.

THE TEXT that came through from her a couple of minutes later confirmed he was right.

Where are you? Tom told me what happened. Call me. I'm worried. I need to know you're okay. Xx

There it was; he was letting her down again, making her worry unnecessarily.

Jack knew he should call her back, text her at the very least, but he couldn't bring himself to do it. Instead he threw his phone down on the sand, ignoring the stab of guilt each time it rang, knowing he was being a complete jerk treating Lila this way.

He didn't deserve her. She was far too good for him and she should find someone who would treat her better.

WHEN HE EVENTUALLY PICKED UP HIS phone again, he counted five missed calls from her, knew she was going to be going crazy with worry. He could end that worry with one text, but he didn't. Instead he pulled up Tiff's earlier message and on a whim hit call. She answered almost immediately, her voice a little breathless, as if she'd rushed to get the phone, and there was no mistaking that she was happy to hear from him, even if she did try to play it casual.

'Jack, hi. Long time no speak.'

'Hey, Tiff. How are things?'

'Good, really good.'

Jack listened as she chattered away, eager to convince him that their break-up hadn't affected her, wanting him to know her life was great, and keen to remind him of what he had lost. She didn't pause to ask him how he was – typical Tiff – but that was fine. He wasn't in the mood to talk about the crap going on in his life. Certainly had no intention of telling her what had happened that night. It was actually nice to be able to switch off from it for a few minutes. But then her voice cracked and the truth came out in four simple words.

'I miss you, Jack.'

And it was in that exact moment he realised he didn't miss Tiffany. That he had made a terrible mistake calling her. Still, he took the coward's way out and when, after a moment of silence, her tone took on an edge and she questioned why he had nothing to say to that and wanted to know if he missed her too, he lied.

'Of course I do. We have a lot of history and I know that matters. We weren't good for each other though. We wanted different things.'

'But we can change. If we both try a little harder.'

'You know we already did that. It didn't work.'

'So we try again and this time make it work.'

'Tiff, I–'

'Why are you so against this, Jack? Is there someone else?'

There was his get out of jail card. He should have ended it right there and been honest with her, but instead he deflected. 'I thought you were happy. You've just spent five minutes telling me how great everything is. Why do you want to go back?'

'Because I love you. Breaking up was a mistake. I realise that now.'

'I love you too, but… Look, I have to go, okay? You take care of yourself.'

He ended the call before she could say anything else, kicking himself for being foolish enough to tell her he loved her. He did love her, in the way he might love an old friend, but he wasn't in love with her, wondered if he actually ever had been.

When the phone rang again, Tiff's name flashing up on the screen, he let it go to voicemail.

What a mess. He should never have called her.

Lila's face flashed in his mind and it hit him hard, a sucker punch to the gut. He didn't love Tiffany, but he did love Lila, and if it was too soon to be in love with her, he was well on the way. He was a stubborn hot-headed idiot, so busy mourning his sister, he was pushing away the best thing in his life. He thought of Lila back at his house, no doubt crazy with worry wondering where the hell he had disappeared to. Yes she deserved better, but that was on him to prove to her he would be better. Instead there he was, sitting on the beach wallowing in self-pity, and ignoring her calls while leading on his ex-girlfriend.

You're a bloody idiot, Jack.

He was, and he needed to fix it.

36

Lila awoke early on Saturday morning despite having barely slept.

She rolled over, looked at Jack. He was still asleep, lying on his belly, head turned away from her and arms hugging the pillow his face was buried in. She watched him for a few moments, the slow steady rise and fall of his broad shoulders, the scruff of thick light-brown hair.

The previous night she had experienced every emotion, the raw sorrow when Tom and Imogen had shown up at the house, telling her what had happened, aware that the knowledge his sister had been raped would be killing Jack. She could see the toll it had taken on Tom, knew Jack and Stephanie had been closer. He would be suffering. That had been swiftly followed by fear. No-one knew where Jack was. He had already been in a weird mood before he left the house. Distant even. It had unsettled her all evening to the point she had barely been able to concentrate on the movie her and Elliot had watched.

After Jack failed to reply to Tom's text, she had tried calling him, texting him when he didn't answer. By the time he finally arrived home, a full two hours after that first call, she was almost frantic with worry. Jack was impulsive, she knew that, and he had been through so much already. What if the revelations about Stephanie had pushed him over the edge?

Relief was swiftly followed by anger – he was okay. She got that he was hurting, but he was still an arsehole, and though he was being overly affectionate to her, that didn't let him off the hook for what he'd put her through. After Tom and Imogen had left and Elliot had slunk off to bed, sensing the shitstorm that was about to explode, Lila had laid into Jack, all of the fear and worry, that awful foreboding panic that he had done something really stupid, coming out all at once. She rarely lost her temper, but when she did she lost it spectacularly, and it seemed she caught Jack by surprise.

It was short-lived though and once she ran out of steam more guilt had followed for yelling at him after what he had been through. Exhaustion hit next, catching them both. It was a second late night, nearly four, when they'd finally sunk into bed, Jack holding on to Lila as if she was an anchor he barely dared let go of. She had been too tired to read much into it at the time. In the cold light of morning though she couldn't shake the ominous feeling that something was off.

Where exactly had he been? He still hadn't told her.

Leaving him sleeping, she slipped out of bed, reached for her bathrobe and crutches.

SHE FOUND Elliot in the kitchen, unsurprised to see he was already up. Her brother had always been awake at an ungodly hour, that big geeky brain of his too active to stay asleep. He was sat at the table drinking coffee and intently studying his iPad. Lila poured herself a cup and went to join him.

Elliot put down his mug. 'You look like crap.'

Lila's lips twisted. 'Good morning to you too.'

'Is it good?'

Elliot's tone had sobered as he studied Lila and she shrugged.

'Honestly? I don't know.'

'Where's sleeping beauty?'

That had her grinning. 'Still sleeping.'

'Has he told you where he was?'

'Not yet.' Lila sighed. She got it that Elliot was annoyed and she appreciated he was being protective of her, but he had to look at the bigger picture. Jack had been to hell and back. Was it any wonder he had reacted badly?

'I'm heading back to Norwich in a bit. I can take you home if you want.'

'Thanks, but no thanks. Look, Elliot, I know you don't get it, but he wasn't thinking straight last night. I'm not giving up on him.'

Her brother studied her for a moment, his eyes huge behind his thick-rimmed glasses. He gave the ghost of a smile and finished his coffee, nodded at her. 'Okay. You know where I am if you need me.'

AFTER HE HAD GONE, Lila let Cooper outside. It was still early, but already a warm bright morning, the sky a cloudless deep blue, and with the exception of a couple of kids who were loading up a rowing boat further along the shoreline, she had the place to herself. It wouldn't stay that way for long though. Being a Saturday and with the weather so good, tourists would soon arrive, parking up along the edge of the creek, many of them heading down to the beach. She wished she had her camera with her, knew while the place was empty was the best time to get the shots she craved.

As Cooper sniffed at a patch of green, she glanced back at the house. The curtains in Jack's bedroom were still drawn and she didn't expect to see anything of him any time soon. As tempting as it was to crawl back under the covers with him, catch up on some much needed rest, Lila was too antsy, knew that sleep wouldn't come.

Something was off about the previous night and she couldn't figure out what it was.

Although she had been furious, she knew much of Jack's behaviour could be put down to what had happened at the restaurant. She knew how close he had been to Stephanie and that it would be killing him knowing what had happened with Giles, but that didn't explain earlier. Jack had been acting weird with her before he had even left the house and that was bothering her.

She turned to call the dog, saw he had made his way down to the creek and was swimming between the boats.

'Cooper!' She hissed his name quietly, not wanting to disrupt the silence of the morning. When he ignored her, she tottered down to the water's edge. 'Cooper! Come here now!'

She could hardly go wading in after him with her crutches and was debating what to do when a female voice came from behind her.

'Cooper!'

Lila turned to see a woman standing on the muddy bank. Although casually dressed, her blonde haircut looked expensive, as did the emerald-coloured silk scarf that was looped around her neck.

The woman whistled loudly and the dog's head shot up. 'Cooper! Come here now.'

He seemed to recognise her, paddling furiously towards the shore.

'Um, thank you.' Lila stood by in surprise, not really sure what else she could say or how she was supposed to react, assuming the woman was a neighbour of Jack's. She watched as the woman took a step back as Cooper shook himself before she stepped in to catch hold of his collar, rubbing him behind the ears.

She glanced up at Lila. 'You must be Jack's wife? Girlfriend?'

Lila wasn't really either, but it would sound odd to explain their relationship and current living arrangement, so she simply nodded and mumbled, 'Yes. I'm Lila.'

'I'm Hayley, Hayley Baxter, one of Jack's neighbours. Well, I say neighbour, I let the house out mostly these days. I know this young man though.' She smiled at Cooper. 'Our dogs used to play together when I lived around here.'

'It's nice to meet you.'

'Is Jack about? I'm on a fleeting visit, but it would be nice to say hello.'

'He's not actually up yet. I can ask him to come over and see you if you like.'

Hayley smiled. 'No, it's okay. I'm actually heading out. I'll maybe stop by later.'

'I'll let him know.'

Lila made small talk with the woman for a few minutes longer then together with Cooper, made her way back to the house, oblivious that she was being watched.

SHE HAD no idea he was there.

He had watched her down by the creek with the spaniel, saw that she was alone and had been toying with approaching her when the blonde woman had appeared. Irritation had coursed through him as he watched them talk, realised he had missed his opportunity.

When the women eventually parted ways, Lila and the dog headed straight back to the house. He didn't dare go knock on the door, knew Jack was home and wouldn't react well to seeing him.

With the chance to get Lila on her own gone, he ambled back to his car. He had driven up to the coast on a whim, had spent much of the night sitting behind the wheel and watching the house, wondering how the hell he was going to make this work. He should have thought things through and come up with a plan, but he had been impatient. That was always his problem. He often acted without thinking about the consequences. It was how he ended up in trouble.

This time he had to do things right.

AFTER DRYING COOPER – not the easiest of tasks with a broken leg, especially as he kept thwarting her efforts, desperate to get the large bone Jack had previously bought him – Lila filled his food and water bowls, and put on the coffee maker.

The house was quiet aside for the sound of Cooper gnawing at his bone and the drip of the coffee filter and when Jack's phone vibrated on the counter, Lila jumped. She glanced at the offending object as it bounced around, stopping when she saw the name on the screen.

Tiff.

For a moment she didn't think she could breathe, her heart in her mouth, a chill on her skin as she watched the phone ring until it finally cut into voicemail.

Why was Tiff calling Jack?

As she continued to stare at the phone, tried to rationalise the call, telling herself she was overreacting and it was nothing, a text came through, and she could see the opening couple of lines on the screen.

I'm so glad you called last night. I love you and now I know you still love me we're going to...

The screen turned black and Lila released the breath she hadn't realised she was holding. She was going to be sick. Jack had called Tiff the previous night and told her he still loved her. When was he planning on breaking this news to Lila?

Or perhaps he wasn't.

Suddenly it all made sense, why he had been acting weird, where he had been all night. He missed Tiff, wanted his relationship back, and when he had found out the truth about Stephanie, she was the one he had turned to. That knowledge cut like a knife.

Jack didn't have a lock on his phone and part of Lila wanted to open the text, read the rest of the message, but she wasn't sure she could bring herself to do so, scared of what it might say. Not that anything could make her feel any worse than she did at that moment.

She glanced at the phone, knew it was a betrayal to read the message, but damn it, Jack had just betrayed her, declaring his love to his ex-girlfriend before coming home and cosying up to Lila. And like a fool, she had fallen for every word he had said, every promise he had made, been weakened by every kiss, believing that he really was sorry for scaring her. Instead it had all been a lie.

To hell with it. With shaking fingers, she swiped the screen, clicked on the text.

I'm so glad you called last night. I love you and now I know you still love me, we're going to work this out, Jack. I'll come up Sunday and we'll talk, make things right again. I've missed you so much. xoxo

Lila had been wrong when she thought she couldn't feel any worse. The pain went deeper than she thought was possible. Tiff was coming to Norfolk the next day? So Jack must be planning on telling Lila things were over this morning.

For a moment she held on to the counter convinced she was going to be sick.

It crossed her mind that perhaps he wasn't really asleep. Maybe he was lying in bed, trying to figure out the best way to tell her things were over.

Screw him. She wouldn't let him humiliate her like that.

While part of her was tempted to go upstairs and bash him

over the head with one of her crutches, violence wasn't her style. Fuck Jack Foley. If it was over, it would be on her terms.

She didn't dare chance trying to catch a bus, had no idea how frequently they ran from Burnham Overy Staithe on a Saturday. She wanted to be gone before Jack woke and couldn't handle the humiliation of him finding her waiting at a bus stop again, like the first day they had met.

Elliot would drive back and get her, but that would take time. Lila couldn't stay in the house. She needed to be gone.

That only left the option of a cab. She didn't have enough money to get one all the way back to Norwich, but she could probably scrape the money together for the fare to Fakenham or Holt.

She googled the number for a local taxi company and gave them a call, emptying her purse on the counter as they quoted her fares. Holt was out, but she just about had enough to get to Fakenham. She would call Elliot on the way. Ask him to come get her. She booked the cab; relieved when they told her they could be with her in ten minutes.

The clothes and toiletries she had brought with her were upstairs, but she would have to forego them. If she went into the bedroom, she would have to see Jack again and she couldn't deal with that. She grabbed her iPad, irritated when she saw the battery was low, knew she didn't have time to charge it before leaving, and shoved it in her bag along with her purse. She left her phone out on the counter and waited for the taxi driver to call.

EIGHT TORTUROUS MINUTES PASSED, each one feeling longer than the last, as she beat herself up for trusting Jack, for being stupid enough to fall for him. Since Charlie, she had been so careful to guard her heart from being stomped on again. How could she have been so foolish? Damn Jack to hell, she had been halfway in love with him, maybe more than halfway.

She pounced on her phone when it rang, announcing the cab's arrival, dropped it on the counter again when Cooper leapt up, hearing the car outside, and started barking.

'No, Cooper, shush.'

He would wake Jack. She had to go before he came downstairs.

Hitching her bag on her shoulder, she grabbed her crutches and made her way towards the door, letting herself out of the house, guilty that she hadn't had a chance to say goodbye to Cooper properly.

She got in the cab as quickly as she could, didn't spare a glance back at the house until they were pulling away from the driveway. Part of her expected to see Jack standing in the doorway, but the door was still shut and there was no sign of him. Disappointment tinged her relief.

It was better this way, not seeing him. She wondered if maybe she should have written him a note, telling him why she had gone. The last thing she wanted was for him to come after her looking for an explanation. If she had left a note he would know she had seen the text, probably be relieved that he didn't have to dump her.

She kicked herself for not thinking about it before then, decided she would send him a brief text when she got home telling him why she had left and not to contact her.

Alone with her thoughts, knowing that she would never see him again, and that knowledge stinging her to the core, her emotions finally got the better of her. She saw the cabbie glance in the rear-view mirror, her cheeks burning as she willed the tears not to fall. She had been humiliated enough for one morning; there was no way in hell she was going to fall apart in the back of the taxi.

When the driver glanced at her again, she forced a tight smile and looked out of the window.

She had planned to call Elliot during the journey, but the cab was so quiet, the driver preferring silence to a radio, she didn't want to have the conversation in front of him. She would call Elliot when she reached Fakenham. It was a warm day and she could find somewhere outside to sit and wait for him. She could probably do with the fresh air and the time alone to help clear her head and put things into focus... brood about the fact her world had been turned upside down.

She told herself to stop being so dramatic. Things were never going to work with Jack; deep down she had known that. They came from different worlds, had been thrown together by tragedy. The feelings they had for each other had come so fast and hard, it should come as no surprise they would die down just as quickly... for Jack at least. Lila had a feeling she may need a whole lot longer.

She was grateful when the cab pulled into Fakenham town centre, relieved to get away from the prying eyes of the taxi driver. She paid the fare; annoyed her hands were still shaking. It was precious money she could ill afford. Without being able to work, her finances had taken a big hit and she knew her bank account was already empty. Ever since being declared bankrupt, she didn't have the luxury of credit cards or overdrafts and all she had was the seventy-eight pence in her purse.

Much as she hated the idea, she was going to have to talk to her brother and ask for a loan. She knew Elliot would give it to her without hesitation, would insist on it being a gift not a loan, but he was her little brother. She was supposed to look after him, not the other way around.

Finding a circular bench under the shelter of a large tree, Lila sat down to gather her thoughts. She had managed to get away before Jack had awoken. The most difficult part of this was over. Now all she had to do was call her brother and sit tight until he came to pick her up. It wasn't such a hardship. She had a pleasant enough seat and with the Saturday morning shoppers and the guitarist busking a few yards away, it should be easy to keep herself distracted.

She reached into her bag for her phone, eager to call Elliot and get home to her flat. When she was finally home and locked away from everyone, she would give into the emotions she was trying to keep at bay. Jack didn't deserve her tears, but she knew they would fall anyway. God damn him for hurting her like this.

She felt the first lick of fear as she rummaged in her bag, couldn't find her phone. Frustrated, she tipped the contents of her bag out onto the bench: keys, iPad, purse, hairbrush, tissues, a couple of loose tampons (that she quickly shoved back in the bag) and a packet of mint Tic Tacs.

Where the hell was her phone?

Frantically she checked the lining of the bag again, tried to recall her movements as she had left Jack's house. She'd had the phone when the cab arrived, had answered it when the driver called. It had been in her hand, so where the hell was it now?

And then she remembered, heart sinking, as she recalled Cooper barking and how she had tried to shut him up, scared he would wake Jack. She had put her phone down on the counter and hadn't picked it up.

You idiot, Lila. How could you be so stupid?

She forced herself to focus, aware she was currently stranded in a market town more than twenty miles from home with no phone and no money to get home.

Her iPad. Some of the shops were bound to have wifi. She would get a signal and send Elliot a message on Facebook. If he didn't see it she could always message Beth or Natalie.

The relief was short-lived as she picked up her iPad, realised it was out of charge.

Fuck!

What the hell was she going to do?

When panic threatened to take over, she drew a couple of deep breaths and tried to calm down. There would be a solution. She had to think rationally.

She had her cash card. Even though she was pretty sure her account was empty, it was still worth checking. Failing that, maybe her bank had a branch in Fakenham. She could ask around and find out. Surely if she explained her predicament they would let her borrow a phone to call her brother. And if that didn't work, could she go to the police for help? It wasn't an emergency, but she just needed to make one phone call.

Feeling buoyed that she had a plan, she reached for her crutches. As she started to get up, she heard a familiar voice.

'Lila?'

HAYLEY BAXTER STEPPED out of the letting agency, spotting Jack's girlfriend immediately. Even from a distance, with her crutches, one leg plastered, the other wearing a cowboy boot, and her brightly coloured dress she was instantly recognisable, and she looked a little distressed, glancing around as if unsure of where she wanted to go.

Hayley had only met her down at the creek a short while earlier. Lila, she recalled. What was she doing in Fakenham? Hayley was about to go over and ask if the girl was okay, perhaps needed a lift back to Burnham, when someone approached her.

At first Hayley thought he was harassing her. Lila seemed a little agitated, almost looked panicked, but then she saw Lila nod at the man and they started talking. It seemed she was okay after all.

37

Stephanie was firmly on Jack's mind the second he awoke. Surprisingly he had slept heavily and seemingly dream free, but now he was back in the land of the living every unwelcome detail from the previous night resurfaced, from what had happened in the restaurant, the knowledge of what Giles had done to his sister, to his ill-judged phone call to Tiffany, to the way he had treated Lila.

He cranked one eye open, saw the crack of sunlight through the curtain, and glanced at his watch, surprised at the time. He rolled over, found Lila's side of the bed empty. From the coolness of the sheets, she hadn't been there in a while.

The previous night when he had finally pulled his head out of his arse, it had really hit him how much she meant to him, and although he had tried to tell her that when he finally got home from the beach, she had been crazy mad at him. And truth was he couldn't blame her. She had put up with his bullshit, been patient with him, for long enough.

Although she had eventually calmed down, he still needed to fix things, planned to do that regardless of how long it took because he knew she was worth it. What had happened to

Stephanie was beyond awful and Jack knew he still had to deal with that, would probably end up grieving his sister all over again, and he would need Lila's support more than ever, but Steph was gone and this was about making things right with the person he needed the most.

As he showered, he tried to figure out how the hell he was going to do that after everything he had put her through. He thought about his phone call to Tiffany, knew Lila would be beyond hurt when she learnt he had called his ex-girlfriend. But he also knew he owed Lila the truth. She was too important to lie to and hopefully, if he was honest with her, they could move past it.

He expected to find her curled up on the sofa, either asleep or reading her Kindle. He knew she had barely slept the past couple of nights – all his fault – and she had to be exhausted. When he saw she wasn't there, he figured maybe she had let Cooper out, but then the dog sauntered over, bone in mouth, and dropped it in front of Jack, Cooper's tail thumping and a wide grin on his black and white doggy face.

Jack gave him a brief rub on the head before heading through into the kitchen, a tiny knot of anxiety tightening his gut when he saw Lila wasn't in there. The doors were all closed; suggesting she hadn't gone outside, but her iPad wasn't on the kitchen table where it had mostly sat and the oversized patchwork handbag she used wasn't hanging over the edge of the chair where she generally left it.

'Lila?'

Jack waited a beat, called again; his panic raising a notch when there was no answer.

Where the hell was she? Had something happened?

Remembering Elliot had stayed over, Jack went to the kitchen window that looked out on the drive, but saw the kid's car was gone. Had Lila left with him?

Needing to know she was safe, Jack grabbed his phone from

the counter, swiped it open, his heart going into his mouth as he read the text from Tiffany that was on the screen.

Jesus! What the hell had he done?

The message was open and there was no doubting Lila had seen it. Jack knew she was paranoid about Tiff, stupidly worried that she wasn't good enough for him. Seriously, she had no idea how wrong she was. But he couldn't blame her for thinking that way, knew that by acting like a complete twat, he had given her every right to be suspicious.

Somehow he had to make things right. Lila was the best thing that had ever happened to him. He couldn't lose her. Wouldn't.

He dialled her number, willed her to pick up, freezing when he heard the opening bars of her ringtone coming from behind him and the instantly recognisable sound of Dave Grohl. *All my life I've been searching for something, something never comes, never leads to nothing...*

He shot around, saw her phone lit up on the counter, and grabbed it.

So if her mobile was there, where the hell was she?

Ending the call, but keeping her phone in his hand, he walked from room to room looking for her, frustrated when he had searched the whole house and she was nowhere to be seen. Her things were still in his bedroom, but it bothered him that her bag was gone.

He tried to put himself in her shoes. She had been mad as hell at him the previous night and although she had eventually calmed down, finding that text on his phone from Tiff would have likely tipped Lila over the edge. She wasn't in the house, but she had left her phone behind, which made no sense. He opened the French doors, searched the perimeter of the house. There was no sign of her in the garden, on the decking or down by the creek and he couldn't picture her wandering further afield without her phone and especially with a broken leg.

Had something happened to her?

Suddenly fearing the worst, Jack dialled Elliot's number from Lila's phone, waited what seemed like an age for him to answer.

'Hello?'

'Where's Lila?'

There was a long pause. 'Uh, with you?' Elliot answered cautiously, sounding suspicious in case it was a trick question.

'She's not here.'

'Okay, maybe she went out for some air or something. She was pretty mad at you last night.'

'I know. I've looked outside for her and there's no sign of her anywhere.'

'Maybe she went for a walk.'

'She has a broken leg! Her bag's gone, her iPad too I think.'

'But you've got her phone.'

'I'm aware of that. She must have left it behind.'

'So where is she?' There was a mild note of panic in Elliot's voice.

'That's what I'm trying to find out!'

The conversation was going nowhere and Jack was wasting precious time when he could be trying to find Lila. He tried to rein in his frustration. 'I'm going to keep searching for her. Can you please do me a favour and go and check her flat, see if she's there? If you hear anything from her please call me straightaway, okay?'

He slipped his own phone in his pocket, kept Lila's in his hand as he did a more thorough search of the house, knowing she wasn't there, but needing to check for his own peace of mind. She couldn't have gone far outside with her crutches, but he checked anyway, wandering up to the main road then back down to the creek. There were a handful of people about and he pulled up Lila's Facebook profile picture, showed it to them. No-one had seen her.

It occurred to him she might have texted or called someone before disappearing. While snooping wasn't in his nature, at this point he was too concerned for her safety to care. He glanced at her text messages. The most recent message was the one she had sent him the previous night at the beach that he had ignored. He bit down on the stab of guilt as he scrolled past it, opening and reading conversations with her brother and a couple of friends, hoping they would offer up a clue. The conversation trail with Beth where his name was mentioned more than a couple of times (and which he knew Lila would be mortified knowing he had seen) might have actually made him laugh out loud if he weren't so worried about her.

Closing the text messages he pulled up her call log, wincing when he saw all the missed calls to his phone the previous night. It was no wonder she had been mad at him.

Top of the log were an inbound and outbound call, both from that morning and both for the same local number. He called it without hesitation, heartbeat quickening when he realised it was a taxi firm. Had she gone back to Norwich?

'Hi, I need your help. My girlfriend caught a taxi with you this morning and I need to get hold of her urgently. Can you tell me where you dropped her off?' He gave the time of Lila's call, rattled off his address as the pick-up point.

The operator seemed a little hesitant to hand out the information so freely, so Jack lied.

'She was meeting a friend and she left her bag behind. It's got her phone in it and also her insulin. I can't call her to find out where they were meeting and I need to get her medicine to her. This is an emergency.'

That seemed to get the woman onside. She asked him to repeat the address again then put him on hold for a second while she pulled up the records. 'Yes, I have it here. The driver dropped her in Fakenham at nine fifty-five. In the town centre.'

Jack thanked her, ending the call and reaching for his car keys. So Lila had caught a taxi to Fakenham, though he couldn't imagine why. Unless she planned to then get a bus back to

Norwich. He knew she didn't have much money, probably couldn't afford the cab fare all the way home.

He kicked himself again for being stupid enough to call Tiffany, hating that Lila had been that desperate to get away from him. What the hell must have gone through her mind when she had read Tiff's message? After the previous night and this, he wasn't sure she would forgive him, but he had to at least try to explain that the call to Tiff had been one really foolish moment in reaction to a crappy night, that he was not still seeing his ex-girlfriend and had no intention of getting back together with her.

As he was heading for the front door, there was a sharp rap on the French doors at the back of the house. Lila? He went back into the kitchen; frustrated when he saw it wasn't her, but recognising the blonde woman standing the other side of the glass. As he unlocked the door, Cooper was already out of his bed, his tail wagging, as he headed over to greet her.

'Jack? It's been a while. How are you?'

'It's good to see you, Hayley. I didn't know you were back.'

'Just for a flying visit. I head home tomorrow night. I couldn't go though without showing my face. Do you have time for a coffee?'

Much as Jack liked his old neighbour, he really didn't have time. Finding Lila and sorting out the mess he had caused was the only thing that mattered. He had to figure out a way to fix things.

Hayley must have read his expression. 'This isn't a good day, is it? Maybe next time.'

'Do you mind? I'm really sorry, but I'm right in the middle of something.'

'No of course not and do say hello again to Lila for me. She seems like a lovely girl.'

'Lila? You've spoken to Lila?'

If she was surprised by the question, Hayley didn't show it. 'We met down by the boats this morning. Cooper was having a whale of a time, weren't you, mister.' She reached down to affectionately rub him behind the ears.

'I don't suppose she said anything about what her plans were, did she? She was gone when I woke and I can't call her. She forgot her phone.'

'I actually saw her in Fakenham a short while ago. I've just come back from the letting agency.'

'Did you talk to her?'

'I was going to. I was going to see if she needed a lift back. But she was with a young man so I left them to it.'

A young man? Had Elliot lied to him about knowing where Lila was?

'Tall skinny kid with dark hair and glasses?' he questioned.

'Tall and dark, yes, but not skinny and he wasn't wearing glasses. He was only young, maybe eighteen, nineteen, her brother perhaps?'

An ominous feeling settled in Jack's gut. Not her brother and he feared he knew exactly who it was. He reached in his pocket for Lila's phone, logged straight into Facebook and found the person he was looking for in her friend requests. He pulled up Aaron Gruger's profile picture and showed it to Hayley. 'This kid?'

She studied the brooding boy in the photo before nodding. 'Yes, that's him.'

Aaron Gruger had been the last person Lila expected to approach her in Fakenham and she wasn't sure she bought his story that he had been running an errand for his mother. It seemed all too much of a coincidence that he was here and seeming so pleased to run into her. Her cynicism though was tinged with the tiniest bit of relief, not at seeing Aaron, because knowing what his father had done made her downright uncomfortable (and she couldn't help but think of him as guilty by association), but because he was a familiar face and he would have a phone.

Her first reaction had been suspicion and all she wanted was to get away from him. Why was he there and what did he want? She was still jumpy about what had happened at his house and reluctant to be near him, but he had over-apologised, seemed downright mortified his father had pulled the shotgun on her and Jack – even if Jack had vandalised their property, he was quick to point out, which reminded her that they had hardly been innocent, the police arresting Jack, and given that Aaron probably had no idea what his dear old dad had been up to, it was a wonder he wasn't giving Lila a wide berth.

'I did actually want to talk to you about the stuff Jack said that night,' he told her, before his voice dropped to a whisper, bottom lip trembling. 'I was bloody angry at first that he had the nerve to accuse my dad, but then I found something.'

He averted his eyes, looked a little embarrassed, and Lila's heartbeat quickened.

'What do you mean you found something?'

'I don't know if I can say. It's so difficult.' Aaron's voice broke slightly. 'He's my dad, Lila.'

'If it's to do with me or the two missing girls from Lincolnshire, you need to come forward, Aaron.' She found a smile for him, even forced herself to reach out and touch his arm. 'I know he's your dad and you love him, but if you have proof that he did something bad, you need to tell the police.'

He seemed to consider that briefly and it crossed her mind how tough it must be on him. He was just a kid, what, eighteen, and she shouldn't blame him for his father's actions.

'I can show you?'

'Show me?'

'What I found.'

'Where is it?' Lila's stance might have softened, but she had no intention of going anywhere with him.

'Back at the house.' When he saw her alarmed expression, he was quick to try to reassure her. 'My dad's not there, he's away this week at a teaching conference. And my mum will be out.'

'I'm sorry, Aaron. I'm not comfortable going back to your house again.'

'I see.' His gaze dropped to his shoes and he studied them as he shuffled his feet. 'What are you doing here anyway? Is Jack with you?'

Lila's throat thickened at the mention of Jack's name, remembering the text she had found. She swallowed hard, tried not to think about him. 'No, and I'm actually in a bit of a muddle if I'm honest.'

'Really?' Aaron sounded interested.

'I forgot my phone and I've realised I don't have any money on me. I need to get back to Norwich.' Her face burned at that admission. Who in this day and age didn't carry basic resources? 'Any chance I could borrow your phone to call my brother?'

Aaron beamed, looking positively delighted at the idea of being her knight in shining armour. 'Why don't I just give you a lift home?'

'No!' The word came out a little too sharply and seeing his face fall, Lila stumbled over her words. 'I mean that's very kind of you, but I couldn't impose, and Elliot was planning on meeting me up here at some point anyway.'

It was a mishmash of an excuse that sounded like a lie even to Lila's own ears. Aaron regarded her with what looked like suspicion, but didn't call her on it.

'You wouldn't be imposing, but if you'd rather call your brother then yes, you can borrow my phone. It's in my car.'

'Where's your car?'

'About five minutes that way.' He pointed his thumb over his shoulder.

Lila was suspicious again. Who wouldn't have their phone on them? Why was he so eager to get her back to his car? 'I'm not sure I can walk that far with the crutches.'

Was it her imagination or did he look a little irritated at that?

She was feeling edgy about the whole encounter, thinking she should make an excuse to get away from him. After all, she was in a busy town centre. As long as she stayed where there were people she would be safe. But then he surprised her.

'Tell you what. There's a coffee shop over there. I'll buy you a coffee and you can sit and wait here while I run back to the car and get my phone? How's that?'

Her relief was palpable, though tinged with guilt at doubting his motives. 'I'd really appreciate that. Thank you.'

She thought back to what he had said about his father and

that he had found something. Maybe when he returned with the phone, he would sit down with her and she could try to get him to open up, tell her what he had found out about his father.

SHE GRATEFULLY TOOK the latte Aaron bought her, set the cappuccino he had got for himself down on the bench beside her. Sipping at her coffee, she watched him disappear down the street to his car, feeling the hot drink hit her empty belly, reminding her she hadn't eaten. Truth was, after everything with Jack she didn't feel hungry, wasn't sure she could force anything down; though the rumble in her gut suggested it disagreed.

Reaching into her bag, she pulled out her purse, rummaging through the numerous business cards she stored in one of the cardholders, grateful she had kept them. She found Elliot's business card, Research Associate in History of Science, glad her geeky brother had insisted on having cards printed up. Lila couldn't even remember her own mobile number, let alone anyone else's.

She would wait for Aaron to return, call Elliot, and then try to dig to find out what Aaron had uncovered about his father. The day had so far gone from bad to worse, but she was about to turn it around.

Screw Jack Foley. She didn't need him. Tiff was welcome to him.

DESPITE IT STILL BEING MID-MORNING, the sun was already warm and Lila could feel beads of sweat on her forehead, her cheeks burning, and although she had no appetite, she was starting to rue her decision not to eat. The emptiness in the pit of her belly was beginning to make her feel a little sick and her head was pounding, though that didn't surprise her when she thought about how little sleep she'd had in the past forty-eight hours.

She closed her eyes for a few seconds, the sting behind them softening, and hoped Aaron would hurry. She was desperate to get home, where she could hide away in her flat and put the day behind her. The place was secure, so she would feel safe there – thanks to Jack.

She braced herself against the wave of emotion as he popped into her head yet again.

After everything they had gone through together over the past two weeks, how could he do this to her?

Her eyes burned with tears and she pressed the heels of her hands to them, furiously telling herself they had better not fall. She forced herself to focus, aware Aaron would be back any minute and she couldn't have him catching on that she had finished things with Jack. The whole situation was just too uncomfortable.

Feeling steadier, she opened her eyes, thrown when her vision swam before her. As everything came back into focus, she saw the busker was watching her, brow knitted in what looked like concern. Little dots of yellow appeared in her vision and she tried to blink them away, glad she was sitting down. Her limbs were heavy and she was too hot, sweat beading on her forehead.

Maybe she was overtired or perhaps she was coming down with something. Or it could just be the shock of what Jack had done to her after she'd opened herself up to him, trusted him completely.

It scared her feeling like this when she was alone in an unfamiliar place. She wanted her brother to come and get her and take her home.

She closed her eyes again, willed herself to feel okay. She had to call Elliot, but she needed Aaron's phone to do that.

What if she couldn't trust him? What if he didn't come back?

No, she couldn't think like that. Aaron had been good to her. He had bought her a coffee and he was going to help her. Despite what his father had done, she couldn't compare them. He was one of the good guys.

But she wouldn't let him drive her home. Although she believed him and was trying to trust him, she wasn't ready to put that much faith in him.

She wasn't aware she had lurched forward until arms caught her.

Although she managed to force her eyes open, it was an effort and her lids were so heavy. She tried to centre her vision on the face before her, but it swam in and out of focus before she could register who it was.

'Come on, let's get you home.'

Elliot? Had he come to get her?

Someone was lifting her, hands slipping under her arms in support. She started to protest that she didn't have her crutches, but the words came out slurred and as they moved, she found her broken leg was no longer hurting, that although the bulk of her weight was being supported, it didn't cause her any pain to put pressure on it each time she awkwardly lost her footing.

'Hey, is everything okay?'

The voice was unfamiliar. Lila tried to focus on the face, but it was too much effort.

'My sister isn't feeling well. I'm going to get her home.'

'Okay, son, you need a hand?'

'It's fine, my car's just over there, but thank you.'

It was Elliot. Thank God he'd finally come to get her. She relaxed into his body, let him half carry, half drag her, tried to focus on her bed, knowing once she was in it she planned to stay there for the whole weekend, brood over Jack, and shake off whatever this nasty bug was that she had picked up.

The first she was aware she was sitting in a car was when the door slammed shut. Lila realised Elliot no longer had hold of her and that she was sat down. She heard him beside her, realised he was fastening her seat belt. Which was good, because she wasn't sure that she had the strength to do it herself.

What the hell was wrong with her? Did exhaustion, hunger and heartbreak really make you feel this bad or was she seriously sick?

'Elliot?'

'Yes, Lila?'

'Are… we… home?'

'Soon, Lila, soon.'

THERE WAS no sign of Lila in Fakenham town centre. Jack knew that Hayley had seen her over an hour earlier, that Lila could be long gone. What the hell had she been doing there with Aaron Gruger?

Jack pulled out his phone, saw he had a missed call from Elliot and rang him straight back.

'Anything?' he barked, before Elliot could speak.

'I'm in her flat, Jack. She's not here.'

'Fuck!'

'Where is she?'

Jack debated telling him about Aaron Gruger, decided to hell with it. Lila was missing and had last been seen with the kid of the man who had tried to hurt his sister. Elliot had a right to know.

'My neighbour saw her in Fakenham this morning with Richard Gruger's kid.'

'What? He's the bloke who–'

'I know who he is!' Jack calmed his tone. None of this was Elliot's fault. 'I'm here now. I'm going to ask around, see if anyone saw them.'

'And if they haven't?'

The Foo Fighters started playing in Jack's pocket. 'Hold on, there's a call on Lila's phone.'

He reached in his pocket, stared apprehensively at Ruby's name flashing on the screen. What the hell did she want? And then he remembered, Lila had called her about Stephanie's French trip.

'Hello?'

Ruby sounded taken aback to hear a male voice. 'Umm, can I speak to Lila?'

'Ruby, it's Jack. Lila's not here right now.' There was an awkward silence and for a moment, Jack thought she was going to hang up on him. After how he had treated her when they'd met up, he guessed he couldn't blame her. He made an effort to soften his tone, not wanting to scare her off. 'Ruby, are you still there?'

There was another long pause before, to his relief, he heard, 'Yeah.'

'Okay, listen to me. Lila's missing and I'm scared this has something to do with Steph and what we were talking about on Sunday. I know Lila called you about the French trip and we've spoken to Jessica Drummond, she told us about the fight Steph had with one of the teachers on that trip, Mr Gruger. If you know anything about what happened, please, I need you to tell me.'

It was as if there was a huge time delay, the girl taking an age to hear his question and respond. Jack forced himself to keep a grip on his temper; aware losing it would only scare her off.

'I remember that trip,' she said eventually.

'And do you remember the argument?'

'Yeah, I do. But Mr Gruger, he wasn't the problem. He was angry with Stephanie, but he didn't understand that what had happened hadn't been her fault.'

'What do you mean?'

'He blamed Steph for the fight.'

'The fight?'

'Yeah, she punched his son in the face. Gave him a black eye.'

'His son?' Suddenly Jack couldn't breathe.

'His name was Aaron Gruger and he was vile. He hit on Steph and when she rejected him, he turned violent on her, attacked her. That's why she punched him, because she was trying to get away.'

And now Lila was with him.

'Ruby, thank you.' Jack ended the call before she could reply. He'd heard enough. Lila was with the kid who had attacked his sister, who was likely The Bishop. Jack glanced around the town centre. She was no longer there, he was sure of it.

And then he spotted the circular bench under the tree, and the pair of crutches leaning against it.

Lila?

He rushed over, grabbed the crutches, almost willing them to tell him where she was. There was no sign of her anywhere, but Hayley had seen Lila there so the crutches had to be hers. There was no way she would have left without them. Unless she had been taken. It was a busy town centre though. How the hell would anyone manage that? He glanced around again, saw the old bloke busking with the guitar looking in his direction and Jack strode across.

'There was a girl here using those crutches. Did you see her?'

The busker continued singing, glancing at Jack a little suspiciously. Jack pulled up the picture of Lila he had saved to his phone from Facebook and thrust it under the man's nose. He finally stopped strumming, a frown on his face as he studied the picture.

'Did you see her?' Jack repeated, his temper rising. 'I know you're busy here and everything, but she's missing and I'm worried something has happened to her. If you've seen anything, I really need your help.'

The busker met Jack's eyes, took a moment seeming to gauge if he was genuine, and eventually nodded. 'Yeah, I saw her. She was sitting on that bench and she didn't look well. I asked her brother if he needed a hand getting her to the car as she seemed out of it, but he said he had it under control.'

Jack pulled up the screenshot he had grabbed of Aaron. 'This her brother?'

The busker nodded again. 'Yeah, that's him. Seemed a nice young fella.'

Thanking him, Jack threw a fiver in his guitar case. He put his own phone back to his ear. 'Elliot?'

'Yeah?'

'I want you to stay in Lila's flat. Call me immediately if she shows up or you hear anything.'

'Should I call the police?'

'No, whatever you do, don't call the police. After what happened the other night, it will only make things worse. Sit tight and wait for me to get in touch.'

'Okay.' Elliot sounded hesitant. 'What's going on, Jack? Where is she?'

'I think she's at Gruger's house and I'm gonna go get her back.'

It was great to finally be in her bed, lying down.

The toll of everything that had happened must have finally broken her, exhaustion sweeping over her like a mist and pulling her under. Lila had no idea how long she had been out for, was just grateful she was home and safe.

She blinked sharply, her vision still swimming, tried to force herself to focus. Someone was in the bedroom with her.

Elliot?

He had picked her up from Fakenham, brought her home, except she couldn't actually remember calling him.

She had been in his car though, she knew that much. He had half carried her down the street, buckled her seat belt and driven her home. The drive back to Norwich was a blur, but she vaguely recalled him helping her up the stairs and into her flat, putting her on the bed.

Her flat didn't have stairs.

That was odd, because she remembered climbing them. More like being dragged up them, the cast on her leg banging as it hit each step. As if the reminder set it off, her broken leg began to throb.

'Elliot?'

'You're awake.' His voice sounded odd, un-Elliot-like.

'Water… please.'

He got up and came towards the bed, and for a moment, she thought back to the hospital. After the accident he had sat in the chair and watched over her, like now.

A glass pressed against her lips and she tried to move, but her limbs were still so stiff and heavy she could barely raise her head. He tipped the glass and she gratefully gulped at the water, could feel it running down the sides of her mouth and dripping down her neck, but she was so tired and didn't have the energy to try to wipe it away.

She blinked again as her brother took his place back in the chair beside her bed. There was a window behind him and that was odd, as he was sitting to the right of the bed where the wall backed on to her living room. The window was supposed to be on her left.

What had happened to her flat?

'I've been waiting for you to wake up. I thought I'd given you too much.'

Too much what? What the hell was Elliot on about?

And why was he still in her room? She was home now and wanted to be alone so she could brood over Jack.

God, yes, Jack. All the anger came flooding back, the betrayal and how he had hurt her. She hated him with every fibre of her body, even if she couldn't properly feel most of it. But as much as she hated him she still loved him. Damn it, why did it have to hurt so badly? And talking of hurt, why was her leg aching so much?

Her crutches. They had been left behind when Elliot had helped her to the car. Had he gone back for them? There was no way she could manage without them. She attempted to sit up again, this time getting annoyed when her limbs didn't comply. Elliot sat in the chair watching her and she blinked hard, tried again to clear her vision. His face swam before her before slowly coming into focus, and she realised with a start that he wasn't Elliot; that the face staring back at her was Aaron Gruger.

Why was he in her bedroom?

She stared at the window behind him, remembered the stairs they had climbed again, and an icy finger of fear stroked down her back as she realised she wasn't in her bedroom, wasn't in her flat. Where the fuck was she?

If she was with Aaron and she wasn't at home, she had to be in his house.

This time she fought the haziness, struggling to sit up. Her good leg complied, her bad one reminding her it had been punished, but her arms wouldn't move. They were stretched above her, something pulling them down. She wiggled her fingers, her hands, trying to ward off the numbness, realised her wrists were bound together and anchored to something above her head. Panic seared through her as she tried to sit up again, with each passing second, the haze clearing and her current predicament becoming all the more real and all the more frightening.

Why had Aaron brought her here and why had he drugged her and tied her down?

'Aaron? What are you doing?' Lila hated how shaky her voice was. She wanted to sound authoritative, but damn it, she was so scared.

'Good, you're coming back to me.' He sounded pleased. 'I thought I had put too much ketamine in your coffee and you were going to be calling me by your brother's name all afternoon.'

'Please untie me.'

She watched him get up from the chair, stride over to the bed, the mattress dipping as he sat down beside her, and she tried to recoil as he softly stroked her hair.

No-one knew where she was.

That sudden realisation shook through her and for a moment, she thought she was going to be sick.

'You know I'm not going to do that.' His fingers knotted in her hair, pulled tightly holding her head in place. 'You had to start asking questions, had to keep digging.' He leant over her and his breath was hot on her face. It smelt of stale coffee. Lila squeezed her eyes shut. 'I can't let you go, you know too much. But we can have a little fun first.' He tiptoed his fingers of his free hand down between her breasts and over her stomach and she tried unsuccessfully to twist away.

He was going to kill her. Pure fear coursed through her veins and, although she tried to stay calm, not wanting to show him how scared she was, her body betrayed her, trembling violently.

'You know I've liked you since that first time I met you, even if you were too stuck up to accept my friend request on Facebook. You're older than my usual type, but when you connect with someone, I don't think age matters.'

Her brain was still a little fuzzy and her whole body leaden. It would be a struggle to fight Aaron even if she wasn't tied up. How the hell was she going to get out of this? No-one knew she was there. She had run out on Jack, hadn't managed to get hold of Elliot. Had they even noticed yet that she was missing? And she didn't have her phone or her crutches. Even if she could somehow manage to get free, find a way out of the house, how far would she get with a broken leg?

'People will be looking for me.'

Aaron shrugged at that, seeming unconcerned. 'I doubt it. If I remember rightly you were stranded in Fakenham and no-one knew you were there. Tell me, why did you want to call your brother and not Jack? Have you lovebirds fallen out?'

When Lila didn't answer him, tried to turn her head to face the wall, Aaron continued sounding amused. 'You have, haven't you. I knew something was up when I saw you leave his house this morning and get into the taxi.'

Her head shot back. 'You were there?'

Aaron looked pleased with himself. 'Yes, I was there for most of the night, watching and waiting for the right opportunity. I didn't dream you would make it so easy. All I had to do was follow the taxi to Fakenham and wait for the right moment to approach you.'

'You planned this.' It wasn't a question.

'I already told you, Lila, you know too much and you're a loose end that needs dealing with.' Aaron cocked his head, looking thoughtful. 'I am curious though, how did you learn about The Bishop?'

Had Richard Gruger put his son up to this? Were they in on it together?

When she didn't answer his question, he shook his head seeming disappointed. 'Cat got your tongue? Never mind, we have the whole afternoon to ourselves and I'm sure I can make you talk eventually. I can be very persuasive.'

As though to make a point, he ran his hand up the bare flesh of her thigh, let his fingers creep under her dress. Lila flinched and drew up her legs, trying to get away from him, which only seemed to amuse him. Mercifully he removed his hand, got up from the bed and walked over to the window. She gave a testing yank on her wrists, frustrated when she realised just how tightly they were bound and that there was no way she would be able to wiggle her hands free. There was no give in the rope pulling them above her head either and the knots to whatever he had secured her to were firmly out of reach.

Aaron had said they had the afternoon together and while she dreaded what he had planned, it suggested he didn't intend to kill her just yet. Was he waiting for his father to arrive home so they could kill her together?

A terrible thought occurred to her. If they thought she was a loose end, did it mean they were planning to go after Jack also? She had to find a way to warn him.

As she renewed her efforts to free herself, she became aware that Aaron was watching her struggle, a part-smile on his face, and she forced herself to still, refusing to give him what he wanted. Her breathing was heavy from the exertion, her skin slick with sweat, and she saw his gaze drop to her breasts, a hungry look in his eyes as he took a step forward.

She had to distract him.

'What about Jack? Are you going to hurt him?'

'Why, are you concerned for your boyfriend?' When Lila didn't answer, he shook his head. 'Jack isn't a concern. He doesn't know what you do.'

'But I don't know anything else other than your dad is The Bishop. Is this why you're doing this? To protect him?'

'You don't get it, do you. You don't remember what you saw that night?'

'What night?'

'The night of the accident.' Aaron tapped his forehead. 'It's all locked away up here and at some point it's going to find its way out. That's why you're here. It can't happen. That's why I can't let you leave.'

'But your dad saved me. He pulled me from the water.'

Aaron slow clapped. 'Bravo, Dad,' he muttered sarcastically before his tone sobered. 'You really don't remember any of it?'

Lila thought back to the car accident. Her last memory before it happened was realising there was another car heading towards the bridge, and she had been screaming at Mark to slow down. After that it all went blank.

'So you're the one who's been trying to hurt me? You're the one who pushed me in front of the bus, broke into my flat, and attacked me at Veronica Crowther's house?'

Aaron didn't answer her. Instead he remained silent, studying her.

'You demand a lot of answers for someone who, let's face it, isn't really in a position to be demanding anything at the moment. How about you answer some of my questions instead?'

He approached the foot of the bed, sank one knee into the mattress, and grabbed hold of her good foot when she tried to wriggle away from him, yanking off her boot. He threw it across the room, locked one hand around her ankle and used the fingers of his other hand to caress the sole of her foot. Lila struggled to pull herself free, repulsed by his touch, but he tightened his grip.

'How did you connect Shona McNamara and Phoebe Kendall to my dad?'

When Lila didn't answer him, his voice dropped to a menacing whisper. 'Have you been lying to me? Do you really remember more about the night of the accident than you've let on?'

She swallowed hard. 'I don't remember anything.'

Holding her legs in place, keeping his eyes locked on hers, he climbed onto the bed and crawled his way up her body, his moves deliberately slow, and sat down so he was straddling her hips, his weight pushing her into the mattress. He leant forward, placed his hands either side of her head, his face inches from hers.

'Suddenly I'm not sure I believe you.'

'I'm telling you the truth.'

'Are you really, Lila?'

SHE WAS LYING, he was certain of it. He kept his eyes on hers, enjoying how scared she was as he reached down and unfastened the top button of her dress.

'Shona wasn't supposed to be here, you know. Phoebe was meant to come alone so I was really pissed off when they showed up together. The only people who know who I am are my clients and as they are as guilty as I am, I know they won't tell.'

'You're The Bishop?'

Finally the penny had dropped. He gave a humourless laugh, amused by the shock on her face. He had really taken her by surprise with that little revelation.

'Not quite as smart as you thought you were, hey, Detective Lila?'

He undid the second and third buttons, pulled the dress open and spent a moment admiring the pretty lacy pink bra she wore, his dick growing hard. She had stilled beneath him, was watching him warily, and he knew she understood exactly what was going to happen, that there was nothing she could do to stop him. When she trembled, he wasn't sure if it turned him on or pissed him off.

'It had been Phoebe's idea to fuck. She needed help, but couldn't afford my fee, so she offered a compromise. At first I turned her down, but the more I thought about it, the more my dick liked the idea. I picked a weekend when my dad was away and my mum visiting my grandparents. It was a one-time thing. Once the day was over, she would leave with the test answers and our transaction would be complete.'

He hadn't planned to tell Lila everything, but she wasn't going anywhere, would be dead before the night was through. Besides, he was enjoying her reaction. She thought she had it all worked out, but she really didn't have a clue.

'That's a lie! What about Stephanie Whitman? You said Phoebe Kendall was a one-off, but you wouldn't take Stephanie's money. You wanted sex and when she turned you down, you blackmailed her.'

Aaron could still feel Lila trembling, but her dark eyes were challenging, her expression defiant. He had already deviated from the original plan by bringing her to the house, knew it wasn't supposed to happen this way, but when he realised she had to die, he just couldn't help himself and had figured why shouldn't he get to have a little bit of fun first. He didn't appreciate her confrontational tone though, acting like she was calling the shots, and to make a point that he was in charge he slipped his hands inside her dress and cupped her breasts, pleased when her eyes widened and her body went rigid beneath him.

Still she jutted her chin out, glared at him. 'Why was Stephanie different?'

He had to give Lila credit. She knew more than he realised. He thought back to Stephanie Whitman, recalled the moment of satisfaction when she came to him for help. The way she had humiliated him in France had stuck with him and he had long dreamt of getting back at the silly little cow.

'Stephanie and I had history. I didn't want her money.' No, he had wanted to finish what he had tried to start with her in France and he planned to make her beg. 'She needed to be taught a lesson. I had no intention of ever giving her the test answers. I just wanted to have some fun with her, a bit like how we're having now.'

'You got the test answers from your dad?'

He could hear the tremor in Lila's voice, understood she was trying to distract him and keep him talking. He would go along with it as there would be plenty of time to fuck her later.

'He's not supposed to keep the answers at home, but he's such an arrogant bastard and doesn't believe the rules apply to him. He thinks he's so smart, keeping his office door locked, but I know where he hides the key. At first, I helped out a couple of friends, but I needed to raise funds and it's amazing how much people will pay to get a head start in life. My dad thinks I'm off to college, but I have other plans, and top of the agenda is getting the fuck out of this place. I still can't believe they made me move here, all because some prissy little stuck up cow back home said I raped her. From how I remember it she had been pretty much up for it until I stuck my hand in her knickers.'

He smirked at Lila, lying incredibly still beneath him and listening to every word. He couldn't decide if it was because she was so engrossed by what he was telling her or was too terrified to move in case he reacted to it.

'My parents ended up paying her parents, promised to move away if they didn't involve the police. I can't believe she convinced them I tried to strangle her too. Okay, so I might have had my hands around her throat, but there was nothing sinister about it. Jesus, we were just sixteen and shagging, and she seemed to like it at the time. Dirty little whore is top of my list of people to visit as soon as I get out of here. Maybe I should finish what I started with her, what do you think?'

Lila didn't react. She reminded him of a rabbit caught in headlights and looked almost too frightened to breathe. Aaron gave her nipples a hard pinch through the bra, pleased when she let out a whimper and strained against the rope. He knew she was trying hard to be brave so he was delighted when a single tear escaped and rolled down her cheek, and he made a point of wiping it away, wanting her to know he had noticed it.

Claire Fox was the girl responsible for his move to this hell-hole. He had loved her once, admittedly from afar, and her name and her face were still engraved in his memory. Though he looked forward to the day he could finally punish her for what she had done to him, for how she had ruined his life.

His parents had told him the move to Filby was to protect him, to avoid involving the police. The Foxes were a poor family and it had been easy to pay them off. As far as Aaron was concerned, they shouldn't have received a penny.

He forced his mind off the subject; annoyed it was winding him up again.

'I'm going travelling. Mum doesn't know yet and I have to find a way to tell her. She's an idiot because she dotes on my dad, even though he's cheating on her... I'm pretty sure it's with one of my teachers. My dad's a vicious bastard and likes to put Mum down, make her feel like shit. Her and me, we've always stuck together.'

For a moment, Aaron was lost in thoughts of his mum and everything she had done for him. Not telling her he was going felt like a betrayal. He just had to find the right moment and the right words. Hoped she would understand.

'What did you do to Phoebe and Shona?' Lila's voice drew him back.

He gave her a measured look. 'You really want to know, given your current situation?'

She hesitated briefly, but then gave a nod.

'It was an accident.'

He could tell by the look on her face that Lila wasn't expecting that response.

'We left Shona watching TV. At first I thought my luck was in and she was up for a threesome, but no, turns out she was there for support, which was a shame, as I actually preferred her. I took Phoebe down to the games room in the basement.'

Aaron glanced down at Lila, made sure she was paying attention.

'We start getting all hot and heavy and turns out she likes it a little rough like Claire did. One thing led to another and I guess I must have squeezed my hands around her neck a little too hard, because she was on the floor and she wasn't moving. Shona came into the room, I suppose she heard Phoebe screaming – in enjoyment you understand – and anyway, Shona freaks out when she sees her lying on the floor and I panicked. It wasn't my fault, you see. You girls, you like to lead us on. You're just as bad, Lila, with your short skirts and your prick-teasing boots.'

'What?'

He saw the panic in her eyes and fed on it.

'You think I didn't notice? You're no different to the rest. I saw the way you looked at me that first time you came to the house, I sent you a friend request on Facebook, thought we would connect, but oh no, you ignored that, left it sitting there, didn't even bother responding to that nice message I sent you, and then you had the nerve to come back here with *him*. What was that all about? Were you trying to rub my nose in it that you were with someone else?' Aaron could feel the rage burning inside of him at the injustice of it all. 'You're just as big a fucking whore as the rest of them.'

THE SMART THING TO do would probably have been to call the police, but given what had happened at the Gruger house a couple of nights earlier, Jack didn't believe they would take him seriously. He had no proof that Aaron Gruger had kidnapped Lila and taken her back to his house – okay, he had a couple of witnesses who had seen them together in Fakenham, but both had said nothing sinister seemed to be going on and unfortunately, from the facts he had been able to gather, that Aaron had attacked Stephanie in France, that Lila had appeared unwell when he escorted her back to his car, the police probably wouldn't worry too much. While Jack didn't doubt they would check up on it, he didn't think it would be a priority.

Mad as she was at him, he could not imagine any possible scenario where Lila would willingly get in Aaron Gruger's car and it bothered the hell out of Jack that Gruger had been almost carrying her. The busker said she had looked sick, was staggering and being supported by him, and he had been pretending to be her brother; add that to the list of reasons Jack should be concerned. No, he couldn't wait for the police, knew it was a risk going back to Gruger's house, but also that he would never forgive himself if anything happened to Lila. If she was trapped in the house, Jack intended to get her out safely by whatever means necessary. He would deal with any consequences later.

There was one car in the driveway and while his immediate reaction was to hammer on the front door again, he held back. That plan hadn't worked out so well last time. Besides, if Lila was in the house and being held against her will, Jack didn't want to give Gruger the upper hand. Instead he discreetly made his way around the perimeter of the property, checking the ground floor doors and windows. All were secure until he reached the back of the house and found the kitchen door unlocked. He hesitated briefly before pushing it open and stepping into the house.

The kitchen was pristine, the surfaces spotless and shiny and empty of clutter, as though it was a show home. What kind of insane high standards did this freakish family aspire to? As he considered the question, his apprehension levels rising as he worried exactly what kind of trouble Lila might be in, a scream reverberated through the house that chilled him.

No longer thinking, he raced out of the kitchen into the hallway, headed for the stairs.

THE MASK finally slipped and in that moment, Lila knew true fear, realised there was no way to rationalise with a monster. Aaron had seemed crazy enough explaining his version of events to her, from the encounter with Claire to what he had done to Phoebe and Shona. Although he had scared Lila, there was part of him that had still seemed human, at moments almost remorseful, which gave her hope that she might be able to reason with him. She had tried to keep him talking, even though the words pouring from his mouth both repulsed and frightened the crap out of her, knowing that unless she could get through to him, he was going to kill her.

She didn't want to think about how he intended to do it, just as she refused to consider what he planned to do to her before he killed her. It was difficult to keep a blank mind, but she knew she couldn't show him any fear, silently cursed when one of the tears she had been fighting to hold back escaped and he noticed it. His touch had been almost tender as he wiped it away, for a moment giving her real hope that maybe she could get through to him, but then the shutters went down, his dark eyes filling with rage, and that was when she knew she was really in trouble.

She screamed when he ripped her dress open to the waist, the sound muffled when he covered her mouth with his, and she squirmed beneath him, trying to fight him off as his tongue slid against hers. As one hand tugged hard on her hair, the other disappeared lower, was suddenly yanking at her knickers.

Lila bucked beneath him, biting down hard on his tongue. He yelped in pain, rolled off her and she managed to pull her good leg free, kicking out and catching him hard with her heel. She heard the snap of bone, for one hopeful moment thought she had hurt him, but then he was back on top of her and he was mad as hell.

'Fucking prick-teasing whore.'

His fist came from nowhere, slamming hard into the side of her face and sucking the breath out of her. For a moment she couldn't see, wasn't sure what had happened, but then came the pain, causing her to cry out, and she tasted blood. She pulled at her wrists as he slipped his hands inside her dress again, begging him to stop.

'Get your fucking hands off her!'

Lila recognised Jack's voice, but took a moment to register he was actually in the room. One moment Aaron's weight was pinning her to the bed, the next he was on the floor, and when she tried to lift her head, Jack was on top of him, holding him down as he repeatedly punched him in the face. She blinked hard, barely daring to believe he was there, screamed out his name when Aaron, who had been stunned by the ambush, managed to recover, getting in a punch of his own and catching Jack off guard. As the pair of them rolled on the floor, she strained on the rope, terrified Aaron would gain the momentum and hurt Jack, desperate to help. But then Aaron went still, his face a bloody puffy mess, and Jack was beside her. He had a cut above his eye, but it was superficial and Lila choked back a sob as he gently stroked her swollen cheek.

'Hey, it's okay. You're okay.'

As he worked at the knots binding her wrists, he kept his eyes on hers, told her she was safe and kept repeating that he was sorry, and when she was finally free, she forgot how pissed off she was with him, flinging her arms around him and holding on tight. In her peripheral vision she saw the shadow, realised to her horror that Aaron was on his feet, saw the glint of something silver.

'Jack!'

Lila pulled him towards her, rolling back onto the bed and ducking to the side just as the knife slashed past Jack's shoulder, missing by an inch, and slicing into the duvet. Jack reacted quickly, catching hold of Aaron's arm, trying to make him drop the weapon. As he forced Aaron to his knees, punched him hard in the gut, the knife finally clattered from his fingers.

Lila reached for it, as Jack prepared to take another swing. A foot stepped on the knife barely a second before she heard a thump and, glancing up the leg of the newcomer who had joined them, she saw red on the golf club.

Jack was on the floor, lying face down, blood seeping from the wound in the back of his head. And that was when Lila really screamed.

'Aaron! What the hell's going on?'

Judith Gruger shook her head at her son in disbelief at the scene before her.

His face was a mess, thanks to Jack Foley, and she didn't doubt he had received the beating because he had attacked Lila Amberson. The girl was on the floor and screaming over her boyfriend's body, her dress ripped open down the front, exposing her bra. When she glanced up, Judith could see where Lila's mouth was cut, her cheek raw, red and swollen, and her eyes puffy from crying.

'What the hell have you done?' she demanded, cradling Jack's head. He wasn't moving and Judith wasn't sure if he was dead. She hadn't intended to swing the golf club so hard, had reacted in fury when she saw her son being attacked.

'You're in my house, Miss Amberson. My husband warned you to stay away.'

'I'm in your house because your son drugged me and brought me here. He was going to rape me, threatened to kill me. He's a fucking psycho.'

The words cut deep, had Judith's hackles rising. How dare the girl speak about Aaron like that? Still, it didn't stop her from being mad at her son. He had promised her he wouldn't do anything and she had trusted him. If she hadn't arrived home early, what would have happened? It didn't bear thinking about.

'Aaron! Look at me.'

Her sharp tone had his head swinging in her direction and her heart almost broke as she looked at what they had done to him.

'I'm sorry, Mum. I was just trying to help.'

'This isn't helping! I told you I would take care of everything.'

And she would. That was her job, to protect her family, to make sure nothing and no-one could hurt them. Aaron had just made that job ten times more difficult though.

Lila must have caught on to what she had said because her expression suddenly changed from angry to wary.

'I need to get Jack to a hospital,' she urged. 'Please can I use your phone to call an ambulance?'

'I don't think that will be necessary.'

The wariness turned to fear and then, as they locked eyes, to understanding, and Judith realised Lila had spotted her dark grey running top, had recognised the hood. 'It was you.' She sounded a little breathless, like she didn't quite believe it. 'You were in my flat. You've been trying to kill me.'

'You've proven very difficult to get rid of, Miss Amberson.'

It should have been a simple job, slipping into the hospital room and giving her a quick injection, but the girl's brother had walked in and had almost caught her. Luckily he was known for having an overactive imagination and no-one had really believed what he thought he saw. Judith had waited in fear until Lila had awoken, not daring to make another attempt at the hospital, especially with the brother standing guard, and had been filled with relief when it seemed the girl couldn't remember anything from the night of the accident. Judith had read up on it though, knew the memories were likely to come back eventually.

After Judith had pushed her in the path of the bus, had been pursued by Jack Foley, she had realised she was going to have to dig deeper, be more creative. While an accident raised little suspicion, she was aware Lila's memories could return at any time, that the most important thing was getting rid of her before she did remember, regardless of the method.

After her break-in attempt misfired, she had concocted the ruse to lure Lila to the Crowther residence. Judith didn't know Veronica personally, but they both followed a couple of the same pages on Facebook and Veronica was one of those types who liked to over share every aspect of her life. Her profile was open to view, her address easy to find, and she was forever tagging herself at different locations, shared hundreds of photos.

When Judith realised Veronica was on a dream trip to Australia, it had been easy to set up a fake profile. The plan had been so simple, to attack Lila and knock her unconscious, bundle her into the back of the van Judith had hired, drive her to a remote location and finish the job. Veronica's stupid brother had ruined everything though by showing up. All Judith had needed was five more minutes and she would have had Lila secured and been on her way.

Killing wasn't something Judith enjoyed doing, but thanks to her son's inclinations, she had been left with little choice. She had actually cried after she had suffocated Shona McNamara. The girl had been locked in the basement for five days and she was aware that she had to do something about her before Richard arrived home from his business trip. Shona couldn't be in the house when he returned. If he caught on that Aaron had attacked another girl, this time killed her, he would be straight on the phone to the police.

He already held it against Judith that they had bailed Aaron out once before. It was the dirty secret that had pretty much torn them apart, though still kept them together. Claire Fox had been asking for it. Judith believed her son when he told her. And her parents were so money hungry they were prepared to turn a blind eye if the offer was right. Judith had made sure it was. She hadn't gone to all that trouble for Aaron to screw it up now. Phoebe was dead and if Shona walked out of the house alive, her son would go to prison for what had essentially been an accident.

But now she had an even bigger problem on her hands, with not just Lila, but Jack to get rid of too. She couldn't let either of them go, but Jack was a well-known writer and came from a wealthy family who would ask a lot of questions if anything happened to him. She needed time to figure out what the hell to do with the pair and also had to somehow get the bloodstain from the wound in Jack's head out of Aaron's bedroom carpet.

When Aaron had found the photos and the fake Facebook profile on her disposable phone, realised what she had been up to, he had confronted her, and she had broken down and confessed, explained to him why Lila had to die and that she was doing it to protect him. He had insisted on helping her, even though she said she would take care of the situation, had begged her to let him be the one to snatch Lila.

Judith wasn't stupid and knew his intentions and what he wanted to do to the girl, had explicitly told him no, but he had gone against her wishes anyway and by doing so he had made things far more complicated.

How the hell was she going to fix this?

'YOU HAVE to let us go. Jack told people he was coming here looking for me. If we don't show up they will call the police.' Lila didn't know if Jack had told anyone, but it was the only threat she had.

Judith wavered for a moment, but after everything that had happened, Lila knew her letting them walk out of the house alive would not be an option. Still she continued to plead, even as she watched Judith take charge of the situation, shocked how the woman she had perceived as meek and fragile transformed before her eyes. There was a hardness about her that Lila hadn't seen before and, from the things she said to Aaron, it was clear she would do anything to protect him.

Jack was unconscious and Lila wasn't sure if he was even breathing. The pool of blood from the wound in his head, that had soaked her hands and her dress, scared the hell out of her. He had come after her, had tried to save her life, and she couldn't lose him. She needed to find something to bandage the wound, stem the blood flow, and she glanced around the room, spotting a football scarf hanging over the back of the chair at the computer desk. It wasn't perfect, but it would do. Easing Jack's head off her lap, she reached for the scarf, startled when Judith grabbed hold of her, jerking her back, easily overpowering her as she pinned her face down on the floor.

'What are you doing?' Lila pleaded. 'He's bleeding everywhere. I need to stop it!'

As she struggled to get free, Aaron threw his mother the rope that was on the bed, and Judith retied Lila's hands behind her back. The strength of the woman scared her; made her realise that the frightened little bird act was just for show.

And then she was being pulled away from Jack, crying out in agony, as Judith grabbed a handful of her hair and dragged her out of the bedroom, down the stairs, and along the hallway to a closed door. Judith loosened her grip briefly to open it then pushed Lila into the room and down another set of steps.

She left Lila on the floor, disappearing back up the stairs and turning off the light before shutting and locking the door.

What were they going to do with Jack?

Lila screamed out for Judith to come back, to please let them go, but no-one answered her, and eventually her voice became hoarse from yelling. The house was remote and no-one was going to hear her. She needed to save her energy. Still it terrified her what might be happening upstairs. Was Jack already dead?

And if he was unconscious, did Judith plan to kill him before he woke, knowing he would be harder for her to subdue?

Lila glanced around the room, her eyes gradually adjusting to the darkness. Aaron had called the basement a games room, and true it had a pool table and what looked like a darts board on the wall, and there was a wide sofa scattered with cushions on the far side of the room, but essentially it was no more than a cellar with a stone floor and brick walls. Shona McNamara had spent five days locked in this room and Lila knew the young girl would have experienced the same terror she was going through.

When Jack had shown up, she had been convinced the nightmare was over. If anything it had gotten worse. As she sat in the darkness, unable to stop thinking about what Judith had planned for her, she heard the sound of the door unlocking again, peered up as light spilt on to the room, seeing Judith and Aaron coming down the stairs. They were moving slowly, struggling between them to carry something, and as they neared the bottom step, Lila realised it was Jack.

Was he alive?

She pleaded with Judith again, begged her to listen to reason, but the woman ignored her, heading straight back for the stairs the moment they had put Jack on the ground. Aaron glanced down at her, managed a grin though it looked almost grotesque with his puffy face.

'I'll pop back later and see how you're doing,' he told her suggestively.

'Aaron!'

He glanced sheepishly at his mother, quickly followed her back up the stairs. Lila heard the door slam and lock, was again in darkness.

She shuffled her way over to where Jack was and twisted around so her back was facing him and she could touch him. He was motionless and his skin was cool, but not dead cold. That said; Lila had no idea how long it took for rigor mortis to set in.

She reached for his hands, realised they were pulled behind his back and bound the same as hers. She couldn't feel past the rope for a pulse, but guessed Judith wouldn't have tied him up unless he was alive. Still, Lila felt along his body and up to his neck, needing to be sure he was still with her, breathing out a sigh of relief when her fingers picked up on the faintest beat.

'Jack? Can you hear me?'

There was no reaction and she suspected his head injury was serious, knew he had to have it looked at soon.

Was his phone in his pocket?

She checked, each movement taking such a ridiculously long time, frustrated when she found both pockets empty. Of course Judith would have removed his phone. The woman was not stupid.

All this time Lila had been convinced Richard Gruger had been her tormentor. Of course it had made no sense. He had pulled her from Filby Broad. Why would he save her life and then try to kill her? Lila didn't particularly like the man, but it seemed she had him wrong and he had played no part in Shona and Phoebe's deaths, and she suspected he had no idea what kind of monster Aaron truly was or the lengths Judith would go to in order to protect their son.

How had Stephanie been caught up in this mess too? Lila knew she had gone to see The Bishop on the night of the accident. Had she actually met up with Aaron and maybe seen something that had made her flee the house? Or had it all been a coincidence?

Feeling tired and defeated, Lila lay down next to Jack, tried to draw comfort from nestling against his body, and gave into the wave of exhaustion that swept over her.

W hen she eventually awoke, it took her a second to realise where she was, why she couldn't move and could barely see, but then the terror and the helplessness all came flooding back, remembering how Aaron had kidnapped her, that Jack had tried to rescue her, but been badly injured, and that they were both going to die.

She had no idea how long she had been asleep for, the dark basement giving away no clues, but her head was heavy, suggesting it had been a while. Of course though the heaviness could be down to the drug Aaron had given her. If she had been out for hours, he and Judith would be coming for them soon.

Needing to do something, unable to bear waiting to die, knowing that she was Jack's only hope for survival, Lila glanced around the room as her eyes adjusted, looking for some kind of weapon or even something she could use to cut through the rope around her wrists. It seemed the room really did only consist of the pool table and dartboard. Cues and balls wouldn't help her, not unless she could get her hands free, but a dart was sharp. Although it was dark, she thought she could make out a couple stuck in the board, but even if she was right, she knew with her hands bound behind her and a broken leg that there was no way in hell she could reach them.

She glanced at the pool cues again, balancing against the table. Could she use one to knock a dart to the floor? It was a long shot, but it beat waiting around to die, and she had to try something.

Getting hold of the pool cue was the easy bit, shuffling over to where the dartboard was, while painful and slow going, was doable, but trying to balance the cue behind her the way her wrists were tied, her hands still slippery with Jack's blood, was almost impossible and she repeatedly dropped it, each time finding it harder to get it in position again. The effort was exhausting and she was sweating from the exertion. After more than a dozen attempts, she gave up, swearing out loud, wanting to curl up in a ball and cry.

Jack desperately needed to get to the hospital. She had to keep trying. Ducking her head, she tried to wipe the sweat off her face with her shoulder, rubbed her bloody hands on the back of her dress as best as she could. She concentrated on picking up the pool cue again, trying her best to balance it as she aimed it up towards the dartboard. She felt it touch a dart, but as she tried to knock it off the board, the cue slipped through her fingers again.

Concentrate, Lila. You nearly had it.

She tried again, determined not to be discouraged, got herself in position, ignoring the strain between her shoulder blades, the rope cutting into her wrists. The cue wobbled and she thought it was going to slip then it touched a dart. Sweat rolled into her eyes and she tried to blink it away, and she took a second, nudged the dart gently then again a little harder when it didn't budge. It dropped along with the cue and she lurched forward to avoid it hitting her, losing her balance and face palming the floor. The sharp end of the dart grazed the back of her bare leg. Her cheek was already stinging and swollen from where Aaron had punched her and smashing against the floor only added to the pain.

With some effort, she rolled over, managed to pull herself upright. She reached for the dart behind her, finally found it, bringing it up between her bound wrists. The way they were tied though there was no way she could reach to cut the rope.

Lila let out a cry of frustration. She had gone through all that effort for nothing.

On the floor in front of her she heard what sounded like a groan and her heart almost stopped, hoping, praying, that her ears weren't playing tricks on her.

The following grunt confirmed to her they weren't.

'Jack?'

She shuffled back over to him, the dart still in her hands, ignoring the pain in her knees and broken leg. He wasn't fully conscious, but he was more alert than he had been. Lila lay on the floor in front of him, getting her face as close to his as she could.

'Jack, please wake up. I need you here with me. I can't do this alone.'

There was nothing and she was beginning to wonder if she had imagined hearing him, then his eyes fluttered open, though his lids were heavy and she could see he was struggling to focus.

'Jack?'

'Lila? What...?'

'Jack, focus on my voice. I'm going to figure out a way to get us out of this, I promise. Please, hold on. Stay with me. I can't... I won't lose you. I love you.'

She meant it. Intended to fight to the end, even though she knew the odds were stacked against them. And she did love him. Despite the text from Tiff, which had been such a huge deal earlier, and perhaps would still niggle if they managed to get out of this, he had tracked her down, tried to protect her. If they were going to die together, Lila was going to do so knowing that she loved Jack and believing that, in his own way, he loved her back.

He was silent, his eyes drifting shut and she held her breath.

Come on, Jack. Several long seconds passed, but then he was back with her.

'Tiff's text.'

'It doesn't matter.' Lila pressed her forehead against his, breathed in his scent, comforted by knowing he was there with her.

'It's not what… you think. She misread things. Lila, I… love you.'

His head slumped against hers and Lila stiffened. 'Jack? Jack, please wake up.'

She couldn't do this without him. Needed him with her.

'Jack, please.'

He didn't respond, his head heavy as it slumped against her shoulder, and tears pricked against the backs of her eyes again. She blinked them away furiously, knew she needed to pull herself together and be strong for them both.

She shuffled her way around him, laid down so they were back to back, felt for his hands. She might not be able to get herself free, but maybe she could loosen the rope around Jack's wrists. Not that he was in a position to do anything, but at least she would be trying something.

Focussing on the sharp end of the dart, careful not to accidentally stab or cut him, she poked at the rope, for a long while worrying that she was wasting her time, but then feeling the twine start to give.

She was finally getting somewhere, the rope feeling like it was about to snap, when she heard a key turn in the lock at the top of the stairs, quickly hid the dart in her fist. With her eyes fully adjusted to the darkness of the basement, the sudden burst of light from the overhead bulb momentarily blinded her and she was still struggling to focus as Judith and Aaron made their way down the stairs.

'We'll get him out of here first then come back for the girl,'

Judith was instructing her son, talking to him as though Lila wasn't even there.

She screamed at them to stop as they attempted to lift Jack, terrified that this was it and she wouldn't see him again, earning herself a sudden and hard slap across the face from Judith.

'Shut the hell up, you silly little bitch, or I'll cut out your tongue.'

They couldn't take him. What were they going to do to him?

Lila continued screaming, despite Judith's threat, as she watched them struggle to get the weight of Jack's body back up the stairs. Eventually though they managed it and the light went out again, the door locking.

Lila fought to get to the knots around her wrists again, but it was no use, the dart just wouldn't reach. Feeling useless and defeated, knowing that she couldn't save Jack, her screams turned into sobs that wracked through her body. There was nothing else she could do, but wait helplessly in the dark.

THEY WERE GONE for what seemed like ages, her mind presenting awful scenarios of how Judith might kill them both. Foolishly Lila had thought she would be with Jack at the end, had managed to take a little comfort from that. Knowing she was now on her own terrified her.

When they eventually returned, she shuffled away from them, screaming and kicking out as Judith tried to grab hold of her. Although she knew she couldn't beat them, Lila had no intention of making it easy for them.

'Where's Jack? What have you done with him?'

'Jack is no longer a problem.'

When Lila screamed again, Judith caught her by the legs, pushing her to the ground and climbing on top of her. In her hands she held a scarf and Lila choked down on her fear, convinced the woman was going to use it to strangle her. As her face loomed nearer, Judith's dark eyes boring into hers, Lila tried frantically to pull free.

The flashback when it came was sharp, clear and sudden.

Lila had jolted awake, took a second to realise she was in the car and it was filling fast with freezing cold water. The accident. Mark had been driving and they had hit another car. She remembered tyres skidding, bracing for the impact then darkness. Her head hurt and so did her chest and shoulder where it was pulling against the seat belt, and there was a sharp pain in her leg. She glanced at the driver's seat. Although it was dark, she could see Mark was slumped against the wheel, his head twisted at a grotesque angle; his eyes open wide in horror, staring at her. He wasn't moving and was pale, and it was then that Lila saw the piece of metal piercing through him and coming out of the back of his seat.

Even as the shock registered and she started screaming, her brain kicked into action.

What was it she had read about sinking cars? Getting the window open quickly was imperative. The water was nearly up to her chest, leaving her with precious little time. She tried the electric window switch, terror gripping her when it didn't open. Panicking, she bashed at the glass with her elbow, realised it was too strong. She needed something to break the glass. Glancing around the car though she saw nothing that would help her. Then she remembered the safety video she had seen online. They had used the headrest.

After some struggling, Lila managed to pull the driver seat headrest free, smashed its metal poles against the window. It took several attempts but the glass finally shattered. Knowing she was fast running out of time, she went to pull herself out of the window, realised she was still wearing her seat belt.

Fuck!

As she fiddled with the buckle, the car submerged enough that water could pour through the open window, cursing loudly for forgetting to undo the seat belt at the outset, a scream pierced through the air. Was it the person in the other car?

The water was up to Lila's neck, already nearly covering her mouth. Why wouldn't the bloody seat belt unlock. Taking in a deep breath, holding it, she wriggled the belt, trying to give it some slack, clicked it again, tears of relief filling her eyes as it unlocked. Finally free, she pulled herself out of the window, managed to get to the surface as the car disappeared beneath her.

Up ahead she could see two other people in the water. It was too dark to make out their features clearly, but from the screaming she could tell they were female. At first Lila assumed they had been in the car together and swam closer, but then to her horror she realised they were actually fighting, that the older of the two seemed to be trying to hold down the other female. She had hold of a handful of her long blonde hair, was yanking the girl's head back viciously and trying to duck her under the water.

What the fuck?

As the girl disappeared below the surface, Lila screamed at the woman. 'What the hell are you doing? You're going to kill her.'

The woman's head snapped round, dark eyes locking on Lila's.

The blonde girl resurfaced, choking on a mouthful of water. She spotted Lila, started screaming. 'Help me, oh my God, please help…'

Her plea was cut off as her head disappeared again.

'Hey!' Despite her injuries, Lila managed to close the gap between them, knew she had to help the blonde girl before the woman drowned her.

Why the hell was she hurting her?

Panic rose when the blonde girl didn't resurface, and Lila ducked beneath the water. The headlights of the sunken car illuminated the girl's figure as she drifted towards the bed of the river, eyes closed and arms flailing upwards. Lila caught her hand, held on tightly as she tried to pull her to the surface, but despite her grip, the girl's fingers slipped through hers.

Frustrated, Lila tried to go back down after her, realised she was almost out of breath and couldn't manage it. As she returned to the surface for air, the woman who had been attacking the blonde girl caught hold of Lila's head, pushing her back under the water. Caught off guard, Lila screamed, taking in a huge gulp of water, fighting against the hands that held her down. She eventually managed to break free, greedily sucking in air as she coughed and spluttered. From the bank of the river, she heard the slamming of a car door, a voice yelling, but before she could register, before she had barely taken her first gasp of air, the hands were around her throat, squeezing hard as they pushed her under again, the blackness swallowing her whole.

For a moment, Lila stilled, back in the basement room, Judith's face looming over her.

'It was you.'

When the woman's eyes narrowed, she elaborated. 'The night of the car accident you were in the water. I saw you kill Stephanie and then you tried to kill me.'

'Bravo, Miss Amberson.' Judith scowled. 'At least you know now why you have to die. I always knew you would remember eventually. That you were the one loose end I had to take care of.'

'But why kill Stephanie?'

'To protect my son of course. I know he didn't mean to kill that girl, Phoebe, that it was a careless accident. The other one was still alive when I found them and at first I didn't know what to do. You have to understand that I couldn't let her go. My son's life would be over. I didn't want to kill her, but she left me with no choice. You see I have to think about Aaron's future. He has so much ahead of him, so much to live for.'

And what about Shona and Stephanie? Why did their lives not

matter? Anger rubbed against Lila's fear. She wanted to ask the questions, but knew Judith was as cold and calculating as her son, that there would be no rationalising with her.

'Stephanie Whitman showed up at the house unexpectedly to see Aaron, her timing was terrible. It was late at night and I had just loaded the bodies into the boot of my car. I had gone back in the house to get a knife and when I stepped outside and saw Stephanie, my heart nearly stopped. She was standing by the front door holding the locket that had been around Shona McNamara's neck. At first I thought she had seen the bodies, but I guess it must have come off when I was dragging Shona to the car.

'I intended to talk to her, tell her Aaron wasn't home and send her on her way. The bodies were in the boot and she hadn't seen them, and I kept the knife hidden behind my back. I told her the locket was mine and I must have dropped it. She was about to hand it over, but the lid popped open on the boot. I guess the latch hadn't caught properly. After she saw the bodies, I knew I had to deal with her.

'She tried to get back to her car, but I managed to grab hold of her, wrestle her to the ground. I had seen her slip the locket in the pocket of her jeans, tried to get it. Little bitch poked me in the eye with her keys though, managed to wriggle out from underneath me. She ran for her car, but changed direction when she realised I was close behind her, that she didn't have time to open the door and start the engine. I chased her round the back of the house and into the woods, managed to catch hold of her when she tripped over a fallen branch. She was struggling like crazy and I was having trouble subduing her, knew I had to kill her there and then. I didn't want to use the knife, knew it would make a mess, but I had little choice. Your friend, the one you were in the accident with, stumbled across us just as I was about to slice her throat.'

Judith sniffed. 'He was not much of a man if you ask me. He

screamed like a girl, but didn't attempt to help her. Unfortunately he did manage to distract me long enough for Stephanie to hit me in the head with a stone and pull herself free again. They bolted in different directions, your friend back to you I presume, Stephanie to the house and her car. I honestly thought it was over. By the time I had managed to get back on my feet, they had both gone and I had two people who were going to go straight to the police. I was actually ready to confess, was going to tell the police that I had killed both girls to spare Aaron.

'But then I heard the crash. I was the first on the scene and when I realised what had happened, who was involved, I understood I was being given another chance to fix things. Stephanie couldn't live and when I realised that you had seen me too, neither could you.'

'But I did live. Your husband–'

'My husband came home earlier than intended.' There was anger in Judith's tone. 'Ironic really given that he's usually late, sometimes doesn't come home at all. He stopped on the bridge and saw me in the water with you. Of course he thought I was trying to save you, not drown you. He came down to the water, helped pull you ashore. By that point, two other cars had stopped and I knew there was nothing I could do. You were unconscious and no-one knew if you would make it. I had to keep quiet, hope that you wouldn't wake up. Another fifteen seconds and you wouldn't have been a problem.

'Of course, Richard took full credit. He might be a private man, but there was no way he wanted anyone knowing that I had already been in the water when he had got there. He's very protective of his family that way. And it was for the best. When you woke, I worried you would recognise me, that the memories would come back.'

The woman was completely mad, perhaps even more so than her sick sex pest of a son. Crazy ran deep in this family.

Lila glanced apprehensively as Judith pulled the scarf taut in her hands, tried to renew her efforts to wriggle free, realising she wasn't going anywhere. Judith was much stronger than she looked.

'Please don't do this,' Lila begged, hating how pathetic she sounded. 'Please, just let me go and I promise–'

Her words were cut off as Judith forced the scarf into her mouth, knotting it tightly behind her head. Lila let out a muffled humph, her heartbeat accelerating. What the hell was Judith planning to do to her?

As though she were a mind reader, Judith smiled cruelly as she yanked Lila to her feet. 'Okay now, dear. It's time to go on a little car journey.'

Lila had fought like a wild cat when they had forced her into the passenger seat of Jack's car, locking the seat belt across her, but now they were moving, she was strangely subdued.

Aaron knew she had spotted the blankets in the rear of the car where they had lowered the seats; that she understood Jack's body was beneath them. It was almost a shame he was dead, finally succumbing to the blow he had taken to the back of his head. After all the trouble he had caused, Aaron had hoped to be the one to kill him, to do it in front of Lila. They still needed to get rid of his body though, which wouldn't be easy, Judith had warned. She had killed Shona at the house before driving her and Phoebe's bodies to the site they were heading towards and admitted she hadn't considered how difficult it would be lugging a dead body. That was why Lila was still alive (and Jack would have been too if he hadn't pegged it). It would be easier to kill her at her final resting place.

It was just the two of them alone in Jack's Land Rover, with Aaron's mother leading the way in her own car. Once the bodies had been hidden, they intended to drive along the North Norfolk coast and dump Jack's car near a deserted stretch of beach. They had his and Lila's phones, planned to set it up to look like a suicide. The coastline was notorious for riptides and strong currents and no-one would be suspicious if their bodies were never recovered. Everyone knew Jack was volatile, even a little unhinged, going crazy over his sister's death. Whether Lila had joined him in his suicide bid or he had killed her first before dragging her body into the sea with him, they would leave people to speculate.

Not liking the silence in the car, Lila appearing to have accepted her fate now she knew Jack was dead, Aaron decided to tell her about the suicide/murder plan. She was restrained and could hardly go anywhere, so there was no harm in her knowing. He wanted her to understand how they intended to get away with it, to know that her family and friends would never know the truth about what had really happened to her.

Of course he didn't tell her what was actually going to happen. That bit was a surprise and he couldn't wait to see the look of horror on her face when they showed her where they intended to hide her body.

She didn't react as he spoke; only to squeeze her eyes shut as though she was trying to block him out, but he didn't miss the tears that escaped, trailing their way down her cheeks, pleased that he had managed to get under her skin.

He removed one hand from the wheel, reached across and ran his fingers up her bare leg. She flinched, eyes shooting open, and mumbled through her gag.

'What was that? Do you like me touching you?'

More mumbling, this time sounding angrier and more frantic, and he grinned; just about able to make out the vile name she had called him.

It was a shame they had been interrupted earlier. He had so been looking forward to his afternoon of fun with Lila and having her beside him was torture. Her dress was still ripped down the front, exposing her pretty pink bra, though much of her was covered in Jack's blood, and with her hands tied behind her, her breasts were thrust forward, caught either side of the seat belt. Aaron had spent the entire journey with a hard-on, knew if his mother wasn't in the car ahead he would pull over on the side of the road, fuck Lila. If he did that though, his mother would kill him. She was already mad enough at him for snatching Lila and bringing her to the house, telling him he had risked everything. Aaron couldn't see how, knew he had been careful, still he didn't want to piss his mum off, understood that Lila was off the table. Not a problem though, he would find himself plenty more girls to have his fun with when he went travelling. Although he couldn't have her, he kept his hand on Lila's leg, liked having the power over her and knew how much she despised him for it.

His mother slowed as they passed through a village. Aaron supposed he should be taking a note of where they were, but he'd been too distracted. As they came out of the other side heading back into the country, thick wooded trees flanking the road, she indicated left, turning down a dirt track.

Aaron followed her, gave Lila a sidelong glance. Her eyes had widened and, although she was trying not to show any fear, he could feel her leg trembling beneath his hand.

THEY DROVE for about half a mile before his mother stopped and opened a gate. As he waited patiently he let his fingers creep up under Lila's dress.

'This is fun, isn't it? The wait is almost over. Are you excited to see your final resting place?'

Another stream of expletives partly made it through the scarf. Although her eyes were damp, they were flashing angrily.

He removed his hand, putting both hands back on the wheel as he followed his mother through the gate, turning off the ignition as she closed it behind her.

This place was perfect. She had described it to him earlier, confessing where she had hidden Shona and Phoebe's bodies. Apparently she had seen the derelict farmhouse one day while out with her running club and in the days when Shona was locked in the basement games room, Judith had done her research, finding out that the place had been abandoned for years.

Past what looked like an old cattle shed, Aaron spotted the well, his blood heating in excitement. His mother had tested the depth with a weighted down piece of rope before finalising her plan for Phoebe and Shona, knew it was over forty feet deep with at least fifteen feet of that filled with sludgy brown water. Once the bodies were submerged, it was unlikely they would ever be found.

Lila struggled again as Aaron dragged her out of the car. Her fear escalating as she spotted the well, understood where they were heading. He roughly dragged her across to where his mother was waiting, pushed her down on the ground beside the well and held her in place while his mother secured her legs together with more rope, winding over and around the cast, before attaching one of his old weights to the other end, the same as she had done to Phoebe and Shona. Although the well was deep and you would need a heavy-duty torch to see down to the water, she told Aaron they couldn't risk the bodies floating to the surface.

They left Lila by the well, returned to the car to get Jack's body.

'WE HAVE TO CALL THE POLICE.'

Dave had said that as soon as they had parked up by the driveway that led down to Richard Gruger's house, repeated it again when two cars had exited the property, one driven by a woman, the other by a kid of about eighteen, nineteen, who looked like he had done a few rounds in the ring with Mike Tyson. Judith and Aaron Gruger, Elliot guessed. He stared at the second car, wondering why it looked familiar. Did a double take. 'That's Jack's bloody car.'

'We have to call the police,' Dave repeated.

'I promised Jack I wouldn't.'

'So where is he? Why isn't he answering his phone? If that's Jack's car and he's not driving it, he must be in trouble.'

Elliot debated. It had seemed like a good idea finding out where the Grugers lived and driving out to their house at the time, but once he arrived, he wasn't quite sure what to do. Did he get out of the car and approach the house or wait there on standby for Jack's instruction? Elliot was hardly a superhero, ready to save the day. Hell, he had never even thrown a punch. Had no idea if he even could. And he'd had to bring Dave along for moral support because he wasn't brave enough to come alone.

This was his sister though and Jack thought she was in trouble. But where was Jack? He had gone to the house to get her and his car was there, so why wasn't he driving it?

'We need to follow them.'

'No, what we need to do is call the police.'

Elliot ignored Dave as he swung the car around, keeping his distance behind the two vehicles. He had no idea where Aaron and his mother were heading, but he had a bad feeling his sister and Jack might be in a lot of trouble.

His fears were confirmed when twenty minutes later, both cars left the main road onto a dirt track. Elliot pulled over on the side of the road, not wanting to alert either driver that they were being followed. He glanced at Dave, who had spent the entire journey telling him what a bad idea it was. For the first time, his friend was quiet.

'What now?' he asked, unsure if he should follow the cars down the dirt track.

Dave shrugged, his round face pale in the shadows. 'Now would be a really good time to make that phone call.'

'JACK'S DEAD... suicide... driven crazy by his sister's death...'

Snippets of conversation filtered through the pain, the blackness and the cold. Damn it, it was summer. Why the hell was it so cold?

At first he couldn't move and his mouth was drier than sandpaper. Where the fuck was he? The conversation became clearer, one voice talking. Aaron Gruger.

'Do you like me touching you?'

A muffled response that sounded like it might be a slew of angry swearwords.

Lila!

Did the fucker have his hands on her again?

Jack was going to kill him. He started to move, realised it was a bad idea, as pain blasted through his skull. Besides, he couldn't move his hands; they were bound behind his back.

And then it all came back to him. Lila tied to the bed, Aaron on top of her. He had beaten the crap out of the kid, freed Lila, but then something had smacked him hard on the back of the head. After that it was mostly blackness, though he vaguely remembered coming to at one point. Lila had been with him, told him she loved him. Or had he dreamt that bit?

He was pretty sure he wasn't dreaming now though. His head was throbbing like it had a pickaxe in it and from the conversation he was hearing Aaron still had Lila, was taking her somewhere where he planned to kill her. And he had help.

At first Jack wondered whom that help was, assumed it had to be Richard. But then the kid mentioned his mother and another piece of Jack's dream slid into place as he remembered looking up to see Judith pacing and panicking, Aaron way too nonchalant about everything, as they discussed what to do with the bodies.

Judith Gruger, the meek subservient wife of Richard. Jack had been convinced she was a victim, had even felt sorry for her. He hadn't fucking seen that one coming.

Jack's dead.

He sure as hell felt like he should be, wasn't sure how he was even conscious, but he was at least for the moment, and he had to figure out a way to get Lila to safety. Even if he didn't survive this, she had to.

How exactly he planned to get her to safety he wasn't sure, but the fact he was covered by blankets, that Aaron thought he was dead, had to be an advantage. Jack tested the rope around his wrists, thought it gave a little when he gave it a test yank. He tried again. Yeah, it was definitely getting looser.

The car stopped.

'This is fun, isn't it? The wait is almost over. Are you excited to see your final resting place?'

More muffled words and though Jack couldn't quite make them out, he could hear the anger behind them.

That's right, Lila. Be mad at him. Don't let the little prick see you're scared.

The car started again, though only briefly then the engine was turned off. Wherever they were, this was the place Jack and Lila were supposed to die.

He heard the car doors open, was aware from Lila's screams and the amount of cursing coming from Judith and Aaron that Lila was putting up a fight. Jack used the distraction to work harder at freeing his wrists, aware he was running out of time.

Where the hell were they?

The door closed and he realised he was alone, used all of his strength to give one final hard tug, felt the rope snap. He pushed back the blanket, tried to sit up, fighting against the wave of nausea that had stars floating in front of his eyes, threatening to pull him under again.

He sucked in a deep breath, held it, tried to sit up again, this time more gingerly. It looked like they were at some kind of abandoned farm and from what he could see they were in the middle of the countryside, though Hell knew where.

As his eyes adjusted, he could make out movement in the distance, realised Lila was on the ground and being held down as something was tied around her legs. And then he spotted the well behind her, understanding exactly why she had panicked and was fighting to get free. Knew what it was they planned to do to her.

Ignoring the pain in his head, he clambered into the front seat of the car; his car he realised, pleased when he noted Aaron, dumb kid that he was, hadn't had the sense to take the keys. Jack snatched them out of the ignition and shoved them in his pocket, quietly eased open the door, closing it again behind him before crossing to the derelict building that had once been a farmhouse. He leant against the wall for a moment, feeling woozy, forced deep breaths as he glanced around for a weapon, aware he had to get to Lila before they threw her in the well.

'WHERE THE HELL IS HE?'

Judith's heart was pounding, fear racing through her veins. She had helped Aaron load Jack Foley into the back of the car, even placed the blankets over him. He was dead, she had checked for a pulse herself. So how the hell had a dead man managed to get up and walk out of the car?

'He can't have gone far, Mum.'

'He shouldn't have gone anywhere. He's supposed to be dead!'

She glanced back at Lila; relieved to see she was still where they had left her.

Aaron was right. So maybe she had been mistaken and had

missed a weak pulse, perhaps Jack was alive and had managed to crawl out of the car. He was in a bad shape and had his hands tied behind his back. They were in the middle of nowhere. He couldn't have gone far. They needed to keep their heads, get Lila in the well then find out where the hell he'd gone. Judith glanced back at the girl again, knew once she was dead it would be one big problem she would no longer have to worry about.

'Go find where he is,' she snapped at her son. 'And when you do, make sure this time he stays dead.'

'Aren't you going to help me?' Aaron whined, seeming unimpressed with the task he'd been given.

Judith kept her eyes trained on Lila; almost fearful that if she looked away the girl would be gone. 'I have another problem I need to take care of.'

LILA SAW Judith striding towards her, could see from the determined look on the woman's face that her time was up. She tried to shirk away, though knew she wasn't going anywhere, that her fight was finally coming to an end.

She had watched with hope as Judith and Aaron had gone for Jack, only to discover he was no longer in the back of the car, had sobbed tears of relief when she realised he was somehow still alive. She hoped he could find a way to safety, expose the truth about Judith and Aaron Gruger, let the police and her family know what had really happened to her. Damn it, she didn't want to die, but it was going to happen. At least her body would be found though and Elliot would have closure.

Judith caught hold of her under the arms, and despite Lila fighting with every last bit of strength she had, Judith lifted her easily, positioning her against the stonewall of the well. As Judith reached down for the weight that was tethered around Lila's feet, Lila purposely threw herself back on the ground, knew Judith couldn't manage both the weight and her body at the same time. She was strong, but not that strong.

Realising what she had done, Judith smacked her hard around the face before pulling Lila back up on her feet. This time she twisted her so she was facing the well, looking down into the darkness. It looked like a pit to hell. Would she die before she hit the bottom or would she slowly sink and drown? Her whole body shook and she fought to free herself, screamed through the gag even as Judith lifted her, knew it was unlikely anyone would hear her and, even if they did, knew they would never get there in time. As she tottered against the edge, she squeezed her eyes shut, willed it to be over quickly.

Something slammed hard into her back then the weight eased. For a moment, Lila thought she was falling, braced herself for the impact, then she realised she was on the ground, that someone had hold of Judith, was pushing her backwards over the mouth of the well, hands around her throat.

As the woman kicked out and screamed, Lila realised it was Jack.

'Please no!' Judith was begging for her life, suddenly sounding much more like the docile woman they had first encountered. 'I'm sorry for what I did to your sister. I'm sorry.'

Jack stilled, for a moment Lila worried he was going to collapse, but then he questioned softly, 'What did you do to my sister?'

He didn't know.

Had Judith in her panic forgotten that he hadn't been there when Lila had her flashback, that he didn't actually know that Stephanie had survived the car accident, but been drowned by Judith as she tried to swim to safety.

'What did you do?'

The woman was silent, clearly realising her mistake. 'I'm sorry,' she repeated, her voice barely audible.

For a moment, everything paused then Lila saw Jack's jaw

tighten, heard Judith gasp as he pushed her further into the well, let her linger there for a second, before letting go. The woman's scream was of pure terror, echoing all the way down and Lila knew she would hear it in her nightmares for weeks, was aware of how close she had come to the same fate.

She glanced up at Jack, hardly daring to believe he was actually there with her, aware he was looking too pale, wobbling on his feet as though he might collapse at any second. He needed to untie her so she could get him help. She couldn't lose him, not now they had come that far.

And Aaron. Where the fuck was Aaron? They still had him to deal with.

As though thinking about him managed to magic him up, he suddenly appeared, charging towards the well and Jack and Lila, clearly alerted by his mother's screams, a look of pure thunder on his grotesquely beaten face. To Lila's horror he was holding an axe.

And then everything seemed to go into slow motion as Jack lurched forward throwing his weight against Aaron, making him lose his grip on the axe. As the pair of them grappled on the floor, this time Aaron easily overpowering Jack, Lila unable to do anything but watch on helplessly, two figures appeared in the distance racing towards them, both screaming like some kind of battle cry, one tall and skinny, the other short and stocky.

Lila blinked, doubting what she was seeing. Was that Elliot and Dave?

They were waving what looked like swords above their heads and heading straight for where Aaron was on top of Jack, hands squeezing around his throat, seemingly oblivious to the fact he was about to be attacked.

If she hadn't almost just died, if her life – and Jack's – weren't still in danger, Lila thought she might actually laugh at the ridiculous sight of Elliot and Dave throwing themselves on top of

Aaron, bashing him over the head with their heavy but very fake swords.

How the hell did they know where to come?

Somehow, by some sheer miracle, between them they managed to triumph, Dave using his belt to lash Aaron's hands behind his back. And then they were freeing Lila, who by that point was laughing hysterically at the two battleground heroes who had saved her life, and she was hugging and kissing them both, so pathetically grateful that her laughter turned into tears and she sobbed all over them.

Jack was still on the ground, looked like he didn't have the energy to move and Lila pleaded with Elliot to call an ambulance then crawled over to Jack and hugged him to her, cradling him in her arms to keep him warm.

'Did your brother just come to my rescue with a fake sword?' His voice was weak and Lila could tell each word was an effort; that he was in a lot of pain. She nodded, though couldn't help it when tears leaked out of her eyes.

He forced a smile. 'Hey, don't cry, it's only a flesh wound. We didn't go through all this for me to die on you now.'

'No we didn't and I have so much to tell you, but when you're better.' She leant down, pressed a kiss against his cold lips.

Where was the bloody ambulance?

'Stay with me, Jack. I won't lose you, not now.'

She thought she saw the faintest nod and then his eyes drifted shut.

In the distance, she heard the wail of the siren and although she wasn't in the slightest bit religious, for the first time in her life she prayed.

EPILOGUE

SIX MONTHS LATER

Lila stood by the grave, a bunch of yellow roses in her hand. She visited regularly, at least once a week, the psychologist treating her urging her to go, believing it was a good way to deal with her emotions and begin the healing process.

She knew people viewed her as a survivor; that she had somehow overcome a horrific car accident then a murder attempt, but she had lost so much in the process, wasn't sure she would ever completely get over the night she almost died at the hands of Judith and Aaron Gruger.

Judith's body had been recovered from the bottom of the well, along with the remains of Phoebe Kendall and Shona McNamara. Aaron had been arrested and charged with Phoebe's murder, along with being an accessory to murder for Shona McNamara. He had also been charged with Lila's attempted murder, plus several other counts. Lila knew that had his mother survived, she would have stood trial for worse crimes.

Lila never told anyone about the conversation that had occurred between Jack and Judith before she fell into the well – Lila's official line to the police. Lila would never blame him for that, understood his motives, and refused to let his name be tarnished. She would take that secret to the grave for him.

She had seen Richard Gruger only once since his wife died and it wasn't planned, they happened to be passing in the corridor at the police station. He had nodded tersely at her and she had averted her gaze. Neither of them had anything to say to each other.

Gruger had disowned his son, seemed keen to distance himself from his wife's crimes. Lila read in the news that he had shacked up with one of the teaching assistants at his school within two months of Judith's death. Not that he worked at Bishop's House anymore. Even if it hadn't been enough that the husband and father of a pair of murderers was serving as their headmaster, the school board was furious that Gruger had kept copies of all the test papers at home, that his son had been able to access them and sell the answers. The parting hadn't been amicable and there were rumours abound that jobless Gruger was currently writing his own tell-it-all book about the murders.

TEARS SPILLED as Lila set the flowers down on the grave, still torn apart for the one life she had tried, but hadn't been able to save. The memories hurt so much.

Like always she said a few words, knew they would never be enough, before she headed back to her car.

As she drove home, she turned up the volume on the radio, made an effort to sing along with the songs she knew the words to. She had survived and even though there were days like that day where she didn't feel she could move forward, she would find a way, knew she had a responsibility to live her life to the fullest on behalf of the ones who didn't make it.

ONCE HOME, she made herself a coffee, sent Elliot a text,

checking he was still on for movie night later. Maybe she would head out with her camera that afternoon, lose herself for a while. It might snap her out of this mood.

She heard footsteps behind her, felt arms snake around her waist, and sunk back into them.

'You okay?' Jack's breath was warm against her ear, immediately making things feel right. 'You went to her grave again, didn't you?'

Lila stayed silent, but he knew, and she got it that he didn't fully understand why she continued to torment herself that she hadn't been able to save his sister.

Sure he visited Stephanie's grave, but the visits were maybe once a month. After her memories had been unlocked, Lila had carried the guilt of knowing what had really happened to Stephanie for three long days, not daring to talk to Jack about it until she knew he was fully on the mend. She was terrified the truth might tear both him and their relationship apart, but knew he deserved the truth.

And at first he had been shocked, took a few days to process the news, though deep down she knew he had his suspicions after that final conversation with Judith.

But he had dealt with it, seemed to move on easier than Lila.

She turned in his arms, hugged him tightly, remembering how at one point she had been terrified she was going to lose him too. But there they were, six months later, and they had survived everything together. Knowing that, Lila would figure out a way to move forward.

TAKING A BREAK FROM WRITING, Jack and Cooper joined Lila down on the beach. It was a chilly December day, but the sun was out, the sky a perfect cloudless blue.

As he watched Lila snap pictures of the sea, some of the dog, even a couple of cheeky ones of him when she'd thought he wasn't looking, Jack wondered if she would feel so guilty about Stephanie if she hadn't been his sister.

It had been hard learning so many secrets about his sister's past and her death, and finding out she hadn't been killed outright in the car accident, that Judith Gruger had drowned her, took a while to process. He had closure though, knew he needed to move on or it would eventually drive him insane. Judith was dead – an eye for an eye – that he couldn't bring himself to regret. Knowing what the woman had done to Stephanie, had tried to do to Lila, ensured Jack had no problem sleeping at night.

And Giles was finally out of the picture. Much to the family's frustration, Stephanie's death meant a rape charge wouldn't stick, but Henry had finally seen his golden boy for who he really was, sacking him and badmouthing him throughout the industry, ensuring he wouldn't find it easy to get another job.

Alyssa had brooded for a week before announcing herself young, free and single, hitting the bars with her friends. After a wild three months, she had started dating seriously again. Jack had met Will, liked him, and was pleased to see his sister's taste in boyfriends was improving.

Alyssa had met Lila a couple of times. Both encounters had been a little uncomfortable, but it was a start. His mother had been a different story, warming to Lila straightaway. Thank God, because he knew Lila had been terrified about meeting her. Knowing what Lila had done, that she had tried to save Stephanie's life, changed things for everyone. Even Henry had softened his stance.

Elliot meanwhile was actually revelling in his new hero status, and Jack knew there was no way he could ever repay him and Dave for what they had done.

INSTEAD OF HEADING BACK to the house, Jack and Lila drove the coastal road to Cromer. Lila still insisted on working shifts at Nat's Hideaway, though Jack tried to encourage her to throw more time into her photography. He knew she was good and that taking pictures was her passion, and he wanted her to have every available opportunity to have a career doing the thing she loved most.

As they entered the café and he saw her excitement at seeing her friends though, he understood why this place was important to her too.

'No dogs in the café, Jack,' Natalie reminded him, her tone stern, though the glint in her eye gave her away.

It was December and the place was empty, and Natalie, Beth and Joe, Natalie's son, had been decorating the Christmas tree when Jack and Lila had walked in. The place smelt of coffee and warm pastry, the tone relaxed and full of laughter. He got why it was popular and Lila liked it there.

'Coop promises he'll be on his best behaviour.' Jack grinned, taking a seat before Natalie could object.

Shaking her head, though struggling to hide her smile, she disappeared behind the counter, returning with a pot of tea, a plate of mince pies and a bowl of water and a couple of biscuits for Cooper.

Jack knew Natalie and Beth had been there for Lila over the past few months, had spent valuable time with her talking through everything that had happened. Although that day spent in the Gruger house had scarred her and she still suffered from nightmares, fortunately they were becoming further apart. He had come so close to losing her that day and it still terrified him trying to imagine his life without her in it.

'THANK YOU FOR THAT.' Lila glanced up at him as they walked back to the car.

When he raised his eyebrows in mock innocence, she smiled

and elaborated. 'For taking me to see my friends; I really needed that pick-me-up today.'

Jack slipped his arm around her, pulled her close. 'We're going to get past everything, Lila. I promise you, we're going to be okay.'

She stopped walking, pulling him around to face her, locking her arms around him and kissing him hard on the mouth, before pulling back slightly, a smile on her lips.

'You mean *are*, Jack.' She nodded at him, her smile widening. 'We're not *going to be okay*, we already are.'

ACKNOWLEDGMENTS

Writing a novel is never a sole effort and, as always, there are a number of people I am indebted to.

Firstly, to my beta team: Jo, Andrea, Paula, Christine, Sally and Jeff, thank you as always for your honest and valuable feedback and for answering the many questions I throw at you.

To my sister, Detective Constable Holly Beevis, for ensuring the police procedural elements of the story have been portrayed accurately. If there are any errors, they are mine, not yours.

Also, to my competition winner, Natalie Mcardle, who has been in my thoughts often during the writing of this book, to Lyn Wells for your wonderful generosity, to my desk buddy, Ness, thank you for your help with the title, to my brilliant and funny editor, Morgen Bailey, whom I have loved working with, and last, but most certainly not least, thank you to the wonderful team at Bloodhound Books.

Printed in Great Britain
by Amazon

LINCOLN
CATHEDRAL